Praise for Reb

Praise for *Divas*.

'Rebecca Chance's *Divas* sizzles with glamour,
revenge. Unputdownable. A glittering page-t...
this debut had me hooked from the first page
Louise Bagshawe

'I laughed, I cried, I very nearly choked. Just brilliant!
This has to be the holiday read of the year'
Olivia Darling

Praise for *Bad Girls*:

'Glitzy, hedonistic and scandalous, this compelling read
is a real page-turner' *Closer*

'A fun, frivolous read' *Sun*

Praise for *Bad Sisters*:

'Blistering new bonkbuster' *Sun*

'A gripping and exciting novel' *Closer*

Praise for *Bad Angels*:

'The perfect bonkbuster for lazy holiday reading' *Star*

'Pure festive escapism' *Heat*

Praise for *Killer Heels*:

'The perfect sunlounger fodder in the form of power games,
illicit romps and some menacing high-heeled shoes'
The People

'A perfect mix of sex, secrets and back-stabbing, this sizzling
bonkbuster deserves a place in your beach bag' *Closer*

Praise for *Killer Queens*:

'I give *Killer Queens* five stars – massively enjoyed the book –
and it's ...   ...having!'

BAD BRIDES

Rebecca CHANCE

**SIMON &
SCHUSTER**

London · New York · Sydney · Toronto · New Delhi

A CBS COMPANY

First published in Great Britain by Simon and Schuster, 2014
A CBS COMPANY

1 3 5 7 9 10 8 6 4 2

Simon & Schuster UK Ltd
1st Floor
222 Gray's Inn Road
London WC1X 8HB

www.simonandschuster.co.uk

Simon & Schuster Australia, Sydney
Simon & Schuster India, New Delhi

A CIP catalogue record for this book is available
from the British Library

Paperback ISBN 978-1-47110-172-4
Trade Paperback ISBN 978-1-47110-171-7
eBook ISBN 978-1-47110-173-1

Typeset in Berling by M Rules
Printed and bound by CPI Group (UK) Ltd, Croydon, CR0 4YY

To all the brides out there – good or bad!
Enjoy your special day!

Acknowledgements

Huge thanks to:

At Simon and Schuster: Clare Hey and Carla Josephson, who've slaved to get this book into print on a very tight deadline. Sara-Jade Virtue and the amazing marketing team – Alice Murphy, Dawn Burnett, Ally Glynn – who work just as hard promoting the books. Dominic Brendon, James Horobin, Gill Richardson, Rumana Haider and Rhedd Lewis are raising my sales with every book, and I'm incredibly grateful. Hannah Corbett in publicity has been brilliantly efficient and very generous with the bubbles!

At David Higham: Anthony Goff, my ever-wonderful agent. Marigold Atkey has been helpful and efficient way beyond the call of duty, and Chiara Natalucci and Stella Giatrakou in foreign rights do a fantastic job of selling Rebecca Chance overseas.

Emma Draude and Sophie Goodfellow at Emma Draude PR, who are getting reams of fabulous coverage for my books. Lucky me!

Antonio di Meglio, whose beautiful chandeliers feature in the book, and Massimo Panuccio, of Sartoria Massimo, who was kind enough to do fabulous sketches for Brianna Jade and Tamra's dresses for the ceremony, you can see them on www.pinterest.com/rebeccachance1/badbrides.

Travis Pagel is my marketing guru, and Marcos 'stop me' Malkmuth is my personal DJ ... Love you boys!

Dan Evans at Plan 9 and Oscar Henriquez for my beautiful new website www.rebeccachance.net.

Marco and Alice Baldini, for getting married with perfect timing for me to use the details in this book! And Gabriella and Leonardo Lenzi of Tenuta Neve d'Agosto for their exquisite taste, plus all the fascinating information about the history of their beautiful venue.

Matt Bates and Karl Frost, fantastic friends, wonderful company and a gorgeous couple!

Michael Devine of www.makethemostofyourgarden.com designed Tamra's ridiculously extravagant Chelsea garden so wonderfully that I almost believe it exists!

My intern, Lydia Laws-Wall, who's an absolute star. I feel so lucky to have her!

Paul Willis, Greg Herren, and Beth Hettinger Tindall gave me amazingly detailed help with the description of Kewanee Hog Days and Illinois corn-fed life. Thank you three so much, you really brought Tamra and Brianna Jade's backgrounds to life.

Emma Louise, aka 'The Harry Potter Girl', Kevin Loh and Emma Beynon for sharing the #bananalove!

I honestly don't think I could have written this book in a very short amount of time without the Rebecca Chance fanfriends on Facebook to cheer me up, distract me and banter with! Thanks, Angela Collings, Dawn Hamblett, Tim Hughes, Jason Ellis, Tony Wood, Melanie Hearse, Jen Sheehan, Helen Smith, Katherine Everett, Julian Corkle, Robin Greene, Diane Jolly, Adam Pietrowski, John Soper, Gary Jordan, Louise Bell, Lisa Respers France, Stella Duffy, Shelley Silas, Rowan Coleman, Serena Mackesy, Tim Daly, Joy T Chance, Lori Smith Jennaway, Alex Marwood, Sallie Dorsett, Alice Taylor, Joanne Wade, Marjorie Tucker, Teresa Wilson, Ashley James Cardwell, Margery Flax, Clinton Reed, Valerie Laws, Simon-Peter Trimarco, Kelly Butterworth, Kirsty Maclennan, Amanda Marie Fulton, Marie Causey, Shana Mehtaab, Tracy Hanson, Nancy Pace Koffman, Katrina Smith, Helen Lusher, Russ Fry, Gavin Robinson, Laura Ford, Mary Mulkeen, Eileen McAninly, Pamela Cardone, Barb McNaughton, Shannon Mitchell, Claire Chiswell, Dawn Turnbull, Michelle Heneghan, Jonathan Harvey, Jeffrey Marks – and Bryan Quertermous, Derek Jones, David W. Rudlin and Colin Butts, the very exclusive (i.e. tiny) club of my straight male readers. Plus of course Paul Burston, the Brandon Flowers of Polari, and his loyal crew – Alex Hopkins, Ange Chan, Sian Pepper, Enda Guinan, Belinda Davies, John Southgate, Paul Brown, James Watts, Ian Sinclair Romanis and Jon Clarke. And the handful of beloved relatives brave enough to read my books – Dalia Hartman Bergsagel, Ilana Bergsagel, Sandy Makarwicz and Jean Polito. If I've left anyone out, please do send me a message and I will correct it in the next book.

Kirsty Mcdonald won the Twitter competition to have her name in the acknowledgements: here it is. Congratulations!

Thanks to Vina Jackson and Stella Knightley for their lovely quotes – fantastic writers and very good friends.

Tarquin's surreally nonsensical lyrics were crowd-sourced on FB but ended up mostly coming from the deliciously twisted brain of Dorcas Pelling.

The gorgeous team of McKenna Jordan and John Kwiatkowski and everyone at Murder by the Book, for bringing my smut to Texas.

And as always – thanks to the Board. We are so lucky to have each other.

Lastly, to the FLs of FB, all of whom are *Gone With the Wind* fabulous. Twirl!

Author's Note

Readers of my previous novel, *Killer Queens*, will recognize members of the royal family that feature in *Bad Brides*. You absolutely don't need to have read that book before starting this one, but for those who haven't read *Killer Queens*, all you need to know is that I created a set of British royals who are definitely not the Windsors – though some of mine may share a few similarities with certain real-life royals! The heir to the throne in my parallel universe is Prince Oliver, whose son and heir Hugo recently married his long-term girlfriend, Chloe Rose. And the character who reappears in *Bad Brides* is Hugo's sister Sophie, who was previously both a brat and a bitch, partly due to the death of her mother Princess Belinda in a ski accident years ago.

However, since the events of *Killer Queens*, Sophie's become much nicer to entertain at an engagement party in your newly renovated stately home – should you want to invite her! Just make sure you have some good-looking young footmen in uniform for her late-night entertainment . . .

Prologue

London, August

'Ladies, gentlemen, thank you so much for coming out this evening!'

Jodie Raeburn, editor of both *Style UK* and its latest off-shoot, *Style Bride* magazine, launching that very day at a hyper-fashionable party in Harrods Bridal Boutique, surveyed the packed room of glitterati with considerable pride. Because shepherding the debut issue of *Style Bride* into print had been, without question, the most teeth-rattling, white-knuckled roller-coaster ride of her editorial life.

In all her years of wrangling temperamental photographers, coke-crazed fashion designers and anorexic models, Jodie had never had to cope with a last-minute crisis this dramatic. She had made a strategic decision to have two celebrity brides-to-be compete against each other for the cover of the magazine and the prestigious title of *Style* Bride of the Year, hoping to garner maximum publicity for her new launch and impress her highly demanding managing editor.

And, as far as publicity was concerned, Jodie had succeeded

beyond her wildest dreams. Two crack *Style* teams had watched in shock and awe as both wedding ceremonies took very unexpected turns, cameras capturing every moment of the drama, prompting an emergency of epic proportions. Jodie had been forced to delay publication of the magazine for several weeks, which would usually have signalled disaster: but her team had worked round the clock, and the press coverage of the competing brides' various meltdowns had been so compelling that *Style Bride* had almost doubled its advertising as bridal designers and cosmetic companies fell over themselves in a last-minute race to appear in a magazine that was bound to fly off the shelves. Even with the huge printers' bill, the first issue of *Style Bride* was already a raving financial success.

As she continued with her prepared speech, Jodie's mind raced back to the choice she had thought she was making months ago. The candidates for *Style* Bride of the Year had been narrowed down to a shortlist of two: on the one hand, exquisitely pretty Milly Gamble, a young starlet on the rise, engaged to Tarquin Ormond, even more famous than her as the lead singer of a folk-rock band garlanded with Brit awards and Grammies. On the other, Brianna Jade Maloney, nicknamed the 'Fracking Princess' by the media, an American ex-pageant beauty, all teeth, hair and golden tan, whose marriage to Edmund, Earl of Respers, had been arranged by her equally gorgeous mother, Tamra.

Tamra was here tonight, the Fracking Queen herself, resplendent in a stunning cocktail dress. And so was Brianna Jade, close to the podium, dressed more demurely than her mother, but still with that polished, American-groomed glow about her, radiantly beautiful as always. Jodie scanned the crowd to see if she could spot Milly or Tarquin, but the head count was so dense that she couldn't pick out their near-identical ringleted blonde curls.

Jodie's heart was beating fast with excitement. Even though many of the guests here knew what was about to be announced – the reveal of the first-ever issue of *Style Bride*, anchored by a photograph of the Bride of the Year, smiling in glorious triumph at her coup in having snagged the cover – Jodie was over the moon at her own achievement. She had turned a tortuous and agonising process into a glossy first issue, so thick with copy and advertisements that its girth measured two centimetres.

Two centimetres! That was huge in magazine terms! And at that thought Jodie's smile spread as wide as the Bride of the Year's. In work as in marriage, size really *did* matter.

Chapter One

Stanclere Hall, July

The Fracking Queen commands and we obey, Edmund St Aubrey, Earl of Respers, thought with amusement as he contemplated the duck-egg blue Tiffany box on his dressing table. Inside it was a four-carat pink diamond engagement ring, the central stone encircled by smaller, no less bright white diamonds; the whole thing had cost over forty thousand pounds.

It was a sum which Edmund would have been quite incapable of affording himself. And even if he had had a spare five figures kicking around – an unimaginable amount! – he would have poured it into some much more pressing need: urgent repairs to the roof of Stanclere Hall, his ancestral home. Or the almost equally vital task of replumbing the Hall and installing a new boiler: the clunks and creaks whenever someone tried to run a bath were frankly terrifying, as if gremlins inside the ancient pipes were hitting them with tiny hammers. Or buying desperately needed new farm equipment. Edmund winced, thinking about his ancient John Deere tractors, so corroded by now that the workers joked that the rust was all that was holding them together.

But you don't need to worry about the roof or the boiler or the tractors now! he told himself, taking a deep breath, fighting back the panic that wrapped around him every time he thought about how much money he needed to keep Stanclere Hall running. *All the jobs in the house and on the estate are safe now, thank God.* Edmund could not separate the interests of Stanclere Hall, its landscaped gardens, its arable land and its loyal staff; they were all essential parts of a whole without which he would never be complete. The Earls of Respers had always lived at Stanclere Hall, and with that privilege came huge responsibility. Edmund did not own the Hall; he held it in trust for the future generations of Respers and also for all the people to whom it provided jobs and a roof over their heads, in the form not only of the Hall itself but all its tied cottages. Some of the families had worked for the Respers as long as the latter had been in residence.

So no pressure, Edmund, as the Fracking Queen would say, he thought, smiling. No pressure at all. Just the wages bill every month, the soaring costs of electricity and gas, a crumbling ancient stately home to maintain, an ornamental lake covered in algae ...

Mercifully, inside the small square Tiffany box was the solution to all his problems. It might be unorthodox for the mother of his future fiancée to have bought her own daughter's engagement ring, but the Fracking Queen had been insistent, and she always got her way. She had demanded that Brianna Jade, Edmund's heiress bride-to-be, was not to be proposed to with some old ring from the Respers family jewels. Edmund had argued that there were some very good pieces of jewellery in the safe: being part of the entail, he couldn't sell them to raise money to maintain the estate. Edmund, who disliked to see so much money thrown away on what he privately considered to be just a bit of shiny carbon, had tried to tell the Fracking Queen that it was much more typical of the English aristocracy to bestow a family heirloom on one's bride. But the Fracking Queen had countered with the fact that when Prince Oliver, the heir to the British throne, had proposed to his late bride, Princess Belinda, he had done so with a ring bought from Garrard's jewellers, and what was good enough for the royal family was damn well good enough for Brianna Jade.

There was really no arguing with the Queen when she was set on something; she would pull out her tablet thingy, whizz around it, tracing a perfectly manicured finger on the screen, and come up with a devastating fact that would stop you in your tracks. And since she hadn't insisted that Edmund purchase the pink diamond ring himself, or even pick it out, but had done all that herself, there was also no denying that she played fair. The box had been produced triumphantly today when she arrived from London, as she and Edmund drank sherry in the library while Brianna Jade supervised the unpacking of her and her mother's weekend wardrobes.

Edmund had blinked at how very bright the ring was. It looked as if it had been cut specifically to refract the maximum light possible, as if you could, in a pinch, use it to spark a fire by channelling sunlight through it, as they did with mirrors in the Boy Scouts. But the Fracking Queen had smiled complacently at the sparkling diamonds she had produced, sculled her sherry in one swift gulp – *my God, she can hold her drink*, he thought respectfully; he'd seen her knock back glasses of good single malt as if they were spritzers – and stood up, announcing that she would send Brianna Jade downstairs in an hour or so and that she expected Edmund to have 'sealed the deal', as she put it, in time for champagne before dinner.

Champagne which she had had sent from Harrods, of course, because Edmund couldn't possibly afford her favourite, Cristal. Cases of it had arrived the day before, together with hampers of foie gras, caviare and vast quantities of bresaola, some sort of Italian beef slices on which the Queen mainly existed for diet purposes. Cook was fascinated.

He raised his eyes from the little blue box and looked at himself in the mirror of his dressing table. Being born an Earl had not made Edmund arrogant in any way. If anything, it had humbled him, the knowledge that he had so much responsibility but lacked the business skill to run his estates profitably. Nor was he arrogant about his looks.

I'm just an average sort of chap, he thought, considering his reflection. He was tall enough – six feet – with nice regular features. *At least I have a decent jawline.* It might be a cliché that many of the British aristocracy were chinless wonders, but it didn't make it any less true. His light brown hair, his grey eyes, his square forehead and straight mouth were all Respers features, seen in many of the family portraits. The men were attractive in a traditionally manly way, but the solid features, wide shoulders and strong jawlines were harder on the women. Respers females tended to be described, charitably, as 'a little on the masculine side'.

Well, Brianna Jade will definitely raise the Respers aesthetics considerably, Edmund thought, picking up the tie that was draped over his valet stand and placing it around his upturned shirt collar. He had never really believed that women as beautiful as her existed outside films and magazines. Or that, even if they did, one of them would conceivably want to marry him. He was the envy of the entire county. Brianna Jade looked like the model for Botticelli's *Birth of Venus*, she was the sweetest-natured girl Edmund had ever met, and she was bringing him a dowry that would literally transform Stanclere.

And what did he have to give her in return? A title, a big delapidated house and – he looked at himself again in the mirror as he straightened his tie – an average-looking man who just happened to be an Earl.

He really was the luckiest chap in the world.

Chapter Two

As Edmund St Aubrey contemplated his good luck, Brianna Jade Maloney sat quietly in the corner of one of the tatty chintz sofas in the morning room of Stanclere Hall, waiting for its owner to come with his sure light tread down the creaky central oak staircase and stride across the tatty old carpets in the Great Hall. Tamra, Brianna Jade's mom, said that as soon as Edmund and her daughter were officially engaged, there would be major, *major* renovations on the Hall, and you'd better believe all the ancient rugs would be the first thing to go, before the moths in them got to her Italian cashmere.

Brianna Jade's hands were folded in her lap, her expression perfectly composed as she pictured Edmund appearing in the doorway of the morning room, smiling at her with his polite, English-gentleman smile, about to say –

But Brianna Jade made herself stop right there, before she actually heard the words in her head. She wanted them to be lovely and new when Edmund said them to her, to have her own reaction be completely spontaneous. This was a luxury she had barely ever enjoyed in her adult life to date: from the age of fifteen, she had competed in one pageant after another

for four straight years, and pageant competitors were pro-
grammed like computers. Even though those days were behind
her, had ended when Tamra married vast amounts of money
in the shape of Ken Maloney, the Fracking King of America,
Brianna Jade had still needed to learn how to behave in her
new life, to follow another set of rules. She was very much
looking forward to a marriage in which her own vast dowry
would allow her, hopefully, just to be herself.

It's the start of a new life now, she thought with great relief.
I'm settling down. Finally, she knew where she belonged: in this
lovely house in the country with farmland all around it. She
had always wanted to live on a farm. And England was so
pretty and green, so much prettier than Illinois. Brianna Jade
loved it here.

She had totally earned this. All those years of walking onto
pageant stages, smiling till her mouth cramped and saying
what the judges wanted to hear without any idea of what she
actually thought about the questions they were asking. And
then, after her mother had married Ken, catapulting them into
the lap of luxury, they both swiftly realized that they had to
learn how to talk right and know how to act classy enough for
Florida high society, which had turned out to be just as
exhausting.

Being the Countess of Respers, by contrast, seemed like
it would be a walk in the park. The London upper crust had
been hugely welcoming to the Fracking Queen and Princess:
no one in Britain cared about what kind of an American accent
you had. US class distinctions were meaningless over here.

Brianna Jade might not have been the brightest bulb in
the chandelier intellectually, but she was richly gifted with
common sense. She was perfectly aware that almost everyone
in London society had been so very friendly because she and
her mother Tamra had swept in on a glittering tide of money,

as if their dollars had been golden coins that her mother scattered from her carriage, like she pictured people doing in the olden days. Of course, some of the younger women hadn't been *quite* so nice to her, but that was only to be expected. Brianna Jade knew all about mean-girls' cliques and how they didn't like a new girl at the best of times, let alone one who was pretty enough to be on the pageant circuit.

And the rich, titled, twenty-something British women, led by some girl called the Honourable Araminta, were complete pushovers compared to the hardcore bitches from back home in Illinois, all scrabbling to win the titles of Kewanee Pork Queen or Watseka Corn Queen. Those were girls who'd rub baby oil into your false lashes so they wouldn't stick on, doctor your shampoo with Kool-Aid to streak your hair, glue up the nozzle of your hairspray can and refuse to let you use theirs, even push you into a stinging-nettle patch or rub poison ivy into the inside of your dress.

Nope, the Honourable Araminta, aka 'Minty', and her girl-friends had no idea how to catfight as dirty as the Kendras, Taylors and Kymbers on the pageant circuit. In the US, Tamra had done plenty of battling for her daughter, but here Brianna Jade was more than equal to the task. What had these Honourables and Ladies ever lacked in their life? Had they ever had to shop at Goodwill or the Salvation Army, make a packet of ready-made grits last a couple of days between two of them, or hitch to school because they had two tyres bald as eagles and no money for gas? No way.

Brianna Jade didn't understand half of what they said, anyway, because of their sharp clipped accents which made their words like stabby little knives thrown too short to reach the target. And she wouldn't have answered even if she had, because she'd figured out early on that what drove them really crazy was if she just smiled back at them with her perfect teeth, her best 'I'm a Christian and I forgive you' pageant smile. For some reason she couldn't work out, they *hated* that smile. They actually recoiled when they saw it, like she had a full water pitcher in her hand and they were the Wicked Witches from every compass point going.

The Honourable Minty and her crew did have one thing in common with the girls back home, though: they were equally wary of Brianna Jade's mom. Tamra provoked that reaction in women. It wasn't her fault; her God-given looks meant that she was catnip to every dad, male teacher and, frankly, a lot of those girls' teenage boyfriends. That had been Tamra's ultimate threat to the really bad mean girls, that she'd flirt with their boyfriends and turn their heads around so they literally couldn't even see their girlfriends any more, they were too dazzled by Tamra Krantz.

Because Tamra was the ultimate MILF. She'd had her only daughter at sixteen: when, at fifteen years old, Brianna Jade won the title of Pork Queen of Kewanee (a fact Tamra *never* wanted mentioned in later life), Tamra was thirty-one and looked twenty-four. She was the perfected version of what Brianna Jade would hopefully become, with her thick mane of strawberry-blonde hair, her big luminous eyes, her skin lightly tanned and so smooth that even the haters couldn't help calling her 'Barbie' as a grudging compliment.

Brianna Jade regularly heard girls at school bitching that Tamra had better legs than they did, a flatter stomach and, for a while, bigger boobs: however, on marrying Ken, which took them up in the world like an express penthouse elevator to Classy Town, Tamra had taken a good look around her, realized that D cups didn't fit into the Armani or Carolina Herrera dresses worn to fundraising Florida balls, and had the implants removed. Ken had bitched and moaned about it, but, as always, he went along with what Tamra wanted.

Like we all do, Brianna Jade thought now, smoothing down
the pleated silk skirt of her Balenciaga dress with its exquisite
chiffon pintucked sleeves. It was totally gorgeous, but she still
couldn't pronounce most designer names right. She suspected
Minty of guessing that fact and trying to catch out Brianna
Jade by repeatedly asking her who had made her clothes, but
Brianna Jade just smiled seraphically in return, flicked her
glossy, perfectly blow-dried hair from one shoulder to the
other, and said:

'Oh, I couldn't tell you. Mom and I have so many pretty
things.'

Foiled, Minty had sneered again, tossed her own hair – the
British society girls were all proud of their hair, though
Brianna Jade's was lusher than any of theirs – and slinked
away. Brianna Jade had heard that Minty had nicknamed her
BJ, but that was water off Brianna Jade's back, rain off her
bouncing, lacquered, hairsprayed locks. It sure wasn't the first
time she'd been teased about that. Tamra had apologized years
ago for not realizing the consequences of naming her daughter after Brianna Jade's dead father – Brian Schladdenhouffer,
who had done the decent thing and proposed when Tamra
got knocked up, only to die in a combine-harvester accident
before he could either get married or see his daughter born –
and after the stone in the engagement ring, a jade he'd given
Tamra till he could afford a Kay's diamond from the local
mall. ('Every kiss begins with Kay!')

Tamra had suggested that Brianna Jade change her name:
Brianna Jade had promptly burst into tears, said that she
wouldn't dream of it, that her name had not one, but two
lovely references to her dad, and that her mom should never
raise the idea again. Being called BJ really wasn't such a big
deal, she had insisted bravely. Tamra had burst into tears as
well, and they'd hugged and cried for a long time before

deciding to hitch into Kewanee and go spend some money they didn't really have on Bananas Foster ice-cream sundaes at Carvel, their favourite treat.

And look at me now! I'm going to be Brianna Jade, Countess of Respers, with the Honourable Araminta and her friends dancing at my wedding!

An ecstatic smile spread over Brianna Jade's face at the prospect of their sour expressions as they saw her walking up the aisle of the Respers family chapel in a couture gown, her train a mile long, her diamonds sparkling and her head held high and triumphant. Edmund walked into the morning room to see her big hazel eyes wide, her glossed lips curving ecstatically, her strawberry-blonde hair tumbling around her face, and her cheeks pink with sheer pleasure at her imminent engagement: she looked so stunning that he almost dropped to one knee there and then.

'You look like a Sienese icon,' he blurted out, unable to take his eyes off her.

'I do?' Brianna Jade directed the full wattage of her smile at him. 'That's a good thing, right?'

Brianna Jade was quite unfazed by her lack of cultural knowledge. Rich, upper-crust people didn't talk about opera or ballet or paintings, not back in Florida and not here in Britain either. When she and Tamra were invited to the Royal Opera House, no one in the private box they sat in would ever say a word about the singing or dancing: they just gossiped about whose husband was looking to upgrade to a trophy wife, or whose wife was taking 'extra sessions' with her personal trainer. She'd worked out long ago that, for these people, culture was either an excuse to dress up, go out and spend money, or a stick to beat the peasants with because they didn't know about ... well, that Siamese icon thing Edmund had just mentioned.

Her eyes softened even more sweetly as she gazed at him.

He'd meant to be nice, and now he was going to explain to her what he'd been talking about. Plus, it was sweet of him to assume that she *might* know what the Siamese thing was ...

'Icons are paintings of saints,' Edmund said. 'Mostly done on a gold background, because they were so special – they were supposed to be worshipped. The ones from the Siena School are all pale-skinned like you, with hazel eyes and blonde curls. I'll find some to show you.'

'I'd love to see them,' Brianna Jade said politely.

'So, um, anyway—' Edmund had planned out where he thought the proposal should take place – 'I was wondering if you'd like to go for a stroll with me in the grounds before dinner? The lake always looks lovely at this time of day.'

Brianna Jade was already rising to her feet, which she had sensibly clad in two-inch Lanvin slingbacks with a square heel. She and Tamra had learnt early that British aristocrats thought it was really 'common' for women to wear high heels when any kind of walking on lawns was involved: that was for what they called 'plebs', which seemed to mean anyone but them. Brianna Jade remembered polo matches where Minty and her crew had audibly mocked young women digging divots in the grass with the heels of their Jimmy Choos. Instead, the posh girls (although Tamra and Brianna Jade avoided saying that word, as posh people loathed it) showed off their skinny bare legs in Le Chameau or Hunter wellies and miniskirts that barely covered their tiny bottoms.

As Edmund held out his hand to her, Brianna Jade noticed his eyes flickering down for a second to assess her footwear, and his almost imperceptible nod of approval that she wasn't wearing stilettos.

Hey, I may not be Ivy League material, but I'm a quick learner, she thought proudly. *I'll do fine as a Countess. He'll never have to be embarrassed by me.*

'Shall we?' he said, the little phrase that posh men used to mean 'Let's go', and he tucked her arm through his so that she was resting on him just a tad. It was very gentlemanly; she loved it. They proceeded out through the French windows, onto the terrace, and down the stone steps to the gravel path that looped scenically around the gardens. They had been designed by someone with the weird name of Capability Brown, who Tamra assured Brianna Jade was like the biggest deal ever in gardening, and they needed a whole lot of maintenance. Edmund had apologized on their first visit because what he called the 'vistas' weren't what they should be; trees and bushes needed to be pruned away so that you could really see the views.

Well, that's what he's got me for, isn't it? she thought now, tripping along happily next to Edmund; after years of stepping elegantly up and down pageant stairs in killer heels, a stroll along a gravel path in two-inch slingbacks was nothing. Gardeners cost money, and that's what she was bringing to the table. Soon this place would have vistas up the wazoo. Stanclere would be vista heaven. They could invite magazines just to take photos of the vistas ...

She giggled a little at her own silliness, and Edmund, looking down at her pretty face for a moment, smiled at how charming she was. They rounded some overgrown shrubbery and the lake appeared, a soft green grassy slope dropping away to the oval expanse of water below, which shimmered gently in the light of the afternoon sun even with the green algae at its shoreline.

'It's supposed to be much more dramatic a sight,' Edmund said apologetically. 'The rhododendrons should really frame the first approach to the lake, and the stand of silver birches has been awfully neglected ...'

'It's a *great* vista,' Brianna Jade reassured him, and he burst out laughing.

'You have truly lovely manners,' he said, patting her hand.

'Let's walk over the bridge,' she said eagerly, looking at the low pale stone bridge that arched so elegantly over the water. Secretly she was thinking how very romantic it would be to be proposed to there, the sun behind her making her hair glow rosy with its golden light, Edmund on one knee ...

'Ah, I'm so sorry,' Edmund said, grimacing, 'but the groundskeeper told me this morning that he's worried about the foundations. It needs shoring up, apparently. He was supposed to put a plank across each side to stop people walking over it, just in case, but he clearly hasn't got round to it yet. I'll have to have a word with him tomorrow. Can't blame him too much though, I suppose – there's just so much to do around here ...'

I am totally getting that fixed first thing! Brianna Jade thought, staring at the beautiful picture – *vista* – before her, the white bridge standing out in front of a background of soft greens, a gentle slope rising beyond, planted with foliage in which mauve and white flowers flashed out here and there in the emerald bushes, the pewter lake like the base of a bowl. *Now I'm seeing myself in my wedding dress standing there, Edmund beside me, with flowers floating in the lake ... white roses ... and white ribbons all wrapped around the bridge, maybe some lavender ones too ...*

'I thought we might walk up to the gazebo?' Edmund was saying. He led her up the short stretch of path to the open stone building that looked like a small temple, with pillars in front of lots of statues of Greek gods and goddesses in stone drapery.

'I love the statues,' she said enthusiastically. 'Mom does too.'

Edmund had extracted the Tiffany box and was holding it behind his back now. 'All from Greece,' he informed her. 'An Earl of Respers brought the statuary back after his Grand Tour in the late eighteenth century.' He coughed. 'Not that the Greek government knows they're here. I'm afraid he bribed a lot of people to be able to take them out of the country. We should probably give them back.'

'Hell, no!' Brianna Jade shook her head decisively. 'That was ages ago, and they look great here. Finders keepers. Plus,' she added, 'I saw on the news that Greece is totally bankrupt, so they'd just sell them to someone else anyway, and they could never look as nice as they do right here.'

'I'm very glad you've taken that position,' Edmund said. 'Because I'm hoping, more than I can say, that you will agree to, um, take up a permanent position—'

Oh God, he thought, *you sound as if you're making a speech in the House of Lords! For God's sake, Edmund, there's a beautiful young woman looking up at you, waiting for you to propose to her – try to sound like a man and not a stuffed shirt!*

He cleared his throat.

'What I mean to say,' he continued, 'is that in the time that we've spent getting to know each other, I've come to appreciate you more than I can say. You are a truly lovely, sweet girl who would adorn any position into which she was placed—'

Position! Why on earth do I keep saying that?

But mercifully, as he seemed to be irredeemably tangled up in unnecessarily pompous verbiage, understanding was dawning on Brianna Jade's face.

'*Oh!*' she exclaimed. 'I get it now.' She shook back her cascades of hair. 'Take your time,' she added reassuringly. 'It's not like we're in any rush. And I want this to be special.'

This helped considerably. *I really am hugely lucky*, Edmund thought. *When Lady Margaret McArdle told me about the most beautiful American heiress London had seen for donkey's years, what were the odds that she'd also turn out to have a lovely temperament and a sensible head on her shoulders?*

'Brianna Jade,' he found himself saying very simply, 'I honestly don't even feel I *deserve* to ask you to marry me. And I want very much for us to be able to be honest with each other, which is why I'm not going to tell you that I'm madly in love with you, and I certainly don't expect you to tell me the same – not right now, anyway. We're both aware that in some aspects this is an arrangement. I'm very happy about it, and I do hope you are too.'

It was formal, he knew, and it was not the romantic declaration that a young twenty-four-year-old woman might want to hear. But it was the truth, and he had resolved beforehand that she – and he – deserved nothing less. It was common knowledge in his circle that Prince Oliver, heir to the throne, had proposed to Lady Belinda Lindsey-Crofter under entirely false pretences, basically tricking a young woman who was genuinely in love with him into thinking that her sentiments were fully returned, that it was a love match; when the truth had eventually dawned on Belinda, she was trapped, not only married but pregnant with the heir to the throne. The general view among the upper classes was that Oliver had behaved very badly by deceiving her. After all, many aristocratic young women would have been more than happy with the bargain he had to offer, a complaisant husband and a royal crown awaiting them.

But that was not how Edmund intended to treat Brianna Jade. No deception, no trickery. They were both going into this with their eyes open.

Hers were indeed wide as he gazed down at her, but not with surprise or indignation. She was listening intently to every word he said, hands clasped in front of her, lips slightly parted to show her extraordinarily perfect American teeth, a string of pearls behind her velvety pink lips.

'I honestly think you're the most beautiful girl I've ever

seen,' Edmund said. 'But you're also very quick, and curious, and spirited, and funny, and I truly enjoy spending time with you. Goodness knows if you feel the same about me—' he grinned self-deprecatingly – 'I know I can't possibly be the most handsome man you've ever met! But I do have all this to offer you.'

He gestured around him, encompassing not just the gazebo and the illegally looted Greek statuary but the entire sweep of Stanclere Hall.

'You would make a wonderful mistress of the Hall,' he said. 'And of course, a wonderful Countess of Respers. But you've got to decide if this really is what you want.'

Her smooth tanned forehead crinkled into the faintest of lines as she looked up at him: clearly, she was baffled by this suggestion. *Of course I want it!* her expression said. *I'm standing here waiting for you to propose, aren't I?*

'I know this is what the Fra— your *mother* wants for you,' he clarified. 'But I do think it's crucial that you're free to make your own decision. Your mother can be very – um, err ... your mother has a wonderfully vibrant and decisive personality, and of course she only wants the best for you—'

Brianna Jade wasn't frowning any more; in fact her lips had parted further into a lovely smile, her teeth flashing in a ray of late afternoon sun.

'You can call Mom bossy if you want,' she said cheerfully. 'She is! But she loves me way too much to push me into something that would make me unhappy.'

It wasn't exactly a passionate declaration of love, but neither was his, and it certainly told Edmund that Thunderbirds were Go. He sank to one knee, simultaneously bringing his right arm round in front of him, so that it ended up just above his eye level. Should he have opened the box first? Probably, but then the ring might have fallen out. He really should have rehearsed this; but then, he'd wanted to be authentic, honest, not over-polished. Luckily, regular winter skiing meant that he had decent enough balance to stay on one knee without wobbling while he held up the box with his right hand and opened it with his left.

'*Wow*,' Brianna Jade breathed out on seeing the ring, a long, slow exhalation of sheer delight.

'Brianna Jade,' Edmund said, 'will you do me the very great honour of becoming my wife?'

'I *will*!' she said, her eyes sparkling now as brightly as the enormous pink diamond. 'I *definitely* will!'

Should he stand up first? No, she was already holding out her left hand, each finger tipped with pale pink nails whose own tips each had a white crescent painted onto them, so perfectly executed that they were like miniature works of art. She had slightly separated the third finger from the others to make it easy for him; in a moment, he had detached the ring from its velvet slot and slid it onto its allotted place. He came to his feet as she turned her hand from side to side in the approved brand-new-fiancée fashion, marvelling at its lavishness.

'You carry that off wonderfully,' he said with complete sincerity. 'It looks superb on you.'

She beamed up at him and raised her arms to wrap around his neck, the ring flashing streaks of colour across the stone pillar next to them; he encircled her waist and bent to kiss her for the first time. His cock stiffened almost immediately. She felt delicious in his arms, her body taut and toned from the runs she took every morning, but her breasts were soft against him, pressing seductively against his chest, her lips equally soft and pillowy beneath his, parting to let his tongue slip in, kissing him back with not a shred of false modesty. His hands tightened around her slim waist, pulling her closer, and she tilted her head up more and slid her hands down his back.

Her breath was fresh and pepperminty; she must have not only brushed her teeth before this crucial encounter, as he had done, but surreptitiously sucked on some sort of mint as well. Neither she nor her mother did anything as vulgar as chew gum, thank goodness. His cock was fully hard now, pressing against her lower body, and he was both mortified – they had barely got engaged and here he was, acting like a rampant bull! – and relieved that the attraction was fully there, that he had committed himself to a woman to whom it would be a positive pleasure to remain faithful. He shifted back fractionally, but she followed him with a lean of her body so his cock was still sandwiched between them, showing him that she, too, was relishing the proof of his instant reaction to her. When he eventually raised his head, they were both breathing fast, pink-cheeked, and smiling rather goofily at each other. Edmund dropped a kiss on her forehead and took a step back, clearing his throat.

'Well,' he said idiotically, 'um, that was very nice indeed.'

Brianna Jade burst out laughing.

'You're not kidding!' she said. 'Wow, what a relief! I mean, I think you're really cute. Mom promised me she'd googled you and you were a hottie before she set us up to meet – but you know, you don't know until you *know*, if you see what I mean.'

'I *do* see what you mean,' Edmund said, grinning and telling his erection firmly to go down. 'Firmly' perhaps wasn't the right way for him to think of that, dammit ...

'Let's go back to the house and tell Mom we're all done and dusted,' Brianna Jade said, winding her left arm through his and admiring her ring once more. 'She'll be dying to know it's all okay.'

'She loves you very much,' Edmund observed.

'Yeah, but don't worry. She's going to be fine letting me go,' his fiancée said with that quick perceptiveness of hers, combined with her American frankness: he was deeply grateful for both qualities. 'Mom's had to look after me since she was just a kid herself, you know? She's due a whole lot of "me" time, and now she's gonna take it. She won't be hovering around here, checking that you're treating me okay, or any shit like that.'

'Don't mince your words on my account,' Edmund said, laughing. 'Do feel free to express yourself.'

'Oh yeah, British humour, I get it,' Brianna Jade beamed. 'You say the opposite of what you mean. Anyway, Mom isn't going to be a hover mother. She said last night she'd been running my life for way too long and she just wants to see me happy and settled. And she wouldn't want to move in here or anything. Mom *loves* London. She wants to buy the house we're renting there.'

Edmund briefly tried to compute what Tamra's Chelsea mansion might cost on the open market. It came complete with a ballroom whose floor slid back to reveal a swimming pool, a climate-controlled wine cellar, billiard room, climate-controlled cigar storage room, cinema, a fully equipped gym and four underground parking spaces accessed through a private tunnel ... He shook his head in disbelief at how much money there obviously was in fracking. It certainly made spending forty thousand pounds on Brianna Jade's ring look like a mere bagatelle. Tamra had wanted to spend six figures, but Edmund had told her that countesses did not wear engagement rings that looked as if they belonged to pop stars, and she had reluctantly yielded.

He was looking at the ring as they strolled arm in arm out of the gazebo, and his fiancée followed suit.

'I didn't—' he started, wanting to be honest about everything, but again, she knew what he was thinking.

'I know Mom picked it out and bought it,' she said simply. 'That's totally cool. Men aren't as good at this kind of thing, and Mom knows just what I like.'

'I wanted you to have an heirloom,' he said. 'We do have some fairly decent family jewels. I was thinking about getting my mother's engagement ring reset.'

'Aww, that would have been lovely!' Brianna Jade said sympathetically. 'Let me guess – Mom nixed that idea?'

Edmund nodded, amused.

'Hah! I know – it wasn't big enough for her, I bet,' Brianna Jade said, grinning. 'Look, I get how things work here. People don't buy stuff, 'cause their families have loads of antiques and they pass them on. But there's no way Mom could give up the idea of me having a big shiny ring.'

She squeezed his arm empathetically.

'I'm sorry. I hope you're not offended. I'd love to wear your mom's ring, if you'd like. Would that be okay? It would mean a lot to me. And I'm sorry you're an orphan, too. I can't imagine what I'd do without Mom in my life. I know you don't like to talk about it much – the whole British stiff upper lip thing – but I'm here if you ever want to.'

Her sincerity was so evident that Edmund, very touched, stopped for a moment, reached for her other hand and pressed a kiss onto it.

'I truly am so lucky to have met you,' he said with equal sincerity. 'And I would be honoured for you to wear my mother's ring. I'll make sure to pull it out of the safe as soon as we get back to the Hall, and if it needs resizing we can easily organize that.'

'That's lovely,' Brianna Jade said happily. 'I'd really like that. Thank you.'

They fell into an easy, companionable silence as they rounded the overgrown shrubbery and started up the path that led back to Stanclere Hall. Edmund, who had been mulling something over, decided that he and Brianna Jade seemed able to talk about things so comfortably that he should raise a nagging concern he had about how their marriage would work.

'I'm wondering though – you must have thought this through already, but you know that I'm basically a farmer, don't you?' he started. 'I spend most of the year here, at the Hall. Not, you know, jetting off to Venice for the weekend or anything like that. I'm very fond of London, and I go to the races, of course, but really, my place is here. And we're in Rutland, not Sussex – you can't just pop up to London for a day.'

'Well, you can if you hire a helicopter,' his fiancée suggested.

'Yes! Yes, I suppose so.' It was an entirely new concept for Edmund. 'Frankly, I'm surprised the Fr— your mother hasn't done that already, instead of driving from London.'

'She loves the countryside here,' her daughter explained. 'She's really into looking at it. We get the chauffeur to take the back roads to see little villages and stuff like that.'

'I had no idea …'

'But Edmund—' It was the first time that Brianna Jade had said his name as his fiancée, and it made her feel happily cosy and intimate. 'You don't need to worry about me being bored here. I love the countryside even more than Mom does. I like London, but I'm not a city girl. Cities are crowded and dirty, and after a few days' shopping I want to get out and breathe some fresh air. Remember, I grew up in pig and corn country. I'd've been a farmer's wife back home, probably.' She sighed in nostalgia.

'Do you miss Illinois?' Edmund asked understandingly. 'I'd miss Rutland more than I can say if I had to leave.'

'I do,' she said frankly. 'Feeding the pigs and chickens, running round finding where they'd laid their eggs ... I really loved it. But it's way prettier in England! Where I come from, it's wide-open country, but here all the little fields are so green, with the hedges and the trees ... I'm going to love seeing the seasons change, I know.'

'And we have pigs and chickens here too,' Edmund teased her. 'Plenty of both. You're welcome to help with either any time you like.'

'I might just do that,' she said. 'Seriously, no kidding. I'd really like it. *That* would make me feel more at home than almost anything.'

'Well!' He grinned. 'I see I didn't have to worry about you minding the prospect of being a farmer's wife. We should probably have talked about all this before – actually, we should *definitely* have talked about this before. I suppose I took a lot for granted. But things were moving so fast ...'

'That's Mom,' his fiancée said reassuringly. 'It's not your fault. She kind of only has one setting, and it's hyperspeed.'

She squeezed his arm again. 'Don't worry – I haven't inherited that from her. I'm much more laid-back. I'm not going to shoot round Stanclere Hall on hyperspeed, driving everyone crazy.'

'Oh, she doesn't drive everyone crazy,' Edmund demurred politely, but he couldn't help but be grateful for Brianna Jade's promise that his married life would be what she called 'laid-back' and he would describe as restful.

They had fallen into a pleasantly even pace, their steps nicely synchronized, as they crested a rise in the gravel path and Stanclere Hall appeared before them. The view of the house was partly obscured by overgrowth and trees that needed pollarding, another of Capability Brown's vistas which required regular maintenance for full, stunning effect. Still, the Hall, its soft golden stone glowing at sunset, its two wings stretching out nobly from the central edifice with its double flight of steps leading up to the massive front door, was still a sight so beautiful that, despite its familiarity, Edmund caught his breath.

'You really love it,' Brianna Jade said, a comment, not a question. The breeze caught the pleated skirt of her dress, lifting the chiffon slightly; she lowered one hand to hold the folds down, her other still linked through Edmund's as they strolled down the path to the Hall, lush green swards spreading out on either side. Like the rest of the gardens, the grass needed urgent attention; the croquet lawn was pocked with mole holes and had gone to seed years ago. But from a distance it was serene, verdant, the perfect setting for a perfect English stately home.

'I do,' Edmund said, his voice quiet as he let his breath out. 'But I'm not a monomaniac.'

'Uh—'

'I'm not someone who's mad about only one thing,' he elaborated quickly for her benefit. 'I really do hope that you and I will come to love each other too, Brianna Jade.'

'Oh, go ahead and drop the Jade!' she said easily. 'It's way too long for everyday use. Brianna or Bri is just fine.'

'Phew,' he said, grinning at her. 'It *is* a bit of a mouthful.'

'Edmund—' She felt the same frisson using his name as before, which was really nice – 'talking about names, now that we're engaged, do I get a title? I was wondering. Do I get to be a Lady? Or an Honourable, like Minty?'

This is why it's such a good thing that we were honest and direct with each other, Edmund told himself. *We haven't pretended that part of her appeal for me isn't her money, nor that mine for her isn't my title. So no one needs to be embarrassed by this at all. Not in the least.*

'I'm afraid not,' he said with regret. 'You have to be born into the peerage to have a title like that. On our marriage, you become the Countess of Respers, and people will call you Lady Respers. Except, I *think*, on legal documents, where you're the Right Honourable Brianna Jade, Countess of Respers. But the lawyers deal with all that sort of thing, so you don't need to worry about it.'

'Oh! I don't get to be Lady Brianna Jade?' she asked naïvely. 'I was sort of hoping I would.'

'Sorry,' Edmund said, charmed despite himself at her lack of pretence. 'It isn't in my power to give you that. Not even King Stephen could. You have to be born into the peerage, you see.'

'Ooh! So our kids—'

'If we have a son, he'll be Lord and then his name,' Edmund informed her. 'Younger son's are Honourables. And daughters are Lady, and then their name.'

'Aww, how lovely – my kids being Lords and Ladies! I can't wait,' Brianna Jade said blissfully. 'And Edmund, don't worry. I won't make a fuss about calling the kids American names like Presley or Kaylee or—' she giggled, 'Latisha. We'll pick proper British ones. I don't want them embarrassed.'

'Good to know,' Edmund managed to mumble: the prospect of the heir to the Respers estates being called Lord Presley had never even occurred to him.

'And I don't want to start having kids straight away, either,' she assured him. 'I think we should take some time to settle down with each other, don't you? Properly get to know each other. Like you said, fall in love.'

There was a shyness in her voice as she said the last words, a shyness that was, however, combined with confidence.

Brianna Jade had no real doubts that she and Edmund would have any problems learning to love each other. He was a truly great guy, and they had so much in common with their love of the countryside; she felt that they were halfway there already. And she had healthy self-esteem: adored all her life by Tamra, Brianna Jade had no trouble believing that even an Earl would find her as lovable as her mother did – hell, she'd happily settle for him finding her *almost* as lovable as that.

They had crossed the lawns and were heading up the stone steps of the terrace now, and he stopped for a moment to kiss her on the lips.

'Taking our time sounds absolutely fine to me,' he said. 'An excellent plan.'

'And Mom won't be in *any* hurry to be a grandma, trust me on that,' her daughter commented. 'Not with having had me so young.'

'Not even to a sweet little daughter called Latisha?' Edmund asked. 'You know, that name is rather growing on me. I think Lady Latisha sounds rather elegant.'

'Edmund! *No!*' his fiancée shrieked, slapping his arm before realizing that he was joking.

'Oh ha ha! *Very* funny!' she said, giggling, and Edmund was laughing too as they reached the top of the terrace to the spectacular vision of the Fracking Queen in all her splendour.

Chapter Three

Tamra Maloney, a champagne flute in her hand, was standing by a table covered in a white cloth which bore not only a bottle of Cristal in a large silver wine cooler, but two more flutes awaiting the engaged couple. Seeing that her daughter's future as the Countess of Respers was not only assured, but that she and Edmund were getting on well enough to laugh together, the mother of the bride's full lips curved into a smile that bordered on a positive smirk of satisfaction. With her slightly slanting dark eyes and mane of red-gold hair, at that moment Tamra resembled a beautiful jungle cat: she could almost have been a lioness after a successful hunt, stretched out along a tree branch, purring with pleasure after having eaten her fill.

Even with his beautiful twenty-four-year-old fiancée on his arm, Edmund could not help the instinctive reaction he always had at the sight of her mother. Tamra Maloney simply took your breath away. She wasn't just beautiful, she had a quality of barely leashed sensuality, a gleam in her dark brown eyes, that had several of Edmund's friends eagerly comparing her to a young Sharon Stone. Dominic, with whom Edmund had roomed at college, was already insisting on being Edmund's best man purely to give him enough status to hit on Tamra at the wedding.

'Sod bridesmaids,' Dominic had leered enthusiastically, 'I want the mother of the bride. Talk about hot cougar action! That woman could fuck me into pieces and I'd die with a smile on my face.'

'*Dom,*' Edmund had said crossly, 'that's the grandmother of my future children you're talking about. *Please!*'

But looking at Tamra now, in a fitted silk wrap Givenchy dress that was perfectly decent but still clung to every lush curve of her body, at her flawless, lightly tanned skin, her strawberry-blonde hair held back with Michael Kors sun-glasses, and around the long stem of her neck a De Grisogono rose-gold necklace set with diamonds, so elaborate and heav-ily worked that only a woman with her height and confidence could have carried it off, Edmund couldn't actually blame Dominic for lusting after his mother-in-law-to-be. She and Brianna Jade could have been sisters, could almost have been twins from a distance, until you saw that Tamra's eyes were bigger, darker, and gleaming with a lust for life and a wealth of experience that Brianna Jade, simpler, sweeter, happy to settle down into country life at twenty-four, would never acquire.

Brianna Jade's a Sienese icon, Edmund reflected, *but Tamra's a Titian; that colouring – the red lights in the hair, the golden skin, the deep brown eyes, she's a classic Titian beauty. I must tell her – I think she'd rather like that. Shame we had to sell our own Titian in the 1950s …*

Tamra's wide brown eyes, framed in ridiculously thick dark brown lashes, not all of which she had been born with, glanced swiftly towards her daughter, taking in the ring on her finger, the smile on her face, the snug link of her arm through Edmund's, and Edmund's own contented expression. Tamra

had had the most discreet plastic surgery money could buy;
her features moved so easily that it was clear she hadn't had
Botox; but Botox, now, was for amateurs, as were fillers, short-
term fixes that messed with one's face disastrously in the long
run. Casting directors in Hollywood were increasingly refusing to even see actors whom their agents couldn't guarantee
were free of both.

The really clever men and women were taking a much
more measured approach, one which required no riskily inva-
sive procedures at all: a double blast of microdermabrasion
followed by gel lathered on the face and a cold laser, like a
little flashlight, trained on the skin for at least forty-five minutes to stimulate collagen production. As Tamra smiled, there
was barely a single line creasing the smooth high forehead or
fanning out from those marvellously compelling dark eyes.
Her lips, infinitesimally plumped by the discreetest of collagen
injections – the only injectable Tamra permitted herself, and
only because her doctor performed them behind the lip,
rather than into it, giving a tiny extra fullness without changing the shape at all – parted as she breathed out a long, utterly
complacent sigh of relief and triumph in equal measure.

She'd done it. Her baby was going to be a Countess. All
Tamra's hard work, the struggle and graft and frustration and
tears and picking herself up off the damn floor every time she
fell down, starting all over again, time after time – everything
had been worth it to see Brianna Jade like this, marrying a
really good guy who would take care of her and who just so
happened – *hello!* – to be a damn Earl! Her grandchildren
were going to be Lords and Ladies! Pretty good for Tamra Jean
Krantz from Kewanee County, Illinois!

She wanted to run towards Brianna Jade and Edmund, to
burst into much-needed tears of sheer happiness, but over
here people seemed to be more stick-up-their-ass, and while

she and Bri were determined not to have their moxie ground out of them by stuck-up Brits, Tamra was okay toning it down a little to fit in. *Go along to get along,* as she'd always said. So Tamra put down her glass and walked quickly halfway across the terrace, met there by her daughter, who had moved just as fast; they didn't cry, but they fell into each other's arms, hugging so tightly that Brianna's four-carat diamond engagement ring left a dent in her mother's firm, tanned bare back below the halterneck tie of her dress when they finally released each other. They looked into each other's eyes, light hazel into dark brown, as they had so many times before, their bond as tight as it could be, and, as so many times before, mother and daughter exchanged an unspoken message.

Don't cry. No tears. We're on top of the world, you and I.

A pageant competitor and her stage mother had no problem at all either crying on demand or controlling the impulse. Both of the women swallowed in unison, took deep breaths and broke into smiles so joyful that Edmund, who, in true gentlemanly fashion, had crossed to the table to pour drinks (by his code, ladies should never have to fill or top up their own glasses when a gentleman was present) was so dazzled by their sheer wattage that he spilled some Cristal on the tablecloth.

'All my dreams for you have come true, honey,' Tamra said to Brianna Jade, reaching out to stroke her hair. 'I got there in the end, didn't I?'

'You did, Mom,' Brianna Jade said happily. 'You really did.'

Clasping her daughter's hand, Tamra turned to Edmund, who had managed to fill the champagne flutes without any more spillage and was waiting politely for his fiancée and future mother-in-law to finish their women's moment.

'Edmund, I know you'll make my little girl a wonderful husband,' she said contentedly.

'I'd better, Tamra,' Edmund said with an amused twist of his lips. 'Or I rather think you'll make my life a living hell.'

Tamra burst out laughing. 'I *will*, dammit,' she admitted. 'You're damn right. Jeez, Bri, I found you a British Earl who tells it like it is *and* has a sense of humour! I never thought I'd manage *that.*'

'And he's very good at serving drinks, too,' Brianna Jade said as Edmund handed them flutes filled with pale straw-coloured Cristal, studded enticingly with tiny bubbles. The three of them clinked glasses. Edmund and Brianna Jade sipped the champagne; Tamra, however, sank the contents of her glass in a single, effortless drag.

'I'd have killed at the keggers if I ever went to college,' she said cheerfully. 'Hell, I needed that. This has been a long time coming.'

She put down her glass on the stone balustrade and took in the scene before her. The sun had almost set now, and dark rose streaks were reaching across the lawns, darkening the leaves of the ancient oaks in the woodland beyond. Those trees had been planted by the first Earl of Respers, centuries ago, a fact that never ceased to make Tamra marvel. She had come from nothing, dirt-poor German immigrant farming stock; now her grandchildren would be Lords and Ladies, would inherit this beautiful stately home, climb the historic trees, play on the lawns, slide, screaming with happiness, down the banisters of the staircase which had been carved with acanthus flowers by Grinling Gibbons himself in 1640 (apparently that was a huge deal as Edmund mentioned it constantly – she'd have to look it up). Tamra was a stickler for detail.

Tamra turned to lean against the balcony, looking up at the golden stone expanse of Stanclere Hall. Edmund and Brianna Jade were finishing their champagne, talking quietly but happily.

Tamra's eyes rested on her daughter's fiancé for a moment.

He's a good-looking, well set-up guy. Nice shoulders, strong bone structure, tight abs. That's all the farm work, I guess – he seems pretty into all of that. Funny that we came from a farm and that's where Bri's ended up. He's not handsome, but he has a real nice face; better that way. Gorgeous guys are nothing but trouble. Yeah, Edmund's one of the good ones. And hell, I should know! The amount of men I've had to size up instantly in my time . . .

She noticed with pleasure that Edmund was actually listening to what her daughter was saying. A man who listened to a woman was worth his weight in gold. Tamra had seriously never thought that she'd hit the jackpot like this. To nail, for her daughter, an Earl who was thirty-four – the perfect marrying age for a guy – and didn't just have his own hair and teeth but was actually pretty hot in a low-key British way; no denying that was like the relentless ring of a casino slot machine flashing a golden horseshoe triple bonus on the screen as coins flooded out into the trough below.

But, she conceded, Edmund had hit the jackpot too. Tamra had more money than God and she was no tightwad about spending it.

She gazed up at the expanse of the Hall, a smile of wry amusement on her perfect lips. Mentally, she listed all the things that urgently needed fixing: the roof, the dry rot, the plumbing, the electrics, pretty much every damn thing. Like the lawns, the Hall looked great from a distance; close up, Tamra could see a whole lot of crumbling window frames, perilously bent guttering and stone that needed repointing – apparently the whole Hall needed repointing, a job that would literally take years. But Tamra was fine with that. It was the deal. And the Hall, after all, was held in trust for her grandkids; it wasn't like she'd plough money into this only to have

Edmund sell it out from under her. He couldn't even if he wanted to because of the entail. Doing up Stanclere Hall was an investment in the future of her family.

Plus, she got to put in en suites all over, with underfloor heating and proper American power showers. *Oh my God, I can't wait! That trickle that comes out of the taps and shower heads here ... ugh, not just a trickle, but kinda yellow too, like washing your hands in pee! The plumbing's going to be the first thing I tackle ...*

'Tamra? May I?'

Edmund was courteously proffering the Cristal bottle, and Tamra never said no to a drink.

'You know,' she said, flashing him her best teasing smile as she held out her glass, 'you should really call me Mom now, Edmund, like Bri does.'

This time Edmund spilled some champagne over his tie as Tamra and Brianna Jade giggled in unison at the appalled expression on his face.

'It's okay, son, I was just messing with you,' Tamra said, sending her and Brianna Jade off into even more giggles as Edmund's eyes widened in horror at the prospect of Tamra calling him 'son' from now on.

'Don't worry, Mom's just playing,' Brianna Jade said, taking the bottle from her fiancé before he accidentally poured the rest of the contents over his handmade Lobb shoes.

'Honestly, Tamra, it's odd enough calling my future mother-in-law by her first name,' Edmund admitted, pink-cheeked now. 'Let alone ...'

He simply couldn't look at the stunning woman in front of him – she was forty, he knew, but she looked ten years younger – and remotely connect the word 'Mom', or even 'Mummy', with her in any way. His own mother, who had died with his father in a small plane crash on a bird-watching safari in Botswana seven years ago (ironically, it had been a cormorant flying into one of the engines that had caused the disaster) had been a considerably more – well, *motherly* figure, with her sensible tweeds and greying hair. Picturing Mummy clad in Tamra's silk wrap halterneck dress, her hair held back with Tamra's designer sunglasses and her liver-spotted arms bared ... the image was so surreal, and Edmund had such a flash of sadness for his parents in that moment, that he couldn't speak another word.

'It's hard that you don't have your own folks still here with you,' Tamra said, reading his mind with disconcerting acuteness. She reached out to pat his arm sympathetically. 'I'm so sorry. They were too young to go.'

Edmund nodded in thanks, took the glass Brianna Jade was handing him and drank some more; he appreciated her words very much, but was too British to be able to respond to them. Tamra understood this too.

'I love the taste of champagne,' she observed, deliberately lightening the mood, 'but those damn bubbles can get up my nose sometimes.'

'You can stir them out,' Edmund said, clearing his throat, glad to have the conversation changed. 'With a champagne whisk. My grandmother had some – they're rather lovely old things. She had one she wore around her neck in a little silver case: you pull it out and all these sort of filaments pop out and you put it in your glass to whisk the bubbles away.'

'Cool,' Tamra said appreciatively.

'I'll make sure we fish them out for you and give them a good polish,' Edmund said, smiling at her. 'The silver here's been awfully neglected, and we don't want to give you a tarnished whisk! We'll have it all ready for you in time for cocktail hour tomorrow.'

'Edmund, I would love that, and you're really sweet to

make the offer,' Tamra said – she had got the hang of saying 'really' instead of 'real', as the English did – 'but I won't be here tomorrow. I'm heading off back to London now. Time to leave the newly engaged couple in peace and quiet.' She winked at them, a perfectly executed gesture, one set of enviably thick eyelashes fluttering for a moment on her smooth cheek. 'Last thing you guys want is Mom hanging around! So I'm going to love you and leave you. I got the maid to pack me up again while you guys were sorting yourselves out. I mean, if Bri turned you down at the last minute, Edmund, we'd be leaving anyway, and if she said "yes", I needed to get the hell out of Dodge. So either way it was a no-brainer.'

'But Tamra, it's getting dark now,' Edmund protested politely, though inwardly he was full of admiration for her skill and excellent manners: leaving the newly engaged couple alone together displayed a sensitivity he hadn't expected from her. 'Why not at least stay till morning? You'll want your dinner, surely.'

She laughed in his face in the nicest possible way, her teeth just as mother-of-pearl and perfectly aligned as her daughter's.

'Oh Edmund, honey, you know I barely eat at the best of times,' she said fondly, patting his arm again. 'I have a hamper ready to be loaded into the car – smoked salmon and bresaola and Cristal all waiting for me on ice. I'll just pick at some protein and drink all the way home.'

'But—' Brianna Jade began, only to be interrupted by her mother.

'Ssh, honey,' Tamra said with huge affection, enfolding her daughter in another tight hug. 'You'll be fine. You and Edmund have way more interesting things to do than sit around and make conversation with your mom, for God's sake! Right, Edmund?'

She winked at him again, a devastatingly appealing wink

that said that she knew that he and Brianna Jade hadn't even kissed before today and that she imagined he had plenty of ground to cover now. Edmund's shirt collar was suddenly tight and damp with sweat; he ran a finger inside it to loosen it up.

'See you very soon,' Tamra said, kissing him lightly on the cheek, her very expensive perfume enfolding him for a moment. 'And don't worry about me being bored in London on my lonesome! I'm seeing Lady Margaret tomorrow for a boozy lunch – Jeez, that woman can drink like me, it's a real pleasure hanging out with her – and I've got a meeting with the publicist to talk about the first set of engagement pictures in *Hello!*'

She beamed. 'Won't take more than a couple of weeks to set that up. Did you propose on the bridge, Edmund? Over the lake? That would look gorgeous if we wanna recreate it.'

'No, it needs some shoring up,' Brianna Jade said, distracted from the shock of Tamra's sudden departure by the prospect of the engagement photos as Tamra had known she would be. 'He did it in the gazebo instead.'

'Lovely!' Tamra said. 'Get the bridge fixed first thing, though. They might want to use it too. *And*, I've got really exciting news – *Style* magazine is going to run its first-ever Brides issue next June, and guess who's going to be on the cover if I have anything to say about it?'

Brianna Jade actually clasped her hands at her breast in excitement. She hadn't done that since her pageant years, and this was the first time ever that she had made the gesture quite spontaneously.

'No *way*, Mom!' she gasped.

'*Way*, honey! I swear, you guys are going to be *Style*'s first ever Wedding of the Year! You have everything – class, title, a good-looking groom—'

'Um, thanks,' Edmund murmured, adjusting his collar again.

'And the most beautiful bride *ever*! I swear, Princess Chloe is a lovely girl, and looked real nice on her special day—' Tamra had actually forgotten to say 'really', such was her level of excitement – 'but you're going to blow her out of the water, Bri, honey! *Style* Bride of the Year!'

Her dark eyes gleamed not only with anticipation, but with infinite menace; woe betide any other bride who might try to snag that coveted title for herself when Tamra Maloney had set her heart on the prize for her beloved daughter.

'As far as I'm concerned, it's a done deal already,' she told the Earl and Countess-to-be. 'I swear, if *anyone* tries to stand in my way—' her eyes flashed with an ominously dark flame 'they'll regret it for the rest of their lives!'

Chapter Four

Latitude Festival, Sussex

> Birds come flying like dreams of kings
> And the seahorses chant of life
> Death paints blue the song they sing
> But dreams can fade where there is stri – eye – ife ...

Tarquin Ormond sang ecstatically into his microphone, his head tilted back to catch the last traces of sunlight, his golden curls, damp with sweat, framing the angelic face of the choirboy he had once been. The huge crowd in front of the main stage at Latitude, hippies and hipsters united in worship of Tarquin's authenticity, his poetic soul, his transparent sincerity, sang along, their heads also tilted back, as if they were all worshipping at some centuries-old rite, with Tarquin as their beautiful and pure high priest.

And in a way, that was exactly what the crowd was doing: worshipping the band's authenticity. Tarquin and his band, Ormond and Co, were mainstays of the folk-rock revival,

sweet-faced boys who wrote all their own songs and not only
played all their own instruments, but dedicated endless hours
to searching out obscure traditional ones to incorporate in
their music. For this song, 'Blue Seahorses', a roadie had
lugged onstage a theorbo, a long-necked lute, which Elden, the
guitarist, was playing with limited skill but great concentration, and a hang – a huge steel hand drum invented by Swiss
sound engineers – on which Lance the drummer was flickering his fingers intently.

Despite it being the height of summer – mercifully decent
weather for once, so the Latitude crowds were in flip-flops
rather than wellies – Ormond and Co were dressed in swel-
tering tweeds. Being posh boys to a man (the band had been
formed at the minor public school they had all attended),
the tweeds were not second-hand from charity shops, which
was where most new-folk bands bought theirs, but had been
handed down through their various families. Tarquin's three-
piece suit had been used by his Great-Uncle Willoughby for
deer stalking and hare-coursing. No matter how many times
it had been dry cleaned, it still smelt, when heated above a
certain temperature by Tarquin's body, sweating under the stage
lights, of stinky dog and hare blood. The young men were all
quite used to their suits by now and barely noticed each other's
odours, but eager journalists rushing to interview them as they
came offstage had often been noticed to rear their heads back
and inhale as little as possible once they took in the full whiff
of the four Ormond members in their damp hot tweeds.

My love's ungiven, my wings are straw
I dip my heart into your life
My waterfall of tears will soar
Seahorses steal my promised wife
For dreams can fade where there is stri – eye – ife . . .

Tarquin sang, and a great many people in the field below the stage, who would have commented, 'But what the fuck does that even *mean?*' if they had seen the words written down, sang along with him with as much conviction as if his lyrics were a Shakespeare sonnet set to music. Tarquin's exquisite tenor voice, together with the melodic cadences of the tunes written by Lance and Elden, elevated the nonsensical words into a sort of broken poetry while sung – with the caveat that as soon as you actually stopped for a moment to ask why sea-horses would want to steal anyone's wife, the whole edifice would tumble like a house of cards.

'God, talk about the Emperor's New Clothes!' Milly Gamble, Tarquin's actress girlfriend, watching from the wings, shouted in her friend Eva's ear. 'This one makes even *less* sense than the last one!'

'It's like poetry,' Eva protested. 'I know what he *means* …'

'You're so nice, Eves,' Milly yelled accurately, if patronizingly. 'You never have a bad word to say about anyone!'

'I do!' Eva was piqued. 'I'm sure I do.'

'I don't mean slagging off factory farming or supermarkets or Third World work conditions,' Milly shouted. 'I mean actually bitching about—'

But she had to cut herself short, as the music had reached a final peak and stopped with a last wail of the theorbo. Onstage, Tarquin had sung the last 'stri – eye – ife …' of 'Blue Seahorses', and was panting, arms spread wide like the golden-haired, blue-eyed martyred saint he strongly resembled, microphone dangling spent from one white hand as the crowd cheered and drummed their feet and wailed their applause. The steel hang was dripping with sweat from Lance's beard; the roadie running onstage to remove the drum had to handle it very carefully in case it slipped through his fingers.

'Fuck, Tark's going to pong of dog even more than ever when he comes offstage,' Milly muttered grimly. 'I'm not going *near* him till he has a shower and changes and hangs those stinky old rags up in the sunshine to air out.'

'I do think it's rather lovely that they all wear their family's clothes,' Eva whispered bravely. 'It's so authentic and *real*. You know, their fans actually know the names of the relatives they belonged to?'

'They *do*? God, how mental of them!' Milly said loudly enough that Elden, handing his theorbo reverently to another roadie and receiving an Arabian *oud* in exchange, shot a cross glance over at Tarquin's girlfriend, whom he rightly considered not remotely respectful enough of her boyfriend's band and their very important art.

Onstage, Tarquin had raised the mike to his mouth again, and was saying: 'Beautiful people of Latitude!'

The crowd cheered this with great enthusiasm. Tarquin was completely transparent: he was like a holy fool, quite incapable of saying anything he didn't mean. If he told them they were beautiful, he was utterly sincere, and they accepted the compliment very happily.

'I just can't hold it back any longer!' he exclaimed, pressing one hand against his heart. 'I wrote "Blue Seahorses" for my girlfriend, and that song means so much to me – it really sums up all my hopes and fears about love, which is, like, the deepest feeling ever.'

The crowd roared its approval of the profoundly meaningful lyrics of 'Blue Seahorses'.

'And so many of you have got in touch to say how much the song means to you as well, which is *so* emotional for me to hear,' Tarquin continued, and the young female fans at the front, all of whom were madly in love with him, squealed at almost bat-like pitch at the idea of Tarquin reading the emails and Facebook and Twitter posts in which they poured out their hearts to him.

'So look, I was planning to do this at the end of our set, but I just can't hold it back any more! I feel your love surrounding me, lifting me up like the seahorses, and I'm just like – the time is *now*!'

Tarquin turned, sweat flicking from the tips of his boyish golden curls, one hand to his brow to block out the sun as he squinted into the wings to spot Milly.

'Some of you may know my girlfriend, Milly Gamble,' he continued, at which the screams dwindled considerably; Tarquin's female fans either pretended that Milly didn't exist or posted screeds of hate on fan-boards about how she wasn't worthy of him.

'*Some* of them?' Milly muttered to Eva, equally unenthusiastic at his words. '*Please*. I was in *Dr* fucking *Who*!'

To be fair, Milly was quite right. Most of the audience would recognize her, and the majority of those who did would be able to put the name to her adorably pretty face, that of a perfect English flower child: big blue eyes, blonde ringlets, round chipmunk cheeks and just a sprinkling of freckles across the bridge of her tip-tilted nose. Because of her looks, Milly was always cast as the innocent heroine. She had already been Hero to Melody Dale's Beatrice in the recent RSC *Much Ado About Nothing*, a Dickens heroine for ITV and a princess in a castle on *Dr Who* (played by Melody's husband James).

It was deeply frustrating for Milly, who was longing to break free of this typecasting and play a scheming bitch for a change, and not just because it would reflect her true personality so much better. But she was intelligent enough to go with what nature had dealt her, and there was no point trying and failing to be cast as a femme fatale when you looked like an innocent Dickensian virgin. She was just twenty-three, and already well-known enough to pose for glossy magazines, usually with the caption 'Britain's Newest Sweetheart' above her delightful little face: if that was how she was going to be perceived, Milly had decided, then why not try for 'America's Sweetheart' too? She was determined to crack the States, had already been compared several times to a young Meg Ryan, and being not just an up-and-coming ingénue, but half of a young and gorgeous celebrity couple to boot, was perfect publicity.

'Milly! Darling, come out here,' Tarquin called, holding out his hand to her.

'She's not going to fucking *duet* with him, is she?' Elden hissed to Lance, one hand covering his mike so his words didn't get picked up, winding his fingers furiously through his beard with the other. All the Ormonds but Tarquin had beards: to his great distress, he was unable to grow anything more than blonde bum fluff. 'Because she can't fucking *sing*, for a start.'

'Everyone! Milly's a bit shy!' Tarquin said, utterly misunderstanding Milly's delay. In fact, she was swiftly adjusting the daisy chain she wore in her hair and checking the embroidered neckline of the white broderie anglaise Temperley dropped-waist mini-dress that looked charmingly simple but had cost over three thousand pounds. 'Let's all call her name to show her how much we want her out here!'

Female voices were not much on display in the chants of 'Milly! Milly!' that rose from the audience; when Milly finally stepped onto the stage in her wedge sandals, the cheers that arose were mostly from men at the front craning to see up the very short skirt of her dress. Milly, quite aware of this, flashed a beautiful smile at the crowd as she picked her way daintily over the various cables on the floor, stepping, perhaps, a little higher than she strictly needed to each time to flash a fraction more upper thigh.

'Baby!' Tarquin said devoutly as she reached his side, slipping into American jargon temporarily, something he never allowed himself in his lyrics. 'I love you so much, I wrote that song for you – *you're* my blue seahorse!'

'Oh, Tark,' Milly breathed, staring up at him with big round blue eyes just as enthusiastic as if she had thought even *he* knew what he meant by calling her that. 'I love you too.'

Tarquin's jacket was unbuttoned; he reached into the pocket of his silk-backed waistcoat, pulled out a little box and dropped to one knee.

'Ah, *bollocks*!' Lance mouthed to Elden. Even Tristram, the bassist, who never said much, shook his head as if trying to cancel out what Tarquin was clearly about to do.

'Milly Gamble, my blue seahorse, will you do me the very great honour of saying yes in front of all these lovely people ...'

Roars of appreciation for Tarquin's acknowledgement of the audience rose from the field. A few girls at the front, tears beginning to pour down their faces, shrieked: 'No, Tarquin, no! Don't do it! Marry *me*!' but their voices were generally lost in the crowd as Tarquin continued.

'Milly, you're my muse, my inspiration for my songs, my soulmate. We're twin hearts, beating together. Without you I was lost, and when I found you I came home. Will you do me the very great honour of becoming my wife?'

Milly's expression never faltered, but as she looked down at Tarquin her brain was racing with calculation. She raised her hands to the sides of her face, pantomiming her surprise without obscuring her features for the TV cameras recording the festival; she knew exactly where they were. Her cupid's-bow lips parted in a round O of amazement that she knew suited her tremendously.

She hadn't seen this coming, hadn't perceived Tarquin as

much more than a very useful stepping stone to someone even more famous and useful than him; but it was quite true that since she'd started dating him a year and a half ago, his profile had done nothing but rise, the awards his band had won around the world had multiplied to the point that they'd fill up countless mantelpieces and still overflow. And with a proposal this public – live on camera, on the main stage of one of the trendiest festivals in the UK – how could she say no? She simply couldn't. And a wedding would be *fantastic* publicity for her . . .

'Oh my God! This is *such* a surprise – but of course I will!' she blurted out in her sweet baby voice.

Beaming from ear to ear, Tarquin jumped to his feet and opened the box. And when she saw what was inside, Milly had to use every single trick in her box of acting skills in order to manage an enthusiastic: '*Oh, Tark!*' and keep the smile on her face.

'I chose it specially to match your eyes!' he said as he slid the turquoise ring onto her finger.

'It's *beautiful*,' she breathed, taking just the right amount of time to look at it in wonder before raising her eyes to her fiancé's face so that he could kiss her for the cameraphones which were now going off in a perpetual stutter of clicks; even the sobbing girls were holding theirs up, wanting to capture the moment so that they could text it to their friends with captions scrawled over the screen like: *I want 2 DIE kill me NOWWWW OMG why why why Tark is MINE!* :(:(:(

The stink of Tarquin's suit was almost unbearable. Milly disengaged herself from it immediately, waved charmingly at the audience and tripped lightly offstage, flashing radiant smiles at Elden, Lance and Tristram. She was perfectly aware that they all disliked her and was highly enjoying their crest-fallen expressions.

'Wow,' Tarquin said to the crowd. 'I'm engaged! Unbelievable! Okay, guys, let's play some music!'

Lance started up the next song on the set list, and the audience went crazy: 'Moon Face' was one of Ormond and Co's biggest hits. Tarquin held out the mike so that the crowd could sing the opening 'Oh, oh oh oh oh,' and they responded with a loud wail.

'Congratulations!' Eva said as Milly rejoined her and, taking her hand, pulled her friend down the rickety steps on the side of the stage. Eva mewed with frustration, as she loved Ormond and Co and wanted to watch the end of the set; but Milly had had psychological dominance over her ever since childhood. They had attended the same nursery school, and their first encounter had been when Milly walked up to Eva, who was docilely brushing the hair of her Little Mermaid Barbie, and started to wrench Ariel from her owner's hands, screaming: 'Mine! *Mine!*' Eva had taken one look at the angel-faced little girl with wrists of steel, released her grip on Ariel, and barely ever said no to Milly since.

'Honestly, a *turquoise?*' Milly said under her breath so that the various other people hanging around the backstage VIP area couldn't hear her. She took a swift look around, spotted a trestle table that was free, and marched across the grass, still towing Eva in her wake. A few 'Congrats, Milly!' were called out as she passed musicians or actors whom she vaguely knew, and her smile never faltered as she said a quick: 'Thanks!' But she didn't slow down till she reached the table and sank onto the bench alongside it, running her hand over it first to make sure there weren't any loose splinters that could catch at her very expensive dress.

'*But* although I'm *gutted* I only got a bloody *turquoise*,' she said crossly, 'what I'm thinking is that we could use this for marketing. It could be a brilliant way to push Milly and Me. I might as well get *something* positive out of it. We could make versions of the ring – like copies, you know?'

Eva looked baffled.

'You want to copy your engagement ring?' she asked, frowning, as she often did. Eva was a very earnest girl who liked to make sure she understood everything about a situation before she moved onto the next one. It was an excellent attribute for her job: she was a perfectionist, and already two fine vertical lines were developing between her thick dark brows from hours spent concentrating on her work.

Without Milly by her side, Eva would have drawn much more attention, maybe as much as she devoted to her work: her face, framed in a curtain of straight, silky dark hair, was not pretty but striking, with the kind of features that were currently very fashionable. The heavy brows, high cheekbones and wide mouth were all those of a high-fashion model, and Eva's thick eyelashes – which Milly had tried to pull out when they were around nine, envious that grown-ups always cooed over them – framed slanting greenish eyes that surveyed the world with a quiet reserve that an observer who took time to study her face would have considered highly intriguing.

But next to Milly, Eva faded into the background. And to be honest, that was what she preferred. Her friendship with Milly was by no means masochistic: with Milly next to her, the spotlight was off Eva. She wasn't expected to chat or flirt or draw attention; she could sit back quietly and enjoy herself watching others, an introvert who used an extrovert as an invisibility cloak. That was how their joint business worked, and it suited Eva much better than people realized.

'Yes! Copy the ring! Like a special, limited edition, charity version. It isn't even new, so the design won't be copyrighted or anything. I might as well get some benefit from it being a bloody *turquoise*!' Milly put her hand flat on the table, stretching out her slim white fingers, looking down derisively at the blue stone set in rose gold and surrounded by small pearls on her third finger. 'To match my eyes ... blah blah, like you can't get blue diamonds? *Honestly!* You can do versions of it, right, Eves? With different stones, of course, so it's not exactly the same.'

Eva bent her head, studying the design of the ring.

'Well, I could do some in those zebra jaspers I've been using recently,' she said slowly. 'And the agates, too. They would look pretty with the pearls. I don't usually use pearls at all, but if you want something as close to this as possible I could order them in. They're not as ethical as our other stones—'

'Oh, that's fine,' Milly said, fluttering her hand to signify that standards could be flexible on this occasion. 'I *love* this idea,' she beamed. 'Talk about great publicity! Not only am I engaged, but I'm actually happy to make versions of my ring as a special charity donation thingywhatsit so I can share the love for a good cause! Wow, that sounds *really* good when I say it out loud. We'll do it as a limited edition for breast cancer – is that big right now, breast cancer? I'll check with my publicist. She's bound to know what the hottest charity is right now.'

Eva was used to Milly's way of talking, accustomed to telling herself that Milly's heart was in the right place, it was just that her words didn't always come out quite the way she meant them. And having Milly's name on the ethical jewellery line that Eva designed was perfect for both of them. It had been Milly's idea, of course. When Eva graduated from art school, having decided she wanted to specialize in jewellery design and work only with companies that used environmentally positive products mined by workers paid a living wage, Milly had pointed out that in order to succeed in that kind of niche market Eva would need publicity, and that quiet, retiring Eva was the last person in the world to be able to drum it up. Milly's brilliant solution was that Eva would design, Milly would 'front' the brand and put her name on it, and they would share profits.

So far, it had worked wonderfully. Eva was more than happy to be left alone to deal with the creative side of things, and Milly was superbly gifted at working Milly and Me, the name of their company, into every interview she ever did. Making the brand ethical naturally meant that she could promote it without seeming pushy, and even Eva, who had no knack for promotion, could see that an interview with Milly where she talked artlessly about how in love she was, how happy she was to be engaged, and how she wanted to share that wonderful feeling by giving back to people whose loved ones had breast cancer would be just the kind of article which journalists from women's magazines would fall over themselves to write.

'How will Tarquin feel about it?' Eva asked, her normally pale cheeks pinkening a little as they did every time she saw Tarquin or even pronounced his name.

Milly, who was perfectly aware that Eva had a crush on Tarquin, smiled at her indulgently and said, 'It's for charity! Of course Tark'll be fine with it! You know what a do-gooder he is.'

'I don't think that's quite fair ...' Eva murmured, but her voice tailed off. She tipped her head forward, pretending to study the ring, but really so that a soft swathe of dark hair could cover her face. She hated it when Milly was dismissive of Tarquin. No matter how much Eva told herself that this was how people in relationships behaved, that you teased each other, you didn't go round all the time with hearts and flowers wreathed around you, holding hands and looking into each other's eyes and only saying lovely things about how wonderful the other was, she couldn't help wishing that Milly wouldn't joke about Tarquin or his lyrics. It made Eva immediately want to jump to his defence, and that would give away the fact that she was madly in love with him, had been ever since she bought Ormond and Co's first CD *For Now the Lion Dreams*, and been carried away by his haunting voice, his cryptic lyrics and, of course, his otherworldly beauty.

So when Milly had met Tarquin backstage at a fundraiser it had been horribly bittersweet for Eva; she got to meet her idol and find out that he truly was as gentle and poetic and honest about his emotions as he seemed in his songs and his interviews. But the price, of course, was that she had to watch him following Milly around like Mary's little lamb, staring at her worshipfully with his big, pale blue eyes – *the colour of powder-blue quartzite*, thought the jewellery designer side of Eva, *just a tiny hint of lavender in the blue* – writing songs about Milly, and now, *marrying* Milly ...

'The wedding's going to be such an amazing opportunity,' Milly was saying. 'Wait till I tell my publicist! Wow, just think of the photo-spreads that Tark and I can do. Is it cool that we've got the same colouring, or is it a little weird? You know, making us look like brother and sister? Some people post comments like that online ... I think we definitely need to work on the styling so we're not dressed *too* alike. Tark's got his new-folk-crusty-whatever thing, which honestly I *hate*, but I can see it's huge right now, so I'm all right with it, and I have a more flower-child vibe, so there's a difference there ...'

Inside her pale suede Isabel Marant crossbody bag, Milly's phone vibrated to signal an incoming text; she pulled it out and gasped.

'It's Katharine!' she said excitedly. Katharine was her publicist. 'She says it's trending on Twitter already! Cool! Oh yeah, I should tweet a photo of the ring. God knows why I didn't do that already, what's *wrong* with me? Everyone *loved* when I posted that pic you took of the daisy chain in my hair earlier today – oh, Eves, that's a good idea, what about doing some daisy-chain jewellery? That would be really on brand for Milly and Me.'

She scrolled down.

'Oh *wow*!' she exclaimed. 'Katharine's going to pitch the wedding to *Style* first thing Monday. They're doing a Brides issue in the UK for the first time ever next June, and she's going to push for me and Tark to have the cover! Can you *imagine*? Oh my God, Eves, this is huge! I'm so, *so* glad that Tark proposed now!'

Milly was so excited that she momentarily forgot about photographing, tweeting, Facebooking and Instagramming her ring: she clasped the phone to her narrow chest as ecstatically as if it were a contract for a leading role in a Hollywood rom-com, her eyes shining as brilliantly as the blue diamonds she infinitely preferred to turquoises.

'Oh,' she added, 'and Katharine thinks the turquoise is fab – *right* on brand, she said. I can't wait to tell her about Milly and Me Breast Cancer – no, that doesn't sound right at all. Katharine will think of how to put it, she's a genius that way. *Anyway*, I'll *totally* put up with having to wear a bloody turquoise if it gets me on the cover of *Style* Brides!'

She gazed at Eva, her eyes so dazzling that Eva almost blinked.

'And Eves, you'll help me do it *all*,' she went on, quite as if she were conferring the most generous of favours on her best friend. 'You *know* how much I rely on you! We'll get a wedding planner, of course, but I want *everything* to reflect my and Tarquin's ethos, you know? Wildflower meadows, home-made lemonade – ooh, maybe we could get Pimm's to sponsor the drinks? Everything has to be right on brand, and you just get that so instinctively. British, ethical, down-to-earth but just sheer luxury at the same time.'

Milly heaved a huge sigh of bliss.

'God, I didn't see this coming at *all*!' she said, deliciously aware that even the VIPs hanging out in the backstage area were taking surreptitious photos of her – Milly Gamble from *Dr Who* looking all blissed-out and loved-up just after Tarquin Ormond had proposed to her. 'This is really going to take me – and Milly and Me, of course – to a *whole* new level of brand awareness!'

Chapter Five

Two hundred miles away from the Sussex fields across which Ormond and Co were blasting out their song 'Moon Face', Tamra Maloney was settling into the hand-upholstered, leather back seat of her Bentley Flying Spur as her chauffeur drove her back to London, blessedly unaware that Brianna Jade now had a rival for the *Style* Bride of the Year tiara. If anything could have improved Tamra's mood at that moment, which probably wasn't even possible, it would have been her Bentley. She just loved this car. There was nothing like it in the States, nothing at all. Yes, you could get hugely luxurious and expensive cars over there, of course, but nothing so elegant and refined. From the 'B' of the Bentley logo hand-sewn into the capacious headrests, to the built-in case of drinking glasses and the tables that slid out so smoothly from the back seats, to the DVD screens and the multimedia remote control that lay discreetly between the seats, everything had been hand-fitted by experts; it was like relaxing into a moving work of art.

Deciding to spend over two hundred and fifty thousand pounds for the Flying Spur had been the easy part. Picking her colour choices for the interior by contrast had been agonizing. Bentley offered a dark-red leather called Fireglow for the seats and upholstery, with a dark stained burr walnut for the wooden veneers that was almost black. Tamra had been seriously tempted by the rich crimson and charcoal combination of one of the showroom models. But the salesman, with exquisite tact, had murmured: 'Very *nightclub*, madam. This colour choice is extremely popular with our Russian and Arab clients . . .' and Tamra, who was very quick on the uptake, had read his meaning instantly.

'I got it,' she had said, flashing him a gorgeous smile. 'Like we'd say in the States, keep walking. What do you suggest?'

The salesman had allowed himself a much smaller smile and advised Tamra that the combination of a damson exterior, plus beige leather seats and matching damson leather interior trim, with the dark walnut veneer, would be the choice *he* would make for madam. Madam was modern and elegant, and the deep purple reflected her style and was contemporary without being – well, *nightclub*.

And she loved it. The purple made her feel positively regal, and the sales guy had been right – the beige seats looked a lot classier than the red would have done. Tamra had no problems flashing her money around, no wish to pretend she wasn't anything but the newest of new multi-millionaires; it was a shame, she often thought, that there wasn't a word that fitted in between 'multi-million' and 'billion'. The former didn't really convey the scale of her wealth, and she wasn't quite in the latter's league. *Yet. Never say never.*

She was perfectly happy to buy everything new and shiny and custom-made: that was her deal. But there was luxurious and there was flashy, and she knew she needed to stay on the right side of that line. It was proving surprisingly easy: the Bentley guy had been typical of the high-end salespeople here, who were very happy to guide you along the right path as long as you learnt their keywords. You went into their shops dressed all elegant and rich-looking – *not* flashy, Armani rather than Versace – and you listened out for key phrases like 'refined' and 'restrained', or their antonyms, 'perhaps a little flamboyant', or the killer 'Arab/Russian/nightclub' trifecta used by the Bentley salesman, which was the biggest warning of all. Having tons of money was fine in the UK, but being vulgar with it was not. Tamra had learnt to focus her love of shiny things squarely into jewellery.

And this kind of shine, she thought, reaching out to run one finger over the surface of the open table next to her, the walnut lacquered in layer upon layer of hand-painted applications till it shone like a mirror. *Look at that glossy finish. There can't be a car in the world more beautiful than this.*

She drank some of the Cristal from the glass she was holding and selected a small canapé from the plate that was resting on the table: smoked salmon, tossed in the lightest dressing of lemon juice, low-fat crème fraiche and chopped dill, served in a Little Gem lettuce leaf cup. No carbs, of course. Barely ever any carbs in solid form, only in liquid: the Cristal, for instance. Tamra was fine never eating solid carbs again in her life, but by God, you'd have to pry the liquor bottle from her cold dead hands, even if it was getting harder to keep the weight off now that she'd gone past the forty mark.

Forty! My God! I still can't believe it!

She resisted the impulse to pull out her pocket mirror and scan her face; she'd told herself to stop doing that any more. It led to paranoia, which led to unnecessary surgery, which led to looking like one of the women off the *Real Housewives* shows, who literally didn't know where to stop. Some of them were like wax models of their former selves, Madame Tussaud's come to life, smooth, motionless, their eyes stretched artificially wide by upper eyelid repositioning surgery: or blepharoplasty, where any excess fatty tissue was removed from around the eyes, making them seem bigger, but also oddly stretched. Like Manga teenage eyes in a middle-aged face.

And once you start, you don't stop. For confirmation, she only had to look back at all the other women in the social circle in Florida into which marriage to Ken Maloney, the Fracking King, had precipitated her. Ken had proposed to her within a week of their first meeting and whisked her and Brianna Jade off to his marble beachfront palace. The levels of nipping, tucking, lifting and liposuctioning in West Palm Beach had to be seen to be believed. If an alien from another galaxy had landed there, it would immediately have assumed that all the women at the country club were engaged in a terrible, suicidal competition to stretch their skin as tight over their skeletons as humanly possible. Tamra, with only a nose job and boob implants, was quite a contrast, and only the deep well of common sense from which she had drawn ever since she'd found herself a pregnant single mother at sixteen had saved her from the temptation to start tinkering with her face.

It had been shockingly unprecedented in West Palm Beach when she'd gone under the knife to actually *reverse* a cosmetic procedure. Ken had whined when she'd had her implants removed, but Tamra had his ring on her finger by then, so there was nothing he could do about it. And since she was a B/C cup anyway he'd had to admit, post-surgery, that there wasn't that much of a difference.

Dr Dubrow did a great job, she thought now, complacently looking down at her breasts. *The girls look great.* Tamra still regretted never having done pageants herself; with her, it would've been Miss USA or die trying. She had the attitude

as well as the looks. Brianna Jade was drop-dead beautiful –
Tamra had been a knockout at sixteen, but she genuinely
thought that her daughter was even better-looking than she
had been at that age. However, Brianna Jade had never truly
relished getting up on that stage and selling her personality
with everything she'd got.

Tamra's perfectly shaped lips curved in a smile of nostalgic
amusement as she remembered the struggle it had been to
find her daughter a suitable talent for that specific part of the
competition. When Brianna Jade had won Pork Queen at the
Kewanee State Fair (prize: five hundred dollars, a pigskin
jacket and the lead place on a tractor trailer in the parade), all
the contestants had been required to prepare a pork dish as
part of the contest, and Brianna Jade's Tater Tots casserole had
been widely appreciated.

*Thank God for Mrs Lutz, our landlady, helping BJ with that
pork casserole. Someone had to – I could never cook to save my
life – and at least BJ did the gruntwork herself. I know damn well
that Barb Norkus, who came second and went on to win Watseka
Corn Queen, didn't do anything with her pork 'n' beans but
carry the casserole – her mom cooked it all.*

But you couldn't hand out your pork casserole to judges
from the stage, nor could you even cook it as you travelled
around the Midwest staying in the cheapest of cheap motels
and living off bulk-bought ramen noodles, yoghurt and take-
out salads from Arby's. And Brianna Jade couldn't sing or
dance, not well enough to compete with the other girls, that
was for sure: most of them had come off the kiddie pageant
circuit and had been taking lessons since they were four. So
Tamra had come up with a comic skit for her daughter,
'Twenty Things You Didn't Know About the Pig', complete
with a slide show, and, after intensive coaching, BJ had managed to pull it off okay.

Never enough to win, though. BJ was beautiful enough to place as a runner-up for the prize money to keep them going, but it wasn't enough for the big time. And Tamra had never blamed her for it. She had pushed her daughter into pageants to get them out of Kewanee, and it had worked.

But Tamra had been getting more and more worried, waiting in vain for that big break that would happen for BJ, the competition she'd win, the nice rich guy who'd fall for her. People would tell Tamra to take BJ to LA and try the acting circuit, but no way was BJ an actress: she only managed that comic monologue with Tamra coaching the hell out of her. And Tamra could easily imagine what pretty girls who weren't great actresses went through in Hollywood to get cast. She'd have taken a rusty old pickaxe to the balls of the first guy who asked her daughter to get down on her knees at an audition.

Tamra wasn't a typical pageant mom, living through her daughter's success, letting her own looks fade in order to channel everything into the younger version of herself, willing to sacrifice her daughter's own wishes ruthlessly on an altar bedecked with crowns and prize money. Tamra had firmly told the many people in Kewanee who'd pushed her to get her adorable little five-year-old into kiddie pageants where they could stick it. Brianna Jade would have as normal a childhood as her mother could manage, though Tamra had to work long days at the feed store and pull night shifts at the local bar, Hogs and Cobs, while she scrabbled to maintain a network of fellow moms who would watch Brianna Jade for her.

No point asking her folks for help: she'd been thrown out of the house when she got knocked up by her boyfriend, Brian Schladdenhouffer, even though he'd swallowed hard, manned up and proposed when he heard the news. And no point looking to the Schladdenhouffers either; they'd blamed her for everything, from 'trapping' their son (whose clumsy condom skills had actually been to blame for the pregnancy) to pretty much causing his death in the combine-harvester accident because, according to them, he'd been so distracted by being trapped that he had slipped and fallen from the machine during refuelling. Not a pleasant way to go.

Well, screw them all, the Krantzes and the Schladdenhouffers both, a sixteen-year-old Tamra Jean Krantz with a bellyful of baby had thought, setting her jaw firmly and not looking back. She'd worked her ass off, schemed with everything she had to give her daughter a big break that would take BJ into a better life; what she hadn't expected was that the break would happen to her, passing through Jacksonville, Florida, pumping gas into her beat-up old Hyundai, which was pretty much held together with duct tape at that point. Ken Maloney, pulling into the gas station in his shiny silver Lexus convertible, had looked over, seen the way Tamra handled that nozzle and fallen in lust on the spot. And after three consecutive nights spent wining, dining but most certainly not bedding Tamra, he had fallen in love as well.

'I fell for your pretty face, honey, but I stayed for what was behind it,' he'd always said to her fondly. Tamra wasn't educated, but she had a brain like a steel trap, and Ken took great pleasure in teaching his new bride all about the intricacies of the fracking industry. Tamra had been thirty-five then, Ken seventy-four; she had been honest with him, had told him that she wasn't in love with him when he proposed, and Ken had responded that if she'd pretended she was he would have taken back the offer. And of course she was grateful to Ken, not just for his kindness to her but to Brianna Jade, who had been nineteen when Tamra and Ken married.

Ken had saved them just as Tamra was really starting to panic about her and BJ's future, but he'd always maintained he'd got the best end of the bargain. Tamra had kept him laughing from morning till night, and proved such a natural in the fracking business that he'd brought her in as an equal partner, tearing up the prenup on their second anniversary. By their fifth, he'd dropped dead of a major heart attack, but he'd always said he wanted to go with a smile on his face and Tamra on top of him – *and bless him, that's exactly what happened*, his widow thought fondly. *His doctor warned him about how much Viagra he was taking, and Ken just said, 'Hey, Dr Katz, you've seen my wife in her bikini at the country club, right?' and Dr Katz sighed and refilled the prescription.*

Tamra had been taken aback at how much she missed Ken. She had come to feel huge affection for her husband, who had adored her and given her so much, and she found herself unwilling to stay in the home that they had shared and in which they had found a surprising amount of marital happiness. So she had decided on a fresh start, even though the highest ranks of West Palm Beach society would still be open to her and BJ as long as Tamra upped her donations to the fundraising charities and benefits: Ken Maloney's widow might not be liked by the women who ran that world, but her money most certainly was.

Still, Tamra didn't want to mope around a marble palace in Florida with memories of Ken everywhere she turned and nowhere further to rise in their social circles. She had much bigger ambitions. Why stay in the States to be patronized by would-be ladies when she could go to the UK and meet the real ones? On that TV series *Downton Abbey*, the whole set-up was based on the American heiress who'd gone to Britain and married an Earl who needed the money to fix up his stately home. Well, Tamra was willing to bet there were plenty of titled guys in the UK whose houses could do with a big cash infusion.

Besides, she could run the fracking business from the London office perfectly well. Their company had fracked wells successfully in the Ukraine and Poland, which were waiting to be fully exploited; plus there was the European Union to be lobbied with assurances that fracking could be done responsibly and without the horror stories of polluted drinking water and natural gas explosions which were rife in the US. The more Tamra considered it, the more she realized that being based in Europe would be a business as well as a personal advantage.

But Tamra needed to see her daughter settled well. Brianna Jade wasn't going to follow her mom into the fracking business; she didn't have the drive or the ambition to run a company, and Tamra was no believer in nepotism. With her sweet nature and domestic tendencies, all Brianna Jade wanted – really, pretty much all she had ever wanted – was to marry a nice guy and start having a home and kids. Fine, but why shouldn't Tamra get the best husband possible for her daughter? Not just nice, but titled too? Prince Hugo was married, and Prince Toby, his cousin, was famously too wild a playboy to make a good husband, but if she couldn't get a prince for her Fracking Princess, a Duke or an Earl would do nicely ...

Tamra's glass was empty. She refilled it from the bottle resting inside the built-in veneered wine cooler, an addition she had insisted Bentley custom-make, and for which they'd billed her a fortune.

Well, I did it. I snagged my baby an Earl, just like on Downton Abbey, *and a lovely one too. He'll make her a great husband – Lord knows, I know men, and I picked a good one out for Brianna Jade. And all those bitches who ruled West Palm Beach and looked down on me and my daughter for coming from hog country are gonna feel like their stomachs are burning up with acid for the rest of their lives every time they read about the Countess of Respers in the society magazines.*

It was the icing on the cake. Tamra would never have insisted Brianna Jade marry an aristocrat simply to spite the West Palm Beach Competitive Starvation League, but hey, if their suffering added whipped cream and cherries to the top of the sundae, Tamra would relish that too. And she sure as hell did. It was time to celebrate.

Let's go shopping, she thought with an even more cat-got-the-cream smile. *Mommy needs some me time.*

She set down her glass, used the remote control to bring up the internet on the screen in front of her – the Flying Spur had a built-in Wi-Fi hub – and navigated swiftly to one of her favourite sites, inputting her search criteria and scrolling through the results with considerable interest. After much consideration, she picked two options, placed her order, specified the delivery time and logged off in the happy certainty of a job very well done. She emailed some instructions to her live-in housekeeper, slid out the wireless headphones from their discreet slot, put them on, clicked again with the remote and loaded the audiobook of what most people would consider a bizarrely unlikely suggestion for a Fracking Queen to listen to: Edith Wharton's *The Buccaneers*.

But, having caught the bug from *Downton Abbey*, Tamra had become obsessed with biographies of American heiresses who had come to Britain in the nineteenth century to find titled husbands. Consuelo Vanderbilt, with a vast dowry garnered from her father's US railways, had married the Duke of Marlborough, while his brother, Lord Randolph Churchill, had snapped up Jennie Jerome. May Goelet, the richest American girl of all, had been sponsored into society by the Prince of Wales himself, and had her choice of European royalty and half a dozen British peers before finally settling on the Duke of Roxburghe. Then there was Winnaretta Singer, of the sewing-machine fortune, who went to France and snagged the

Prince de Polignac. It turned out it was way easier to find princes on the Continent, but Tamra was very grateful they hadn't had to cross the Channel to find BJ a nice aristo husband – it was foreign enough for her in Britain sometimes.

And as well as the biographies, there were not only the novels, but the films and TV series adapted from them. The American heroines in fiction all snagged their peers by being bright, sparky, charming and spirited, like Isabel Boncassen in Anthony Trollope's *The Duke's Children*, who married a Marquis who would be Duke one day. Bettina Vanderpoel in *The Shuttle* fell for an Earl, Lord Mount Dunstan – unlike her poor sister, who only managed a baronet, and a nasty one into the bargain.

To her own surprise, Tamra, who had barely picked up a book in her life before, was finding all this literature utterly absorbing. She was almost sorry to turn off the audiobook when the Flying Spur pulled to a halt outside the discreet mechanical gate around the corner from her Chelsea mansion. Teodor, the very efficient Slovak chauffeur, pressed the remote that activated the gate, sliding the car down the passageway that led to her own private parking garage below the house.

'Thank you, Teodor,' Tamra said as he held the door open for her. 'Once you've cleared the drink and food from the car and taken it to the kitchen, you and Marta can have the night off.'

'Thank you, Mrs Maloney,' Teodor said politely, and stood waiting, hands folded, as Tamra walked over to the garage lift; he wouldn't have dreamt of doing anything so crass as beginning to clean out the Bentley until his employer was on her way up to her three-floor, thirty-room mansion.

The opulent master suite – *mistress suite*, Tamra liked to call it – of the Chelsea mansion which Lady Margaret McArdle, Tamra's newly made British friend, had nicknamed the White

House, spread across a large part of the third floor. Like Tamra, Lady Margaret was perpetually irreverent, one of the many common factors that had made them fast friends. When Tamra had first come to London, she had, in true nineteenth-century style, hired an indigent aristocrat, a divorcée who had manoeuvred her short marriage to a baronet into writing puff interviews for *Hello!*, *Tatler* and *Majesty* magazine, and was regularly engaged to chaperone rich Americans around London, introducing them into society.

But as soon as Tamra and Lady Margaret had met, at the bar at the House of Lords reception after the Berkeley Dress Show, the first official event of the London débutante season, the two women had bonded instantly, snapping together like magnets. The American newly minted multi-millionairess from Kewanee, Illinois and the Duke's daughter with the bluest Anglo-Irish blood running in her veins were sisters under the skin, bawdy women who could drink most men under the table without blinking an eye. They could have run a bar in the heyday of the Wild West as a team, and managed the brothel upstairs too.

So the baronet's divorcée was now distant history, and Lady Margaret McArdle was Tamra's BFF: they were practically joined at the hip. Tamra had been very amused by the 'White House' comment, and it was never more apt than in the 'mistress suite', which comprised not just the huge, pristine white bedroom, but two walk-in dressing rooms for summer and winter wardrobes, a fur closet, and two bathrooms – because it could certainly not be assumed that a couple who shared a bed would ever want to share a bathroom. Both were walled and floored in almost-translucent Tuscan grey-veined marble, with walk-in rainforest showers, gigantic travertine sinks and, to Tamra's great pleasure, sunken jacuzzis: she loathed the fashion for freestanding baths in the middle of the room.

Where did you put your soap? Your body brush? Your glass of champagne? Your waterproof vibrator? Even your book?

Because Tamra was genuinely surprised by how much pleasure she was taking in reading ever since she had come to London. She had never had time before to stop and smell the roses, had been way too busy driving from one pageant to another, coaching her daughter, calculating strategies by which they could save a buck or two; and then, after marriage to Ken, she had thrown herself into learning the ropes of the cutthroat world of the fracking industry, Ken her enthusiastic guide. There had barely been a book in the whole sprawl of their entire Florida home, apart from maybe Warren Buffet's authorized biography and a couple of Tom Clancys.

But now, I really love books. Who the hell saw that coming? I honestly think folks in Kewanee would be as surprised to see me reading a big English novel with tons of long words in it as they would Brianna Jade getting married to an Earl, Tamra reflected as she stepped out of the lift and turned into the opulent surroundings of her own private heaven. She exhaled in sheer bliss, not only at having so much space, but at being able to be alone in it.

Mine. All mine. For the first time in my life, a home I don't have to share with a single living soul.

She'd always totally got the appeal of white interiors. They told people, straight away, that you were dripping in money, because you could afford the whole squad of cleaners it took to keep every surface free of the tiniest little stain or imperfection. The stately homes she'd visited, Tamra had noticed, were the opposite: they had dark wooden floors, elaborate rugs, tapestries, chintz upholsteries, tons of prints and patterns and stuff that hid the dirt. They kept the warmth in too, all those rugs and hangings, because the Dukes and Earls couldn't afford to heat their stone walls any more – *well, if they ever could.*

But when you were new-money rich, you didn't need to worry about that. You had underfloor heating beneath the marble expanses, so that you could walk around naked all day if you wanted and still feel deliciously warm in your glittering white ice palace. Which was precisely what Tamra did; entering her summer dressing room, she kicked off her shoes and stripped off her clothes, posting the latter down the built-in laundry chute to the utility room where Marta would sort out hand-wash from dry cleaning, unfastened her big rose-gold necklace, pinned up her matching red-gold hair and, naked as the day she was born but considerably more decorative, turned slowly in a full circle, examining her body in the array of angled mirrors in the hexagonal room.

She was a knockout still. Her skin was pale-golden tanned from Florida, topped up with spray treatments in London, and almost as smooth as Brianna Jade's. Tamra had put on a few pounds during her marriage and she had settled into them. There was a slight rounding of the hips and buttocks, even a little convexity to her stomach. *But fuck it, who cares? I'm forty, I look better than most twenty-year-olds and I don't ever need to worry again about whether a man wants to fuck me*, she thought with a wicked smile of anticipation. Her boobs, since the reduction, were perky and full but in proportion with the curves of her lower body, and you could barely see the scars below their round swell; she'd rubbed rosehip oil into them every day for two years, and now you had to go looking to even try to find them.

Tamra glanced up at the clock: *only twenty minutes to go! I can't wait!* Strolling through the huge bedroom, over the white soft-as-snow alpaca rugs, she relished again the fact that all of this space was hers. That no one would or could come in without her say-so, even her beloved daughter. She adored Brianna Jade more than life itself, would put BJ's welfare over her own in a heartbeat, but she had shared a bedroom with her daughter ever since she was born, until Tamra moved into Ken's California King bed. Ken, bless him, had been uxorious, a word he had taught her; he'd wanted to fall asleep every night with his heavy, old-man, liver-spotted arm across the slender, chiffon-and-lace-clad waist of his miracle younger wife, a woman who had the body of an expensive hooker and the brain of a CEO.

But boy, that arm was real heavy sometimes, Tamra thought now. *I'd lie awake and listen to him snore and think how lucky I was to be with him, and still sometimes it was all I could do to wait till I was a hundred per cent sure he wouldn't wake up before I slid out from under and ran down to the water's edge and walked into the ocean naked and just stood there, staring at the stars and the lights of the boats on the water, telling myself to suck it up, that it wouldn't be for ever.*

She smiled, remembering.

And then sometimes, God help me, I'd go back upstairs, pull back the covers, suck Ken's dick till it got hard and climb on top of him to give him another ride to weaken his heart just that little bit more, tip him over to the other side. Till finally, bless him, he got there.

He was a real good husband, Ken. He gave me everything I wanted, left it all to me with no strings attached, and all he asked was that I stay faithful to him. He said I'd have plenty of time to fool around after he was gone.

And boy, was he ever right!

In the bathroom that Tamra preferred, because it overlooked the gardens behind the house, Marta had done everything she had been asked to do in the email. A bottle of Cristal rested in one of the chilled wine coolers, a bottle of Ketel One vodka in the other: Tamra had had the coolers built into a travertine slab beside the curved, upholstered window seat, just as she'd added them to the specs for her Bentley. She liked her drink chilled and within easy access at all times. Frosted glasses, fresh from the freezer, were lined up in the wine fridge next to the coolers: on a silver plate lay a range of Charbonnel et Walker Marc de Champagne truffles, pink, milk and dark, displayed around a mound of hulled strawberries.

Just a couple more things to do . . .

From one of the opaque glass-fronted cupboards, Tamra extracted a sheet of black slate and a small suede case, both of which she placed on the marble next to the wine coolers. Then she pulled the Ketel One from its silver sheath, poured herself a shot, and sank it in one swift, practised go, staring at herself in the huge oval mirror above the sink. The ice-cold spirit burnt deliciously down the back of her throat; it would be the first of many.

Me time, dammit all! My daughter's finally settled and out of the house, my own life can start. Wow, I've waited a long time for this . . .

Sliding open a drawer beneath the sink, she studied its contents before pulling out a ribbed purple finger-stall vibrator. *Start small and build up. We've got a way to go tonight.* In a couple of seconds, it was between her parted legs; she leant forward, gripping the marble edge of the sink surround with one hand, the other working on herself, never taking her eyes off her face and upper body, reflected back at her by the large mirror, refracted behind her by several others set around the bathroom to give her views of every angle. Her red-gold hair, piled on top of her head, her big dark eyes with their thick lashes, her parted lips, her perfect teeth, her perfect smooth pale golden skin . . .

Tamra ate very carefully, worked out like a maniac with a whole series of personal trainers; now, the mini-vibrator buzzing against her, she watched her boobs bounce, her eyes grow darker, her lips part even further, turned on by her own beauty. As she came, she still watched herself gasp and moan and shove her clit even harder against her finger, relishing that she could bring herself to orgasm so easily, and that she loved the sight of herself in the throes.

I'm starring in my own porno, she thought with great satisfaction. *Fuck it, why watch anyone else when you can turn yourself on like this?*

But even a star needs supporting actors . . .

Right on time, she heard the elevator rising to the third floor. Marta had let in Tamra's guests, given them directions to their destination, and would now be retreating to the staff flat at the far end of the house which she shared with her husband Teodor. Tamra straightened up, taking a look at her face, now glowing with the flush of orgasm, her cheeks dewy and pink, her lips moist; crossing to the coolers again, she poured icy vodka into three shot glasses, lined them up and stood there, waiting. The jacuzzi was filled and bubbling softly, fragranced with rose and chypre, underwater chromatherapy lights set to a deep pink which bathed the water with a deliciously suggestive colour. Neither of the two young men who could be heard crossing the bedroom, accurately directed by a very discreet Marta, had been here before, and, experienced as they were, their eyes widened at the sight of their surroundings, the sheer lavishness of the setting, the exquisite scent in the air and, of course, their client herself, naked and American-smooth, not a hair on her body apart from the glorious mass of red-gold hair pinned above a face that was as breathtaking as her figure.

'Hello, boys,' Tamra purred, slipping her dark gaze up and down their bodies, very pleased to notice that they had both reacted instantly to the sight of her. 'This is our playroom. Come over here and do a shot with me before we get started.'

Eagerly, the young men crossed the room and took the glasses she was holding; Tamra clinked hers with theirs in a toast, then downed her vodka in one, giving them the cue to follow suit.

'It's Bruno and Oliver, right?' she said, looking from one to the other.

Bruno was dark-skinned, with striking light green eyes and full, sensual lips; Oliver taller and much fairer, his features Germanic, his blond hair clubbed at the back of his neck in a short ponytail. Both young men were as handsome as the models that the escort site promised and, side by side, they presented an exotically delicious contrast. Oliver wore a tailored suit, Bruno a slim-cut shirt and equally fitted trousers. Tamra could have taken them both out to dinner, to the opera, been seen anywhere in public with them without anyone realizing that both young men were pay-to-play. They were absolutely five-star escorts all the way. Lady Margaret had recommended this agency to Tamra, and, as with so many things, Lady Margaret had been, as she would put it with a wink at the double entendre, 'absolutely bang on'.

'That's right, um—' Bruno began.

'Call me Tamra,' she said, smiling at them both with blinding force. 'No formality here, boys. Now, I'm sure you don't want to get those lovely clothes wet. Go into the bedroom, take 'em off and come back in here looking pleased to see me, okay?'

'No problem at *all*, Tamra!' Oliver said fervently. 'Oh, and Diane said to bring you this ...'

From his jacket pocket he pulled a bulging baggie of pre-sieved cocaine, no rocks or lumps in it, powdery as icing sugar. Diane, who ran the escort agency, was more than happy to provide extras for trusted clients.

'Would you like to—'

'We'll save that for after Round One,' Tamra said, winking
at them so seductively that Bruno swallowed hard, his Adam's
apple swelling along with the already prominent bulge in his
trousers. 'No sense rushing things. We've got plenty of time for
me to do lines off both your cocks and then watch you lick
each other clean ...'

Both Bruno and Oliver turned and almost ran to the bedroom, so eager were they to strip naked; they practically
jostled each other in the doorway. Tamra did one more shot as
she listened to the sounds of zips being unfastened, shoes
kicked off, near-jumping from one foot to another as they
pulled their underwear off. The anticipation was making her
so wet she was almost dripping on the marble floor. After all
those years of having to grab sex where she could, a quick fling
here and there on the road in the rare times Brianna Jade was
safely looked after elsewhere, and then the time in purdah
with Ken, the joy of being able to have sex pretty much whenever she wanted, with young men who looked like underwear
models, was simply dazzling. Tamra had been asked out by
every eligible bachelor over thirty in London and quite a lot
of non-bachelors as well, but no way was she ready to date
seriously, not at all. Boyfriends tied you down, and the idea of
getting married again nearly brought her out in hives. She was
much too busy being the merry widow.

'Oh *yeah*,' she said contentedly as Bruno and Oliver re-
entered the bathroom, both stark naked and sporting the large
erections she had already seen on the password-protected,
security-encoded section of Diane's website. Both young men
were almost completely shaved, what they called in the US
'slip-and-slide', and trimmed and waxed pubic hair on men
made their cocks look even bigger. Bruno's was longer, Oliver's
wider. *Decisions, decisions ...*

Tamra let out another long sigh of absolute bliss, spread her arms wide along the marble shelf behind her, and opened her legs.

'You,' she said, pointing at Bruno, 'come here and eat me out. Then you get a turn,' she said to Oliver. 'The one who makes me come hardest gets to fuck me first.'

She judged Bruno the winner, but it was a close-run thing, and she could barely even get a word out once both young men had given it their best shot. Instead she pointed at Bruno, her eyes filmed with pleasure, her lips parted and moist.

Professional as he was, Oliver couldn't help groaning in disappointment at having lost the competition. But a few minutes later, the party having moved to the bathtub, the noises he was making were considerably more satisfied. Bubbles pumped up from the jacuzzi's powerful jets, surrounding Tamra, who was holding onto the edge of the bath for dear life, and Bruno, behind her, gripping her slippery hips. His cock thrust in and out of her as Tamra simultaneously sucked off Oliver, who was standing on the marble floor next to the jacuzzi, his feet planted wide, his moans of pleasure audible even over the motor of the whirlpool bath.

Unfortunately, Oliver was being too gentle with her. That was the thing with some escorts – they'd hang back a bit out of professional courtesy. You had to show them how you liked it. Managing to balance as Bruno's cock slammed in and out of her, Tamra let go of the bath, grabbed Oliver's hands and dragged them to the back of her head, still sucking his cock with everything she had. Oliver got it straight away, twisted his hands in her hair, started fucking her mouth hard, and Bruno picked up the rhythm, his hands digging into her now as he pounded away behind her, Tamra's muffled moans rising to an absolute scream of pleasure that came out through her nose, because her lips were sealed so tightly around Oliver's bobbing, throbbing, girthy cock—

'Ah *fuck*! *Fuck* yes!' Oliver screamed too as he dragged his cock from Tamra's mouth just in time, Tamra rearing back to take the explosion of come over her perfect tits, water and hot young male spunk dripping from her hard pointed nipples; behind her, Bruno dragged his out too, shooting into the condom. He was a grunter, not a yeller. The sounds he made as his orgasm hit were right from the back of his throat, loud and wordless. Tamra watched Oliver, her eyes bright and wide: the sight of his cock spasming, his hands now white-knuckled on the bath again to keep him from falling, his hips rocking as he squirted his last drops on her wet skin, was so erotic that she licked her lips in sheer pleasure. She loved watching guys come, loved watching them lose it completely; that was why women liked gay male porn, of course. If you were into guys, that was where you saw them really going for it, giving it, taking it, shooting their loads, their faces convulsed, their lips open as they gasped and groaned ...

'Nice going, guys,' she said, approvingly. 'Time for some coke, some liquor and Round Two.'

Oliver, who couldn't be more than twenty-three, was already recovered enough for his cock to bob in excitement at the mention of Round Two: he held out a hand to steady Tamra as she climbed out of the bath, white bubbles mounding on the water-slick curves of her body.

'What did you have in mind for Round Two?' he asked, his eyes sparkling.

Tamra reached up and kissed him, pressing her wet body against his dry one, rubbing her crotch into his, feeling his cock curl awake. She drove her tongue deeply into his mouth, making him take it just as his cock had filled hers just now, her hands behind his head, removing the elastic from his hair, twisting her fingers through it, pulling it deliberately, hurting him just enough, hearing him moan in excitement and stiffen even more.

'You want me to fuck you with a strap-on?' she said, pulling back, still holding his head, her lips touching his as she spoke. 'Or you want me to tell Bruno to fuck you while you eat me out?'

'Oh *man*,' Oliver breathed. 'I want *both*.'

Bruno, out of the jacuzzi too, pressed up behind Tamra; he wasn't that tall, and his cock and balls squashed into the split of her buttocks, the cock, stiffening again, pressing into her arse. He bit and kissed the back of her neck and she writhed in excitement; his wide lips were so soft, his teeth so deliciously sharp on her wet skin, she was ready to go again right now, needed a cock inside her now, *now*—

Bending over, she grabbed Oliver around the waist for balance, widening her legs.

'Put it in me!' she commanded Bruno. 'Fuck my ass this time, and give it to me good. I want it fast and furious. Jesus, you boys are fucking *gold*!'

As Bruno quickly grabbed another condom, she reached back with one hand and started to rub herself; by the time Bruno slammed into her, she was already coming, screaming her orgasm against Oliver, who had dropped to his knees to support her: he held her up, kissing her mouth frantically, his arms flexing to take the impact of her body rocking forward every time Bruno slammed into her with another hard furious stroke. Tamra's fingers never stopped all the time that Bruno fucked her; orgasm smashed into orgasm, overlapping so completely that she didn't stop coming the entire time. Instructed to give it to her good, Bruno obeyed his client with the complete professionalism of an expert. By the time his grunts reached the pitch of a wild boar about to charge, and his cock finally pumped its second load, Tamra literally could not stand up.

She collapsed into Oliver's arms, and he caught her with

the reflexes of Prince Charming catching a fainting Cinderella, lowering her to the thick plush rug on which he had been kneeling, her head resting on his thigh. She was so thoroughly fucked that even the sight of his cock pointing straight up to his belly button, looking even wider and thicker with veins from this angle, didn't make her turn to take it in her mouth. She was panting like a sprinter, her chest heaving, her breasts jiggling; Oliver bent over to kiss her nipples, lick and nip at them, and she moaned softly and stroked his hair, her hips still jerking a little as she came down from the crazy orgasm high.

'This is *so* not like work,' Bruno said as he disposed of the condom and washed his cock in the huge sink. 'And believe me, I *never* say that to clients.'

'He really doesn't,' Oliver confirmed into Tamra's breasts.

'I need a drink,' she said, managing to catch her breath. 'One the size of Lake Ontario. And I need a line the size of – of—'

'Pall Mall?' Bruno suggested. 'Coming right up.'

'Champagne,' she specified. 'Jesus, help me up!'

Oliver did one better; he picked her up, carried her to the soft towelling-upholstered chaise longue, and laid her down there as Bruno brought her a brimming champagne glass and the black slate with a whole series of big fat lines now decorating its surface. Inside Tamra's suede pouch had been a razor and several silver straws: each young man, showing excellent manners, took a straw for himself and kept them separate.

'Whooh!' Tamra said, tilting back her head as the butter-soft cocaine slid down. 'This is *smooth*.' She grinned at the two young men kneeling by the chaise longue. 'Diane has the best drugs *and* the best boy-toys.'

'Not to boast,' Oliver said seriously, 'but everyone says that.'

Tamra nodded appreciatively. 'My friend who recommended Diane is gay, and she says your girls are top-notch.'

'Do you want me to ring for one?' Bruno asked. 'It's no problem ...'

Tamra waved a hand dismissively, finished her champagne and handed the glass to him for a refill.

'No thanks,' she said. 'I like a *lot* of cock. And I don't share nicely like they tell you to in pre-school.'

She plumped up the towelling-covered pillows behind her and pulled herself up to sit a little higher, her long slim legs stretching out in front of her. And yes, her stomach pooched out just a bit when she didn't lie completely flat, and no, she didn't give a damn about it. She reached up and stretched her arms, a long sigh of contentment issuing from her lips, the coke buzzing through her bloodstream. Bruno returned with the new glass of Cristal, and she took it, sank two fingers into it and then into Oliver's mouth. He licked the fizz off eagerly, his red lips parted, asking for more; he was such a good kisser that she filled her mouth with Cristal, bent over, let it flow slowly into his, feeling him kiss and swallow, kiss and swallow ...

'Bruno, you ready for Round Three?' she asked. 'I want you to fuck Oliver's ass when you are. Just like this.' She stroked Oliver's cheek. '*Just* like this,' she purred, sliding three fingers into his mouth now, feeling him suck on them hard, her other hand delving into his hair. Bruno was already unwrapping a condom, picking up the lube which she had laid out on the counter, squirting some onto his hand. She knew both young men were fully on board with fucking each other as well as her, had chosen them specially; Oliver's eyes were already wide with anticipation as he braced himself, knees on the rug, hands on the chaise longue, to take Bruno's cock.

'And if you take it all, right up your ass, every inch of him ...' Tamra filled her mouth with Cristal again, let it flow into Oliver's, felt him swallow every drop – 'you can fuck me after. Any position you choose. Wherever you want to put it.'

Bruno was working lube into Oliver's ass, his hands dark on Oliver's paler skin, his cock distended as he slid the condom on. Oliver was already moaning, both at the pounding he was about to take and the prospect of fucking Tamra afterwards; she kissed him, plunging her tongue into his mouth as Bruno started to work his cock inside, and Tamra felt that too, felt Oliver shudder and buck as the cock slid inexorably further into him, Tamra kissing him so hard now he could barely breathe, had to gasp for breath through his nose, as she had had to when his cock was jammed right up to the roof of her mouth ...

'How are you going to fuck me?' she whispered against his lips as Bruno started to move faster, beginning to slam Oliver's more slender body against the chaise longue. 'Where are you going to put that big fat cock of yours? You better keep it hard for me, you better not come now with Bruno's cock up you ... you better save it for me or there'll be trouble ...'

Oliver wrenched his head back.

'Now,' he pleaded. 'I want to fuck you now, *now*, let me do it now ...'

Tamra felt an actual spark between her legs, as if a vibrator with a faulty connection had given her a tiny, very pleasurable electric shock.

'*Awesome* idea!' she said, jumping up and going to grab a condom; a bare minute later she was stretching out on the big rug, Oliver above her, his big cock, meaty and wide, making her scream as he drove it into her in one shocking, almost painful stroke. Bruno was deep inside him, waiting for his cue to start moving again, and now he did, plunging in and out of Oliver in the same rhythm that Oliver fucked Tamra, a chain of fucking, Tamra's legs spread as wide as they could go so that Oliver could kneel between them, and Bruno behind him. Oliver's fair hair hung round his handsome face, his cheeks bright red, his eyes almost glazed with the intensity of what they were doing; Bruno's dark curls damp with sweat.

Thank God they both came already, Tamra thought, her back arching, her hands grabbing onto the legs of the chaise longue, determined not to close her eyes for a moment, to watch this whole thing, Bruno fucking Oliver fucking her. *I want this to go on for ever. I want them to hold out as long as they can, the dirty fuckers! My God, Oliver's cock is huge, it's like a battering ram – Jesus, this is so fucking hot* ...

'Don't either of you *dare* fucking come for *hours*, you bastards!' she panted, as her head bounced up and down on the rug with the vigour of their efforts. 'Don't you fucking *dare*!'

Chapter Six

The Century Club, London

'Ethereal! Other-worldly! Fairy tale!' Milly read from her pale blue leather Mulberry notebook. 'Spiritual! Poetic!'

Her round blue eyes lifted from the book, fixing limpidly on her wedding planner.

'You said to think of five buzz-words for this meeting, and that's what I came up with,' she said. 'That really encapsulates how I feel about this wedding.'

Ludo Montgomerie, wedding-planner extraordinaire, who had a client list as packed full with celebrities as Spago's during the Oscars, raised his Botox-arched, manscaped brows as high as his injectables would let him.

'Dearie *me*,' he commented in his sing-song tenor voice. 'I had no *idea* I was taking on an *elf*-themed wedding. Shall I see if Cate Blanchett will stick her pointy ears back on and officiate at the ceremony?'

Milly bridled indignantly and Eva jumped in to keep the peace, reaching out to refill the glasses of rosé from the wine cooler on the wooden table between Milly and Ludo. They were ensconced in a cosy niche on the rooftop terrace of the Century Club, five storeys above Shaftesbury Avenue and a world away from the bustling workers and tourists who cluttered the pavements like slow-moving cattle badly in need of herding. The sun filtered through the draped white canvas overhead that billowed gently like sails in the breeze; only a few golden rays angled through the chinks between the fabric, striking the floor and tables here and there like divine illumination. The terrace was wide and generous. It was really an open penthouse, the whole top floor of the building, with a bar to one side, big tables in the centre, and a series of fashionably low and saggy leather sofas grouped around the edges.

The tables were for public dining, business meetings whose participants were very happy to have snippets of their conversations about shows they were pitching or films they were auditioning for be overheard by fellow members of the private club whose membership was mainly composed of actors, film and TV producers, screenwriters and dissolute novelists. The sofas were for more intimate, discreet encounters, like planning a wedding whose details needed to be kept hush-hush so that magazines could compete to buy the exclusive photographs and spend paragraphs listing all the delicious minutiae: the flowers, the canapés, the bride's hair and make-up, the invitations ...

'I know you were joking about the elf theme, Ludo,' Eva said in her soft voice, 'but actually that's a really good perception off what Milly wants. She and Tarquin do both have that other-worldly Cate Blanchett look, you know? And they share very strong ethical principles, as I'm sure you're aware. I've brought the latest portfolio of our jewellery line to show you the kind of sustainable styling we do ...'

'Oh, I did my research,' Ludo said, waving his hand in a queenly gesture of dismissal at the portfolio that Eva was bending to retrieve from her large, hand-sewn, faux-leather satchel; Milly would never have dreamt of lugging the heavy bound book around herself.

'I'm familiar with your ethos,' he continued. 'Believe me, bleeding hearts and hippie vegan bicycles *aren't* exactly my usual vernacular. But I'm aware that this whole beardy-weirdy, eco-folk trend is *terribly* fashionable at the moment, which is why I agreed to meet you and see if I could find a way to, erm, polish off the rougher, hand-crafted edges and give you a Ludo Montgomerie wedding. We all have to move with the times, don't we?' His eyes brightened. 'And I *love* your fiancé!' he said directly to Milly. 'You're a *terribly* lucky girl! He's positively gorgeous. Frankly, the *visuals* of the two of you are the main reason I said I'd have this chat. Will he be joining us?' he asked hopefully.

'He's on tour,' Milly said. 'But he's totally okay with any decisions I make.'

'Like ninety-five per cent of couples I deal with,' Ludo sighed, picking up his glass and settling back in the sofa, preparing to console himself with wine in the absence of the handsome Tarquin. 'Do you know that French expression – *entre deux amants il y a toujours l'un qui baise et l'autre qui tend la joue?*'

Eva, her forehead corrugating with concentration, followed along: like Milly, she had gone to an expensive girls' private school, but unlike Milly, she had been a swot. Though the science and geography teaching at St Paulina's had been very sketchy, the more acute pupils had had a thorough grounding in more ladylike subjects, which included French.

'Oh, that's very ... depressing,' she blurted out. 'If I understood it right?'

Ludo smiled complacently.

'In love,' he translated, 'there's always one person who kisses and the other who lets themselves be kissed. Literally "gives them their cheek". As it were.' He tittered in amusement.

'Cynical, but that's the French for you, isn't it? Cynical, and just a little soap-dodging, bless them. Well, in weddings there's one who does all the arranging and the other one who just turns up. I barely ever see the grooms, just the brides and their mothers.'

He grimaced.

'The gays are the big exception, of course – the lesbians are obsessed with details, but at least they *agree*. Nothing worse than two queens squabbling over whether they're having peonies or forsythias in the flower arrangements! *But*, I just did Wayne Burns' marriage,' he added, naming the top English footballer who had come out a couple of years before, 'and that was much more pleasant. His partner used to be a luxury concierge and he has *much* higher taste levels than the average WAG, I can tell you! Did you see the *Hello!* cover? I must say, they really did me proud, those two. It was the chic-est footballer's wedding *ever*.'

'I *did* see them,' Milly said brightly: she loved any association with celebrity. 'I want a *Hello!* cover too. You can get that for me, right? I mean, that's an absolute *must*.'

'Hmm, hmm . . .' Ludo put down his glass and steepled his long, elegantly manicured and be-ringed fingers together. 'A little birdie told me that we were after *Style Bride* for this, no less? If that's the case, you can forget about *Hello!*, dear. *Style Bride*'ll want a *total* exclusive.'

'Do you think you can manage that?' Milly's eyes were huge now, and as luminous as if they had been lit from within. She was clasping her hands together, like Ludo, but her grasp was prayerful rather than contemplative. 'Oh my God, I would *die* to get that cover! I'd do *anything*!'

Ludo snorted a little laugh out of his nostrils.

'Oh, I'm sure you *would*, dear,' he commented, looking Milly up and down. 'Actors – I know *just* what you're like! Well, the *supreme* editor you need to impress at *Style* is of course Her Majesty Queen Victoria, Editrix Supreme, and she's certainly not averse to the lady-loving side of things ...'

'*Really?*' Milly was agog with this juicy piece of gossip.

Ludo nodded gleefully.

'But you've got no chance of a little casting-couch advantage there, my dear,' he said chattily. 'Victoria's boringly faithful to her girlfriend, by all accounts. Lesbians! They really are a different breed.'

'Oh, Milly wouldn't *dream* of anything like that. She's *madly* in love with Tarquin and he just adores her,' Eva stammered, her words tumbling over each other and crashing to a halt as Ludo and Milly turned identical expressions of surprise, laced lightly with disdain, upon her.

'Ludo was *joking*,' Milly said, reaching over to pat Eva's hand. '*Honestly*. Eva's really nice,' she explained to Ludo.

'How absolutely charming for her,' Ludo said smoothly. 'Well, *revenons à nos moutons*, shall we? Let us return to our sheep, as the French say. I really do need some notes for this wedding beyond elf ears and trailing white nighties, which, frankly, I can tell you, will *not* be a plus point for *Style Bride* ...'

Milly swallowed down her resentment at the mocking tone and elf ears comment: Ludo's reference to the Wayne Burns marriage, combined with his nonchalant familiarity with Victoria Glossop, the famed and feared editor-in-chief of the *Style* magazine empire, had put her on alert. She didn't want to lose the chance to have Ludo Montgomerie, wedding planner to the stars, oversee her own ceremony.

'Well, Eva and I were watching *Pride and Prejudice* the other night,' she started, 'and we both thought it would be perfect for me and Tark to sort of base ourselves on that—'

'The Greer Garson/Laurence Olivier one?' Ludo sighed. 'Gorge! But you know those costumes weren't at *all* historically correct! Or Jennifer Ehle and Colin Firth? I love the white linen shirt idea for Tarquin, with his slender build – *so* much better for clothes, Colin can skew a *leetle* stocky ...'

Milly frowned.

'I don't know what you're talking about,' she said frankly, but with no embarrassment: one of the many advantages of an expensive private education was that its beneficiaries were so cushioned by privilege that they were totally comfortable admitting ignorance on any subject. 'I meant the film with Keira Knightley, of course! That bit at the end when Matthew McFadyen comes towards her in the meadow with his greatcoat billowing out at sunrise ...'

'Oh *lawks*!' Ludo rolled his eyes. '*So* ahistoric! He looked like the 1970s crashing straight into a boyband ... but hmm, I do rather see what you mean there. What was ludicrous for Mr Darcy would actually be rather wonderful on Tarquin – and you *certainly* have the figure for Regency, dear,' he added, casting an approving glance at Milly's almost completely flat chest. Her lack of breasts was crucial for a leading lady; any overly visible curves were considered vulgar, much more suitable for the cheery maid parts than the refined aristocrats whom British ingénues were so often called upon to play.

'Daisies and wild flowers!' Milly rhapsodized eagerly, having finally had some approval from Ludo of what she was aiming for. 'English country-style, with cider and lemonade in jam jars! Maybe a butterfly greenhouse? Or release butterflies over us when we say our vows? Much more original than doves, right? But I want it to be super-chic! Like an Italian film! Think about Keira Knightley's wedding – she had a Chanel strapless frock with matching shoes, but it was really simple, like a prom dress, and just a little flower garland thingy in her hair, and the shoes were flats, and then they drove away in a Renault Clio, so it was really shabby-chic simple, but *really* chic – Karl Lagerfeld was there and he said it was perfect! We can't do France, because Keira did that already, but maybe Italy? We could get lots of Cinquecento cars instead of Renaults ...'

'And *breathe*!' Ludo commanded, waving his hands in front of her face to stop the breathless flow. 'Right! *So*—' he reached for his glass and drank some more wine, 'it has to be English and Italian, super-chic but country-style, shabby-chic but smart enough for Karl Lagerfeld to attend ...'

'Yes, exactly. Perfect!' Milly rose to her feet, as light as a feather, and picked up her cigarettes and lighter from the coffee table. 'I'm *so* glad you get what I'm after. I'm going to have a fag on the smoking terrace – talk about the details with Eva, she's really going to be your liaison for all the day-to-day stuff. She's the designer and she knows exactly what my brand needs. You can run everything through her.'

Refilling her glass and picking that up too, she wafted away in a cloud of pale pink, the layers of her Alice + Olivia silk georgette dress rippling around her narrow frame, the metallic fabric of her flat Charlotte Olympia sandals glistening subtly as she went; heads turned, acquaintances waved to her, and Milly smiled at them all as she floated away and up the stairs to the open smoking terrace.

'I wish *I* could have a fag on the terrace, and I don't mean a cigarette,' Ludo muttered sardonically. 'She didn't *quite* get that I was joking, did she?'

'Um, no,' Eva admitted. 'She doesn't really get it when people tease her.'

'You know, I've dealt with a *lot* of spoilt young madams who think they can order me around as if I were a flunkey,' Ludo said, perfectly poised. 'Really, *vast* amounts of them over the years. The moment they realize that I'm *utterly* prepared to turn my back and walk away is when they start apologizing profusely and knuckling under. I can pick and choose who I work with, believe me. You've seen my recent client list.'

'Oh, please – Milly and Tarquin really want you to organize their wedding!' Eva said swiftly. '*Please*. I think I can clarify what she's trying to say ...'

'I do *not* do lemonade in jam jars!' Ludo sniffed.

'No, of course not – but maybe a Lemon Drop cocktail made with organic Meyer lemons served in recycled Venetian glasses?' Eva suggested. 'I honestly think the butterflies could be an amazing idea, too. I'm doing a butterfly range for the next Milly and Me collection, we could look at the colours for those ... I thought Milly could have her hair all dotted with little butterfly pins, and I love your Regency idea. You could dress Tarquin in a frock coat, he'd look wonderful ...'

'Hmm,' Ludo said, and went very quiet for a whole minute and a half. Eva started to say something after thirty seconds had elapsed, but he held up an imperious hand and she fell instantly silent, something he noticed with a nod of approval.

'*Linen*,' he pronounced eventually.

'I'm sorry?' Eva asked nervously.

'Linen! And cotton!' Ludo announced, staring up at the canvas sun-curtains overhead. 'White draperies billowing everywhere! Yards and yards of lovely crisp white cotton, like sheets in the wind – scented, we'll get some old ladies to starch and iron them all and spray them with lavender and thyme ... fresh, fresh, fresh! Young, clean, new, a *modern* look. Wild flowers planted in the centre of the tables. Poppies and cornflowers. I'll even consider the butterflies, but no promises on that. Of *course*, this would all be *ghastly* for a bride and groom a *day* over twenty-five or with visible signs of wear and tear, if you know what I mean? Your friend Milly's *very* lucky that she looks like a Christmas-tree angel,' he added firmly. 'And that she's marrying a grown-up version of Little Lord Fauntleroy.'

'Oh *phew*!' Eva almost sagged in relief. 'I'm so glad you'll do it. Milly'd set her heart on you planning the wedding, and I love the white linen idea.'

'Covering the tables, blowing in the breeze … starch and fresh flowers, Sicilian lemons, geranium and citronella oils burning in torches …' Ludo rhapsodized. 'I'm going to attempt something really difficult, taste-wise. You know what's hardest? Simplicity! It's so easy to slip into parody. And yet I have a *very* good feeling about this. Beach chic in the Italian countryside. A Tuscan landscape – that stunning Chianti countryside, green hillsides, lines of cypresses, vineyards stretching away down the hill, everything *alfresco*, maybe a prosecco fountain with people dipping little cut-glass antique punch glasses in, those very old-fashioned ones that nobody uses any more – when you said Venetian glass, I had an *epiphany*, I could see it all.'

His voice trailed off. Eva waited to see if he was going to say anything else, but he just sipped some rosé and smiled at her encouragingly, so she ventured to ask, 'don't they need to get married in the Town Hall if they want to do it in Italy?'

'No, dear,' Ludo said dismissively. 'Legally it has to be a civil wedding conducted by the mayor, but it can be anywhere you like nowadays. I have the perfect location in mind, but I'm not going to say another *word* yet until I have it nailed down. Oh, I see it *all*. Even the little Italian ladies behind the scenes, ironing all my lovely linen.'

'Could we organize a religious blessing as well?' Eva asked. 'Tarquin's family's Catholic, so I know they'd appreciate that. Could you maybe find an Italian priest?'

Ludo smiled complacently.

'Oh, no problem there,' he said. 'I know *just* the man for the job. Father Liam Wiles – he's *charming*, believe me. Tarquin's family will be more than happy with him.'

'So, is everything sorted?' Milly was back, her step so light they hadn't seen her approach, beaming seraphically above them and trailing a smell of Marlboro Ultra Lights. 'I can see you two've put your heads together and got all your ducks in a row, right? I'm *so* excited!'

'I have to talk to Jodie Raeburn about the timing,' Ludo said, not deigning to respond directly to his client's wittering. 'I *definitely* need to know her deadline for the *Style Bride* cover and launch. I imagine we'd need to have the ceremony by the end of May at the latest.'

Victoria Glossop was *Style*'s New York-based editor-in-chief, but Jodie Raeburn, the editor of *Style UK*, was directly responsible for editing *Style Bride*, and her approval would be crucial when pitching for the coveted cover of the magazine and the title of *Style* Bride of the Year.

'Oh, *whenever*!' Milly said enthusiastically. 'Whenever! I don't care if I'm standing in the cold shivering my tits off as long as the photos are fabulous and I get to be on the cover of *Style Bride*!'

'Well, *that's* the attitude I like to see,' Ludo commented with the most approval that he had given to anything Milly had said so far.

'And—' Emboldened by this, Milly perched girlishly on the arm of the sofa beside him, spread her pink skirts around her and bestowed on him a pearly, perfect smile, tossing back her golden locks. 'I was rather hoping that you'd be nice to us about the whole question of your fee? I mean, we *are* a very promotable and photogenic couple, and then there's the whole *Style Bride* possibility. After all, if that comes off we'll be absolutely all over the papers, which is *great* publicity for you – really help to build your business.'

Ludo's smile had deepened as she went on, becoming so openly satirical that Milly faltered to a halt, no longer able to look at him as she made her pitch for a discount. When she had wound down, he waited a long three beats before he said, very gently: 'My dear, you're aware of my two biggest-profile weddings last year? Wayne and Andy Burns, Melody Dale and James Delancey? Or, as I like to call them, Wonder Woman and Dr Who?'

These were the roles for which the two actors were respectively known best.

'Of course, you know Melody and James, don't you?' Ludo continued. 'You were in *Much Ado About Nothing* with her – lovely girl. Such a natural beauty now she's had all that awful plastic surgery reversed. And you were in *Dr Who* with James. But despite all that, you weren't at the wedding, though, were you, dear? No, I didn't think so. It was *very* exclusive. Would you like to speculate on the reduction I made in my fees for either of those two couples? Hmn?'

He tilted his head, still smiling at Milly as he landed this series of killer blows.

'Not. A. Penny,' he continued. 'I wouldn't have reduced my fees if I'd done Prince Hugo's wedding to Chloe Rose, let me tell you. I don't do that for *anyone*, and certainly not you! Believe me—' He stood up gracefully, smoothed down the folds of his royal blue shantung silk harem trousers, and gathered up his Hugo Boss bag and iPhone. 'If I wouldn't give a discount to Wonder Woman and Dr Who, I *certainly* won't do it for you!'

He twiddled his fingers in the air in a farewell gesture, sketched a wink at Eva that came and went so fast she wasn't even sure whether she'd actually seen it, and turned to go.

'Toodles!' he said over his shoulder as he made his exit. '*So* looking forward to working with you!'

Chapter Seven

Stanclere Hall

I need to find something I can actually do here, Brianna Jade thought as she carefully picked up her breakfast tray and moved it to the side of the coverlet. Carefully, because it was as ancient and rickety as everything else in this house; one of the little carved feet was bent at an odd angle. It was really cool, like a little table that went over your legs, so you could sit up, prop yourself against the tapestried headboard of the bed with the Harrods hypo-allergenic pillows your mom had had shipped down here on emergency after one appalled night spent on the nasty old feather ones, eat your egg whites scrambled with spinach and lean turkey slices, and sip your non-fat-milk cappuccino without ever leaving your bed.

And yes, Tamra and Brianna Jade had swiftly imposed their dietary requirements on the rapidly expanding staff at Stanclere Hall. Or rather, Tamra's dietary requirements; Brianna Jade would really not have minded putting on a few pounds, now that her days of competing in pageants which had a swimwear section were well and truly behind her. Tamra had been too responsible a mother to let her daughter live on yoghurts, cigarettes and Red Bull, like many of the other girls; she had always been very strict about Brianna Jade maintaining reasonably healthy eating habits and working out, and – unlike most of the other mothers – she had led by example.

But sometimes I'd really kill for a sausage, instead of turkey slices that don't really taste of anything, Brianna Jade thought wistfully. *Mom says we can't get those low-fat chicken sausages over here that we used to live on back home. Which sucks, 'cause I loved those.*

She was getting restless, her toes twitching. Time to get up. But the trouble with getting up was that then she'd have to decide what she was going to do all day, a problem that was becoming increasingly acute. Normally, a bride-to-be would have been thoroughly absorbed in all of the many and various details of planning her wedding: Brianna Jade had known girls back in the US who literally quit their jobs a year before the wedding date in order to devote themselves entirely to the process. However, Tamra had insisted on taking over all of the wedding organization so that Brianna Jade wouldn't be so distracted by it that she lost sight of what was much more important – bonding with her fiancé.

That had made sense on many levels: Tamra was a highly skilled organizer, whereas Brianna Jade's skills most definitely didn't extend in that direction. But the trouble was that it left Brianna Jade with very little to occupy her time. She went up to London every now and then to look at flower-arrangement ideas, to Milan for initial fittings for her dress, but frankly, she trusted her mother's ability and taste much more than she did her own, and simply ended up agreeing with everything that Tamra had chosen.

Nor did Brianna Jade have much to do with the renovations of Stanclere Hall. They were being planned by a team of structural engineers and architects, with Tamra, again, serving as designer and project manager. Brianna Jade was more than happy for her mother to take control, while duly consulting Edmund, of course. She herself wouldn't have known where to start when it came to building works. But again, it left her with barely any involvement, apart from picking out her favourites from the array of paint, wallpaper, carpet and tile samples pre-selected by her mother.

The depressing revelation slowly dawning on her was that, apart from the pageant requirements of keeping herself in optimal physical condition, maintaining perfect grooming, smiling beautifully and walking up and down steps in ankle-length dresses, she actually had very few useful skills or interests. In West Palm Beach, the ready-made social life of young people her own age had swept her along on a wave of shopping, morning-to-night parties, and dating. Here the nearest shops were miles away, the parties were only in the evening, and – well, she was engaged. She was no intellectual, had never regretted not going to college, and wasn't remotely tempted to take courses now, or even pick up anything more demanding than a magazine.

So the problem wasn't settling into Stanclere Hall, becoming used to it being her home now, per se: the problem was that she didn't have enough to do. She hadn't had much in common with the West Palm Beach crowd, but the social whirl had at least kept her busy. Here, for the first time in her life, Brianna Jade would have to generate her own entertainment, build her own interests, and she had no experience in how to even start going about that.

'You need to get involved in running the house,' Tamra had said to her on the phone yesterday: the internet connection at Stanclere Hall wasn't good enough for them to Skype yet. 'There's nothing to stop you. It's not like Edmund's got a pos-

sessive mom living there who wants to run everything her
own way, like Lady Lufton in *Framley Parsonage*. Or a mean
old housekeeper who's obsessed with Edmund's dead wife,
like Mrs Danvers in *Rebecca*, with a huge bunch of keys she
won't give you, hanging on a chatelaine from her waist. That's
why the mistress of a house is called a chatelaine, did you
know? Because she has all the keys—'

'Mom, do you do *anything* right now but read British novels
about stately homes and Lords and Ladies?' Brianna Jade
asked impatiently.

Her mother had laughed, a long, dirty laugh that was very
familiar to her daughter.

'Oh honey, don't you worry about me,' she'd said happily.
'I'm getting my oats.'

'GreatMomgladtohearityoudeserveit*please*don'ttellmeany-
deets, okay?' Brianna Jade rattled off.

'No worries, honey,' Tamra said. 'I've got Lady Margaret for
that side of things. We're pretty much BFFs at this point. She's
really cool. I didn't know Duke's daughters had such dirty
minds.'

Brianna Jade sighed. 'I wish *I* had a BFF down here,' she said
wistfully. 'Edmund takes me to lots of parties and dinners and
stuff, but I haven't really clicked with anyone yet.'

'Oh, hang on in there, honey,' Tamra said easily. 'It'll come,
I promise you. You just keep going to the parties and being
your sweet self, and you'll find some nice girlfriends sooner or
later. You know, you're engaged now – you're not a threat to
any of them, and once they realize that you're not going anywhere, they'll settle in and want to be friends with the new
Countess-to-be. Then you can pick and choose the best ones.
Like Mary Gresham in—'

'Mom! No more people from novels!' her daughter wailed.
'*Please!*'

'I'm going to send you a box of books,' Tamra promised ominously. 'I'll put Post-Its on 'em so you can see which are the easiest to start with. That could be something for you to do, you know? In between going round the Hall, making notes about everything that needs doing! I know we've got the roofers coming in next week, but honey, there's *so* much you could get on with. What about planning your whole master suite? His and hers bathrooms? Go ahead, order a whole bunch of bathroom magazines and start picking stuff out! You can run it past Edmund if you want, but honestly I think he'll be pretty much Rhett Butler about it as long as you don't go crazy with the marble and gold. They really don't like that over here. It's like the opposite of West Palm Beach.'

'Rhett Butler?' Brianna Jade's perfect nose crinkled up charmingly.

'He won't give a damn!' Tamra said impatiently. 'Jeez, BJ, we've seen *Gone With the Wind* tons of times!'

'I don't remember stuff like you do,' Brianna Jade said, not at all daunted; she knew that Tamra's brain was faster and retained more information than hers did. Brianna Jade could never have taken over Ken's Fracking Crown, nor would she have wanted to. *But Mom's pretty much cleverer than anyone – it's just that people don't realize it for a while because she's so gorgeous.*

'I really miss you, Mom,' she said wistfully. 'Maybe we can watch *Gone With the Wind* again in your screening room when I come up to London next week?'

'Sure thing, honey,' Tamra said happily. 'I'll go order it now. Oh, I'm so looking forward to seeing you! I've found some great new boutiques to take you to.'

'I actually don't need any more clothes, Mom,' Brianna Jade said. 'Things aren't that dressy in the countryside. I'm mostly in my workout clothes and jeans and wellington boots.'

'Hush your mouth!' Tamra said, laughing; clearly she thought her daughter was joking. 'Oh, and I've joined this club called Loulou's where *everyone* goes – George Clooney and Mick Jagger *and* Princess Eugenie were in the other night! Mind you, it's so damn dark in there you can't tell who everyone is until you fall over 'em ...'

'Oh, that sounds fun,' Brianna Jade said gamely, to which Tamra giggled more.

'Oh please, you can't fool me,' she said. 'I'm way more into that kind of thing than you are. You'd be happier in the screening room eating popcorn and watching a movie. Now go off and take a stroll round your new home and figure out how many bedrooms you're going to have to lose to make them all en suites, okay? I've got an architectural consultant all booked in to make sure we're not ripping down anything precious, but you should have a sense of what you want before this lady starts, so we know what we're working with ... oh, and let me know how the new kitchen ranges are, will you? They were supposed to get delivered today. We got two and they cost, like, nine grand each, *plus* the tank, so they'd better be perfect!'

The thing is, Brianna Jade thought as she slipped out of bed, *Mom cares about all that stuff so much more than I do. Bedrooms, bathrooms, architects, roofs, kitchen ranges, plumbing, pipes, guttering – or maybe it's not that she cares about it more, it's that anything she takes on, she gets real – really – thorough about. I've got no idea how many bedrooms we should lose! I'm actually way more interested in the gardens than the house. And the farms. I want to explore the farms.*

Okay, that's something that's actually got me excited! She threw on a dressing gown and went to shower. Her mom's bathroom improvements couldn't come too soon; the shower was three doors down the corridor, its tiles chipped, its fittings rusty, its water a trickle compared to what she was used to in the US – *and Mom's house here. And every single London hotel we've stayed in. It's not a British thing, it's a stately home thing. Poor Stanclere Hall, it won't recognize itself after Mom gives it a makeover!*

Then she pulled on a sports bra, running shorts, a loose Stella McCartney pale pink tank and her running shoes, tied her thick strawberry-blonde hair back into a ponytail with one of the No-Snag elastics she and Tamra shipped over in bulk from the States, and headed along the rickety corridor and down the creaking front stairs, leaving her bedroom door open to signal that one of the new maids hired from Stanclere village would know to clean the room and bring down her breakfast tray.

It still made Brianna Jade feel weird, having staff around the house. Even though she'd lived for years in Ken Maloney's Florida mansion, with its discreet fleet of Hispanic maids in black dresses and white aprons slipping silently from one room to another, always smiling, doing their work so invisibly they almost seemed like magical elves, she had never quite got used to it. And back in West Palm Beach, the staff had been employed by her stepdad and her mom; now they were her fiancé's employees, soon to be hers, and that felt, honestly, even weirder.

The kitchen was bustling with activity. Mostly workmen, putting the final touches to the magnificent new pale yellow Smallbone kitchen that Tamra had ordered at vast expense. The two ranges, Rayburn oil-fired, top of the line, anchored the huge room, enormous cast-iron mammoths in British racing green. Mrs Hurley, who had been the cook at Stanclere Hall for twenty-odd years, was standing, arms folded, staring at them with her lips tightly pressed together, looking so grim that Brianna Jade, who usually found her very friendly, hesitated on the threshold, debating for a long nervous moment whether she should just turn tail.

Don't be a coward, she told herself firmly. *Like Mom says, you don't work for them, they work for you.*

'Is everything all right, Mrs Hurley?' she said feebly. 'I mean, with the stoves? My mom asked me to check.'

Mrs Hurley turned to look at the Earl's fiancée, a ridiculously pretty and incongruous figure, her long tanned glossy limbs shown off by her pink and grey running gear, and it became clear that the grimness of the cook's expression had actually been an attempt to repress the strength of her emotions at seeing her kitchen so radically transformed for the better.

'Oh, Miss Brianna,' she said – there was absolutely no way Brianna Jade could induce her to drop the 'Miss' – 'it's just like a miracle, it really is. Not just one, but two! After the old Aga – honestly, you should have been here to see them cart it out. The state it was in! It half fell apart when they were getting it on their fork lift.'

'All grease and rust, it were,' came the muffled agreement from a young man wedged behind the second Rayburn, fitting the oil-supply pipe and fire valve. 'You're well rid of that.'

'I was having a bit of a moment. Silly of me to be sorry to see it go, when I know perfectly well it was only fit for the scrapheap,' Mrs Hurley said, sniffing. 'But I knew all its quirks better than my own cooker at home. I could coax it to do anything I wanted. Well, almost anything. The last time I tried a soufflé was ten years ago, and oh dear, what a disaster that was! The previous Earl didn't let me forget it for years. Mr Edmund's such a sweet-tempered man, he's not fussy at all, but his father was *quite* another kettle of fish. He was *very* particular about his food, just like your mother. Oh, don't think I'm saying a word about *that*, Miss Brianna! Mrs Maloney has high standards and knows exactly what she prefers, and a compliment from her really means something.'

'I'm afraid I don't have standards as high as my mom,' Brianna Jade admitted.

'Oh well.' Mrs Hurley smiled at her tolerantly. 'Hopefully it'll come with time, and you have a very good example in Mrs Maloney. But goodness, there'll be no excuse for any mess-ups with my baking now, will there? I thought I'd do ham and cheese mini-soufflés for a starter tonight. I could leave the cheese out for you, Miss Brianna, and make yours with non-fat milk?'

'That's fine, Mrs Hurley,' Brianna Jade said quickly. 'I'm not actually *that* fussed about dieting. I know my mom's very careful about it, but it's not that huge an issue for me.'

'Are you sure, Miss Brianna?' Mrs Hurley frowned. 'Mrs Maloney was nice enough to sit down with me, right here at this table, and take the time to run through all of her and your requirements and make suggestions for how to adapt my recipes for both of you. I must say, she's an example to all the ladies who aren't spring chickens any more! You can see she's very concerned to keep her figure, and who can blame her?'

One of the workmen who'd helped to bring in the Rayburns, a labourer in Stanclere employ, whistled long and appreciatively at the mention of Tamra's figure.

'That's enough from you, Gideon Banks. And you young enough to be Mrs Maloney's son!' Mrs Hurley snapped, flapping him out into the yard with both hands. '*Anyway*, Miss Brianna, I wouldn't want your mother coming back and telling me I've been feeding you the wrong things and getting all cross with me because you won't fit into your wedding dress any more, would I?'

'I'll run for half an hour extra,' Brianna Jade said, torn between frustration and amusement that even when Tamra wasn't here, her forceful personality prevailed. She sighed. 'Mom's right about the wedding dress.'

If I'm going to be on the cover of Style Bride, *my figure needs to be perfect. Model-perfect.*

'That's right, dear,' Mrs Hurley said comfortably. 'After the wedding you can let things slip a bit, put on a few pounds. But not before. Oh, I can't *wait* to see you in your dress! There won't have been a more beautiful bride at Stanclere ever. So it's a low-fat soufflé for you, then a nice roast with all the trimmings on the side for Mr Edmund, and summer pudding for him. If you pick the bread off, you can have all the berries you want. Your mother said berries are anti-aging. I've been eating plenty ever since she told me that, but I can't say I've seen any difference myself.'

Outside in the yard, Gideon Banks sniggered loudly, but Mrs Hurley pointedly ignored him. She was a scrawny, big-boned woman with greying hair scraped back from her forehead and a twenty-a-day cigarette habit which had miraculously not affected her excellent palate.

'Great,' Brianna said, crossing to the gigantic Siemens American-style fridge-freezer, pulling a glass from the brand-new cupboard and holding it first against the ice and then the water dispenser. 'I'll just grab some water so I'm hydrated before I go for my run—'

'And for lunch,' Mrs Hurley overrode her, 'your mother gave me a recipe for low-calorie crêpes stuffed with courgette. She said she got it from a healthy-eating magazine. We've got so many courgettes from the kitchen garden, and I'll make your batter with non-fat milk and grate a very little low-fat mozzarella on the top. Mr Edmund can have his with a nice béchamel.'

'Lucky Mr Edmund!' Brianna Jade muttered resentfully into the fridge door.

'And a tomato salad,' Mrs Hurley finished cosily. 'With lots of balsamic vinegar and basil. Your mother says you only need a drop of oil in the dressing with that.'

'You know,' Brianna Jade turned round and propped her hips against the yellow wooden panel doors behind which the fridge-freezer was concealed, a discreet rectangle cut into it by the Smallbone kitchen fitters for the ice and water dispensers, 'I really don't need a cooked meal in the middle of the day, Mrs Hurley. Not if it's too much trouble with all of Mom's recipe suggestions. I can easily fix snacks myself. In fact, I'd sort of *like* to. It'd give me something to do, and I never really learnt how to cook. Maybe you could show me how to make those crêpes ...'

Her voice tailed off as she sensed a sudden drop of temperature in the kitchen. It was as if she had opened both panel doors, allowing an icy-cold blast of chilled air to flood into the room, filling it with frost: quite an achievement, considering that the kitchen was big enough to host a fireplace in which a whole pig could be roasted on a spit and a double-height gabled ceiling in which, until very recently, a drying rack had been hoisted for all the kitchen towels, napkins and cleaning rags. Tamra's installation of an entire laundry room, complete with industrial washing machines, had rendered the rack obsolete, and the ceiling had been scrubbed and freshly painted in a pale green that chimed nicely with the yellow Smallbone wooden panelling and the dark racing green of the Rayburns.

In consultation with Mrs Hurley, Tamra had decided that the original flagstones should be kept, but they had been power-washed and now gleamed as bright as grey stone could; Tamra had, as she put it, fast-tracked the kitchen, and this alone would have been enough to make Mrs Hurley her loyal devotee from that moment onwards. The bright clear colours, the new paint job and the thorough clean of the flagstones made the kitchen look enormous, a positive empire in one room over which Mrs Hurley ruled supreme.

Which was why, with Brianna Jade's last words, all the men who worked on the Stanclere estate, and had been in the kitchen either to admire the new ranges, help ensure that the oil-supply pipe had full access to the elevated steel storage tank outside, or slack off hoping that Mrs Hurley might have some baked goods that needed eating up before they went stale, disappeared out through the back door in a flurry of movement. Almost instantly, they could be heard outside tapping on the side of the new tank and muttering meaningless jargon in the way that men did when they suddenly needed to look busy. The only two men left in the kitchen were the Rayburn employees, who didn't understand the gravity of the situation.

'*Fix yourself something?*' Mrs Hurley repeated, her voice even colder than the water Brianna Jade was drinking. The latter shivered right to the base of her suddenly clammy spine.

'I didn't mean—' she began, as the Rayburn installer who was not trapped behind the ranges mumbled something about needing to check the radiation barrier that protected the house from the tank, and hustled outside to join the other men as fast as his heavy work boots would take him, ignoring the agonized expression of his colleague.

'That means "prepare yourself something", if I'm not mistaken?' Mrs Hurley asked Brianna Jade, picking up a tea towel and starting to wring it between her large, gnarled fingers. 'Even Mrs Maloney, who eats like a bird, has *me* prepare her a plate with her special Italian beef slices and her non-fat crème fraiche and her Little Gem salad without dressing! *Mrs Maloney* doesn't want to come into my kitchen and "fix" anything for herself. She tells me what she wants and I make it for her, which is my *job*, and has been for over twenty years!'

The installer behind the ranges managed to squat down far enough that his body was now barely visible behind the bulk of the cast-iron stoves.

'I just meant . . .' Brianna Jade said feebly. 'I just wanted to save you trouble, with all these extra diet versions of regular food – and it sounds like Mom's been going on and on at you about it. I just meant I could go into the fridge and pull something out if you're busy.'

She flinched back at the expression on Mrs Hurley's face.

'Of course I'm *busy*,' Mrs Hurley positively snapped. 'I'm always *busy*. A cook's work is never done. You shouldn't go into this line of work if you mind being *busy*.'

Only Brianna Jade's long experience in pageants kept her legs from buckling under her at this stage in the confrontation; Mrs Hurley's eyes were fixed on her beadily, her head jutting forward like a T-Rex bending over a vulnerable vegetarian stegosaurus. Very luckily, at that point Jennifer, one of the new maids, appeared in the kitchen door with Brianna Jade's breakfast tray, and the interruption allowed the Rayburn man to pop up from hiding, boost himself frantically over the range and scramble for the back door.

'I was meaning to say thank you so much for a delicious breakfast,' Brianna Jade managed to get out, thinking frantically: *What would Mom say? How would she handle this? She'd start with a compliment.* 'The eggs were, uh, scrambled really nicely.'

The hard lines of Mrs Hurley's hatchet face softened fractionally, and Jennifer, crossing to the new, brushed-steel commercial Miele dishwasher and putting down the tray, provided even more distraction. The cook's head swivelled and she said sharply: 'Jennifer, there's a wonky foot on that tray! Take it out and get Gideon to look at it after you've cleared it. He's doing bugger all at the moment, so he might as well have something to get on with, the lazy sod!'

Okay, now Mom would follow up with something smooth that shows she understands the situation.

'I totally get that you're happy to do diet meals for me as well as everything else, Mrs Hurley,' Brianna Jade said, taking the opportunity to cross the kitchen, heading for the back door, which also meant strategically putting the length of the kitchen table between herself and the cook. 'I won't worry any more about you—' *don't say 'working too much', or 'being busy'!* – 'uh, being driven crazy by all my mom's suggestions.'

Mrs Hurley's features tensed up again.

'Which you're not! You're not, and that's great,' Brianna Jade said swiftly. 'My mom's great and really cool and I bet after all these years of just kicking around here with Edmund, Mr Edmund – the Earl – *anyway*, I bet that it's really great to have a lot of new challenges in the kitchen and of course my mom's made sure that you have loads of new stuff to cook with … and on … and put stuff in …'

She trailed off rather desperately, but Mrs Hurley's face was now wreathed in smiles.

'She's ordered me a Gaggia ice-cream maker – the professional one!' Mrs Hurley said. 'And don't worry, Miss Brianna, I can just as easily make you frozen yoghurt in it too. With a little fruit in it and Hermesetas for sweetening.'

'Sounds great!' Brianna Jade said, now almost at the back door. 'So, lunch at one, right? Cool! Off for a run now – lovely talking to you – really glad you're happy about the ice-cream machine. Back for lunch, courgette crêpes, sounds totally yummy—'

Outside! Into the sunshine, moving swiftly, not looking back, passing the group of men gathered around the huge oil tank, their voices low, clapping the second Rayburn installer on the back in congratulations at his successful escape. They averted their eyes respectfully from her Lycra-clad figure as she walked swiftly by; she was followed by Jennifer carrying the tray out to Gideon for repairs, and she heard the guys bursting into relieved banter with the maid, letting off steam as they teased her and tried to get her to bring them cups of tea and biccies.

There's nothing men hate more than women fighting! she thought, waiting until she'd rounded a corner, turned into the farmyard and was out of view before she hoicked one leg up on a fence and stretched out her hamstrings. *I mean, if it's not a pillow fight between two Victoria's Secret models, they're more scared of that than almost anything in the world. They'd rather face a charging bull.*

She started to run, slowly at first, five minutes just to warm up, past the old stables, which were now the garages, as Edmund couldn't afford the expense of keeping horses to ride. She skirted the huge lorry which had brought the two Rayburns and the oil tank and turned onto the gravel drive that looped around the whole front wing of Stanclere Hall. By the time she had reached the façade of the house, she was hitting her stride, crossing the lawn, dodging and dancing around the mole holes, taking long leaps over them for extra shits and giggles, as they'd said back home.

Make the most of it, she told herself. *This is the biggest fun you're going to have today.*

Which was … depressing. And also, not quite true: she and Edmund were spending tonight in, i.e. not going out to one of the many dinner parties or 'drinks dos' to which they were constantly invited, and they'd planned to watch a film after dinner. Brianna Jade was definitely looking forward to that. Tamra had been quite right on the phone yesterday: Brianna Jade was much more of a homebody than her mother was, much more inclined to stay in and watch a movie than go out to the latest hot club and fall over George Clooney in the darkness.

I mean, what would I say to George Clooney anyway? Mom would know just the right thing. She'd be rattling away with him in a minute, saying something funny and making him burst out laughing. I'd just mumble 'sorry' and stare at him, making an idiot of myself looking star-struck.

But that's why I'm in the country and she's in the city. Which is cool, I love it here, but I have to find something to do.

Her lame attempt to ask Mrs Hurley if she could give her some cooking lessons had been thrown back in her face. Which was a real shame, as Brianna Jade genuinely wanted to learn to cook, and had barely had the opportunity. The only real lesson she'd ever had was when she begged Mrs Lutz, their landlady, to show her how to make that casserole for the Kewanee State Fair Pork Queen pageant. Tamra, working her two jobs, was rarely home long enough to be able to make home-cooked meals, not that she had ever been the domestic type anyway. On the road, mother and daughter had pretty much foraged. And after their miraculous elevation to multi-million-dollar status under the aegis of Ken Maloney, they had still not been free to do exactly as they wanted.

Which was fair enough, considering all Ken was giving us, Brianna Jade thought. *Ken wanted me to be his perfect princess. He loved me to dress up, go shopping, get my hair and nails done, have beauty treatments, take tennis and swimming and dance lessons so I could join in the junior and débutante cotillion balls. Boy, I don't miss those at all! All the girls being competitive with me because I hadn't grown up in their so-called high society, most of the guys thinking I'd be easy because my mom and I weren't as classy as they were. Well, they soon learnt their mistake. I hated all those preppy boys, acting like they were the cream of the crop in their polo shirts with the collars turned up ...*

Ken's previous two marriages had produced no offspring, something that had never bothered him. It had been an unexpected, but charming bonus that with Tamra he had found not only a gorgeous trophy wife, but a pretty, affectionate, grateful daughter: he had lavished money and attention on Brianna Jade in order to turn her, Cinderella-like, into a sophisticated glowing blonde princess fit for the highest circles of West Palm Beach society. But cooking lessons would not have fallen into the princess category. Maybe a Cordon Bleu course would have been acceptable, but Brianna Jade would have to have known her way around at least the basics of a kitchen before she dared to go near something as smart as that.

Well, so much for Mrs Hurley teaching me how to cook, she thought wistfully. *Maybe I should take up embroidery. That sounds very aristocratic. Ladies are always embroidering on those wooden circle things in the movies. And it might not be exactly practical, but it would be something to do. I'm not brainy like Mom, I can't lose myself in a book like she does. I need a hobby I can do with my hands . . .*

She was over the lawns now, heading at a long, easy lope down the slope that led to the ornamental lake. Even before it came into view, she heard the clash of chisels on stone, the whine of machinery which was hoisting replacement blocks into place to substitute some that had been found to be dangerously cracked. The work on the bridge was well under way, would be completed in plenty of time for the wedding. Brianna Jade skirted the lake, waving cheerfully at the men labouring below, who stopped, shading their eyes with their hands, to watch the blonde vision that was the lucky Earl's bride-to-be flit past in her trainers, her long tanned legs lifting and falling effortlessly, her bosom strapped down with a sports bra but still with enough of a jiggle to keep them hypnotized.

'Lucky bugger – all that and pots of money too,' one of them commented, shaking his head.

'You seen her mum?' another one asked, whistling long and low as Brianna Jade's bouncing ponytail disappeared around the back of the gazebo. 'If he's *really* lucky he'll be doing 'em both!'

'You filthy bugger,' the first one said happily. '*That*'ll be summat to think about later ...'

The gardens were separated from the farmland beyond by what was called a ha-ha, which Brianna Jade had thought for ages was some sort of in-joke of Edmund's: eventually she had looked it up and discovered that it was actually a real word, meaning what they'd call a 'drop-off' in the States. The land fell away sharply below the gardens so that animals grazing, or farm workers toiling away below, could see the boundary, but the Respers family and guests strolling in the pleasure gardens would merely perceive a long green stretch of lawns and plantings flowing gently into the rolling fields beyond. Combine harvesters were ticking away in the distant fields, the air crisp with warm summer scents, the perfume of linden trees and freshly cut hay; it was a glorious perspective, a perfect English late-summer panorama, and Brianna Jade stopped for a moment to appreciate it. She was incredibly lucky that all of this was so soon to be hers, inherited by her children, this countryside that had to be among the most beautiful in the world, these lands so rich and verdant that she couldn't see why anyone would ever want to live in town when you could be surrounded by this pastoral bliss instead ...

And then another scent reached her nostrils, and she inhaled it with even more delight than the smell of fresh hay and linden. It wouldn't have appealed to many people, but to Brianna Jade of Kewanee, Illinois, the smell of a pig farm was as delicious and familiar as lavender to a girl who had grown up in Provence. She was too young to have seen the Bisto gravy ads where eager children with pug noses followed the visible brown trails of meaty gravy smell to their point of origin, but what she did now was just the same; sniffing the air like a bloodhound, she jogged around the ha-ha, tracking the odour of pig as it grew stronger, eventually spotting the farm buildings and fenced pens up ahead where her quarry had to be located.

Pigs! They were her favourite animal. She'd grown up around them: everyone had pigs in Kewanee. People laughed at the current fashion for keeping pot-bellied pigs as pets, but why not? Pigs were friendly, loyal, and very clean. They recognized people and their voices just as much as dogs did, and they sure as hell never tried to hump your leg.

'Oh *wow*!' broke from her lips as she reached the first pen. Forgetting all about needing to cool down and stretch after a run, she hung eagerly over the railing, staring at the animals inside. They were huge, with wide-set lop ears that drooped over their eyes, almost covering them completely. The dirty white colour of their hair, dappled with big black spots, made their forward-thrust noses seem even pinker; snuffling with excitement at seeing a new human, several of the sows trotted forward to greet Brianna Jade and see if she had any scraps to throw them, oinking happily in greeting.

'Hey, ladies!' she said, squatting on her haunches to scratch their backs, digging her fingers in just the way she knew they would like, utterly careless of her shellacked nails. Their hair was silkier and straighter than the pigs she'd known back home, but they were every bit as friendly, jostling to get close to her even when it was clear that no mid-morning snack would be forthcoming. Their noses were soft and smooth against her knees as they pushed their faces through the bars.

'Oh, you're *lovely*!' she cooed at them. 'Good girls, lovely ladies ...'

She could have stayed there all day hanging out with them, and they would have been very happy; when one of them eventually wandered off to flop down on the short grass with a heavy grunt, another came over to take her place. It was only an awareness that she had lunch at one, and would need to be back, showered, and nicely dressed in time for it which made Brianna Jade, reluctantly, climb back to her feet; even then, she noticed a stick propped against the railing and, knowing exactly what it was for, picked it up and started scratching the sows further down their backs, which sent them into fresh snuffles of excitement.

Happy memories were flooding back to her. Days in Kewanee, when she was old enough to roam around with her friends, or even on her own, hanging out on the local small-holdings, helping the farmers with the farrowing sows, lugging pails of slop and dumping them into the troughs, cleaning out the sties. Tickling their tummies as they rolled over enthusi-astically and waved their trotters in anticipation. Sweeping the wood shavings they slept in into neat piles that they would burrow in happily, watching them wallow in the summer mudslicks, as Mrs Lutz explained that pigs didn't sweat and wallowing was the only way for them to cool down in the heat ...

Winning Pork Queen at the Kewanee Hog Day fair had been the highlight of her life, the best thing that had ever hap-pened to her; being the crowned queen, standing on the tractor trailer, her sash arranged over the pigskin jacket she wore proudly over her cheap blue pageant dress, hearing the crowd cheer as she scattered Oreo cookies on the finish line of the hog race, the signal for the competing pigs to be released and scamper as fast as their trotters would carry them towards the enticing black-and-white cookies ... oh, how happy she'd been at that moment! Her heart had literally been as full up with happiness as a trough brimming over with potato peelings.

And of course, the irony was that my winning Pork Queen was the thing that made Mom think I could compete in pageants and take me away from Kewanee and all the lovely pigs.

She sighed. *Mom never lets me say a word about Kewanee. She took away that pigskin jacket, and all the photos of me in my crown holding a cute little piglet and kissing it. Those were such cute photos ... Okay, I know why she doesn't want us talking about it any more. I do get it. We'd get so teased about it – no, way more than teased. Torn to shreds. We'd never hear the end of it.*

But it's hard not talking about some of the happiest memories I've ever had. Maybe the happiest.

'Ooh-arr,' came a deep male voice, and Brianna Jade, who hadn't realized there was anyone else around but the pigs, jumped about a foot and looked around her wildly for the origin of the sound.

'Ooh-arr,' the voice said again, and this time she located its origin: an enormous, muddy man standing inside the pen, having just emerged from the shed. He was wearing ancient, faded dungarees over a T-shirt, and he was leaning on a big, equally muddy spade; she couldn't quite understand how he had got so filthy. It was only later that she would realize that there was a wallowing patch out behind the back of the shed that needed to be watered and turned over in the absence of rain.

He raised a hand and brushed it across his face, probably meaning to push his hair back, but only succeeding in plastering brackish mud across his forehead in a thick diagonal stripe; there were already splashes of mud up his legs and over his arms from vigorous work with the spade. The sun was behind him, and mostly what Brianna Jade could see was a looming, hugely muscled shape, his biceps swelling like melons below the short sleeves of his T-shirt, his wellington-booted legs spread as wide as his massive shoulders. It looked as if it would take the forklift that had transported the Rayburn ranges to move him if he didn't want to budge.

'Um, hi?' Brianna Jade said, putting down the stick and resting it against the railings. 'The pigs are *great*.'

He just stood staring at her. It was beginning to feel like a confrontation in a Western movie, as if he were the local lawman, she were new in town, and he wasn't sure whether to trust her with the pigs or not. Like, uh, a pig sheriff.

'I was just scratching their backs,' she said a little nervously. 'I really like pigs – I kinda grew up around them. Anyway, I should get going! Uh, nice to meet you.'

'Ooh-arr,' the man rumbled again without moving a muscle.

She turned and started to walk away, then broke into a jog, heading back the way she'd come; after a few minutes, with the ha-ha coming into view in front of her, she turned to look back. The man-mountain was still there, huge hands planted on his spade, staring after her.

Jeez, she thought. *I've never seen anyone nearly that big over here. They don't usually come that size in the UK.* Back home in Illinois, they bred on a massive scale: it was all the German and Scandinavian stock, large farmers who had emigrated from Europe in search of land, been nourished on the abundant protein so easily available in the New World, and grown even larger, like a race of giants. When the Future Farmers and Future Homemakers of America conventions rolled into town, hotels trembled for their furniture. The looming silhouette of someone whose hands were almost as big as his spade made Brianna Jade oddly nostalgic: she had always been one of the tallest girls at pageants, the wide square shoulders inherited from her farmer father perfect for carrying off elaborate draped dresses, but she'd often felt big and awkward next to the smaller Asian or Hispanic-origin contestants, with their small bones and delicate frames, the dancers who did ballet or rhythmic gymnastics for the talent section, tiny and flexible in their leotards.

While back home in Kewanee, I was normal. Hell, next to that guy back there, I'd be positively petite! She couldn't help grinning as she skirted the ha-ha, heading back to the Hall. *I should have told Mom to take me to Germany instead of Britain, snagged a whatever-they-have over there. A Prince, maybe. Hey, maybe even a King – Herzoslovakia has one going free!*

The main entrance of Stanclere Hall, with its double-winged stone staircase and impressive carved oak doors, was only used on formal occasions. It seemed weird to Tamra and Brianna Jade to have such an impressive front door and barely use it, but Edmund had looked so taken aback at the idea that they access the house by anything but one of the side doors that they had given up any attempt to change his mind. If they were going to join British society, Tamra had observed, they had to figure out the non-negotiables. En-suite bathrooms, kitchen overhauls: no problem at all. Using the main door on a regular basis: absolutely out of the question.

So Brianna Jade looped round the façade of the house again. She was too sweaty by now to be comfortable going in by the terrace which overlooked the lawns and led to the main suite of entertaining rooms. The drawing rooms might be dilapidated, the stucco on their ceilings peeling, their rugs faded, their draperies moth-eaten, but they were still too formal to walk through in damp, tight Lycra exercise wear. She was making for a side door with glass panels that led to a back hallway that would take her up a staircase to the first floor, directly to the bedroom wing. Stanclere Hall, unlike many other stately homes that had been added to with each new generation, had been built in one well-planned swoop, and the interiors were not the confusing maze that others had become with the addition of new wings over the centuries.

But as she swung around the side of the Hall, having slowed to a walk to cool down, she saw her fiancé's battered old Land Rover pulling up by the stables, Edmund coming back from his morning's work to join her for lunch. Before she had more or less moved in, he had stayed out in the fields all day, taking a packed lunch like the farmhands did; but, to keep her company and build up their relationship, he had deliberately changed his routine. She was sure it was an inconvenience for him but was too grateful to tell him not to do it. The lunches were a lifeline to her, broke up the monotony of her days enough that she could get through them successfully.

Edmund swung down from the Land Rover, not seeing her walking towards him, and stood there for a moment, rolling back his shoulders, as hot and sweaty as Brianna Jade: his T-shirt was sticking to his chest, his ancient, stained jeans clinging to his legs. The Earl of Respers pulled up the hem of his sweat-stained T-shirt to wipe his face and revealed his torso, lean and muscled, but not overtly, the body of a man who did regular physical work, not a gym rat. Her trainers crunched on the gravel and she stopped, wanting suddenly to watch Edmund when he wasn't aware that she was there.

They hadn't had sex yet, a joint decision that they had come to that night of the proposal, over dinner, after Tamra had left; it had been a huge relief to both of them when Brianna Jade had got up the nerve to raise the subject over the lemon syllabub that Mrs Hurley had served for pudding (weirdly, they called dessert 'pudding' over here, even if it wasn't anything like one). Sipping Muscat de Beaumes-de-Venise ('pudding wine') by candlelight, the conversation tailing away as the evening grew later and the whole question of how the night would end became even more acute, Brianna

Jade had felt that Edmund was waiting for her to set the pace, to indicate how she wanted things to proceed.

She was hugely grateful for that, would have hated his assuming that once she had agreed to marry him she would just fall into his bed. But of course, the fact that he wasn't taking her for granted meant that she would actually have to work out what *she* wanted, and that was easier said than done. Part of her had thought that they should just get it over, do it the first night and settle down to being comfortable without the fact that they hadn't had sex looming over them. But when she opened her mouth, what came out was a request that they go slowly, get to know each other better, not take each other for granted. Work towards falling in love, as Edmund had said to her earlier.

And his instant reaction had told her that her instincts had been correct; he hadn't been able to hide his relief.

'You know I find you very attractive,' he'd said at once, reaching across the table to take her hand. 'It isn't that, not at all. It would just feel, tonight – well, a bit forced, I suppose.'

As if he were bought and paid for, Brianna Jade had thought then. *Because that is sort of what's happening. Mom's bought me him, the title, the house, and doing it tonight would be almost like – well, like treating him as a stud boar on a pig farm!* It had been really hard not to giggle at the idea, partly because there was a core of truth to it; Edmund wanted children too, of course, but a huge part of the appeal of a British aristocrat for Tamra had been that her grandchildren would inherit the title, that the money she was pouring into Stanclere Hall would be an investment in her family's future.

'I really liked what you said earlier, about love coming as we get to know each other,' Brianna Jade had said gratefully. 'I mean, I know this is arranged, but we still feel that we could—'

'*Definitely*,' Edmund said quickly. 'You're beautiful, sweet, charming, intelligent – sorry, that sounds like an awfully staid list, and I didn't mean it to be. I just meant that you have all the qualities any man would fall in love with …'

'You had me at "intelligent",' Brianna Jade said, now able to giggle. 'I mean, if a man calls a blonde "intelligent", he can always get her into bed.'

'Really?' Edmund's grin was adorable; it lit up his usually solemn grey eyes, gave his straight mouth a curve that softened his squarish features. 'Gosh, I wish I'd known that years ago. I've always liked blondes, I must admit.'

'Gentlemen prefer me!' Brianna Jade had said cheerfully, reaching forward to clink her Muscat glass with Edmund's, and they'd finished the evening on a truly happy note, walking up the main staircase arm in arm, and Edmund kissing her goodnight, a kiss just as satisfactory as the one that afternoon in the gazebo.

Since then, that had been the pattern; a passionate kiss goodnight, sending them both to bed very happy with the bargain they had made, and a daily routine that they fell into – though less fulfilling for Brianna Jade than for Edmund, who, as a farmer, was fully occupied all summer with the coming harvest.

Tamra had asked her daughter recently whether she and Edmund were having sex yet, and when Brianna Jade had told her no, her mother had tilted her head and said that they didn't want to leave it too long. Think of the pressure on Edmund, she said, if they waited almost half a year until the wedding. And though Edmund seemed really nice and normal, Brianna Jade didn't want to wait till her wedding night to find out that he was weird in bed in ways she didn't like. You heard lurid stories about these British aristos and a kink factor from their private schools. Maybe it was all just rumour and gossip, and God knew, Tamra said, she wasn't judgemental – but you wanted to make sure that whatever they liked, you liked too.

Or what if he had a tiny dick? Just because she had set her daughter up with a storybook-perfect Earl with a stately home, it didn't mean that Brianna Jade needed to have bad or weird sex, let alone with a tiny dick, all her life: she should try before buying, make sure she was okay with the deal she was making.

Plus, it never went well when you put men under pressure sexually, Tamra informed Brianna. The last thing they wanted was a wedding-night disaster with Edmund getting performance anxiety or, as Tamra had tastefully added, blowing his load too soon. Relieved as she had been to hear her mother's assurances that she didn't have to marry Edmund if the sex was awful, this was going too far. Brianna Jade had clapped her hands over her ears and screamed at Tamra to stop, that she didn't want her mom talking about her husband-to-be like that, and Tamra had obeyed. For once.

But now, staring at Edmund, as he gave a surreptitious sniff to his T-shirt, winced, dragged it off and, bare-chested, walked over to the old iron water pump in the courtyard to sluice himself down, those words of her mother's came back to Brianna Jade with considerable emphasis. She had known that Edmund had a good body, slim and toned, but his English tendency to wear clothes that weren't as fitted as some of the European men she'd met at parties meant that she hadn't realized how well-developed he actually was. His pectorals were firm and tight, his abdominal muscles nicely defined, hollowing down to his narrow waist; as he pumped the water up, his right arm rising and falling, the play of muscle from his lats to his swelling bicep was a steady ripple of strength easily exerted.

He bent forward, splashing the water in the bowl onto his face and upper body, his bare back lean and muscled enough to have served as a model for an anatomical drawing. As he stood up again, drying himself off with his balled-up T-shirt, water trickled down his body, catching in the fine gold-brown hairs scattered over his chest, a light trace on his upper arms, darkening on the forearms and in the surprisingly thick line of hair that drew straight down to his belt buckle, disappearing behind the fly of his faded jeans ...

Brianna Jade swallowed hard, watching his biceps flex. It was what she had been waiting for, this physical click with her fiancé; not a *we should probably do it, we're engaged and I like kissing you*, but an *I want him, right now*: unforced, completely spontaneous.

Jeez, I should just have asked him to take his shirt off weeks ago!

Edmund was raising his arms to shake drops of water from his hair, and that very particular bulge that a man's arm muscles get when they're lifted with the hands up to the head, the armpits fully exposed, the darker hair a little shock against the whiter skin, made Brianna Jade's mouth go dry. Edmund had a working man's body and a working man's tan, his forearms and neck sun-kissed, his chest and upper arms white as his armpits, and the contrast was just like the boys she'd dated in Kewanee, achingly familiar and attractive. Unexpectedly, she found herself remembering Marty Boetz from the trailer park who'd been her first. They'd done it in a cornfield – that was pretty much where all the kids went to make out, with the crop so high and thick that you only knew what was going on by the unmistakable sounds muffled by the heavy ears of corn, the thick surrounding leaves. You kept walking till the noises the couple were making faded behind you, and you found a place of your own to spread the blanket and lie down under the stars.

Sounds romantic, but Marty wasn't. It was his first time too, and he made a real mess of it. Literally. It got a bit better, I guess, but it was never anything to make a fuss about. Still, I loved how big and strapping he was – almost as big as the pig sheriff guy back by the pens. Huh, I suppose it's that guy who made me think of Marty. Boy, I wanted him real bad. Even though the sex itself was never great, every time I saw him I'd get the shivers all up and down my back. When he took his shirt off I'd just melt like cheese all over a burger, all sticky and wet …

She must have shifted: Edmund heard her feet on the gravel, swivelled to see who it was, and stopped dead, meeting her eyes. He was experienced enough to see exactly what was in them. The accidental pose, twisted around with the T-shirt in one hand, made him look like one of the Greek statues in the gazebo, a discus thrower; even his hair, sticking to his forehead in curls, was reminiscent of those athletes, with their lovingly detailed musculature, their sinewy bodies, bodies sculpted for sport by rigorous exercise. Brianna Jade thought of the discus thrower's torqued waist, the quadricep of his front leg stretched and tense, and swallowed again.

He wouldn't move, she knew that. She would have to be the one to signal that this was the time, that she was ready. And though it wasn't now or never – there would be plenty of other opportunities for her and Edmund to finally consummate their engagement, as it were – the moment that she actually felt dry-mouthed, wet-pantied excitement for him was surely the best of all possible moments …

Walking towards your sweaty, hot fiancé, who was looking at you as if he couldn't believe his luck, was hugely exciting, but it also made her feel incredibly self-conscious. If anyone had come out into the courtyard, if the Rayburn lorry had driven through, the spell would have been broken instantly; but she reached Edmund without any interruptions, though she was seriously afraid that the flanges of her running shoes would trip on the gravel, was torn between holding Edmund's steady grey gaze and looking down to ensure she didn't fall over.

She stopped just a couple of inches away from him, her face almost on a level with his. His lips were parted and he was breathing fast, his chest rising and falling, the damp hairs so close she could have touched them just by lifting her hand. And she wanted to so much. She was hoping that Edmund would make the first move, but he just stood there, staring at her, and it was Brianna Jade who eventually lifted her hand and pressed the fingers against his smooth damp pectoral, lightly dappled with moles, the hairs a deliciously coarse contrast with the pale skin below, her palm settling against his nipple, which hardened instantly at her touch ...

It wasn't the only part of his body that was hard. She stepped in fractionally and felt his cock against her, the buttons of his fly each standing out in relief, pressing into her crotch, the thin Lycra of her jogging shorts a very flimsy layer between her and his jeans. She gasped, and Edmund's hand came up, took hers in a firm clasp, pulled her towards the house with him; they went in a stumbling rush through the side door, down the corridor, up the back stairs, too narrow for them to walk together; ever a gentleman, Edmund gestured for Brianna Jade to go first, and she felt stupidly embarrassed knowing that he was watching her barely covered bottom, maybe seeing the line of her thong. She would so much rather have followed him, let him set the pace.

At the top of the staircase she took a step, stopped, didn't know where to go for a moment. Then she thought: *Edmund's room. I'm going to be his wife, and then I'll be moving in there. It's the main set of rooms, where his mother and father lived, where the Earls of Respers have always lived – we should go there.* She turned and led the way, Edmund right behind her, putting his arm around her waist, courteous as always, even when they were about to take their clothes off and finally do it.

Through the private sitting room, into the huge bedroom,

right up to the four-poster bed with its massive black oak frame, its heavy dark red brocade draperies suspended from the huge carved finials above; turning to face him, standing frozen for a moment, looking right into his eyes, feeling the shock: *It's here, it's happening at last, after all the waiting. Edmund and I are actually going to have sex ...*

'I should probably shower, shouldn't I?' he said, his voice hesitant. 'I'm covered with sweat, we've been heaving bales around today – I probably have hay all over me too. You won't want me in all of my dirt ...'

'Oh. Okay,' she mumbled.

Brianna Jade would have been very happy to peel her clothes off and go at it right now, right here, have him throw her on the brocade bedspread, cover her with his hot sweaty body, lick the salt from his shoulders as he drove inside her, smell his scent, which was fresh and clean, with a faint hint of the Imperial Leather soap he'd used that morning. She was more than ready, but hesitated to say that.

What if he thinks I'm too forward? Or gross, for wanting to do it right now, with me all sticky from running and him from work?

'Uh, shall I shower too?' she asked, as he turned towards the bathroom.

'Oh, my God, of course you'll want to!' Edmund looked horrified. 'I'm so sorry – you must go first.'

And of course she couldn't suggest that they shower together, soap each other down, because the damn plumbing in this damn house was so messed up that they would literally never get clean if they stood under that trickle together. So she headed alone to his bathroom, a large space but pitifully bare, an expanse of ancient white tiles with a couple of small threadbare mats making the room look even bigger, the battered old bath with the rickety shower head above it at the far end of the room. She turned on the shower, pulled off her nasty, sweaty, clammy Lycra, and climbed into the bath. Of course, Edmund, being a straight man, had the most pitiful selection of bath products, just a two-in-one shampoo and conditioner, a medicated shower wash and a bar of Imperial Leather soap.

Brianna Jade got herself as clean as she could under the dribble of water, washed her hair as well – in for a penny, in for a pound, as Mrs Hurley said – and then realized that there was only one bath towel, as threadbare as the mats. It had been exquisite quality once, with hand-crocheted lace trimming it, but now it was worn so thin that she could see right through it in parts. Tamra had brought down stacks from Harrods, but, ridiculously, Edmund seemed to have been too scrupulous to use the lavish Egyptian cotton bath sheets before marriage.

So Brianna Jade dried her hair as best she could on the hand towel, wrapped herself in the other, which barely reached from the top of her breasts to the top of her thighs, and padded out in bare feet to find Edmund standing by the bed, naked apart from a towel knotted around his waist.

'I nipped down the hall to another bathroom and had a quick wash,' he said, blushing. 'I thought it would be weird to go in one after the other – but then I thought I was probably taking your water, and I felt awful, so I stopped ... but I think I got fairly clean.'

'Oh, I'm sure you did,' she said at random, convinced that she was blushing too. 'You *look* clean. I mean ...'

Thank God – good legs! she thought, glancing down at them. It was ridiculous to realize that she had got engaged to a man without ever knowing if he had skinny chicken legs. She'd read in a gossip magazine that Brad Pitt in *Troy* had bulked up to play Achilles, but had been unable to expand his calves in proportion to the rest of him; he'd apparently needed a calf double.

Well, Edmund definitely wouldn't need a calf double. The trouble was that now she'd looked down to check out his legs, she had to look up again, her gaze passing over the white towel wrapped around his hips; it was with a mixture of relief and embarrassment that she noticed him tenting against it, reacting to the sight of her in her own skimpy towel.

'Hi!' she said, blushing harder. 'So, uh, here we are.'

'It feels like a nice place to be,' Edmund said, bright red now. 'Doesn't it?'

'Yes! It does!'

And she realized, again, that she would have to step towards him. *Jeez, are all titled guys like this? He's standing there with a boner and he can't even kiss me, let alone throw me on the bed and ravage me like the Earls do in romance novels?*

Oh well, I guess husband material isn't exactly the same thing as the hunk on the cover of Love's Tender Fury ... *and he gets hard every time he kisses me or sees me with not many clothes on, so that's half the battle right there.*

Stepping towards him, she put her arms up, wrapping them round his neck, pulling him down to kiss her; he responded with such eagerness that she was hugely relieved. Maybe some sort of gentlemanly scruples were making him nervous about initiating the first move. She hoped to hell he'd loosen up, learn that it was okay to reach out for her too, but right now, with his arms closing around her, his cock firm and hard between them, his lips on hers – *oh damn, he brushed his teeth and I didn't, I hope I don't taste too bad* – everything was exactly where it was supposed to be.

She gasped as his hands slipped down to her bottom, his arms flexing as he lifted her easily off her feet, took a few steps across the room and placed her carefully on the bed.

They were facing each other, looking into each other's eyes; she pulled him on top of her, all worked up again and ready to go, wanting him inside her, but not knowing the words to tell him that he could do it right now, just pull the towels away and slide between her legs; somehow she couldn't just whisper 'Fuck me!' to an Earl who'd just carried her in true gentlemanly style to his four-poster bed. Romance-novel heroines didn't say 'Fuck me.' Well, *historical* romance heroines didn't. And how modern could she feel right now, with deep crimson brocade hangings all around them, blocking out the daylight, hangings that had probably been draped around this bed for centuries?

So she kissed him, and he kissed her right back, and, greatly daring, she reached down to ease his towel from his bottom; he wriggled to let her do it, his cock bumping out against her, and then he unwrapped her towel too and they were naked against each other, which felt so good it made her gasp and throw her head back and arch her crotch into his. He slid down her, careful to go slowly enough to give her time to tell him to stop if she wanted him to, which she didn't, and started to lick her. It was rather too careful and worshipful for her liking, definitely the way a man went down on his wife-to-be, rather than, say, his mistress. But he was doing it without even being asked, which was great, and at least she knew that she was fresh and clean – that had been smart thinking of Edmund's – and his tongue on her felt good, good enough for her to reach down and stroke his hair encouragingly, showing him she liked what he was doing. His eyes tilted up towards her, checking on her reaction, which always made her self-conscious, so she closed her own and concentrated on what he was doing and tilted her hips more so that he hit just the right place with his velvety wet tongue, synchronizing her breathing to his rhythm in a way she'd practised over the years when making herself come.

With little moans and pants and 'yeses' and tilts of her hips, she let him know what she liked, her panting building to a crescendo, breathing into every lick and nibble with increasing strength, letting her orgasm rise to breaking point and flood through all the nerve endings that spread out through her groin, suffusing all of them with pleasure, crying out in delight, her hands gripping fistfuls of the brocade coverlet and then eventually letting go as the throbbing began to subside.

She could have come again and again, wanted Edmund to keep going, but she was wordless, collapsed for a little while, eyes closed, and she felt rather than heard him climb off the bed, open a drawer, pull out a condom packet and rip it open.

'I'm on the Pill,' she managed to say. 'It's okay.'

'Oh *wonderful*,' Edmund said with huge relief, climbing back onto the bed again. She managed to open her eyes, scooch back to the pillows so her head was raised, and she could see him kneeling in front of her, face serious, his cock red and swollen as he looked down the length of her long slim body.

'You're so beautiful,' he said reverently.

Yes yes yes I know fuck me now, fuck me hard! she was dying to say, but still couldn't quite manage; the setting, the ancestral bed in which the Earls and Countesses of Respers had had marital sex over the centuries, was weighing on her as heavily as the brocade draperies hung on the carved oak frame. It seemed rude, wrong, to talk dirty in this hallowed room – Respers heirs and spares had doubtless been born in this very bed, a thought which didn't help the situation.

Jeez, I'm going to lose my lady boner if this keeps up! Come on, BJ, there's a gorgeous guy about to fuck you, get with the programme . . .

Brianna Jade held out her arms to Edmund, the signal that he had clearly been waiting for; eagerly, he shuffled forward on the mattress, taking his cock in one hand. She widened her legs to give him more room as he knelt between them, pressed the tip against the absolute centre of the delicious wetness of her pussy, and began, tentatively at first, to slide inside her; the moans she was making encouraged him, and in a few seconds he was filling her. She had known already that he was well-hung, had felt it when they kissed for the first time, but it was still a huge relief to know that any worries about performance anxiety or coming too soon could safely be dismissed.

Edmund was on top of her now, her arms around him, her legs wrapping around his lean hips as he pumped away at her with a regular steady pulse that showed no indications he might come too soon or lose control. She could trust him, give herself up to the rhythm completely, let it build and build: God, it felt so good! It had been ages since she'd got laid; she'd screwed around in West Palm Beach, of course, but those preppy boys hadn't really been her type. She liked guys who worked with their hands, whose muscles weren't gym-built but natural, and the fact that Edmund defined himself as much as a farmer as an Earl had, ironically, been a big part of his attraction for her.

Her head was tilted to the side, her lips pressing into his shoulder; she kissed him, smelling the Imperial Leather soap he had just used, the tang of his skin, licking the hairs that curled in whorls, pressed down flat by the shower water. She dragged herself back a little, grabbed his head with her hands, made him kiss her as he rose and fell between her legs, his tongue driving in and out of her lips in synch with his cock; it was hypnotizing. They were gasping into each other's mouths, Edmund groaning wordlessly as he worked away, holding himself to an even pace that let them both settle into the shock of a new body so intimately close. He was propped on his elbows, taking some of his weight off her very considerately, and that gave her just enough space to slip her hand down between their bodies, sensing if she wanted to come again – which she *very* much did – that it would be up to her to deal with it.

As soon as he felt her move, he lifted to give her room; she couldn't fault him, he was sensitive to anything she wanted to do. He reared above her in a push-up, watching her expression as her head tilted back as she started to work on herself, her fingers moving quick and frantic between her legs, easing his cock out a little so she could reach the exact wet nub that she needed to just stroke and flick that little, little extra that made all the difference in the world, trying not to catch her nails on his or her tender flesh – they were too long for this, really; usually she used a vibrator, had a couple in her room, she'd have to see if he was okay with that—

She screamed, hitting the spot, arching back even more, and she was going to go for it again, to come and come with his big cock inside her, but he took that to mean that she was done and plunged back into her so eagerly that she had to pull her hand away so it didn't get crushed between their bodies: she couldn't tell him to stop, that she wanted to come again. She fell back, limp, Edmund following her, kissing her frantically now, his mouth glued to hers as his hips drummed a final tattoo between her thighs, his cock swelling inside her, a last strong stroke as it jerked and began to come in spasms.

Edmund didn't yell anything, didn't make any noise but a long deep grunt of satisfaction. He collapsed on top of his fiancée, almost instantly sliding his body weight to the side to make sure he wasn't too heavy for her. Brianna Jade wouldn't have minded, would actually have welcomed the weight, but she wrapped her arms around him, held him close and kissed his shoulder again and again, grateful that the man she was marrying was this considerate of her. To her great surprise, he mumbled, 'Thank you.'

'You don't need to *thank* me!' she said, taken aback.

'I just wanted to be polite,' Edmund started.

'Polite! But why?'

'Well, you know ...' Edmund writhed a bit in embarrassment. 'Thanking the woman after – it's sort of the right thing to do if one's being courteous.'

Brianna Jade couldn't help giggling. Just when you thought you cracked upper-class British manners, something new popped out at you – like thanking your fiancée after sex, as if women were still supposed to be less interested in it than men.

'But I wanted it as much as you did,' she said frankly. 'And it was great!'

'It was?' Edmund had buried his face in a pillow out of awkwardness, but now he turned to look at her, their eyes very close, his features out of focus. 'Really?'

'Jeez, Edmund, you heard me screaming!' she said, smiling at him, her entire body feeling happily released. Not *completely* sated; she could have done with coming a few times more, but hopefully that would sort itself out in future.

'Well, *that's* a relief,' he said, smiling back at her, leaning forward to drop an affectionate kiss on her lips. 'I thought it was more than great. My God, Brianna, the sight of you naked! I don't think I've ever seen anything more beautiful in my life.'

'Oh, thank you!' She kissed him back.

'I'm a very lucky man,' Edmund said, his grey eyes clear and sincere. 'I'm probably the luckiest man in the world, frankly. I honestly don't know what I've done to deserve you, Brianna, but I'll spend the rest of my life doing my best to make you feel you haven't made a bad bargain.'

'Oh!' She almost felt tears rising to her eyes. 'That's so lovely!'

They kissed again, and Edmund, with a visible effort,

propped himself up once more, his cock sliding out of her, slippery and bringing a rush of hot liquid with it.

'Bugger, the coverlet!' He jumped up and off the bed, galvanized, and ran to the bathroom for toilet paper, loping back to mop up his come and hand her another wodge of paper for herself. Then he took one of the discarded towels and rubbed vigorously at the stain. 'It's such hell to wash ... I'll pull it off in future. Maybe I can sponge it and hang it up over a window to dry in the sun? I feel a bit awkward about asking Mrs Hurley to get one of the girls to wash our, err, our—'

Despite her frustration at the mood having been broken – she certainly wasn't going to get her extra orgasms now – Brianna Jade couldn't help smiling at the earnestness of his expression, at his concern for Mrs Hurley's sensibilities.

'Honestly, I wouldn't like to ask her either,' she admitted, pressing the toilet paper against her crotch, feeling his come ooze pleasurably out of her. 'I could help you with the coverlet?'

'Certainly not,' the Earl of Respers said firmly. 'I made the mess, I'll clean it up. God, I'm starving. That definitely worked up my appetite. What about you?'

'We've got courgette crêpes for lunch,' Brianna Jade said. 'Mrs Hurley told me.'

Edmund grimaced.

'I hope she's serving loads of potatoes with that,' he said. 'Or bread. Or both. I've been shovelling shit all day and I've got more of the same this afternoon.'

'Were you at the pig farm? I went there today,' Brianna Jade said, sliding off the slippery coverlet and to the floor, Edmund very solicitously grasping her waist to steady her as she found her footing.

'No, chickens,' Edmund said. 'Fantastic fertilizer. But that's an extra reason I wanted to shower. Did you see Abel at the pig farm? You couldn't possibly have missed him.'

'Huge guy? Yeah.' She walked towards the bathroom to wash herself. 'He said "ooh-arr" to me. Like, lots.'

'It's a standard greeting round here,' Edmund said, grinning. 'I can do it for you if you'd like. I slip into the local accent pretty easily, though my mother always hated it.'

'You really don't have to.' Brianna Jade was laughing now.

'There's a dressing gown on the back of the door,' he said. 'Why don't you put that on so you can go back to your room and get dressed? I'll wait for you and escort you down to lunch.'

'We *really* need to get you a new robe,' she called, dragging on the ancient faded near-rag she found hanging from the hook. 'I'm going to order one for you, and I don't want any argument, okay? I'm throwing this one away as soon as the new one comes. Plus the towels! Why aren't you using the new ones?'

'They were my grandmother's,' Edmund pleaded. 'I know they've seen better days, but—'

As he protested, Brianna Jade re-entered the room, walked to the bed, picked up one of the discarded towels and held it up in front of her face so that he could see how worn it was: her features clearly showed through it.

'Okay,' he said, yielding. 'You do have a point. New towels it is.'

'Hey, I have lots of money,' she said with disarming frankness. 'We might as well enjoy it!'

How great is this? she thought happily as she kissed him on the lips and went back to her room. *Having sex, then talking about actual domestic stuff together, like we were married already. This is real now.* Not that it had ever felt fake to her. She had liked Edmund from the moment she met him, would never have agreed to the proposed marriage if she hadn't known she could have feelings for him; but somehow, the combination of good sex followed by a mutual agreement to throw out threadbare towels was a confirmation that they were embarking on genuine married life, not just a mutually beneficial arrangement.

She was humming a cheerful tune when she emerged from her bedroom in a fresh linen dress and pretty summer sandals, her hair loose around her shoulders in golden waves, diamonds in her ears. Edmund was waiting outside for her in the blue and white finely checked shirt tucked into pressed jeans that was the Englishman's version of smart casual.

'You dressed up for me!' she said, delighted. 'That's so sweet.'

He took her arm and tucked it securely into the crook of his as they walked towards the main staircase, which was wide enough to descend side by side.

'Really,' he said seriously, 'it was the absolute *least* I could do.'

Chapter Eight

It was still, occasionally, a surreal experience for Jodie Raeburn, editor of *Style UK*, to walk into her office and realize that it did in fact belong to her. In her previous incarnation as Jodie Raeburn, lowly assistant to Victoria Glossop, the then-editor, Jodie had sat in the anteroom to this office, a jealously loyal gatekeeper, guarding access to Victoria as preciously as if it were an audience with royalty, but also, paradoxically, terrified to enter it herself: for every ten times Victoria summoned the assistant she had renamed 'Coco' into her office, nine of those were to haul her comprehensively over hot coals for some tiny infraction of the Victoria Glossop Code of Perfection.

There had been an interim *Style* editor between Victoria and Jodie, of course. Jodie had moved to Manhattan as Victoria's assistant and had swiftly climbed the job ladder there, from junior editor to launching and editing *Mini Style*, the teen *Style* spin-off, proving herself fully as an editor. She'd changed her name back to Jodie, establishing her own identity, before she'd returned to London, ready at last to sit in an office once occupied by Victoria.

Filling her killer heels, Jodie thought, smiling to herself at the thought of the stilettos that, along with the miniskirts and her blonde chignon, were an intrinsic part of Victoria's signature look. *As if I could!*

After a near-suicidal attempt in New York to starve herself down to a size zero, Jodie had resigned herself to not being as thin or polished as her mentor. She had had the office completely redecorated when she arrived back in London, deliberately altering the white and greiges and gleaming transparent glass that had been Victoria's tonal palette; the previous editor hadn't dared to change them. Now the décor was fun, playful, as befitted a young editor. Jodie had been barely twenty-eight when Victoria, now CEO of Dupleix Publishing and editor-in-chief of the entire *Style* empire, had sent her protégée to London to not only edit *Style UK*, but also simultaneously launch a British *Mini Style*.

'Sink or swim, and you'd better paddle bloody hard!' Victoria had said gleefully, relishing her choice of words. 'You're taking over at a year younger than I was when I first edited *Style*, *plus* you have a launch to oversee as well! But then of course, you've had the inestimable benefit of being apprenticed to me, so we'll call it a wash. I'm giving you the keys to the kingdom. Don't fuck this up.'

Well, I haven't yet, Jodie thought, looking round her office – *her* office! – with its cream walls, orange and red Marimekko rugs, twin burgundy Fritz Hansen 'Egg' chairs on tripod steel bases, the flashes of gold in the shelving system and framed prints on the walls; a lavish arrangement of salmon-pink roses on the desk, sent by her fiancé, were yet another burst of colour that toned with the rest of the room. *I've put my own stamp on* Style UK, Mini Style*'s flourishing, and, of course, that means Victoria promptly decided to throw another plate at me to juggle. I know all too well how she loves to test people.*

Pulling up her Vitra state-of-the-art chair, she took a seat at her gleaming white laminated Knoll desk, uncapped her bottle of Vitamin Water, took a deep breath, and then activated the video-conferencing screen which every *Style* editor had been required to install in her office as soon as Victoria had taken the helm at Dupleix. Victoria liked to be visually in touch with all her minions, perfectly aware that she was even more intimidating when she was both heard and seen. This was a scheduled call, which at least meant that Jodie had had time to prepare for it, but you still never lost the nerves that fluttered in your stomach at the anticipation of seeing your boss on screen, as perfectly groomed as ever.

Like actors say about performing live – you never stop getting stage fright, Jodie thought as the screen loaded up and Victoria's custom-made white leather chair came into view. It was unoccupied, of course: people waited for Victoria, never the other way around. Ten seconds elapsed, long enough to make the point; and then a swish of fabric was audible, a blur of crisp white shirt came into view, and Victoria Glossop, editrix-in-chief and mistress of her universe, sat down, crossed her long slim tanned legs in their sharkskin beige miniskirt, and tilted her haughty features sideways momentarily to take the glass of water her assistant was handing her – *Fiji water, chilled to seven degrees, with a fresh slice of lime dropped into it with silver tongs*, Jodie remembered all too vividly. She had learnt Victoria's needs so efficiently that even after several years she knew her boss's tastes as well as she knew her own.

'Too cold, Monika,' Victoria said to the assistant as icily as the offending water. 'Take it away and get me one at least three degrees warmer.'

Thank God, the assistant didn't say a word; you never answered back, that was Lesson Number One. You just nodded, whipped the glass away, considered for a split-second buttoning the glass inside your shirt and hoping that would warm it up a bit before realizing that your emaciated, starving frame emitted no heat whatsoever. Then you shoved it into the microwave and hoped that just a couple of seconds in there would fix the problem, which was non-existent anyway since you had taken the Fiji bottle out of the temperature-controlled drinks fridge which was set to the precise seven degrees that Victoria specified ...

'Hi, Victoria,' Jodie said, grinning with great affection at the fact that her boss would never, ever change – *and that I don't have to get the bitch her water ever again.*

'Ugh, I miss Coco!' Victoria complained, looking down her long aristocratic nose at the young woman who, as Coco, had been the best assistant Victoria had ever employed. 'Why couldn't I just clone you? My God, what are you *wearing?*'

'Preen blouse,' Jodie said, her grin deepening. 'Frame jeans. *And—*' She leant back in her chair and raised her legs just enough so that Victoria could see her feet – 'Isabel Marant Bekket hidden-wedge trainers.'

'Sneakers at the office!' Victoria almost gagged. 'My God! Thank Christ at least they have a heel, but—'

The assistant returned with Victoria's water, her slim café-au-lait hand trembling visibly in the corner of the screen as she set it down. Luckily, Victoria was so distracted by the deliberately oversized pale green suede and light brown leather trainers into which Jodie's tight jeans were tucked that she completely ignored her hapless PA.

'They're absolutely positively the latest thing,' Jodie said with considerable glee.

'*Sneakers!*' Victoria repeated, relishing the horror with which she pronounced the word; she and Jodie had fallen over the years into a kind of older sister/younger sister relationship, where Victoria ritually mocked Jodie's clothing choices while secretly acknowledging that Jodie had her finger firmly on the pulse of current trends. 'They look like you stuck your feet into a pair of gigantic marshmallows and then spray-painted them the colour of vomit. Model-vomit, the kind that comes up when they haven't eaten anything for two days and then they do vodka shots, the silly little bitches.'

'Don't hold back, Victoria.' Jodie sipped some Vitamin Water. 'Tell me what you really think of my shoes.'

'I don't *understand* her as a designer,' Victoria complained. 'I don't get her *ethos*, her *philosophy*. Who wants to make women's feet look *bigger?*'

'Hey, she's very European,' Jodie said cheerfully. 'And big shoes slim the legs.'

True as that was, Jodie had deliberately started a policy of annoying Victoria by dressing in Marant and other designers like Acne whose shabby-chic aesthetic drove Victoria crazy; it was a clever ploy to distract Victoria from complaints or gripes she had with Jodie or her staff.

'Sometimes I suspect you of wearing ghastly things in meetings as some kind of calculated provocation,' Victoria said with frightening perception, her grey eyes flashing as sharply as the matching grey diamond of her engagement ring as she picked up her glass of water.

'So, *Style* Bride of the Year,' Jodie said quickly, wanting to move Victoria on from this dangerous line of speculation. 'You want to know where I am with that. I sent through a briefing email earlier – what did you think?'

'It's fun, this, isn't it?' Victoria sat up straighter, eyes flashing even brighter. 'Not the wedding part – God, I really could care less about weddings, they're like a taste *vacuum*, a *black hole* of tacky. All these bias-cut satin dresses the women wear over here make me want to *stone* them with *rocks*. They think they're chic, but all they are is *bland*.'

Jodie shivered: pretty much the worst insult Victoria could possibly throw at anything was 'bland'.

'Well, good news,' she said, deftly taking this and spinning it to her advantage, 'my two front-runners are *definitely* not bland! They're both young, stunning, *super*-photogenic. The grooms are gorgeous too – very different styles. I think the key question here is, what do we want the first issue to say about us? Who's going to encapsulate our brand? I mean, last summer was totally the royal year – first Queen Lori of Herzoslovakia.'

'Fabulous jewellery, *lovely* long neck,' Victoria muttered in parentheses.

'Princess Chloe, of course ...'

'Safe, safe, *dumpy* – a size *twelve*, for God's sake.' Victoria yawned like a cat, perfect white opalescent teeth sparkling between coral-glossed lips.

'So this summer, maybe a Countess is too much like the royals? Is she too beauty-queen?' Jodie clicked on the screen of her laptop, swivelling it round to show Victoria a picture of Brianna Jade in a recent shoot for *Hello!*

'Teeth and hair and tan,' Victoria said dismissively.

'Great bones,' Jodie countered. 'Look at those cheekbones. And she's curvy, but actually she's barely a ten.'

'Photographs bigger,' Victoria muttered, but she was still staring at the picture of Brianna Jade, and she hadn't said no.

'That's muscle tone. She's very fit – she'd jump for you,' Jodie said, a code between them: Victoria loved action modelling shots, had made her name on *US Style* with dynamic, vigorous photographs of models running, leaping, twirling in whirls of fabric and colour.

'Hmm,' Victoria mused. 'Well, she's polished. I like polished. And the other one? Bit insipid, isn't she?'

Victoria knew perfectly well who Jodie's other shortlisted candidate was, had been fully briefed, but she liked making people pitch to her so she could tear at their proposal with claws as sharp as the dragon painted on the six-fold screen that dominated her Manhattan office.

Jodie clicked on Milly's photo.

'She's a full-on It girl here in the UK,' she reported. 'Incarnates boho chic. If she puts on a Top Shop dress, it sells out straight away. Definitely the fashion-forward option.'

'I smell *hippy*,' Victoria spat with gusto, which was barely better than 'bland'.

'English style, fresh, young, Alice Temperley vibe, groom even more up-and-coming than she is – actually he's up and come: his band's won tons of Grammies, swept the Brits this year,' Jodie practically chanted. 'We could style her fantastically – she's *tiny*, she can wear anything.'

This perked Victoria up, as Jodie had known it would; slim, toned Brianna Jade might not be model-skinny, but Milly most definitely was. And that was a huge point in her favour; it was much more work to find clothes for a model who wouldn't fit into the child-size samples designers sent out.

'So who's your front runner?' Victoria asked, sitting back, finishing her Fiji water, setting down the glass, throwing back her head and yelling: 'Monika! More water!' in a shriek so high-pitched that Jodie automatically flinched; after all these years, she still expected the glass to break.

Jodie's secret was that she didn't actually *have* a favourite in this race. There wasn't an obvious winner. In Jodie's opinion, either girl would make a cracking first *Style* Bride of the Year. Her real fear was that Victoria, who was notoriously capricious, would discard both of Jodie's choices and make her go searching for a third candidate, which would take up way too much time when Jodie already had *Style* and *Mini Style* on her plate. And after Jodie had sweated cobs dancing like a madwoman to Victoria's tune, Victoria would probably, perversely, finish by circling back to choose either Milly or Brianna Jade.

And time was of the essence. Yes, the ceremony would be next spring or early summer, in order for the photographs and copy to be ready for the three-month lead time a glossy magazine usually demanded. But the idea was to start tracking the wedding now for the *Style* website, to tease readers with photo shoots of engagement parties, updates on the latest location scouting and dress designs, building into a diary of the most elegant wedding of the year.

Monika practically ran into the office, teetering on the crystal heels of her suede Miu Miu over-the-knee boots but managing to keep the fresh glass of water steady; she whipped the empty glass away, substituting it with its replacement, and dashed out of the room again. Victoria looked at the water and pushed it away as impatiently as if she hadn't just shrieked at her assistant to bring it for her.

'I'm on the fence,' Jodie said frankly. 'I don't usually say this, but they're both very evenly balanced.'

'Pick one!' Victoria snapped, sitting up even straighter, if possible, than she usually did; even after having two children, her posture was as perfectly erect, her stomach as flat and sucked as tightly as ever into her 'Pilates corset' of highly trained muscle. 'Come on, do it! I haven't got all day.'

Jodie opened her mouth, swiftly scanning the pros and cons of each candidate, about to make a decision – but just as she did so Victoria interrupted: 'No! Wait!'

She leaned forward, picking up the silver Tiffany pen that Monika had to polish every week, tapping it on the spotless glass desk that Monika had to wipe smooth three times a day.

'We'll pick *both* of them!' Victoria announced.

'You mean multiple covers?' Jodie asked; this was often done, though never before with *Style*. 'I thought you hated—'

'No, I *loathe* editors who do that! Like the pull-out *Vanity Fair* covers, I hate those too! You *know* I *despise* people who can't make their minds up. Here's what we'll do: we tell these two that they're both in the running,' Victoria said, eyes gleaming, raising one hand to her perfectly smooth blonde hair. 'We'll set them against each other – make them jump through our hoops. That way, we'll have *much* more editorial control. If we commit to one of them, that gives *them* the power, and we want the wedding to be perfect – but if they know they're not a definite yes, they'll bend over backwards to please us. Yes, I *love* this! It's perfect!'

Why don't we just make them cage fight? Jodie thought. *Victoria would love that!*

But watching her boss positively lit up at this idea, she was certainly not going to say a word to counter it. Given the mood she was in, Victoria might actually take duelling brides as a serious suggestion.

Chapter Nine

'Stare up at him – yes, great – like you're offering him the basket thingywhatsit. *Awwight there, 'ave a noice plum, Tarquin me love!'*

The photographer lapsed into a mix of faux-Cockney and faux-Mummerset which was instantly understood by Milly, to whom he was talking, as an instruction to pose like a cross between Nell Gwynne with her oranges and an innocent damsel about to burst into a sung rendition of 'Cherry Ripe'. She was bearing a trug, handmade in Sussex with a chestnut frame and handles and a base of woven willow treated with linseed oil; the *Telegraph* magazine, which had organized the shoot, was very keen on country-chic detail.

The trug, an oval basket specially designed for carrying freshly picked fruit, was exactly the kind of thing that *Telegraph* readers ordered from advertisements in the sponsored gardening section. Milly raised it higher, smiling coyly as she displayed its contents of early autumn apples, damsons, plums and blackberries for the benefit of her fiancé. Tarquin, who was posed next to her under a Worcester Pearmain apple tree, looked down worshipfully into her adorably pretty face.

'Perfect!' The photographer lapsed back into his normal RP tones. 'Okay, I think we've got this set up, everyone take twenty while we get the picnic lighting sorted.'

Hair and make-up and stylist bustled over to Milly and Tarquin, taking the trug away from her, ready to whisk them back to the big RV parked on the farm track that led into the Somerset orchard in which they were shooting. Milly turned to look over one pale shoulder, her golden curls, tonged into perfect ringlets, falling down her back.

'Eva!' she called. 'Come along, I need you.'

Eva, who had been watching and snapping photographs on her phone for the various social media accounts run by Milly and Me, nodded and duly followed, catching a couple of great behind-the-scenes photos as Milly, leaning on Tarquin, slipped off her scalloped pink leather Chloé pumps, handed them to the stylist, and stepped instead into the pair of Hunter wellies waiting ready for her. The cream macramé lace Dolce and Gabbana dress Milly was wearing had a tight pencil skirt, and the sight of Milly waddling awkwardly in the slim-fitting dress and oversized Hunters made even the naturally sober Eva stifle a smile.

'Don't photograph this,' Milly called imperiously, still leaning on Tarquin's arm as they picked their way across the orchard, squelching on some early windfalls. 'I look really stupid.'

'Darling, you could *never* look stupid,' Tarquin said admiringly.

'Aw,' the make-up girl sighed. 'You're so lucky, Milly. My boyfriend would never say that to me.'

'Wait till we're married and he'll change his tune,' Milly said, but her self-satisfied tone belied her words; she was very well aware that Tarquin's devotion to her was rock solid.

Eva ducked her head and sipped her coffee, which was

going cold now but still provided an energy boost. The shoot had started very early, just before dawn, to capture the morning mists, the atmosphere of delicate, febrile romance that Milly and Tarquin incarnated: the whole crew had stayed at a hotel nearby in order to be up for the 5 a.m. call. Three set-ups later, it was eleven-thirty now, the rose-gold sunrise now faded, and the autumn sun was beaming gloriously in the pale blue sky. Milly and Tarquin had already run through a cornfield hand in hand, picked fruit together, balancing precariously on ladders propped against a giant pear tree, and now they would lie in each other's arms on a picnic blanket. The photo spread and interview were provisionally titled *First Love, Last Love*.

'*Very* teen magazine,' Milly had said derisively when the *Telegraph* rang her PR to propose it. 'But as long as we can use Milly and Me jewellery, and the clothes are proper designer, no highstreet crap or someone's rubbishy cheap line for H&M ...'

The Matthew Williamson gown that the stylist was now reverently removing from its zipped sheath, draping it over her arm as if she were selling a bolt of hand-embroidered silk, was definitely 'proper designer'. The stylist proffered it to Eva first, as per Milly's strict instructions that Eva's approval was crucial for the overall aesthetic of the photo shoot. Eva, a designer herself, instinctively knew exactly how Milly should be styled and presented to achieve the perfect branding of Milly's image that would represent both her look and the jewellery line.

'It's *gorge*,' Milly breathed. Eva had shown her photos of all the dresses selected for the shoot, a long list of floaty stunners interspersed with a couple of more fitted lace ones for variety, and this was definitely the *pièce de résistance*. It was made from ivory silk-chiffon, sleeveless, with an asymmetric neckline, ruffles clustered heavily on one shoulder and tumbling down the fitted bodice diagonally in a soft fall to the narrow waist.

The skirt, a glorious riot of cascading tiers embellished with pearlescent sequins and delicate beads, was as full as the bodice was slim, but not ballgown-wide, which would have dwarfed Milly's small frame.

'It's actually from his bridal collection,' the stylist said enthusiastically. 'But it's like *so* much more sophisticated than like one of those awful strapless wedding dresses, you know? I mean, if this were mine I would like *totally* consider hand-dyeing it afterwards and wearing it to openings. It's really an *investment* piece, which for a wedding dress is utterly like *profound* and really speaks to the whole *symbolism* of weddings.'

Eva had learnt over the few years she'd been in business to tune out the way in which most stylists talked, and she let this one's stream of consciousness roll over her. She had come to realize that everyone in fashion now considered themselves artists in their own right. Fashion exhibitions were very prestigious now: the Victoria and Albert Museum in London, plus the Fashion Institute of Technology and the Metropolitan Museum in New York, regularly assembled hugely successful displays, from the costumes of David Bowie to the couture wardrobe of Daphne Guinness to the *Punk: Chaos to Couture* show at the Met. All had drawn huge amounts of press coverage and sell-out crowds.

So stylists feel they've got to talk like they're perpetually interviewing for the job of junior curator at a museum costume department, Eva reflected. *And, ironically, there's a journalist here from the magazine who's going to write the copy, but she's not listening to a word of this drivel any more than I am.*

'Oh Tark, you're not going to think it's bad luck, are you, me wearing a wedding dress?' Milly cooed for the benefit of the journalist, who was scribbling away making notes of the dialogue between the young lovers.

'We make our own luck,' Tarquin replied poetically, pushing back his own tangle of fair curls. His blue eyes were soft as he gazed at his fiancée. 'No, wait – *you* are my luck, Milly.'

'Stop!' the hairstylist muttered sarcastically to Eva. 'It's just *too* beautiful. My withered old heart will burst.'

'He really means it,' Eva said to him under her breath. 'Honestly, it's not for the journo.'

'He needs a good rogering if you ask me,' the hairstylist hissed back. 'Tie him up and suck him dry. See what lyrics he comes up with after *that*. Maybe they'll even make sense for once.'

Eva went bright red, dropping her head forward so that her thick hair fell over her face, hiding her embarrassment at the vivid image this conjured up. She found herself imagining kneeling down in front of Tarquin, hearing him groan as she licked him reverently, feeling his hands twine lovingly in her hair, maybe pushing it away from her face so that he could watch her as she performed what she would consider an act of love and worship on him. It was by no means the first time she had had erotic fantasies about Tarquin, but now was a particularly mortifying time for it to happen. She knew it was a terrible idea for her to let her imagination run rampant about the fiancé of her best friend – *not just terrible, the worst idea in the world!* – and she was desperately hoping that her love for Tarquin would burn itself out naturally with time.

But when someone talks about sucking him dry, how can I help it? It makes me think about all sorts of things I know I shouldn't!

Even through her heavy curtain of hair, she was miserably aware of the hairstylist's sly, knowing gaze on her. People bustled around the small interior, seating Milly at the lighted make-up table built into the specially converted RV, the make-up artist swivelling Milly on the chair, squatting on a step stool to have her hand steady enough to pat Milly's Cupid's-bow lips with a tiny brush dabbed with Chanel gloss. The hairstylist, who had been curled up in a padded recess by the window, unfolded himself and stood up, leaning over Eva, taking the coffee cup from her. He reached into his travel case, took out a silver hipflask and, uncapping it, slugged a little of its contents into the cup, returning it to her.

'There you go, dear,' he said. 'Get that down you, it'll help.'

One step brought him to Milly's side, picking up her hair and twisting it to the top of her head, his lips pursed in consideration. Eva downed the coffee in one go recklessly. It had been rum in the flask, and it did the trick, jolting her effectively back into the present moment. She gasped, swallowed, sat up straighter, threw back her hair and rejoined the buzz of activity in the RV.

They were on a tight schedule, and the team of freelancers were at the top of their game: Milly was already stepping into the Matthew Williamson dress, which was puddled on a special throw cloth on the floor of the vehicle to avoid any marking. The stylist and her assistant were easing the silk-chiffon up Milly's narrow torso, her bony shoulders, cooing softly as they did so; they pulled up the concealed zip at the low waist, slipped the covered buttons at the side of her waist into their little silk loops. The back was open, two overlapping panels at the shoulders exposing her shoulder blades.

Close up, the blades were too sharp, the tiny vertebrae too visibly knobbled. But from a distance, the harsh edges blurred by sunlight, Milly looked like a perfect princess bride. The hairstylist piled her curls to one side, high and over one ear, echoing the asymmetric neckline, taking the look from simply beautiful to high-fashion elegance: Milly's lips had been painted in a daring fuchsia, glossed with gold, which drew the focus to them, again turning the ridiculously pretty dress into something more cutting-edge.

Eva picked up her suede jewellery roll and unfastened it, spreading it out on her lap, no doubt at all in her mind about the earrings the dress needed: she and the stylist had already agreed upon them. They were a new interpretation of the classic chandelier style, slender silver chains dangling from a horizontal hoop, each chain bearing a sculpted leaf made of bluebell and powder-blue quartzite, the leaves tinkling like tiny fountains against each other. The bluebell leaves were the colour of Milly's eyes, the powder-blue quartzite a perfect match for Tarquin's otherworldly irises, and the earrings were shown off perfectly by the high-piled hairstyle which left Milly's white neck bare.

As Milly stepped down from the RV, the make-up artist handing her down the steps, the stylist and her assistant positioned on either side, ready to take swathes of the dress in their hands so that it would never touch the dirt of the farm track, Tarquin's indrawn breath of awe was clearly audible. The hairstylist glanced at Eva sympathetically and reached for his hip flask again now that this part of his job was perfectly done. Tarquin, wearing a linen shirt, a white and blue silk Paul Smith waistcoat in a chintz print, and a tailored pair of white Armani trousers, came forward to take the hand that his fiancée was extending to him. Milly's dazzling smile said that she was perfectly aware that she had never looked quite so beautiful.

'I can't breathe,' Tarquin said, staring at her in wonder. 'You literally take my breath away.'

'So how are you managing to talk?' the hairstylist muttered to himself, filling the cap of his flask and tossing its contents back with a practised dash of his wrist.

'Milly, you were telling me before about the muffins you like to bake for Tarquin?' the journalist asked as they walked slowly and carefully over to the cashmere rug that had been laid (with two more sturdy rugs underneath it for protection) beneath the spreading branches of an apple tree.

Milly was being closely trailed by the stylist and assistant as if they were bridesmaids carrying her train, but Tarquin was ahead, his invisible mascara being touched up by the make-up artist, so Milly could reply confidently: 'Yes, I love to bake. I've definitely got a housewife side to me whenever I get the chance. I actually got a great idea from *Devon and Cesare's Baking Battle* recently – she made a batch of muffin mix and then baked it in a cake tin for a bit longer than the muffin recipe with lots of icing sugar on top. It was delicious – Tarquin loved it! I served it with whipped cream and raspberries.'

Word for word, this was what Eva had done at the weekend, baked a muffin cake for a brunch that Milly and Tarquin had hosted. Trailing behind them, Eva heard Milly's words with incredulity. She had heard Milly parrot her own deeply felt speeches on the difficulties of ethical mining, or sustainable resources and healthy water supplies in the Third World, many times before in *Guardian* or *Independent* interviews, and had had no problem with that; Eva was quite aware that Milly's principles were not yet as fundamentally rooted as her own, and if Milly needed to use Eva's words in the process of working her way into the heart of the issues, that was fine.

But going so far as to say that she baked something I made? Which, actually, was from a Delia Smith recipe – but Delia isn't trendy enough for Milly. She put Devon and Cesare in there instead because they're so much sexier.

Eva must have cleared her throat, made a noise of some sort, because Milly glanced back, the earrings dangling from her lobes chiming like fairy bells at the movement, and said quickly to the journalist: 'Oh, and you will get in a bit of bumf about the earrings, won't you? They're made from recycled silver, melted down. We're trying to get a Fairtrade classification for the process – there really isn't any way to source silver ethically yet, though you can get some from a mine in Bolivia without using cyanide or mercury. Right now though, we prefer to use recycled from a closed-loop process.'

Eva realized she was nodding seriously. Milly was hitting all the important points, explaining the difficulties of morally sourcing metal and the solutions the Responsible Jewellery Council were evolving. Milly then moved onto quartzite, fingering one earring for emphasis, and by the time they reached the picnic area and Milly was lifting one thin white leg from the Hunter welly and waiting while a pale leather Reed Krakoff strappy sandal was fitted to her foot, Eva had filed the muffin cake anecdote away to be discussed with Milly later.

Though she did sidle up to the journalist as Milly was lowered by stages to the cashmere rug and say: 'Actually, it was a Delia Smith recipe Milly used for that muffin cake. Not a Devon one.'

'Oh, really?' the journalist said blankly, looking down at her notepad but not bothering to make a note of the correction.

Feeling relieved at having set the record straight, Eva turned to see Milly, who was by now stretched out on the rug, her head in Tarquin's lap, his long legs extended in front of him. Milly was being positioned to lie in a curve wrapping around him, her arms outspread, her legs together, the myriad tiers of the skirt opened like petals by the stylist and the assistant for maximum effect. From an aerial view, it looked as if she had been dropped there from the sky, an angel fallen slowly and gracefully to earth, caught by the arms of her lover: the photographer was climbing a stepladder held firmly still by two of his sidekicks as a third reached up to hand him a Polaroid for the first shots. With Milly and Tarquin's golden hair, blue eyes, pale skin, and reddened lips – Tarquin's had been very lightly stained by the make-up artist to echo Milly's – they were absolutely ethereal, a perfectly matched pair.

'Feed her some blackberries,' the photographer instructed. 'Let's get a really nice-looking one.'

'Not over the dress! Not over the dress!' the stylist yelped like a terrified Chihuahua. 'The stain will *never* come out!'

The assistant picked out a rich, purplish-black berry, fat with juice, and placed a newspaper underneath it as she leaned cautiously over the fringed edge of the blanket, handing it to Tarquin; docilely, he took it, holding it over Milly's parted, glossy lips. The deep rich colour against the fuchsia lipstick and the pastels of the rest of the scene immediately drew the focus.

'Oh *wow*,' the make-up artist breathed in appreciation. She spoke for the entire group, who were all sighing at the exquisite tableau in front of them.

'It's like an eighteenth-century painting,' Eva observed. 'A Watteau or a Boucher.'

'Yes! Perfect, yes!'

The *Telegraph* journalist scribbled away furiously: Eva's comment would end up in the opening paragraph of the adulatory interview that would run alongside the photo shoot. Milly tilted her head to cast Eva an approving smile: she didn't have the faintest idea who Watteau or Boucher were, that they were famous for beautiful pastoral paintings, decorative allegories of nymphs and their swains picnicking in the countryside, but she knew that, yet again, Eva had said the perfect thing, had steered Milly's image into exactly the place it needed to be.

Tarquin, however, knew precisely what Eva meant, and his sky-blue eyes rose for a moment to Eva's face, his reddened lips parting in a sweet smile.

'Gosh, what a compliment,' he said. 'Thanks, Eva! I was

thinking this is sort of like a *fête galante*, isn't it? Or is it more like a *fête champêtre?*'

Eva considered this, the thought process on her expressive face.

'*Galante*, I'd say,' she concluded. 'You're both dressed so beautifully. *Champêtre* is more country-style.'

'Um – could you just clarify the distinction,' the journalist whispered to Eva: this was pretty high-level intellectual stuff, even for a *Telegraph* writer.

'They both have outdoor settings. A *fête galante* really translates as "gallant party" and describes eighteenth-century aristocrats at leisure in the beautiful grounds of their chateaux. *Champêtre* is pastoral, more in the countryside rather than in a landscaped garden,' Eva explained.

Milly, never happy when she wasn't the centre of attention, wriggled a little and said seductively to her fiancé in a baby voice: 'Sweetie, feed me – feed me the yummy blackbewwy.'

'Oops! Sorry, darling.'

Tarquin returned his gaze to his beloved and the photographer promptly started snapping away. Milly altered her position every few seconds, little moves of the head, twists of her body, offering a whole range of different poses and angles just as professional models did to maximize the effects of the set-up. When she raised one slender white hand and hovered it just over Tarquin's cheek, as if caressing him adoringly – you never actually touched in photographs, to avoid denting the skin or smudging any make-up – the photographer was beside himself.

'Oh come on, cover shot, cover *shot!*' he exclaimed. 'This is bloody *perfect . . .*'

And it was. A month later, that very image was the cover of the Saturday magazine, Milly reclining beautifully in Tarquin's lap, the skirts of her dress spreading over the pale blue rug, her eyes half-closed in ecstasy as she seemed to stroke her lover's face. Ironically, the picture editor Photoshopped in a Gala apple instead of the blackberry, deciding that the proportions worked better, and that it echoed the ripe apples on the branches of the tree just visible in the shot; Tarquin, who had written a song about blackberries and beloveds in the meantime, was rather cast down for a while, but Milly consoled him in the way outlined by the hairstylist, which definitely helped to cheer him up.

Some extra set-ups had been sketched out, and there were more dresses to be worn, but after the runaway success of the picnic rug photographs, the consensus was that they were done; the early start was beginning to tell on all of them, the sun was now fully overhead and casting too much light for the hazy effect they had wanted to capture, and everyone packed up. Milly kept her full hair and make-up, however. She had a meeting with Maitland Parks, the celebrated film director, later on that day, and wanted to walk in looking as stunning as possible. She also made a spirited attempt to 'borrow' the Dolce and Gabbana lace dress, but the stylist was far too experienced with the manoeuvrings of young actresses to allow any such thing; she knew perfectly well that Milly would claim a few days later that she'd accidentally burnt a hole in the dress, or spilt Coke on it, and it wasn't worth returning to the magazine.

'If she wants to *borrow* something,' she said in an aside to her assistant, 'she can call Dolce's PRs directly, get them to bike something over, and then *they* can have the fun of chasing her to get it back in one piece.'

'What if she actually hangs onto it?' the assistant asked.

The stylist's eyebrows shot practically to the roof of the RV. '*Please!* Dolce'll just blacklist her if she doesn't give something back,' she said pityingly. 'And she doesn't want that to happen.

None of the major labels are giving her stuff for free yet. Angelina Jolie she *ain't* – she's just another little starlet on the make.'

The stylist was quite right: Milly was very much on the make. The afternoon appointment with Maitland Parks in the penthouse suite of the Charlotte Street Hotel was of great importance to her, and she was determined to create the best impression possible. Maitland Parks was barely in his thirties, but had already directed two very well-received arthouse films in the mumblecore genre – hyper-naturalistic, partly improvised movies about young adults, recently graduated from college, loafing around waiting aimlessly for their lives to start.

Now, with backing from a major studio, he had the budget to step up to the big leagues, and was planning a film set in Portland, Oregon, dimly understood to be about a group of postgraduate students researching aspects of human behaviour while falling in and out of love with each other. The cast was to be a roster of young, beautiful actors in their early twenties, and there was already a big buzz around *And When We Fall*, the working title of the screenplay. Milly had been on the phone to her agent almost every day for the last few weeks, insisting that she get a chance to meet Maitland when he came to London for casting.

He wasn't doing anything as overt as conduct auditions; mumblecore was too laid-back and cool for that. No, he had taken the suite in the small, quirky Charlotte Street Hotel, a favourite of television and film people who wanted a boutique experience in Fitzrovia, and was engaging in a series of what he called 'meeting-slash-encounters' with a selected flurry of the latest British crop of actors. None of them knew for which part they were being considered, whether they'd be expected to put on an American accent, what, if anything, would be required of them; they all went in highly nervous, trying to give Maitland Parks exactly what he wanted without any idea of what that might be. It made them even more insecure than actors usually were, which was precisely what he intended.

'Hey,' he drawled as Milly came through the front door of the suite. 'Milly, yeah?'

He was sprawled on the big, brightly striped sofa placed underneath the gabled windows of the top-floor suite. The light streamed in behind him, giving him an excellent view of Milly but turning him into a skinny dark outline. It was a classic power play: he could see her, she could barely see him. But it was by no means the first time Milly had encountered something like this. Directors loved to throw pretty young actresses off-balance emotionally.

Milly had already decided not to seem too bright and confident – the characters in Maitland Parks's films were the opposite of those qualities – so she murmured softly: 'Hi! Yes, I'm Milly,' flashed a shy sweet smile, and looked for where she should sit down.

'Yo,' Maitland said, lifting a hand limply and flapping it at the matching sofa facing his, its pink, lime, burgundy and navy stripes clashing with the white pillows on which big coloured flowers were splashed. Presumably that was a deliberate design decision, but Milly thought that if you were hungover it would give you a shocking headache.

'This place is like, really freaky,' Maitland drawled, as Milly moved one of the pillows, sitting down and wedging it behind her back.

'The colours don't really match,' she agreed.

'Don't they?' Maitland sounded surprised; she could still not make out his face. 'I actually meant the ceilings. They're so low. And the walls all slant in. Which is weird. I feel like they're trying to squash me in the night.'

'It's the top floor,' Milly said carefully. 'You know, with a gable roof.'

They must *have those in America*, she thought doubtfully. *Don't they?*

'Yeah,' Maitland said. 'My assistant told me the penthouse had a gable roof when she booked me in. I guess I just didn't know what it ... meant.'

He fell silent. Milly followed suit. This was how she always handled this kind of not-audition-just-a-meeting-slash-encounter; she tried to pick up the mood of the director or producer or casting director and to echo it. The whole point was to demonstrate that she could take direction. So she folded her hands demurely in her lap and sat quietly, her gaze directed to the surface of the shiny laminated black and white lace-print coffee table, on which was a large vase of flowers and a tray on which was set a bottle of water, an ice bucket and three glasses.

'You want something?' Maitland asked after a while, shifting on the sofa. Milly had researched him before today, of course, knew what he looked like, the archetypal skinny white indie boy with long bushy sideburns contrasting oddly with his cadaverous cheeks. He had a scrawny chest and long stick-like legs, his eyes bulging thyroidally behind the thick lenses of his 1970s-repro black-framed designer glasses.

'Maybe some water. Shall I pour you a glass?' Milly responded politely, lifting her eyes to his face, projecting the image of him she had seen photographed in magazines onto the dark outline in front of her.

'Nah, I meant pills,' Maitland corrected her laconically. 'We got Adderall, Ritalin, Valium, Xanax, Oxy, Darvon, Ambien.' He ticked the list off on his fingers. 'Maybe other stuff too. You want some?'

'Oh, um, sure!' Milly said gamely, feeling that she was

expected to say yes; she'd have had a drink or five with a director, she told herself, so this really wasn't any different. 'What do you think I should have?'

'Man, I dunno,' Maitland said, sounding genuinely taken aback by this. He sat up, leaning forward to look at her more closely. 'You like uppers or downers?'

I like champagne, actually, you American weirdo, Milly wanted to say. But she bit her tongue and said as sweetly as before: 'A little bit of an upper, I suppose? I don't want to pass out while we're talking.'

Not that you're doing much talking, she added silently.

'Oh, you could totally pass out if you wanna,' Maitland Parks said casually. 'No worries. Yo, Kumiko!'

Maitland raised his voice a couple of decibels higher, from a drawl into an almost normal pitch: this seemed to be what passed for a shout with him. Milly started. She hadn't realized they weren't alone. Because from the bedroom of the suite emerged a slender, flower-like Japanese-featured woman, her body a pale stalk, her face the centre of the blossom, her hair an explosion of dark petals cascading down to her waist.

Clearly this was Kumiko. As far as Milly could see, the wonderfully thick black mane was the only hair on Kumiko's entire body. And Milly was very well placed to judge, because Kumiko was not only entirely naked, but so unself-conscious about her nudity that she came over to the coffee table and bent over it to place the bowl that she was carrying onto its surface. Her back was to Milly and her nether regions, because of her slimness, were almost entirely exposed as she bent forward.

'So yeah, this is what we got,' Maitland said, gesturing at the bowl, which was full of yellow plastic vials and paper packets of prescription drugs. 'Help yourself. Kumi?'

'I already did my Xanax,' Kumiko said, smiling at him and

Milly in turn, and curling up on the sofa next to him. 'I'm *so* mellow.'

'Cool!'

Milly had been going to opt for an Adderall – she'd heard it was the prescription version of cocaine, fantastic for weight loss, and she was interested to try it – but the appearance of a naked Kumiko had changed her mind, made her decide that she might need to take the edge off. She reached out, pulled the bowl closer to her and selected a vial containing Valium, shaking two pills out into the palm of her hand and washing them down with some water from the jug.

'You're *super* lucky,' Kumiko said languidly. 'Mait hasn't offered anyone else some of our stash yet, and he's seen three people already today.'

'Yay me!' Milly said. 'That makes me feel pretty.'

She flashed a smile to show she was joking – you could never tell how much people from LA would pick up on British humour.

'Funny,' Maitland observed, which was, Milly had noticed over the years, the way that Hollywood types reacted to someone being comic; they didn't laugh out loud, or even smile, simply acknowledged gravely that the attempt to amuse had been successful.

'You *are* pretty,' Kumiko said, crossing her legs and giving Milly a very explicit flash in the process. 'I love your make-up too. It's so dramatic.'

'I did a shoot for the *Telegraph* magazine this morning,' Milly explained.

'Yeah, your agent told me,' Maitland said.

He fell silent after that, staring at Milly, and Kumiko did too. If Milly hadn't been an actress, she would have been extremely uncomfortable, but Milly was both an actress and a raving egotist who put herself squarely at the centre of the universe, and there was nothing that made her happier than a film director who wanted to sit and look at her. His naked girl-friend, or whatever she was, didn't bother Milly in the slightest. She was fine with nudity, knew that Maitland Parks's previous films had involved it, and was quite prepared to strip on screen. Or off it, if necessary.

'Kumiko's not an actress,' Maitland said after a long while. 'She's the embodiment of the spirit of *And When We Fall*.'

The only possible response to this was 'Oh, that's really cool,' and that was exactly what Milly said, widening her baby-blue eyes and tilting her head in the classic tell-me-more pose.

'I'm the total freedom that the characters are trying to reach,' Kumiko added languidly. 'You have to let yourself go – fall – to get there.'

Milly nodded enthusiastically.

'That's really interesting,' she said. She had noticed that there was no screenplay anywhere that she could see, not on the coffee table, the desk, nor on the deliberately not-match-ing chairs scattered around the large living room. Turning her head a little, she tried to glimpse the bedroom through the open door, acres of cream carpet leading to a wide gilt-framed bed with a mirrored headboard and carved posts at each corner topped by large gold finials, a padded backless bench at its foot. She couldn't spot a script there either.

'You're wondering about a screenplay, right?' Maitland said with impressive penetration. 'I don't work like that, showing actors a script. I'm sort of the new Woody Allen.'

'Only I'm not his adopted daughter,' Kumiko observed, which made Milly stifle a laugh and say gravely: 'Funny,' instead.

'Woody sends his actors their scenes the night before they're going to be shot,' Maitland informed Milly. 'And he tells them they can change any of the lines if they want, to get it into their voice. Then he collects the sides the next day. I mean, not him personally, of course. A runner does it.'

'Do they know the story?' Milly asked, thinking that she could risk a question.

'Barely ever,' Maitland said, relaxing back in the sofa. 'Just their own interactions and their characters. It's deeply cool.'

Yeah, for him and for you, Milly thought. *Not so much for the actors, I bet. It sounds like a total nightmare.*

'Wow, how fascinating. I'd so enjoy working that way. What an adventure,' she said with the utmost sincerity: no one could have told what she was really thinking.

'I work in a very improvisational style,' Maitland said, to which Milly nodded earnestly. This was good, this was very good; he was talking about his process, making her sound as if she might be involved in it eventually . . .

'Can you take your clothes off now?' Kumiko asked.

Milly had been half-expecting this, but she'd thought the request would come from Maitland rather than Kumiko. She looked swiftly at Kumiko and then back at Maitland, judging the mood of the meeting; she was able to make out some of Maitland's features now, her eyes having acclimatized some- what to the shadow in which he was sitting, and as far as she could tell he was looking at her with a very interested expres- sion. Kumiko was clearly speaking for him.

'Sure!' Milly said brightly, bent down and started to unfas- ten her suede high-heeled Miu Miu stacked sandals. Kumiko and Maitland watched her intently as she undressed, and, as before, she relished the attention. She knew she was thin enough even for Hollywood's demanding tastes: she watched what she ate but didn't need to starve herself, was lucky enough to be naturally skinny, which meant that she didn't have the telltale signs of an eating disorder which betrayed many actresses. No bulimic points to her jaw from repeated throwing up, no dangerous hollows on her body where the flesh had been starved away.

And she was young enough to wear her thinness very well. In about fifteen years' time, Milly would need to choose between her face and her bottom, as the French said; she would need to eat more or look scrawny. But now, she was a UK size four, perfectly fitting into designers' sample sizes, as Victoria Glossop had already noticed, and Milly knew, as she stood up in the space between the coffee table and the sofa and reached back to unzip her pretty floral Whistles dress, arching her back so that the points of her little-girl breasts were even more visible, that neither Maitland nor Kumiko, would have any criticisms at all of what they were about to see.

She let the dress puddle to the floor and stood, hands by her sides, presenting herself. This, too, was part of the job, taking your clothes off in hotel rooms in front of directors, and really, hotel rooms were the nicest place for it, as far as Milly was concerned. You had to do it in hired rehearsal rooms, in casting directors' offices, in much starker and less upholstered and welcoming environments than this. She'd much rather drop her dress on a cream carpet, stand in her expensive, lacy Myla matching underwear set and let herself be admired by people in a penthouse suite at the Charlotte Street Hotel.

The underwear was truly spectacular, a pale pink set called Delena, mesh and geometrically patterned French lace with rose-gold fittings. The bra plunged deeply; it would have given Milly cleavage if she had anything to cleave. The skimpy thong had a low-rise cut, showing off almost all of her flat stomach, and it had an extra, decorative strap of lace which looked designed for someone to hook their finger through and pull the wearer towards them. Sensing from the quality of the attention radiating from the other sofa that she could spin this out a little, Milly turned slowly, rotating a hundred and eighty degrees, giving them a good look at the way the gusset of the thong slid between her small white buttocks, the material scrunching together as it covered her folds, at the criss-crossing straps at the damp crease at the top of her bottom, also offering an opportunity for someone to slide their finger beneath them, feeling the skin below, pulling the thong slowly down ...

She unfastened the bra first, dropping it to the sofa, before she hooked her thumbs into the lace straps of the thong and started to ease it over the almost infinitesimal curve of her hips. She didn't wiggle or make any movement to sexualize what she was doing, to make it into a striptease. If you set aside Kumiko's nudity, there was nothing overtly sexual about her and Maitland's bearing, and Milly sensed that any bump and grind would be a complete turn-off for him, at least.

The thong fell to the ground, and she bent down to pick it up, giving them the same view that Kumiko had given her earlier that afternoon. When Milly stood up, she was about to place the thong on top of the bra – it had cost fifty-five pounds, she definitely wasn't going to leave it on the floor – but Maitland finally spoke.

'I'll take that,' he said, reaching out his hand, and Milly leant across the coffee table to place it in his palm. He unfolded the delicate scrap of lace, took the straps and hooked it across his ears, placing the gusset over his nostrils. His black-framed glasses gleamed above them like a doctor wearing a surgical mask; since he was now inhaling entirely through his nose, the sound of his breathing was louder in the room, exaggerated, as if it were an oxygen mask hooked up to a tank.

Kumiko seemed unfazed by it – *but then it doesn't seem like anything fazes her*, Milly thought. *I wonder if I can ask them to put on some music? Maitland sounds asthmatic now – it's really off-putting . . .*

Kumiko rose, smiling at Milly, extending her hand to her. Milly had known this was coming, in some variation, for a while now; she smiled back as she took Kumiko's hand and followed her through into the bedroom, Maitland tailing them closely, huffing and puffing like a heavy breather in the middle of a phone stalking session. *Which isn't that far from the truth*, Milly thought, very relieved to see that he was taking a seat in one of the upholstered armchairs, pulled over awkwardly close to the bed, clearly in anticipation of any bedroom encounters, and that Kumiko was guiding Milly onto the mattress. They were performing for Maitland; he wasn't going to be involved in the action. Or so she hoped.

This was, without a doubt, how Milly would have preferred the audition to take place – with Kumiko alone. Because by now it definitely was an audition. Peter Mandelson had once declared himself to be 'intensely relaxed about people getting filthy rich', and Milly Gamble was intensely relaxed about whatever she had to do to get a coveted part that would put her on the Hollywood radar. Given a choice, however, Milly would definitely have chosen Kumiko over Maitland, even before he'd masked himself up with her thong – *I hope I get that back, it's part of the set* – and started breathing like an emphysema sufferer.

Light poured in through the huge windows set into the slanting gable roof; hopefully the clearly illuminated spectacle of Kumiko pushing Milly gently back to the pillows and spreading her legs was distracting enough to help Maitland ignore the sensation that the angled walls were closing in on him. Milly arched back picturesquely, stretching her arms behind her, raising her waist so she looked even slimmer, wishing there was something to grab onto behind her, as stretching out into an extension was extremely flattering. But the headboard was a smooth sheet of mirror set into the gilded wood, and she had to content herself with arching more, head back, so she could glimpse her reflection as Kumiko knelt down, bent her lips to Milly's lower ones, spread them apart with very practised fingers, and started to put on a show for Maitland.

No question, that was what it was. Whatever Kumiko was to Maitland, it was clearly he who would make the decisions, and Kumiko who was doing the work. This wasn't Milly's first time with a woman; like many actors, she was very open to any kind of new experience, especially when a role might be dangling tantalizingly at the end of it.

But Kumiko was by far the best lover she'd ever had, so skilled that Milly would not have been at all surprised to find out that Kumiko had done this – or *was* doing this – on a pro-fessional basis. Her short fingernails opened Milly up for her darting tongue so comprehensively and explicitly that Milly's hips jerked right up off the coverlet in shock as Kumiko touched her tongue to Milly's centre. The burst of sensation was so intense it felt as if Kumiko had burnt her, held a fizzing sparkler right between her legs, her clever fingers holding Milly's delicate folds apart so that they couldn't give any pro-tection, offer a layer between Milly's clitoris and Kumiko's hot wet pointed tongue.

Milly bucked in panic, thinking that she would be over-whelmed, that the intensity might even flip to pain, but Kumiko was surprisingly strong. Her elbows secured Milly's knees, her steel fingers held Milly's pelvis in place, and two seconds later Milly was coming fast and furious, hugely relieved that Kumiko knew exactly what she was doing. Milly managed to get her head back far enough to watch her orgasm face in the mirrored headboard, and the sight of her fuchsia lips parted in a gorgeously seductive O as she wailed and screamed her pleasure was an extra turn-on for her; at home, she always masturbated in front of a full-length mirror, and preferred sex with Tarquin somewhere she could view the entire spectacle.

This was the fastest she had ever come. She wondered, even as she came again, screaming as prettily as she could, if she could teach Kumiko's technique to Tarquin, without, of course, saying where she'd learnt it. Tarquin thought she was faithful, would be very distressed to ever find out that she wasn't, which was fine, as she had no intention of ever letting him discover this or any other extra-curricular activity that she engaged in to further her career. Tarquin – *bless his sweet heart*, she thought a little contemptuously – was possibly the only rocker in the world who intended to be faithful to his wife. Which was ironic, as Milly certainly wouldn't be bothered if he did let the occasional groupie suck his cock in his trailer ...

'Shit!' she yelled, as Kumiko slid two, then three fingers into her, her tongue flicking Milly to another orgasm. 'Shit, that's so ...'

It was really hard to know what words she should use. Who was she playing? What was her role here? Slutty or innocent? Eager lesbionic – as she and her friends at boarding school had nicknamed their after-dark licking games – or first-time convert, seduced by Kumiko into a world of new experiences? She had managed to catch a glimpse of Maitland's face in the mirrored headboard, but with the goggle glasses and the thong over his nose and mouth, any attempt to read his expression was impossible.

And in the next second, she genuinely found herself the amazed innocent, as Kumiko's whole slender hand, the fingers pressed tightly together, began to open her up, slide up inside her. It felt ... amazing. This was *definitely* outside anything a woman had done to her before; they'd never dreamt of this at boarding school. Milly was jerked out of any attempts at acting, was dragged fully into the intensity of the moment as she felt Kumiko's hand inside her, the thumb of the other hand rubbing circles around her clitoris, waves upon waves of pleasure building as each orgasm sucked Kumiko's wrist further inside Milly, who was dripping wet and practically begging for more; it was extraordinary, the sensation incredibly strong, nothing she would have dreamt of wanting, but now she would die if it stopped ...

Kumiko's fingers flickered inside Milly's hot wet walls, exactly on her G-spot, and Milly felt herself letting go completely in a gush of orgasm that was so strong she thought afterwards that she might even have lost consciousness for a few moments. Her body spasmed again and again, clenching around Kumiko's hand and wrist completely involuntarily, the powerful muscles clamping hard, lubricated by the rich surge of come flowing from Milly. Nothing like this had ever happened to her before; she felt completely opened up, turned inside out, worked like a machine that had functioned to maximum capacity because of the highly trained operator.

She wasn't aware of Kumiko's easing her hand out gradually, only dimly felt the mattress move as Kumiko crabbed over to the beside table, pulled some tissues out of the silver box there, and wiped her hand down. Milly lay there, eyes closed, legs open, her own breathing so loud that, mercifully, it drowned out Maitland's, feeling her chest rise and fall so heavily that it almost hurt with each inhalation. Her entire body was a mass of sensation, as if the vaginal orgasm were a flash fire that had spread through her whole chest, up to her face, bathing her in flames that would take long, delicious minutes to subside ...

Maitland was unsnapping the thong from his face, rolling it up and putting it in the pocket of his baggy hipster jeans.

'So?' he said to Kumiko, who was lying back on the bed now, stroking concentric circles on Milly's stomach with a fingertip.

'Completely open,' Kumiko said seriously, rendering a verdict. 'Totally present. She fell, definitely.'

'Yeah, that's how it looked,' Maitland agreed. 'She has a really nice range of expression when that potentiality's unlocked.'

Milly, hearing herself talked about, raised her head, looking from Maitland to Kumiko, registering that her thong had disappeared and deciding, reluctantly, not to mention it. She smiled at Kumiko, would normally have pulled her head down to kiss her, but the scene felt so choreographed that Milly hesitated.

Instead she said: 'Can I return the favour? I'm not as good as you, but I bet practically no one is . . .'

It was exactly the right thing to say. Kumiko smiled complacently as she answered: 'Not how I roll. But thanks.'

Milly had absolutely no idea what Kumiko meant by that, but she was relieved that she wouldn't be expected to perform herself. She was naturally lazy in bed, much preferring to receive – while viewing herself – than to give. She stretched, tossing back her fair curls and smiled at Kumiko, waiting for a further cue: she knew it would come. They had decided everything up till now. They'd tell her what they wanted next.

'You can get dressed,' Kumiko said, exchanging a glance with Maitland, who nodded slightly. 'Take your time, we're cool. No rush.'

Kumiko slipped off the bed and went through into the large oak and granite bathroom, where she could be heard relieving herself; she didn't bother to shut the door. Milly sat up, arched her back, looked at Maitland still sitting on the chair, very close to the bed, so close that she'd have to brush against him if she went that way, and decided not to risk it. Instead she rolled off the far side, giving him a nice action view of her little white buttocks as she went, passed the striking view of Fitzrovia's skyline through the huge window, and walked at a normal pace into the living room to reassemble her outfit, minus thong.

By the time she was dressed, neither of them had come back into the living room; unsure of how to handle this, she peeped back into the bedroom to see that Maitland hadn't moved from the chair. Kumiko was now curled up in his lap, and he was stroking the thick mass of her hair with regular, rhythmic caresses.

'Maitland's keeping your thong,' Kumiko said to Milly. 'That's good. You should be pleased.'

'Great,' Milly said. But Maitland wasn't even looking up: it was clearly her cue to leave, and she duly slipped out of the suite, pressing the button for the lift, her brain racing. She'd call her agent, say that things had gone really well, ask her to do a follow-up call tomorrow, get the lie of the land ...

And what's Maitland Parks going to say? 'She was so good I kept her thong'?

Normally, Milly would have sniggered at this, but she was taking the possibility of a part in *And When You Fall* too seriously for anything but a brief smile to cross her face. It could make her, be the breakout vehicle that Bertolucci's *The Dreamers* had been for Eva Green, in which that actress had had explicit sex scenes with two actors. Nowadays it was no-holds-barred, though it was usually a European director that wanted the actresses to spread their legs, like Michael Winterbottom with *Nine Songs*; still, after Paul Schrader had cast James Deen, an actual porn star, in *The Canyons*, and

Sasha Grey, another porn star, had taken the lead in Steven Soderbergh's *The Girlfriend Experience*, the boundaries were really blurring.

Look, as long as it's called an art film and puts me on the map, I could care less about having sex on screen, Milly thought happily. The lift whisked her down to the lobby, and she stepped outside into a gloriously warm early September evening. Heads turned in her wake, not just because they recognized her, not just because of the still striking hair and make-up, but because her eyes were shining, her expression transcendent, her limbs loose and suffused with the aftermath of an out-of-body orgasm.

God, I love my job! she thought blissfully, holding out her hand for a passing cab. *And I should just have time to nip to the Myla boutique on Oxford Street before it closes to pick up another thong so Tarquin won't wonder why I'm coming home without my knickers on ... hmm, I wonder if I can write them off as a business expense?*

Chapter Ten

'So it's war,' the Fracking Queen said, her beautifully shaped lips setting in a firm line, her eyes glittering darkly in a way that made Lady Margaret McArdle, sitting opposite her at the table in the garden of Tamra's Chelsea mansion, raise her eyebrows in anticipation of the conversation to come.

'Well, *war*'s maybe a little—' began Veronica, the publicist who had just broken the news to Tamra that Milly Gamble was her daughter's rival for the title of *Style* Bride of the Year.

'Oh no, it's war,' Tamra corrected her firmly. 'Only one of them can be on the cover. There's a winner and a loser. It's definitely war.'

'A battle to the death,' Lady Margaret drawled, swirling the ice cubes in her gin and tonic. 'I do love watching you get all excited, Tamra. We just don't do that over here in Britain. We pretend we don't remotely care about anything and then we secretly fester with resentment and stab our rivals in the back.'

'Oh, I'll stab her in the front if I need to!' Tamra said, stirring her champagne with such vicious twirls of the silver whisk Edmund had found for her that the fine silver tines clattered dangerously against the glass.

'Tamra, I – errr ...' Veronica said nervously.

'Ah, she's just letting off steam,' Lady Margaret said, sitting back in the white-painted wrought-iron chair and crossing one leg over the other, ankle to knee. 'Let her have her head.'

Lady Margaret, as always, was wearing trousers. Even for the recent royal wedding of Prince Hugo to Chloe Rose, which Lady Margaret had naturally attended, having been the best friend of Hugo's mother, Princess Belinda, she had worn an ankle-length printed silk divided skirt, wide-cut enough to swish around her ankles, with a tailored jacket and matching navy top hat. It was the perfect compromise: Lady Margaret had been able to tell herself that the culotte-like design meant that she was really in trousers, and if anyone at Westminster Abbey had noticed that the folds of her 'skirt' divided a little suspiciously, Lady Margaret had paid enough lip service to the conventions that nobody was brave enough to tell her that she needed to go home and change.

Had she not been a Duke's daughter, and godmother to the future King, matters would have been different, but what would be absolutely taboo for commoners was just about permissible for an aristocrat who had always been known to be on the eccentric side. And though King Stephen and Queen Alexandra were sticklers for protocol, certain events leading up to the wedding involving them, Lady Margaret and some other key players meant that neither the King nor the Queen would have dreamt of going *mano a mano* with Lady Margaret over what she chose to wear to Prince Hugo's wedding.

Many jokes had been made in the *gratin* of London society – the highest echelons – about Tamra and Lady Margaret's close friendship, as Lady Margaret's sexual preferences were entirely Sapphic. Lady Margaret had warned Tamra that if they closed down the bar of every party they attended, roaring with laughter at each other's jokes, assumptions would inevitably be made, but Tamra had shrugged that off with magnificent disdain.

'Hell, *I'm* not the one husband-hunting!' she had said. 'And no one's going to turn down Brianna Jade just 'cause they think her mom's rug-munching the daughter of a Duke, are they?'

'If *only*!' Lady Margaret had grumbled wistfully, clinking glasses with her friend.

Tamra was perfectly well aware that Lady Margaret was a little in love with her, and had made it perfectly clear to her friend that nothing would ever transpire on that score; but Lady Margaret was much too sophisticated for that clarification to make any difference to the friendship, and had been more than happy to recommend the very discreet and very expensive escort agency from which Tamra had hired Bruno and Oliver. Their sexual needs very well taken care of by Diane's young ladies and gentlemen, Tamra and Lady Margaret were free to run riot at the best parties London had to offer. Lady Margaret also ensured that Tamra was invited to all the house parties that her set threw in the countryside – not the stuffy formal shooting or hunting ones, but the chic, gay-friendly, urban-weekenders, where guests drank expertly mixed martinis, played poker for high stakes, watched the latest films in home-cinema rooms, and neither Labradors nor small children ever made appearances.

Now, Tamra's eyes, dark and full of resolve, met her friend's over the rim of her champagne glass as she took a long sip of the de-bubbled Cristal and set the glass firmly down on the glass table which grew out of the glass terrace beneath it, as did the chairs. It was an extraordinary piece of design, conceived by Michael Devine, the most fashionable garden designer in London. Money had been no object, and Devine had really let himself run wild. Beneath the terrace was a tropical aquarium, providing guests with fascinating glimpses of the shoal of Convict Cichlid fish, which were genetically engineered in Taipei to glow blue in the dark. Devine had pointed out to the owner that the reflections from the sheet of glass by night meant that one could catch the occasional glimpse of other guests' underwear from time to time, depending on the lighting, angle and whether they were wearing any. *Always a useful diversion if there happens to be a lull in conversation,* he had drawled.

Dramatic as the terrace was, with the fish beneath and the spreading, Dali-esque table and chairs extruding from it, the focal point of the garden was a fifteen-metre-tall Niwaki 'cloud-pruned' tree, handcrafted entirely out of glass by Venetian glass-blowers, which towered at its centre The branches and leaves were suffused with thousands of tiny lights which provided warm ambient lighting over and around the dining terrace. The only living plants in the garden were a perfectly manicured circular lawn beyond the dining terrace – hand-trimmed with scissors on a daily basis to maintain its pristine condition – and behind that, a forest of Niwaki *Cryptomeria japonica*, several hundred years old, sited at the far end of the garden to create a private space for quiet contemplation.

Behind a sheath of black glass trellis, a veil of water flowed continuously down the opaque glass walls of the garden. Fibre optics running through the trellis gently glowed blue in the evening, to tone in perfectly with the flickering Cichlids. This was why Tamra preferred the bathroom overlooking the garden; sometimes she sat in its window seat in the evenings, sipping a drink and contemplatively watching the fish circle dreamily in their huge aquarium, their soft blue echoing the lights of the fountain, muted by the black glass. Right now, however, was not the time for contemplation, but for action, and she didn't glance down at the fish, but kept her gaze as steady as if her eyes were twin black barrels of a double-barrelled shotgun aimed at the face of her publicist.

'We need to know our enemy,' Tamra said decisively, 'strategize, and take her down. What do you know about Milly Gamble?'

Despite Tamra's intimidating stare, Veronica was prepared for this: she rattled off Milly's CV to date, covering all her career highlights as well as the ethical jewellery line. Tamra greeted every role that Milly had played with theatrical snorts of derision; Lady Margaret watched the spectacle with great enjoyment.

'Honestly, who *is* she anyway?' Tamra snorted at the end of Veronica's short summary, tossing back her glorious rose-gold hair, picking up her Dior 'Demoiselle' hand-painted sunglasses from the table and sliding them onto the bridge of her perfect nose. 'How could the wedding of some little actress who's never had a lead part *possibly* trump my daughter marrying an *Earl*, for Christ's sake? Who *is* Milly Gamble in this world?'

It was Lady Margaret's turn to snort. This was a line from *The Real Housewives of Beverly Hills*, a reality show to which they were both addicted. Tamra had introduced Lady Margaret to all of the various *Real Housewives* franchises, with Beverly Hills and New York their favourites. They had a regular night where Lady Margaret would come round to watch the latest episode, downloaded from the internet. Tamra set up a whole row of lines and shots, and they would snort and sink them according to a complicated scoring system they had evolved.

'Rather, my dear, you should be asking who her fiancé is,' Lady Margaret said, leaning forward to ring the silver bell on the table. '*That*'s the really interesting point here.'

'What do you mean?'

Behind the big lenses of the sunglasses, Tamra's eyes

narrowed in concentration. The huge French doors of the living room stood open, and Marta, Tamra's housekeeper, came through them, dressed in her pale grey uniform with white apron. Without a word needing to be said, she refilled her mistress's and Veronica's champagne from the cooler on the table, then picked up Lady Margaret's empty glass, taking it to the living room bar to be refilled.

Lady Margaret's attractive weatherbeaten face – as a true English aristocrat, she scorned the use of any sunblocks or moisturizing regime more elaborate than Pond's cold cream morning and night – creased into a smile of pure self-satisfaction as she said: 'Tarquin Ormond, Milly's fiancé, is—'

'He's the lead singer of Ormond and Co,' Veronica interrupted eagerly, keen to show that she was earning the very large monthly retainer Tamra paid her. 'It's sort of folky pop music. They win lots of awards—'

'He's *Edmund's second cousin.*' Lady Margaret overrode her effortlessly; a Duke's daughter who rode to hounds had no difficulty drowning out a mere hired publicist. 'Which opens up a *lot* of possibilities, doesn't it?'

Tamra's head snapped round like a snake about to strike.

'But Tarquin doesn't have a title, does he?' she said acutely. 'Edmund's way higher value!'

'In our world, of course,' Lady Margaret said. 'But Tarquin's really quite famous now, I think. And *Style*'s a very different animal from *Tatler*, which is really the *gratin*'s in-house journal. No question that Edmund and Brianna Jade would absolutely take priority if it came to *that* cover. Hmn. Oh, thank you.'

She took the fresh tumbler of Hendrick's gin and tonic from Marta, ice cubes tinkling against the paper-thin slice of Meyer lemon, tiny triangles cut into its rind to release more of the fragrant oil, and sipped her drink with great satisfaction.

'But if Edmund has higher social status, which clearly he does, then we really need to hammer that home,' Tamra said.

'That's a very good point,' Veronica agreed, sipping her own champagne and reaching out for one of the miniature freshly made canapés which Marta had also placed on the table, tiny blinis topped with sour cream and tea-smoked salmon, quails' eggs dusted with pink salt, little bresaola packets filled with a dollop of low-fat crème fraiche, tied with chive bows, for Tamra.

'This really makes me want to throw a bridal sh—' Tamra went on, but Lady Margaret raised her voice imperiously to silence Tamra, slicing a hand through the air to cut her off.

'You can*not* have a bridal shower in Britain!' she said. 'I've *told* you, Tamra! It's unspeakably vulgar to host a party and require people to bring presents! Really, the mere *thought* makes me shudder with horror.'

'Some brides in the States have multiple ones,' Tamra said, unable to avoid grinning at Lady Margaret's reaction. 'With different themes and different lists.'

'*Lists*,' Lady Margaret muttered in disgust. 'As if that should *ever* be pluralized in this context.'

'We do these huge bridal showers in the States,' Tamra told Veronica. 'Way more elaborate than you guys have over here. You play games like making the bride a dress out of toilet paper, or you get someone in to teach you flower arranging or cupcake making – those were pretty popular in West Palm Beach. They have lingerie showers too, all sorts of themes, and then you have to bring a gift according to the theme. One girl Brianna Jade knew, Megan, had four different showers – a garden one, a lingerie one, a wine-tasting weekend in Napa and an English tea one.'

Veronica was staring at her, totally appalled: even Lady Margaret was goggling at Tamra now, not having heard this information before.

'And you're supposed to bring presents to *all* of them?' Veronica asked.

'Oh, at the minimum!' Tamra was thoroughly enjoying herself now. 'Megan's mom and dad were super-rich, so they paid for everything, even the Napa weekend on a private plane. But, you know, in return for that they expected gifts that cost three hundred dollars a pop, minimum. Each time.'

'And that's instead of the bridal present?' Veronica asked.

'Hah!' Tamra tossed back some Cristal. 'You're kidding me, right? Being a bridesmaid or a groomsman is a huge money pit. You pay for your dress, your hotel, plus your flight to the wedding if you don't live close by. And if you have a destination wedding in Hawaii or the Caribbean, say, that's a ton of money right there for everyone. Plus, often you're expected to fly for the bachelor or bachelorette night – which isn't ever a night, it's a whole weekend, and then you have to plan and host those completely, treat the bride and groom for everything. For the whole weekend. Oh, and "dress" means the whole outfit – shoes, jewellery, accessories. The bride usually pays for hair and make-up, though often they book the top-notch stylist for themselves and get some low-level trainee for the bridesmaids. That happens a *lot*. Not just to save money, but to make sure they look better. And then there's the rehearsal dinner – the groom's family's supposed to pay for that, but I've heard of people asking for contributions from guests for that as well.'

She looked from Veronica to Lady Margaret, relishing their stunned expressions; she did enjoy shocking the Brits with information about American cultural habits that they found outrageous.

'What?' she said, drinking more champagne. 'You never saw *Bridezillas*?'

'Clearly I have to,' Lady Margaret said, awed. 'This sounds

like an absolute hoot! Tell me, if people have a – what did you call it, a "destination wedding" – are they expected to give a gift as well as hauling themselves to Hawaii or the Caribbean?'

'Sometimes,' Tamra said with a wide, beautiful smile, 'they're asked to contribute to the bride and groom's travel expenses as a gift.'

'Oh my *God*!' Veronica shook her head in disbelief. 'So, basically, they're getting married just to squeeze as much money from their family and friends as they possibly can?'

'Exactly. It's all about the money – well, and about being the centre of attention,' Tamra said. 'Megan was beyond obnoxious. She kept holding up hoops to make her poor bridesmaids jump higher and higher. Luckily BJ was just second-tier – because,' she added with an even more beautiful smile, 'Megan didn't want my gorgeous girl anywhere near her in the wedding photos. Her daddy bought Megan a new nose and a personal trainer, but you can't buy what Nature gave my girl.'

Her eyes narrowed once more.

'And *that*'s a point,' she said. 'You put this Milly thing next to my Brianna Jade and she'll blow her right out of the water. BJ photographs like a dream. That tiny little thing'll look dull as ditchwater next to her.'

Lady Margaret and Veronica nodded in agreement with that statement. Tamra adored her daughter, but she wasn't doting in any way; she was perfectly clear-sighted about Brianna Jade's strengths and weaknesses.

'That's why I was thinking a bridal shower,' Tamra said glumly. 'We could've invited her and a lot of other girls who aren't very pretty and posed them so BJ just pops out of every photo. That'd show *Style* who they ought to pick.'

'Darling,' Lady Margaret drawled, 'I have two words for you: engagement party! Throw it at Stanclere, invite Tark and

Milly and a ton of others. Lots of press, lots of photos. Edmund won't like it much, but he'll quite understand that it's part of the deal, as you say.'

Veronica nodded. 'Things are really changing with the aristocratic world. It's the younger generation. Posh people who wouldn't have dreamt of having their weddings in *Hello!* are seeing their children on the covers now. Lady Natasha Rufus Isaacs – she's the daughter of the Marquess of Reading,' she added for Tamra's benefit, 'had a ten-page spread in it when she got married last year. Royalty attended, it was very high-level. She even namechecked Boodles the jewellers in the piece – they lent her a diamond parure – and she got publicity for her ethical clothing line. Of course, she snagged a nice donation from the mag for the line, blah blah, but you know, the social rule about only wanting to appear in the papers when you're born, marry and die is totally gone now.'

'Hatched, matched, dispatched,' Lady Margaret mumbled through a mouthful of blini. 'How we used to put it.'

'I love it! An engagement party!' Tamra's eyes sparkled so brightly that they might have been made from the backlit black glass of the fountain wall. She clapped her hands, her cuff bracelets jangling. 'Over a weekend, right? We'll plan it like a military operation for the photo opportunities and make sure that Milly and Tarquin can come.'

'He might have tour dates we'll have to build around?' Veronica mentioned.

'I was at school with his mama,' Lady Margaret said cheerfully. 'Head prefect when she was a weedy little fourth-former. Put the fear of God in her on multiple occasions. I'll ring her up and tell her to get me some dates from her son, pronto. Don't worry, they'll be there.'

'Milly's an actress, she may have commitments,' Veronica warned.

Tamra rounded on Veronica, but Lady Margaret was there first.

'Please – all actors are absolute tarts for publicity,' she said, taking another blini. 'You tell her she'll be photographed for a glossy magazine. She'll be there, even if she has to fly in for the night.'

'*Exactly!*' Tamra said. 'Veronica, you're bringing me problems and Margaret's bringing me solutions!'

Veronica quailed under her employer's stare.

'I'm not paying for negatives,' Tamra continued to the hapless publicist. 'What I want is non-negotiable! I'm damn well going to see my daughter on the cover of *Style Bride* with a tiara on her head and the words *Style Bride of the Year* plastered across her skirt in gold lettering! You get that, right? Believe me, there'll be a nice bonus for you *when* you pull it off – not *if*, but *when*! Because you're going to do it. Ever heard the expression "going Indiana on your ass"? I swear to God, Veronica, you'd better give this everything you've got or I'll open a can of whoop-ass on you like you've never even *imagined*!'

Veronica's mouth was open, her eyes wide and frightened. Tamra's voice was loud enough that as it rose, a squirrel which had managed, somehow, to scale the glass wall and was crossing the circular lawn, jumped, looked around in panic and shot up one of the cloud-pruned japonica trees as fast as its tiny feet could scamper.

'I simply *love* it when she shouts,' Lady Margaret observed, polishing off the blinis. 'You'd better do what she says, you know. I have no idea what a can of whoop-ass is, but I doubt very much that you want to find out.'

Chapter Eleven

The private members' drinking club in a basement beneath a side street tucked away behind Old Street roundabout was as plush, dimly lit and richly upholstered as Tamra's Chelsea garden was shiny and bright. It was impossible to imagine daylight here, let alone visualize Tamra, Veronica and Lady Margaret sitting in the sunshine, glittering in thousands of tiny sparkles from the leaves of the huge glass tree spreading above them. The club was called the Den, though its décor was den-like only if you imagined its inhabitants as the most pampered and sleek of Burmese cats, strolling on silky paws over the thick carpets, jumping up with easy springs to the burgundy velvet love seats and curling up there, staring with cold green eyes at the waiters bringing them Martinis to lap, their fur glowing softly in the flickering light of the candles set into recessed iron wall sconces.

Ludo, a founding member, was certainly as sleek as any Burmese with his slicked-back blond hair, pale blue Savile Row-tailored shirt, Ralph Lauren linen suit and Dunhill cobalt silk knit tie: as always, his entire appearance was as polished as his Burberry silver cufflinks. His companion was much more soberly dressed, in head-to-toe black with a flash of white at the neck, but his handsome face was creased with amusement as he watched Ludo wave his hands around theatrically, describing the meeting he had had with Milly and Eva earlier that day.

'Lily of the valley!' Ludo was saying impatiently with a very telling roll of his blue eyes. '*So* expensive, *so* delicate, barely *grows* in Italy, where they want to have the wedding – we'll have to fly it over and *honestly*, it costs so much that I can't make much of a mark-up on it, which is the worst of all!'

'Ludo, *really*,' his companion remonstrated.

'This whole thing is so *cutesy*,' Ludo said in disgust. 'Peonies, stock, veronica, *sweet peas* in vintage teapots — you won't believe this, but Milly actually had the idea of arranging flowers in old jars from sweet shops.'

'Oh, I rather like that,' murmured his friend, picking up his stemmed glass and sipping at the pale orange liquid inside. The cocktail was called a Wildcat, a blend of cachaça, pisco, mezcal, blood orange, kumquat and lime juices, with a touch of gooseberry jam and Tokay wine: it had been garnished with a physalis, whose tiny bright orange fruit with its crisp, winglike dried leaves was the perfect visual counterpoint to the drink. The Den prided itself on its avant-garde cocktails and considered each new creation a feast for the eyes as well as the taste buds. Given the eye-watering proportions of mixed alcohol in the glass, however, sipping was definitely the way to go.

'Oh *please*,' Ludo said. 'Can you really see me sourcing vintage sweet jars?'

'Dear, I can see you commissioning them from a factory with faux-vintage labels if there was enough profit in it for you,' his companion said with great amusement.

Ludo burst out laughing and clinked his own drink to the Wildcat: his was a Tango No. 2, a mixture of rum anejo, amber

vermouth, absinthe, Benedictine, mandarin and grapefruit
juices with a champagne float, served in a deep champagne
coupe, and decorated for some reason rather cheesily with a
little yellow and white gingham napkin round the stem, which
Ludo had promptly discarded with a muttered: '*No*. Just *no*.'

'I absolutely banned the sweet jars,' Ludo said now, taking
an equally judicious sip of his drink. 'We're walking a delicate line here pitching for the *Style Bride* cover, you see. I
somehow have to pull off a blend of the rather saccharine,
wild-flowers-in-antiqued-birdcages, running-through-the-
meadows-hand-in-hand wedding that Milly wants, and something chic enough for *Style* to snap it up. It's by no means
impossible, and if anyone can manage it, it's me.'

'Always blowing your own trumpet,' his friend commented.

'Oh, I *wish*!' Ludo said naughtily. 'But I've had a little word
with Jodie Raeburn, the editor – we bumped into each other
at a do at the Langham the other night. She says that she's
very keen on fresh and modern, and this whole faux-simple,
Keira Knightley eloping-with-the-daisy-chain-and-Chanel-
and-Renault thing *does* feel very fresh. So there's that. Ooh!
News! *And* she told me who Milly's competition is – that
American heiress who's marrying Edmund St Aubyn! You
know, the stunning blonde, all teeth, hair and tits? God, I *love*
her. I'd *so* much rather be doing her wedding than Milly's. Her
mother will just *throw* money at it, *millions* probably, and it'll
be old-fashioned classic glamour, which is *so* much more me
than wretched scrawny little Milly and her pissing lily of the
valley and fresh herb displays in vintage china. God, I *loathe*
that word "vintage". It's just a way of selling barely recycled
old tat to idiots! It's almost as bad as "shabby chic", which, you
know, *ditto*.'

Ludo's friend settled back in the embrace of his red velvet
armchair, plucking up the trouser fabric over one knee with

long pale fingers so that he could cross that leg smoothly over the other, a flash of black silk sock showing between the trouser hem and the suede Gucci loafers.

Ludo took a sip of his Tango No. 2.

'I'd *really* prefer to be planning the glamorous wedding, not the eco-chic one,' he sighed. 'And the Yank girl is absolutely perfect for *Style*. I'm sure Victoria Glossop will be signing off on the final decision, and she just loves that all-American, *Sports Illustrated* swimsuit issue look. I mean, who doesn't?'

'But Milly's marrying a pop star,' his friend said comfortingly, resting his hands on the wide padded arms of the chair. 'They're famous, and they're young. Everyone loves youth. It's the terrible curse of our age, this tendency to set youth up as a cult and worship at its shrine, when it knows nothing of the real challenges that humans face with the ravages of age and time.'

'Oh, please, Father, take off the dog collar,' Ludo said pettishly. 'I'm not in the mood for a sermon.'

Father Liam Wiles, Ludo's close friend and officiator of all the Catholic blessings at the weddings planned by Ludo, smiled gently, not a whit offended.

'I was attempting, perhaps rather clumsily, to console you, Ludo,' he observed. '*Style*, like almost all glossy magazines, literally idolizes youth and inexperience, and I was pointing out that you may well be advantaged by having the younger clients.'

Ludo sniffed, muttering, 'Tarquin strikes me as a little inexperienced, but *Milly's* been stretched out on the casting couch more often than young Piers over there.'

He nodded at the passing waiter, a slim and handsome would-be actor, who flashed him a swift smile and wink as he skimmed by their table with a tray borne high. Ludo warmed to his theme.

'I hear Milly's wedged her ankles by her ears for producers more times than a novice in a nunnery waiting for Mother Superior to come in with a big altar candle and—'

'Ludo, *please*!' Father Liam ran a finger impatiently under his stiff white dog collar.

'Oh come *on*,' Ludo pouted. 'You know what all those nuns are like. Why did they go into it in the first place? They're worse than female prison guards, and *they're* all utter and complete lesbians.'

'Well, I can assure you that I did not enter the priesthood for that reason,' Father Liam said coldly.

'No,' Ludo said irrepressibly, 'but the new intake of fresh young Jesuit meat every year at your lovely Mayfair training centre is a *delicious* little extra bonus for some of your colleagues, isn't it?'

'*Ludo*, I'm shocked by the sacrilege of your conversation sometimes!' Father Liam uncrossed his legs, planting the soles of his loafers on the carpet, his handsome brows lowering.

'I'm sorry.' Ludo reached out to touch Father Liam's knee. 'Father, forgive me, I'm such an awful sinner ... my wicked tongue just runs away with me sometimes.'

'It seems that it could be *much* better occupied than satirizing men and women of the Church, who've taken very serious vows of poverty, chastity and obedience,' Father Liam said with immense severity, reaching for the cocktail that would cost £18, plus service, when the time came to sign the bill, and taking another sip. 'I can't imagine you having the dedication or sense of vocation to make such sacrifices for a spiritual calling, Ludo.'

Ludo hung his head theatrically as he listened to this lecture.

'Make penance, Ludo,' Father Liam said, setting his Wildcat on the table, sitting back in his armchair. 'Atone for your irreverence by putting that wicked tongue of yours to good use, and silence your unholy mouth in an act of reverence ...'

Ludo was already tucking the end of his tie into a gap

between shirt buttons, easing the beaten-bronze table to one side, careful not to spill the expensive concoctions upon them, then kneeling down eagerly in front of Father Liam, who sighed in anticipation as Ludo unzipped the fly of his trousers, pushed up the black clerical shirt, eased Father Liam's already hard cock out of the slit in his peacock-print silk boxers – the only touch of colour he allowed himself – worked up the juices in his mouth and then lowered his lips to the tip.

With the exemplary self-control that befitted a man of the cloth, not a sound escaped Father Liam's lips as Ludo began to work his mouth up and down the curving cock, dancing his tongue, as instructed, up and down the bulging vein. The priest's hands clamped on the arms of the chair, the veins on their backs standing out too in relief against his pale Irish skin, blue and prominent. He was maintaining silence for himself, not because he and Ludo felt the need to conceal what they were doing for other members of the club; Ludo was partially hidden by the big bronze table, but anyone giving Father Liam more than the most fleeting of glances would have seen immediately from his wide-legged stance and expression of imminent ecstasy that this was a man in the process of getting his cock thoroughly sucked.

Piers, clearing a table in another niche – each seating area was carefully designed to give its occupants their own semi-private space – did in fact glance over and smile at the sight of Liam and Ludo engaging in their favourite little game: Ludo would 'sin', Liam demand a penance. It was a weekday after-noon, and this very exclusive gay club was very quiet. After a swift overview of the premises, Piers sank into a padded chair, having assessed that the few other members had no pressing needs that required his attention for a few minutes. Reaching down to rub his own cock through the smart black apron tied round his waist over his slim-cut trousers, he was as soundless as the priest as he watched Ludo's head pumping up and down, Liam's face contorting more and more, his lower teeth closing over the plump flesh of his lower lip.

Ludo's hand was cupping his lover's balls, his thumb stroking the tender skin in exactly the way he knew would drive Liam crazy: this was another game they played, Ludo trying to coax a sound from Liam in public, Liam holding off as long as he possibly could. Ludo raised his head, pulling back, looking up at the priest's handsome face, his own flushed with pleasure, and begged: 'Say it, say it!'

Oh yeah, Piers thought, his own cock pushing painfully against the fabric above it, knowing what Liam was being entreated to say: it was incredibly hot, and he'd only had the chance to watch this once before. The club rules at the Den allowed members to have their needs seen to discreetly: no nudity, no actual fucking, and other members – a word which always amused the club tremendously – were not sup-posed either to gawk or to attempt to join the proceedings. Piers was usually busier than now; it was rare that he had the chance to watch one of the hottest couples in the Den finish their business. He ached for them to take him home and sandwich him in every way possible, but, despite Ludo's jokes about seminarians, he and Liam were entirely monog-amous.

Don't come! Piers commanded his penis, trying to think of the most unpleasant image he could – the Prime Minister naked usually did the trick – *don't come!* even as Liam yielded, on the verge of orgasm and knowing that Ludo wouldn't lower his mouth again until he said the precious words.

'Bless you, my son!' the priest panted, and gasped, his hands now tight straining fists in the velvet of the armchair as Ludo lowered his head once more and, lips stretched over his teeth, closed so snugly over the red, bulging cock that it promptly exploded in his mouth, hot come surging out so fast that Ludo's cheeks bulged as he swallowed it down in a series of greedy gulps.

It took imagining the Prime Minister not only naked, but hog-tied and sobbing, for Piers to restrain himself from following in Father Liam's wake. He closed his eyes, summoning up that revolting picture instead of the extremely hot scene that was coming to a close, as it were, in front of him; his Adam's apple bobbed as he also swallowed, though nothing half as satisfying as Ludo's haul. By the time he got himself under control, his cock still hard but his situation no longer desperate, and slipped back to his duties, Ludo was rising to his feet, bending to kiss his lover's lips, and settling happily back onto the love seat.

'Better now,' Ludo said, licking his lips. 'I was getting a little too wound-up there, wasn't I?'

Father Liam nodded gravely.

'Sucking cock always calms you down, Ludo,' he agreed. 'And it's *much* healthier than relying over-much on alcohol or other forms of self-medication. I'm happy to be able to provide you with an alternative ...'

But he couldn't sustain the holier-than-thou pose, not so soon after having come; he broke into laughter, and Ludo joined in as they raised their glasses and toasted their long and happy relationship.

'Here's to a *wonderful* wedding,' the priest said, 'full of eco-chic and stratospheric bills and culminating in the *Style* Bride of the Year!'

He smiled.

'You always get what you want, darling. I just *know* you're going to pull this one off too.'

Chapter Twelve

'There you go, my love, get that down you ... ooh-arr, you're a lovely big girl, aren't you? And getting bigger by the day!' the deep voice cooed.

The snuffling and squelching sounds emanating from behind the pig shed were louder than anything Brianna Jade had heard before. She had been visiting the pigpens regularly every day during her morning runs, spending longer and longer with their inhabitants, finding comfort in their smells and noises, so familiar to her from her childhood. The pigs recognized her now, positively scrambled up to the edge of the pen as soon as they saw her brightly clad figure jogging towards them, eager for not only the back-scratching but her voice crooning compliments to them.

Being very sociable animals, pigs loved company, actually made very good pets, and Brianna Jade almost felt as if she'd adopted them; she and Edmund had discussed getting dogs, but couldn't agree on a breed so far. The breeds Brianna Jade preferred were what Edmund called gun dogs, ones bred to stick very closely and lovingly to their humans, while Edmund would rather have shepherd dogs: much more independent, used to working on their own.

So there was an impasse, and Brianna Jade was beginning to think that maybe she should just get a dog on her own account. Train them up from puppies, breed them when they got old enough. It would be something she would genuinely enjoy doing, and, as a bonus, it would be a subject which she would have in common with lots of people at the County dinner parties to which Edmund took her. Once people had realized that she was interested in animals, it had been like an Open Sesame to the county set: she was invited on visits to their kennels, had a standing invitation to take a pair of Irish wolfhounds on her jogs, and was now regularly taking riding lessons so that she could join the local drag hunt.

She had been remembering, with much amusement, how she had misunderstood the term 'drag hunt' originally, making the entire dining table convulse with laughter at the image of its riders all cross-dressing: old Lord Uppingham, charmed by the idea, had proposed that they do it for charity at the Boxing Day meet, and a small group had immediately formed to organize it. Apart from learning that a drag hunt was one where a scent was laid for the hounds, rather than chasing foxes, Brianna Jade had also been informed in detail by a chuckling Lord Uppingham what a 'vicars and tarts' costume party entailed: it had been a very successful evening, and, driving home, Edmund had said very fondly to her how happy he was that she was settling into Rutland society so well, and how well liked she was by the County.

As if it was just one person, the County, she had been thinking as she approached the pen. *I guess in a way it sort of is – these families have known each other since forever, they've all inter-married. It's nice in a way, like I'm coming into a group that's really pretty welcoming, apart from the girls who wanted to marry Edmund* . . .

And then, even over the snuffles and snorts of the pigs, she had heard louder grunting – human, it sounded like – and the squeak of a wheel that needed oiling, and the unmistakable liquid-and-solid plopping of a whole wheelbarrow-full of pigswill being dumped into a trough by Abel the pigman. She had seen his enormous silhouette from time to time in the distance on her near daily visits, but it was almost as if he were avoiding her since that first encounter a month or so ago, and that idea, which had just popped into her mind, made her suddenly curious.

Why would he be steering clear of me? Plus, he's talking to just the one pig – yet that sounded like a whole load of food, enough for a pen-full. How can one pig possibly eat that much?

Brianna Jade had no pressing reason to hurry back to the Hall. Later that afternoon, her mother was coming up from London, together with Lady Margaret, to go over the plans for the engagement party. Brianna Jade was very excited both about the party and about seeing Tamra. She had woken up that morning literally counting the hours until Tamra's Bentley would pull up outside the Hall and Tamra and Lady Margaret would climb out, Tamra bitching at having to go in by a side door, Lady Margaret teasing her for being a nouveau riche American, both of them having a lovely time with the back and forth banter.

I can't wait to see Mom! And I honestly don't know what to do with myself till she gets here. I'd just sit in my room and watch downloaded TV till lunchtime, which is getting pretty boring . . . so I might as well wander along the side of this pen, pick my way round the back of the shed, find out if all that food I heard getting dumped into the trough really was just for the one pig.

'Oh my God!' she exclaimed, as she rounded the shed, took a few steps down an old cart track, and saw the smaller pen which backed onto the central shed: until now, she hadn't realized it was here, or she would have popped around to visit its occupant as well.

But she couldn't possibly have imagined the sight in front of her. It was as surreal as a scene from *Alice in Wonderland* where the main actors had eaten the cake, or drunk from the flask, and grown to giant proportions. Hanging over the top rail of the pen was the enormous Abel, his arms like huge meaty hams making the wooden bars of the pigpen look flimsy as matchsticks, and inside was a sow so colossal that Brianna Jade's first thought was that she must surely be on some sort of specially invented pig steroids.

Or been blown up like a balloon. I mean, I've seen some fat pigs in my time, but I've never seen anything like this one.

'Wow,' she breathed, coming to a dead halt, unable to keep walking and to fully take in the spectacle before her at the same time. Abel and the pig were built on very similar lines: he was hefty with muscle and the pig with lard, but they both shared barrel chests and very solid limbs. It was the normal-sized pen that looked miniature by comparison.

Both Abel and the sow turned to look at the new arrival. The sun was behind him, as with the first time Brianna Jade had met him; it was the same time of day. So she couldn't see how red he got at the sight of her, right up to his scalp under his thick thatch of brown hair. The sow, chewing an apple, stared at Brianna Jade inquisitively, waiting to see if she had brought anything to eat: when Brianna Jade didn't move, didn't walk towards her holding out something tasty, the sow dropped her head and continued slurping placidly from the brimming trough that Abel had just filled for her.

'She's, like, *huge!*' Brianna Jade blurted out as the sloping, snorting sounds of an enormous pig working her way through a vast quantity of food once again filled the air.

Then Brianna Jade bit her lip: what if he took that badly? After all, most people didn't appreciate your saying that their animals were the size of a house. And yes, animals for the slaughter needed fattening up, but this sow was beyond that, was positively *obese*.

'She do be precious big, don't she?' Abel rumbled shyly, his head ducked to avoid looking at Brianna Jade directly. 'She took the silver medal at the Rutland Agricultural Show last year for fattest pig.'

'My God, there's a pig *bigger* than her?' Brianna Jade came forward to the side of the sty, her eyes wide, still staring at the gigantic black pig with bristly white legs and snout, now buried in kitchen peelings in the trough. 'You have got to be kidding me!'

Abel straightened up, looming over her, completely blocking out the sun: she couldn't help flinching back a little as his shadow fell over her.

'She *won*!' he said, a distinct edge in his deep voice now, annoyance trumping his shyness. 'She took the silver medal!'

'Oh, silver's the top prize? I get it, sorry,' Brianna Jade said quickly. 'I was thinking of, like, the Olympics.'

'Ooh-arr,' Abel said, nodding, his huge head the size of a cannonball. 'I see what you mean, miss. No, silver's the highest prize. First time ever that Stanclere Hall's won the Fat Pig medal, and right proud we are of it. She beat out Sir Gregory Parsloe's Pride of Matchingham, this old girl, and he weren't happy about it at all, I can tell you.'

Luckily he spoke slowly, as she was having a hard time following his accent; it was much broader than the light Rutland accents of the people who worked at the Hall. His 'i's became 'oi's, so 'highest prize' became 'hoighest proize'; she was concentrating very hard in order to understand and not to offend him.

'That's really cool,' Brianna Jade said, smiling at the pig. 'The Earl must have been pleased about that.'

Abel brightened. 'He were, miss. Right pleased, he were. All of us at the Hall were.'

'So I guess that's why she's got all this food, right?'

'Ooh-arr,' Abel said, nodding again vigorously: it was an expression, Brianna Jade was beginning to realize, that served dual purpose as both 'Hello' and 'Yes'.

'She needs nearly sixty thousand calories a day,' he added, and at Brianna Jade's gasp of horror, he grinned for the first time, resting his arms back on the top bar of the pen and reaching out to scratch the sow's head. 'Bet that's more than what a skinny thing like you eats in a month, eh?'

'It's more than my mom eats in a year!' Brianna Jade said frankly, grinning back at him. 'She's always on a diet.'

'Bring her down here if you want to give her a fright then,' Abel said, his smile widening.

Brianna Jade managed swiftly to translate 'froight' into 'fright', and giggled at his quip.

'Oh, I *couldn't*,' she said with the utmost sincerity. 'She'd have a heart attack at the sight of all that food.'

By now she felt comfortable enough to come right up to the edge of the pen.

'Is it okay if I scratch her?' she asked. 'I don't want to put her off her feed.'

Abel turned such an approving look upon her that she felt positively warmed by it. His face was squarish, with a wide jaw and a dusting of freckles across his snub nose; apart from the nose, his features were definitely craggy, rather than hand-some, but his eyes were bright with much more intelligence than his slow drawling accent might lead one to expect, and his smile was as open as the blue cloudless skies above them.

'Good girl,' he said to her. 'There's many as 'ud just reach over without asking. Just scratch her behind the ears while she's eating, eh?'

He shifted over, his great arms sliding along the rail to make room for Brianna Jade in front of the sow; she couldn't help noticing the size of his forearms and biceps, bulging below the rolled-up sleeves of his faded check shirt.

'Yeah, I know,' she said, stepping up onto the bottom rail so that she could lean over enough to scratch the bristly skin between the sow's large, forward-slanted ears. 'I grew up round pigs. I come from Illinois – that's pig and corn country.'

'Is it now?' Abel said, bending to pick up some straw and angling it into his mouth, chewing it, his eyebrows raised in interest. 'You got Berkshires over there, then? In America?'

'I don't know what a Berkshire is,' Brianna Jade confessed.

'This lady's a Berkshire,' Abel said, chewing away. 'It's the breed.'

'Oh! I get it! We've got Yorkshires, Durocs, Hampshires, Landraces, Spots ...' Brianna Jade frowned in concentration. 'Those are the main ones I can think of. Lots of English breeds that you guys brought over when you came to settle.'

'What's a Duroc, then?' Abel asked, head tilted. 'Never heard of that.'

'They're the only native American ones I know,' Brianna Jade said eagerly, very happy to be talking about a subject in which she was genuinely interested: try as she might, she just couldn't find Edmund's discourses on arable farming half as fascinating as pigs. They're big and dark red – real red, and real gentle too. Very easy-going.'

'Ooh-arr,' Abel said, nodding. 'I know the ones. We just call 'em "reds" over here, leastways that's what I've always heard 'em called. Nice friendly beasts.'

'What are the ones up front, the spotty ones?' Brianna Jade asked. 'I keep meaning to look them up. They're real friendly too.'

'Those're Old Spots – Gloucester Old Spots, to give 'em the full name,' Abel informed her through his straw. 'You won't have seen them over in America, I'd guess. They're a rare breed nowadays. Dunno why – lovely beasts, they are. We feed 'em from the cider and perry orchards here – they love the fruit, they do, and it makes the meat taste sweet as sugar. If you've had pork up at the Hall that melted in your mouth, miss, that's Old Spot.'

'Mrs Hurley made pork and apple medallions the other night with cream and cider,' Brianna Jade said. 'Oh my God, that was so good!'

Though I didn't have the cream, just a tiny smear off Edmund's plate, because of fitting into my wedding dress, she remembered gloomily. *How I wish everyone was like Abel and thought I was skinny already.*

'There you go!' Abel said, grinning. 'I can see that you grew up round farm animals, miss. We breed 'em to eat 'em, and that's the truth.'

'They have great lives here, I can see that,' Brianna Jade said sincerely. 'And I really love pork! We ate so much of it back home. Our big fair's called Kewanee Hog Days, and you should see the barbecue pits they have there – oh my God, the ribs are *incredible*. When I won the Pork Queen pageant, we all had to make a pork dish as part of the competition, and I made this Tater Tots casserole. I don't suppose you can even get Tater Tots over here?'

'Never even heard of 'em,' Abel said cheerfully.

'They're *way* yummy,' Brianna Jade said wistfully, quite forgetting her British language lessons. 'They're sorta like hash browns in little crunchy bites – you buy them frozen in big bags.'

'Ooh-arr – like potato crunchies from Iceland!' Abel said, nodding vigorously again. The straw was chewed down now: he spat out the end lustily and it shot over the sow's back and onto the ground.

'You get potatoes all the way from Iceland?' Brianna Jade was really confused. 'Don't you, like, grow them here?'

Abel threw back his head and laughed, a deep rumbling noise like the Jolly Green Giant, a huge bellow that literally did sound like 'Ho ho ho!' Even the pig looked up briefly before lowering her snout once more and recommencing her feed. He was laughing at what she'd said, Brianna Jade knew, but she didn't feel at all offended: there was no mockery behind it.

'Iceland's the name of a supermarket,' Abel explained, turning fully to face her, rocking back on his heels, his hands in the pockets of his dungarees. 'Most of the food's in freezers, so that's why they called it—'

'Iceland! I get it!'

They grinned at each other in complete amity, and then Brianna Jade jumped as if she'd been electrocuted. Suddenly she realized that her Lycra exercise clothes were clammy with sweat, her stomach rumbling with hunger, she was thirsty and she needed to stretch: hanging out with Abel and the pig had completely distracted her from anything else. But that wasn't the source of her real discomfort. She had been so relaxed in this conversation, more relaxed than she had been during her entire stay at Stanclere Hall, that she had not only slipped back into Americanisms that she was trying to eliminate: much worse, she had let slip the information about being Pork Queen of Kewanee, something that Tamra had banned her pretty much on pain of death from ever repeating.

'What is it?' Abel said, frowning deeply, his thick eyebrows drawing together. 'You look like you seen a ghost!'

'My mom – I'm not supposed to—' Brianna Jade took in a deep breath. 'What I said about being Pork Queen – I'm not supposed to tell *anyone*! It's not what the Earl of Respers wants people saying about his wife, you know?' She looked up at him, and an even scarier thought struck her. 'You know who I am, right? Oh boy, I didn't even think of that!'

Now Abel was laughing again.

'Who else would I think you were, miss? We've never seen anything like you round these parts. Running round like you're always in a hurry. I saw you with the Old Spots many a time, but I thought it wasn't my place to talk to you, seeing as you're going to marry Mr Edmund. But then you came over here to see the Empress, and we got chatting away, all easy-like, just like I might with Mr Edmund. I wouldn't repeat a word that you told me, miss, if you'd rather not. Not to a living soul.'

'*Thank* you,' Brianna Jade said with huge relief, sensing without a shred of doubt that he was telling the truth.

'But I *would* like to tell my gran what you put in that casserole, though,' he said, and he winked at her.

She giggled, turning to leave.

'You take cream, cheddar cheese, eggs,' she said over her shoulder. 'All beaten up together. You cook pork sausage and slice it in and then bake it with the Tater Tots on top. I used to spike the cream with a little bit of Tabasco.'

Abel nodded. 'I'll tell Gran,' he said.

'Wait, what did you call the pig?' Brianna Jade pivoted back on the rubber heel of her running shoe, just catching up to something he had said.

He winked again.

'She's called Empress of Stanclere,' he told her. 'So that makes one empress and one queen right here, doesn't it?'

Brianna Jade flinched, and he made a swift, reassuring

gesture, a wave of his hand that said she had nothing to be concerned about.

'Don't worry, miss. It's our secret.'

'Thank you,' she said again, and paused. 'You're Abel, aren't you? Edmund told me a while back.'

He nodded. 'Abel Wellbeloved, at your service.'

He reached up and tugged at the front of his hair, like pulling a forelock, a gesture that Brianna didn't understand.

'And I'm Brianna Jade,' she said. 'I mean, you probably know that. Call me that, please, not "miss". It's been so nice hanging out with you just now. I'd like *someone* here to call me by my name.'

'I could give it a try,' he said doubtfully.

She flashed him a gorgeous pageant smile that rocked him right back on his heels.

'Thanks, Abel!' she called over her shoulder.

It was only as she was rounding the lake that it occurred to her that of course she had someone at Stanclere Hall who already called her by her name: her fiancé.

But that's the thing – Edmund's my fiancé, and Abel's like – well, almost like a friend. A fellow pig-loving friend. Who I can see most days when I visit the pigs. And talk to about pigs, and Tater Tot casseroles, and life back home in Kewanee . . .

Brianna Jade felt a huge, happy smile spread across her face as she jogged back to the Hall. Despite the fact that Abel was one of her fiancé's employees, and a lowly one at that, she'd felt more relaxed, more normal in that conversation than she had with anyone since she'd come to live at Stanclere Hall.

Even with Edmund, a little voice said to her disloyally. *You don't chatter away as easily with Edmund as you just did with that pig farmer.*

Well, that makes sense! she told herself firmly. *There's no pressure on you and Abel to fall in love, is there? He's probably married already with tons of kids. Country people get hitched young. I'd be married with kids too if I'd stayed back home in Kewanee.*

And to her horror, a wave of nostalgia hit her hard, harder than she could possibly have expected. Memories of running round barefoot, the soles of her feet like leather, chasing the landlords' chickens and piglets: the Lutzes had always been nice about keeping an eye on Brianna Jade while Tamra worked all the hours God sent at the feed store and then put in a shift at the local bar at Hogs and Cobs.

Tamra had been so proud of the house she'd rented for her and BJ, a rickety old two-bed one-storey behind the Lutzes' place which Dieter Lutz had jerry-rigged with a totally illegal electric cable running perilously from theirs. But it had a proper porch, with a rusty old swing on it to boot, even if they were too scared to both sit on the swing together in case it broke. Plus, the main thing, it wasn't a trailer. No one would ever say that she had raised her daughter in a trailer park, Tamra had always said, her jaw set, her beautiful lips pressed tightly together: she'd work three jobs before she ever let herself and Brianna Jade end up there. To be honest, living in a trailer wasn't the stigma people familiar with the cliché might think: there were some pretty nice trailer courts in the area, not cheap by any means. They were a lot cleaner and neater than the tumbledown shack the Lutzes charged Tamra peanuts to rent. But it was a house, and to Tamra that meant the world.

And it had been a wonderful childhood for Brianna Jade. Kids didn't care about rickety floorboards, pipes you had to bang with a hammer to get the water to flow, the crawl space below the house being a squirrel colony: what Brianna Jade remembered was the long summer days spent entirely outdoors, playing with the Lutzes' cats, learning where each hen liked to lay her eggs, helping feed the turkey being fattened up for Thanksgiving and the pigs for Christmas. She and Dorothy Lutz had cried and hugged each other and been very sad to say goodbye when, after Brianna Jade won Pork Queen, Tamra packed up her and her daughter's scanty possessions and took them on the pageant circuit.

Jeez, BJ, you're remembering Kewanee like it was paradise, and that's crazy! she told herself firmly as she crested the rise and the glorious spectacle of Stanclere Hall, bathed in soft September sunshine, came into view, breathtaking as always. *Look where you ended up! You're not missing the freezing winters when it was colder in the house than outside, or those Converse sneakers Mom bought for you at Goodwill which were so torn up it was easier to go barefoot and pretend you preferred it. You're not missing that part at all. You just loved the farm life, the livestock, how simple it all was.*

Even jogging along, she heaved a sigh. *I do miss not worrying about what I wear, or how much make-up I have on, or how much I weigh. But actually, I still have to worry about all that, and I suppose I always will as the Countess of Respers.*

She had to stop this line of thought. It wasn't remotely helpful. Brianna Jade was going to be Countess of Respers, which was her mom's dream, but after her marriage she'd take things in a different direction than her mom might anticipate. Tamra was hoping that Brianna Jade would be a high-society Countess, moving in the best circles, throwing fabulous house parties, skiing in the winter, summering in Antibes in luxury villas. Brianna Jade, however, was envisaging a much more rural existence. Breeding dogs, learning to ride well enough to join the local hunt, visiting the pigs and the Empress of Stanclere on a daily basis; she was figuring out ways to fit into Edmund's farming life, and thought that her plans were going to work out pretty well.

'Cause after I get married, Mom's going to realize that I'm not going to want to do as many photo shoots for glossy magazines as she'd like. Of course, I'll go along with some to keep her happy, but I refuse to spend the rest of my life dolling myself up and watching my weight. I've been doing that since I was fifteen, and I'm really looking forward to being able to hang up my curling irons, spend whole days without a lick of make-up, and eat as much cream sauce with Mrs Hurley's pork medallions as I want.

The last image, in particular, cheered Brianna Jade up so much that as she slowed to a walk for her post-run cooldown, she was smiling again. Ready for a long drink of water, and for lunch in a couple of hours, if her rumbling stomach could wait that long; but she had sugar-free gum in her room, that old pageant trick to make you feel like you were eating when you weren't, and hopefully it'd keep her going until the cold roast beef and salad Mrs Hurley was making her for lunch.

'Miss Brianna! There she is. Miss Brianna, there's a phone message for you.'

It was Mrs Hurley herself, craning out of the kitchen door to catch Brianna Jade on her way back into the Hall.

'Really?'

Brianna Jade turned towards Mrs Hurley, her perfectly shaped eyebrows rising a little in surprise. She had her own mobile, which no one else would have dreamt of answering; it was unprecedented for anyone to ring her on the main Stanclere Hall phone line, which was used mainly by Mrs Hurley for placing orders and communicating with tradespeople.

'Yes, miss! I made a note of the name, but she said she'd ring back in half an hour, and it must be around that by now. You've been at your running longer than usual, haven't you? Let me see ...'

Mrs Hurley rummaged in the pocket of her apron and fished out a piece of paper.

'Very odd name it was. I had to get her to spell it out to me. Here you go—'

Brianna Jade took the paper from Mrs Hurley's hand, and caught her breath at the sight of the name.

'*Norkus?* Did I get that right? She said you'd know it, but I must say, it seemed funny to me . . .' Mrs Hurley was saying, but just then the sound of the house phone could be heard ringing, and Brianna Jade, muttering a 'Thank you,' dashed back to the side door and down the hall to Edmund's office, which was the closest extension where she could take the call in privacy; the phone in the main hall was nearer, but there everyone wandering by – builders, newly hired maids and kitchen staff – would be able to overhear the conversation she was about to have.

God, I wish Mom were here! she thought, sprinting into the office, shutting the heavy door and lunging across the desk to grab the receiver. *Why on earth is Barb getting in touch after all these years? No way is she making a pricy international call just to congratulate me on being engaged. Jeez, no way can she come to the wedding, if that's what she's after! Mom'd bust a gut at the mere idea!*

'Hello?' she said cautiously into the receiver, settling herself into the huge, ancient leather wing chair that had probably been in the Respers family for generations, and which Edmund really should replace with a posturally supportive desk chair. 'This is Brianna Jade Maloney speaking.'

'Well, get *you* with your fancy accent!' snapped the unmistakable tones of Barb Norkus, who had been runner-up to Brianna Jade in the Kewanee Pork Queen pageant and had never forgiven her rival; in fact, Barb had surreptitiously tried to push Brianna Jade off the tractor trailer as it carried her and the two runners-up on their triumphal procession down Main Street. 'I bet you think you're *way* better than all of us now,

Brianna Jade Krantz! Marrying an Earl, like something out of a movie!'

Brianna Jade was actually relieved, sort of, that Barb was being all snarky and mean from the get-go. Barb on the attack was something Brianna Jade recognized and was used to: Barb pretending to be nice and friendly, sucking up to her ex-rival, would have made Brianna Jade even more nervous.

'Not exactly *better*,' she answered warily. 'But, uh, different, I suppose.'

'You sound all British and stuck up!' Barb said angrily, her Kewanee accent so strong and familiar to Brianna Jade that the nostalgia washed over her again, even in these very unpleasant circumstances.

'Well I was doing pageants for years, Barb,' Brianna Jade said carefully. 'I had to smooth out my accent for those too.'

'I'm sitting here looking at you on the CelebrityPics site!' Barb broke in, her voice as nasal as ever.

Brianna Jade had forgotten how some American girls' voices sounded, as if they had had clothes pegs clipped onto the bridges of their noses at birth to train them to speak in the highest register possible; there was a babylike inflection that went along with the squeaky voice, as if they were trying to sound like nine-year-olds. She had realized, almost as soon as she and Tamra moved to London, that she was going to have to work on her vocal range, lower it considerably, and she'd been surprised how easy it had been. Just because she'd got used to speaking in a certain way that people in the States liked to hear women talk, it didn't mean that it was her natural voice; she'd been taken aback to find out that she'd been, as it were, faking it for all those years.

'You're posing in this stone thing with pillars in a pink frilly dress by Versayce,' Barb said even more angrily, as if Brianna Jade had set up the photo shoot as a deliberate insult aimed directly at Barb. 'With your fiancé next to you, all lovey-dovey, and your hand on his shoulder showing off your gigantic ring to make the rest of us feel like shit.'

Brianna Jade couldn't really argue with that. Naturally, she hadn't posed with Edmund to make Barb specifically, or anyone in general, feel awful, but she did know what Barb meant; when you weren't feeling great about your own life, those perfect, airbrushed, Photoshopped images of people with more money and beauty and fame than you would ever possess could make you want to go shove your head in a septic tank.

'I'm sorry it made you feel bad, Barb,' she said empathetically. 'That sucks.'

'Fuck you!' Barb screeched: clearly, empathy had not been the best tack to take. 'Fuck you, Blow Job! That's how you got that Earl, I bet! Down on your knees sucking cock! As well as the money your mom got on her knees sucking nasty old-man cock!'

Brianna Jade promptly hung up. She didn't have to sit there and listen to Barb insult her and, much more importantly, her mother; Brianna Jade could have cared less what Barb said about her, but Tamra was totally out of bounds. Plus, Barb had dragged in Ken Maloney, who was also out of bounds; he'd been nothing but lovely to his young wife and her daughter. And, frankly, Brianna Jade had spent a great deal of time during Tamra's marriage trying very hard not to think about what Tamra was doing with Ken in return for his money and social position. It had utterly and completely grossed her out, and even now she was feeling a bit like throwing up in her mouth at Barb's unpleasantly vivid image ...

The phone rang again. Brianna Jade snatched up the handset, and without thinking that it might be a tradesperson, said furiously: 'Barb Norkus, I'm telling you right now that if you say one word about my mom I'm hanging up on you and blocking this number and reporting you to the British police, and since I'm engaged to be married to an Earl, I just *bet* that they'll take it seriously and tell the Kewanee cops that you're making harassing phone calls to me!'

'Ah, don't get your panties in a twist,' Barb said with an unpleasant sneer that Brianna Jade could visualize perfectly; she knew that look of Barb's all too well, having seen it very many times behind the backs of teachers or random adults when Barb, having finished kissing their asses, relieved her feelings by reverting to her true expression.

'How am I supposed to—' Brianna Jade started indignantly, though managing to get her voice down a few notches from soprano to mezzo. But Barb cut through her.

'Don't you wanna know why I'm calling?' she asked.

'No, I don't,' Brianna Jade snapped. 'Knowing you, it won't exactly be to congratulate me on my engagement.'

'Well, it sorta *is*,' Barb said, which put Brianna Jade even more on her guard. ''Cause if you weren't engaged to marry an Earl, I wouldn't be thinking that it made a real good opportunity for me to email CelebrityPics or the *National Enquirer* or some big magazine like that and tell them I've got a real good story about the girl who's gonna marry the Earl of Whatever once being Pork Queen at Kewanee Hog Days! I bet they'd love that!'

Brianna Jade's stomach sank like a stone. But she wasn't an idiot. She had been half-expecting something like this ever since she'd seen Barb's name in Mrs Hurley's handwriting.

'Big deal,' she said as lightly as she could. 'I mean, come on, Barb, the *National Enquirer*? It's not like you've got any photos of me with my clothes off! Why would they care that I won a beauty pageant years ago?'

'OK, maybe not them,' Barb said, undaunted. 'Maybe some British paper. I see links to the *Daily Mail* on loads of my gossip sites. I could try them. They'd be real interested to see how the Countess of Whatever got her big break.'

'*Big break?* Jeez, Barb, you sound crazy! It's just a little country fair!' Brianna Jade said unguardedly, yet another mistake.

'Hey, fuck you! How dare you look down your nose at us!' Barb snapped.

'I mean, you won Corn Queen of Watseka that same year,' Brianna Jade said quickly. 'We each got a title, didn't we? I don't get why you're so pissed at me—'

'I want money,' Barb said, finally getting to the point of her call. 'I want you to send me a big old load of money or I'll go to the *Daily Mail* or somewhere in Britain with my photos and a story about what a nasty back-stabbing bitch you were back in the day. I know, I know,' she added before Brianna Jade could protest, 'you were actually a stupid little suckup idiot, but they'll like it better if I make you out all trashy and back-stabbing and slutty. Those papers always like that kinda dirt. And believe me, the photos I have are gold. It's not just a couple from the Hog Days website, with you looking all smug in your sash and all. My mom took scads. There's you making your Tater Tots casserole, dropping the Oreos for the pigs, nearly falling off the trailer like you were drunk in your pigskin jacket—'

'Because you pushed me!' Brianna Jade said indignantly.

'Yeah? Well, I'll tell the papers you had a couple Jack and Cokes before you got up there and that's why you tripped!' Barb said triumphantly. 'I'll give 'em every trailer-trash detail I can find. I'll go over to the old Lutz place and take photos of that shack you and your mom lived in – believe me, it looks even more like shit now than it used to. I've been googling you guys, and all the stuff that comes up is fancy photos of you two in Florida after Tamra got married, or you posing in tons of pageants. No one's got hold of *this* stuff at all.'

There was an audible smirk in her voice.

'Think if they sent someone over here to snoop around!' she added. 'No one liked your mom, BJ. She was way too pretty. Can you imagine what they'll say to a journalist who comes round asking about what she was like working at Hogs and Cobs back in the day? They'll make up all kinds of shit just to get their own back on her for being all high and mighty now.'

Brianna Jade shivered. This was something they had never had to deal with before. Ken Maloney socialized with the owners of the local Florida papers: their writers wouldn't have dreamt of digging up Tamra and Brianna Jade's dirt-poor past. And in London, Veronica, Tamra's PR, had been busy emphasizing Tamra's investments in environmentally friendly fracking procedures and her large donations to charity. Besides, Tamra and Brianna Jade had always been known as Maloney over here; no British journalist had any idea that tracking down the Krantzes' humble origins would yield a motherlode of embarrassment for them.

Silence fell. Brianna Jade knew that Barb was more than capable of carrying out her threat, and that British tabloids would salivate over her story – probably entering into a bidding war for it, and, more importantly, the photographs. Every detail of the Pork Queen competition would seem hilarious over here, with all its attendant details about pigskin jackets, Tater Tot casseroles and dropping Oreo cookies to make the pigs race. A skilled tabloid hack would wring every last embarrassing detail out of Barb and make hay out of it. It would be all over the *Mail Online* for weeks.

I don't care about myself, Brianna Jade realized at that moment. *I really don't. I mean, it'd be embarrassing, sure. But here at Stanclere Hall, I barely even see a newspaper. I mean, Edmund gets them, but I don't read them. And I can just make sure I don't get any magazines either, the gossipy ones. Sometimes I pick one up in the village – well, I don't have to do that any more. I'm not much of a reader at the best of times, and I've got no problem staying off the internet.*

And I don't think the County will care much either. I mean, the girls might snigger at me behind my back, but they do that anyway. People like Lord Uppingham might actually find it pretty funny if I make a good story out of it, pigskin jacket and all. If I show that it doesn't bother me, people in Rutland won't give a shit after a little while.

It never even occurred to her to worry about Edmund's reaction, which was to his great credit. Even before his proposal, she had been very well aware that he wasn't a snob in any way; he would hate the extra publicity, but he wouldn't blame her for it. In fact, like old Lord Uppingham, he might even be tickled by the jacket and the Oreo-throwing.

No, it's Mom I need to protect. She's the one who'll really get the fallout.

London society, Brianna Jade had already observed, was a very different beast from the small, cohesive county of Rutland. London had a level of snark and cattiness and competition, of scheming to get into the right parties and look down on people who settled for the wrong ones, which was infinitely more cut-throat than life in the countryside. The highest echelons even mocked people who got photographed too much: that last one utterly baffled Brianna Jade, as all the West Palm Beach social set cared about was having their picture in the papers every single day of the week. But Lady Margaret had counselled Tamra that quantity, over here, did not at all mean quality, and that Tamra should be very selective about what invitations she accepted if she wanted to be part of the highest echelons. Hence Tamra's membership of Loulou's, the nightclub below the private members' club, 5 Hertford Street; the whole point about clubs like Loulou's, Annabel's and George's, all in Mayfair, was that absolutely no cameras were allowed inside their hallowed precincts.

Like Las Vegas, what happened in those clubs stayed there. The very top of the *gratin* disliked being in the press at all; Edmund certainly would be much happier never doing one of those photo shoots again, though he knew what he had signed up to and was a very good sport about it. Lady Margaret was helping Tamra walk the line, work out what was 'good' publicity – i.e. could be passed off as charity work – and 'bad' – seeming to court it for one's own ends.

But no way is this good publicity! It'll just give everyone who dislikes Mom and me for being so rich a way to tear us down, and Mom will just hate it. It'll mess up so many things she's worked so hard for.

Oh my God! No way will I get Style *Bride of the Year if this story breaks before the* Style *editors have made their decision and locked it all down!*

And Mom will die, she'll just die if I lose that because of some shit that Barb Norkus, of all people, is pulling.

Brianna Jade made a decision. She had no choice. If it were just for herself, she'd tell Barb to go take a running jump: she didn't even care all that much about being *Style* Bride of the Year, but she knew that for Tamra it was the cherry on the icing on the cake, the culmination of everything she'd hoped to win for her adored daughter when she'd brought the two of them to London. Even Lady Margaret had said that there couldn't be any social objection to such a prestigious magazine cover, which had naturally made Tamra more determined than ever to snag it.

Brianna Jade had heard how Chloe Rose had been mocked by the upper classes when, as a commoner, she started to date

Prince Hugo: Chloe had even been called 'Dog Rose', which had both insulted her looks and tagged her as a social climber. How easy would it be for Tamra to be nicknamed 'Hog Mom' by some jealous rival who envied Tamra's beauty and riches? Or for Brianna Jade to be dubbed 'Tater Tot'? Again, safe and happy in the country, Brianna Jade wouldn't give a shit what the tabloids called her: but for Tamra, papped on a regular basis, to have names like that yelled at her to provoke a reaction would be intolerable.

Mom's done so much for me. Now it's time for me to look after her.

A horribly vivid memory of Ken Maloney's sagging old-man body by the pool, covered in white hairs, mostly where they shouldn't be, was all Brianna Jade needed to confirm her resolve. Much as she hated to buckle under to a blackmailer, this was to protect Tamra, and not on her own behalf. That was what convinced her to open her mouth and say: 'Do you have a bank account, Barb?'

As it turned out, Barb didn't have a bank account, something that Brianna Jade had pretty much guessed already. And the maximum you could send via Western Union was four thousand pounds, which converted roughly into six thousand bucks, which was a fortune to Barb Norkus, even though she pretended that it wasn't enough, not at all, and attempted to convince Brianna Jade to send that sum on a weekly basis. Brianna Jade countered with the very good point that the IRS would be all over Barb like white on rice if she sent that much money so regularly, and Barb had reluctantly agreed. Brianna Jade had said she'd make a transfer every month for that amount, at which Barb had whined and moaned, but Brianna Jade, sensing a weak point, had mentioned the IRS again, knowing that there was no way Barb was going to declare any of this to the tax people, and Barb had folded.

'You'll need to keep sending this every month,' Barb warned firmly. 'I can open my mouth just as fast as I can close it, you know?'

Just till the wedding, Brianna Jade had thought. *After that, and after the* Style Bride *cover* – she had no doubt that Tamra would secure that for her daughter: hadn't Tamra got everything that she'd set her heart on in life? – *Barb Norkus can eat my lily-white ass.*

And, in the pull-behind Scamp camper in her stepmom Hailey's front yard, which she was calling home for now, Barb Norkus stretched out her legs and lit another of the Marlboro Lights she'd boosted from her stepmom's bag the other day. They were a rare luxury, and she had been saving them for special treats; now, however, she could smoke 'em as much as she wanted. And she could get the hell out of this nasty thirteen-foot space, so cramped that, with the double bed down, you were sleeping right next to the kitchen unit, the stinking toilet just a couple of feet away, and washing yourself in the kitchen sink.

Gross, but free, as Barb's dad wouldn't let her stepmom charge her rent for living in the camper, even though Barb's presence there meant that Hailey had to either lock her doors or put up with the knowledge that Barb was helping herself to sessions on her dad's computer and to the household supplies every time Hailey's back was turned. Hailey had insisted that Barb do something in return for free accommodation, and Barb had been tasked with watering the geraniums Hailey had cultivated in the tractor tyre planters around the camper's parking area: of course she'd never done that once, complaining that she'd been way too busy working the recent state fair.

She looked down complacently at the hand holding the cigarette. She'd had her nails done for the fair, but that had been a while ago, and Barb had been hanging on to those overlays like grim death, trying to get another few weeks out of them. She'd got her hair coloured when her tax return came in, but now she must have at least four inches of roots: it had been a while. She'd boosted one of Hailey's home dye kits to cover the roots, but it hadn't been as good a match as she thought, so she actually had bi-colour hair now, and it was really bugging her.

She'd been waiting to pick up farm jobs mid-September for cash; they always needed people to be 'management' over the migrant workers. You got paid more if you knew some Spanish, but Barb didn't see why she should have to learn another language in America, land of the free English speakers, and she'd never exerted herself to try. She preferred working the farm stands on weekends and evenings selling peaches, apples or strawberries, logging the baskets people brought from the You-pick-it.

That was where she'd got the phone which she'd used to call Brianna Jade. Some big-city idiot woman in designer jeans, thinking it was so cool to pick her own fruit – *like that wasn't a back-breaking job for wetbacks!* Barb thought unpleasantly – had been so busy rattling onto her spoilt brats about how great it was to choose your own peaches – *which you could do just as well at Fairway* – that she'd left her phone on the counter and not realized. *Dumb bitch, serves her right. And extra dumb for having left it with an international calling plan on it, too.*

Well, now Barb could chuck the phone and get a new one. Whatever she wanted. She could get her nails and her roots done, she could move out of this shitty camper with its cheap fibreglass walls and thin-as-paper fake wood panelling. She could rent somewhere real nice in the upscale trailer court: a forty-footer RV with central air, a home theatre, a dinette that seated four people, an electric fireplace and a tub/shower –

her eyes positively sparkled at the prospect as she jumped down from the bed and headed out of the camper.

She'd hitch a ride to Wal-Mart, or to the Dollar General on the Illinois Highway: there were Western Unions in both places. Brianna Jade had looked on the website and said the transfer should happen straight away.

Six grand a month! That was seventy-two grand a year – unimaginable riches. Seriously, Barb had never thought she'd make that much in her entire life, let alone in one year! She could get Brianna Jade to make the transfers to Western Unions all over the States, travel around to collect the money from different locations, find some people to buy fake IDs from so the IRS wouldn't catch up with her. Plus, that would mean that all the Kewanee folks wouldn't figure out why she suddenly had so much money and try to ride the gravy train along with her; if Brianna Jade got a deluge of calls from back home, all threatening to sell their snaps of her up on that tractor trailer with the Hog Queen sash across her blue satin-covered boobs, she'd more than likely just throw in the towel and tell 'em to go ahead and do it.

No, this gold mine was all Barb's: she wasn't going to share it with a living soul. On her way to the main road she threw the butt of her Marlboro into the closest tractor tyre planter, kept going, then turned round, pulled the half-empty packet from her pocket, extracted a last cigarette and placed the packet in the centre of the planter, squashing down the geraniums. Hailey couldn't fail to see it there when she came home from her shift at Walgreen's pharmacy counter. It was the perfect fuck-you to her stepmom, acknowledging that Barb had stolen her cigarettes and didn't give a shit that Hailey knew it. Plus, it said that Barb didn't give a shit about Hailey's damn trashy tractor tyre planters either.

Barb's tri-colour hair flapped behind her in the breeze as

she strode away from the family who had taken her in a couple of months ago when her boyfriend kicked her out. It wouldn't have occurred to her for a moment to give a single cent of the six grand to her father and Hailey. In Barb's world, you took care of yourself first, foremost and for ever. Even saying thank you was for suckers.

Chapter Thirteen

Stanclere Hall, November

'God, look at the old place!' Tarquin exclaimed as he turned the car into the drive that led up to Stanclere Hall and the occupants of the eco-friendly had their first glimpse of the newly done-up house. 'It's like a luxury hotel now!'

The Hall had undergone a titanic renovation process in order for it to be spruced up in time for the arrival of the party guests: repairs to the roof had been put on hold in order to focus on more cosmetic aspects. The stonework had been repointed where it most needed it, the window frames refitted, the moth-eaten carpets replaced only where necessary – now that there was staff to polish the mahogany floors every day, they could be shown off – and, in a heroic effort, several of the key bedrooms had been converted or extended into others to allow en-suite bathrooms to be installed.

This was work that had been planned for the wedding at the end of May, not an engagement party in late autumn, and the stampede to speed up the process had been horrendous for everyone involved; with no neighbours to complain about noise, shifts of workmen had toiled away on double pay from six a.m. to ten at night, every day of the week. Edmund had been banished to a tied cottage on the estate, Brianna Jade to Chewton Glen Spa Hotel in the Cotswolds, and Tamra, who cared much more about the revamp than either one of them – ironically, as she would never even live at the Hall – had camped out in a side wing, supervising the works with an iron hand in a velvet glove, and causing the project manager and architect, by the end, to regard her almost as a demi-goddess come to earth, beautiful, capricious, and probably capable of literally smiting them with a lightning strike from her perfectly manicured fingers if they failed to carry out any of her many and various orders.

Certainly, however, the Hall had been transformed: it was Cinderella at the ball. The lime trees lining the wide avenue that approached it had been freshly pruned, and the lawns were so green and lush, the shrubbery so immaculately shaped, that Tarquin's comment was perfectly judged. The sheer amount of money that had been thrown at the seemingly magical transformation bespoke five-star hotel rather than private residence.

'It's rather a shame, in a way,' Eva murmured from the back of the car, looking at Stanclere Hall gleaming in the afternoon sunlight, partly because every single one of its windows was now perfectly clean and they reflected the sun much more than they had when dusty and cobwebbed. Tarquin mm'ed a yes of agreement.

'Oh, you're both just silly nostalgics!' Milly said briskly. 'What's so glamorous about a crumbling old house no one can afford to heat? I bet if you visited before the Fracking Queen threw millions at it, it would have been all draughty and freezing and probably infested with mice, too.'

'Not *glamorous*, Milly, but maybe romantic?' Eva said dreamily. 'Faded tapestries, pulling on extra sweaters in the evening, sitting around the fire, cooking over a big range in the kitchen ... Can you imagine the attics full of old furniture, trunks with stacks of old letters and family photographs, dresses in rickety old cupboards that go back centuries? Rocking horses, maybe, covered in cobwebs ... Think how lovely it would be to explore ...'

'Ugh, the *dust*,' Milly commented, but neither of them were listening.

'Rooms no one's gone into for absolutely *ages*,' Tarquin chimed in. 'Wow, that's so evocative. I can just imagine it. Like layer upon layer of history, a sort of palimpsest of the Hall going back through time. *That's* what we mean, darling,' he said to Milly with his sweet smile. 'When you clean everything up, you sort of sweep those layers away for ever, if you see what I mean.'

'Exactly!' Eva added with great enthusiasm. 'It's like you're whitewashing away the past. The house is like a memory keeper – almost like its own diary going back through the ages – and when you lose that, it's almost like you lose its essential essence—'

'Oh, for God's *sake*!' Milly interrupted impatiently as the Prius followed the sweep of the drive as it curved towards the Hall. 'You're both talking absolute nonsense! Honestly, Tark, you'll end up presenting some TV show on stately homes for American heritage nostalgics, the way you go on.'

'I wouldn't mind that, actually,' her fiancé said thoughtfully. 'In fact, I think I'd rather like it.'

But, as so often, Milly had tuned him out. She didn't just invite Eva almost everywhere she and Tarquin went because she loved Eva's company; she had realized, quite early on when she started to date Tarquin, that the more Eva was around, the less Milly herself had to even pretend to be interested as Tarquin wittered on about poetry and *fêtes champêtres* and layers of history. It worked wonderfully. Milly took care of Tarquin's romantic and physical needs, Eva his intellectual ones. This made life ridiculously easy for Milly, who needed to keep Tarquin happy. Getting engaged to him, planning the wedding, had catapulted Milly into a much higher level of celebrity: snagging *Style* Bride of the Year would be a pinnacle for her – not just being on the front of the magazine in itself, but the flood of media coverage that would disseminate her image to the rest of the world.

This weekend, Milly was perfectly aware, had been set up by Brianna Jade, her rival for the magazine cover, and her scheming mother. They were planning to make Brianna Jade the star of the show, position her front and central for the *Style* shoot that was planned, make it seem inevitable to Jodie Raeburn, the editor, that she should choose the future Countess of Respers as her Bride of the Year. But Milly had her own plans, her own posse lined up, and she was fully preparing to destabilize her rival. And although her fiancé was happily distracted chatting away about essential essences to her best friend, Milly didn't have the slightest worry that Tarquin would start swapping real essential essences with Eva. He was naturally faithful, and Eva, though obviously in love with him, was far too morally evolved to do anything like trying to seduce an engaged man.

More fool her! I'd totally give it a go if I were in her shoes, Milly thought cynically as the Prius came to a halt in front of Stanclere Hall.

Two footmen had been stationed at the base of the double-winged stone staircase which led up to the entrance, and they were coming forward to open the car doors for the new arrivals. On formal occasions, like the party to celebrate the

Earl's engagement, it was perfectly acceptable to use the main entrance, though it was certainly the first time in the history of the Hall that two liveried footmen were assigned to wait outside, one to organize the luggage, one to perform a valet parking service for the arriving guests.

'Good Lord, it really *is* like a hotel. They've got doormen. Um, do I tip?' Tarquin said, seeing their approach. 'One would never normally do so, of course, but if it's being run in an American sort of way . . .'

'You probably should,' Milly said, shrugging.

'No, you *never* tip till the last day when you're staying with people,' Eva, whose own background was Welsh country gentry, said swiftly. 'Just because this looks all five-star hotel doesn't mean we're not private guests, so it's the same rules.'

'Yeah, you're right, Eves,' Tarquin said, relieved. 'Good call.'

He threw her a quick smile over his shoulder as one footman opened the car doors while the other went to the boot to unload their luggage. Tarquin thanked the closer one as he handed him the keys and gave their names to be checked off on a list.

But as they walked up the entrance stairs and into the transformed Great Hall, it became harder and harder to keep in mind that they truly weren't entering a boutique hotel. Milly actually gasped in open appreciation, and Tarquin shook his head in amazement. The heavy oil landscapes hanging ponderously on the walls had all been cleaned, and their details were clear for the first time in at least half a century. Previously, the Hall had never contained much furniture, being more of an antechamber to showcase the superb cantilevered staircase, whose double wings were larger versions of the stone ones outside, creating a satisfying sense of symmetry for the arriving guests, but making them want to move through it as quickly as possible. Big open rooms make people feel very uncomfortable, and perhaps that was the effect the Hall's architect had intended, to create an entrance so imposing that it would remind almost all the guests that they were of a lesser rank than the Earls of Respers.

Now, however, Tamra had transformed the big, draughty, intimidating space into something that did so closely resemble the lobby of a country-house hotel that it was hard not to look around for the check-in desk. Deep emerald velvet armchairs and sofas were artfully arranged around low coffee tables, bearing folded newspapers and magazines. Behind them stood the enormous Chinese vases that had collected dust for centuries by various fireplaces around the Hall, now full of giant arrangements of elegant branches; an applewood fire crackled invitingly in the huge marble grate, while scented diffusers against the walls infused the air with an extra, delicious perfume of orange zest and cinnamon.

The centrepiece was a gleaming Bechstein piano, a giant silver candelabra on its lid; it was mid-afternoon, so the candles were not yet lit, but clearly, a maid would be tasked to come around at dusk and light them and the candles in the matching candelabra on the mantelpiece, so that their flames could reflect enticingly in the gigantic silver mirror above. The pieces of furniture were deliberately placed to create an asymmetry that balanced out the two even wings of the staircase, turning the unwieldy space of the long, echoing hall into the most inviting of sitting rooms.

It was, in short, a masterpiece. It signalled instantly and perfectly to any new visitor that the Hall had been pulled firmly into the twenty-first century with immaculate taste. Tamra might as well have hung out an 'Under New Management' sign outside by the huge oak entrance doors.

'Oh my God, I *love* it!' Milly breathed despite herself; she was perfectly aware that she was visiting the home of her rival, the girl who was up against her for *Style* Bride of the Year, but she couldn't hold back for this brief moment. From now on, however, she decided that she would copy Eva and Tarquin's more aristocratic attitude, swan around with a series of faint sighs for the more nostalgic and bygone past of Stanclere Hall.

I'll need to google that word Tark just used, she thought. *Palimpsest, wasn't it? I'll look that up and drop it into conversation with the Americans, pump Eva and Tark for more of their pretentious guff to wind up the Fracking Queen and the Fracking Princess . . .*

'Hi! Welcome to Stanclere Hall!' came a voice, and they all looked up to see Tamra standing at the top of the stairs, just as if she were the chatelaine. Sunshine flooded in from the high windows on either side of the staircase, bathing her red-gold hair in light, turning it almost into a halo. She descended the stairs like a Vegas showgirl, never looking down, using the trick of swinging one long leg in its black leather high-heeled pump a little backward with every step so she would be sure to find a solid, newly carpeted riser beneath her foot without having to glance down to check. In a cowl-neck pale grey Lanvin dress cinched with a wide black leather belt low around her waist, Tamra's only jewellery was a huge layered gold necklace which perfectly echoed the shape of the cowl neck. Her make-up was restrained but perfect, her hair caught back from her face in a simple clip; she didn't look suitable for any kind of traditional country afternoon, but, equally, she was clearly not pretending to be anything but what she was, the drop-dead beautiful American multi-millionairess mother of the bride.

'You must be Tarquin and Milly,' Tamra said with a smile that flashed her perfect teeth, her hands outstretched in greeting as she finished her descent of the stairs and walked towards their little group, bunched together just inside the doors where they had stopped to marvel at the transformation of the Great Hall. 'How lovely! Brianna Jade and Edmund were so glad that you could make it. I'm Tamra, Brianna Jade's mom, as you must have already guessed.'

Even Milly, reluctanctly, had to admit that Tamra had made an entrance worthy of the Fracking Queen title that London society had bestowed upon her. The nickname might have been acid-lemon, but Tamra had made lemonade from it, behaving regally enough – in public, anyway – to turn what had been meant as an unpleasant little comment on her lack of breeding into a backhanded compliment.

'Yes, I'm Tarquin,' he said, returning her smile with one of his own that was so blindingly charming that Tamra's eyes widened as she took in not only the full extent of his beauty, but also his natural charisma. Gliding towards him, she took his hands and kissed him on either cheek, turning to Milly and doing the same.

'This is—' Milly started, but Tamra cut her off.

'And you must be Eva, the jewellery designer,' she said to Eva, who duly came forward to be kissed too, the other two shuffling back to make room; clearly, Tamra was in charge, would coordinate every aspect of this social encounter. 'How lovely of you to come! Your luggage is being taken up to your rooms, and Jane will show you where you're sleeping. Why don't you all freshen up and then come down to the Rose Room for cocktails? I'm sure Tarquin remembers where that is, but if not, just tell Jane to come back when you're ready and she'll take you down. Brianna Jade is just *longing* to meet you all.'

There was nothing to say to this highly polished speech but 'Thank you,' which they all mumbled, sounding and feeling rather like pupils new to boarding school being granted a brief audience with an improbably glamorous headmistress. Tamra flashed another smile at them, turned to glide away, and then paused with one hand on the piano, turning to look back at them, her figure so gloriously shaped that Eva was horribly conscious of her own imperfect posture, her slightly hunched shoulders, her bony frame, compared to Tamra's exquisite curves and straight spine.

'Oh, just to say, I'm *so* sorry that we couldn't accommodate you in the wing that's been newly refurbished,' Tamra said, her tone entirely unapologetic. 'But we simply couldn't do it all in time, and Edmund said that as you were family, Tarquin, and Milly and Eva are kind of family by association ...' – another wonderful smile accompanied these words, flashing between the two girls – 'that you wouldn't mind what he calls "Spartan living quarters". Jane will show you where the bathroom is, too. You share it with the rest of the floor. Well, see you later!'

And with those last words, she swept away as graciously as Scarlett O'Hara across the ballroom of Tara.

Oh, I see what that bitch just did, Milly thought grimly. *It's definitely war.*

It was insult to injury that she had to listen to Tarquin and Eva's coos of happiness that they were being accommodated in the pre-upgraded wing of the Hall, the one that was indeed so Spartan that its facilities were almost as poor as those at the boarding school which they had briefly pictured on thanking Tamra.

Even Jane, the maid, looked visibly apologetic as she pushed open the door of the room where Tarquin and Milly were to sleep, saying: 'It's all spick and span – and you have nice clean towels,' as if this were the only thing she could find to give a positive spin on the state of the bedroom.

'I think I actually slept here when I was a boy!' Tarquin said appreciatively, looking around at the faded engravings on the walls, the bare floorboards, the pitifully inadequate rugs, the

very basic wrought-iron double bed, the window seat with its
equally faded and patched cushions. The bed itself was covered with a yellowing candlewick bedspread, on which was a
flimsy stack of equally yellowing crocheted lace-trimmed
towels, which had been good quality once, a long, long time
ago.

'Oh, how lovely!' Eva practically pounced on the towels,
stroking the lace between her fingers, admiring its quality.
'Look, I think this is all hand work.'

'How wonderful!' Tarquin marvelled, as Milly pulled a horrible face and muttered something vicious about Tamra.

A footman carried in their suitcases from the car. Tarquin's
ancient leather carry-all looked much more appropriate when
placed on the equally ancient trunk at the foot of the bed than
Milly's matching set of beige Mandarina Duck cases, each decorated with raised padded stripes in paler beige thermoform
rubber – modern, chic and bound to pick up any speck of
dirt – a far cry from Eva's own battered canvas and leather
duffel, which the footman took next door to a smaller single
bedroom.

He then disappeared immediately, showing that Tarquin
and Eva's instincts had been correct. Tamra had learnt from
Lady Margaret that the correct procedure for a guest staying
in a country house was to tip the staff on the last day, not as
they went along, and all of the new employees at Stanclere
Hall had been firmly instructed that any lingering, that silent
moment of stasis where a hotel worker indicated by stilling
their body and smiling hopefully that they were waiting for a
tip, would be considered a sackable offence.

'Oh, look at the bathroom!' Milly heard Eva exclaiming
from down the hall – *far* down the hall – and she gritted her
teeth.

'I wouldn't have come if I knew there wasn't going to be a

bathroom en suite,' she said angrily to Tarquin. 'This is just
totally *slumming.*'

'Darling, no.' He enfolded her tenderly in his arms. 'Think
of the festivals – surely they're worse. No en-suite loos there!'

It was true that at Latitude, at Glastonbury and many, many
of the other festivals that Milly had attended with Tarquin, she
was sometimes required to queue up to use the Portaloos and
Port-a-Showers if they weren't staying in an RV. But what
Tarquin wasn't taking into account was that those toilets and
showers were in the Boutique Camping area of the VIP backstage section, that Milly was sleeping in a top-of-the-line yurt
with wooden floors, wooden beds with Egyptian cotton sheets,
thick-pile towels, dressing mirrors, and handily located power
points for her heated eyelash curling irons and hair tongs.
They were the most luxurious accommodation available at
festivals, giving Milly a huge advantage over almost all the
other women there; she could emerge from her yurt looking
ready for a modelling shoot, having slept wonderfully on a
proper mattress, all her clothes fresh from hangers rather than
crumpled on a tent floor.

At a festival, when they stayed in those boutique yurts,
Milly was at the top of the pecking order, just how she liked
it. Here at Stanclere Hall, she was very much at the bottom.

*It's as if Tamra's deliberately put me where it's going to be
really hard to get dressed and ready and all done-up,* Milly realized as she surveyed the bathroom which, like Edmund's,
was unnecessarily, even mockingly huge, considering that
its entire contents were a sink, a towel rail and a bath with
a rickety showerhead above it and a plastic curtain running
round it which was bound to stick to the occupant clammily
as they tried to soap themselves. The toilet was next door,
and had a wooden seat (*very* unhygienic in Milly's opinion),
old blue and white tiles, and an ancient chain with a ceramic

handle that matched the tiles, sending Tarquin and Eva into fresh ecstasies of appreciation and making Milly's palm itch to slap them both.

She was in such a bad mood when she and Tarquin returned to their room after exploring the facilities that she made Tarquin go down on her for a good twenty minutes and then told him that he'd have to bring himself off if he wanted to come, because she still wasn't relaxed enough to do it for him. His mute expression of disappointment and frustration – because she knew that he was much too gentlemanly to lie there and do it in front of her, and from the door-banging down the corridor as other guests all scrambled for the loo and bathroom before dinner, he'd be lucky to get into either one of those and have a private moment before his erection dissipated – cheered her up enough for her to get up and start the elaborate process of dressing and doing her hair and make-up to look as artlessly charming as if she had spent the afternoon wandering through an apple orchard in fairyland.

Her better mood lasted, however, only until she realized that the one power outlet in the room was situated next to the bed, miles away from the huge cheval mirror. Any chance for Tarquin to finish himself off was lost as he scrambled to drag the heavy mirror, squeaking and groaning, across the creaking floorboards, Milly cursing like a sailor. She broke off the swearing to tell him that by tomorrow he'd have to get her an extension cord or she was walking out of this bloody fucking shitheap, and added grimly that she was willing to bet that Tamra, Brianna Jade and the VIP guests had en-suite bathrooms with rain-shower wet rooms and slipper baths, plus walk-in dressing rooms with adjustable lighting and power points next to the dressing tables. In which supposition she was absolutely right.

Milly would have been much happier, however, to know

that Brianna Jade was in almost as miserable a mood as she was at that moment. It wasn't just that the Countess-to-be was in a high state of nerves about the upcoming party, though that was certainly the case; understandably so, as it was shaping up to be one of the high points in the autumn high-society calendar. Royalty was coming, in the person of Princess Sophie, who was Lady Margaret's goddaughter and particularly close to her, as Princess Sophie's mother had died tragically young and Lady Margaret had been the nearest thing to a substitute. The presence of a royal princess naturally elevated the entire event to a whole other level, including security precautions. The footman stationed at the entrance checking the guest list was actually part of Sophie's protection detail, and the grounds of the Hall were full of lurking, black-clad men talking to each other on Bluetooth earpieces, as Brianna Jade had found out when she fled the Hall for refuge as her mother and fiancé engaged in a shouting match earlier that day.

It had been Edmund who started the fight, though quite inadvertently. He had simply been reassuring his fiancée that she didn't need to worry, that the party would not only go smoothly with her mother and Lady Margaret and Mrs Hurley all supervising it, but that Brianna Jade would not be called on to host many events like this in the future.

'We really don't go in for this kind of thing that much,' he'd said, sitting next to her on one of the new smart outdoor sofas on the terrace; they were trying to keep away from the inside of the Hall, as it was in such a bustle that you fell over someone as soon as you tried to take two steps. 'Honestly, my parents barely threw parties at all. We'd have people over to dinner, but that's more like the sort of thing you've been to already around the County, twenty people for drinks and dinner, and most of them ones you've known for donkey's years. Noting remotely on *this* scale, I promise!'

Brianna Jade and Edmund had been apart for several weeks now, and their reunion two days ago had been very welcome for both of them; they realized that they had missed each other, their growing companionship, Brianna Jade's increasing interest in the Hall's farmland and piggeries, and their physical connection, which they were both definitely enjoying. Edmund, who had not had a girlfriend for a long time, had thrown himself into the joys of regular sex with gusto, and there was a sense with both of them that they were very happily making up for lost time; the weeks apart had been frustrating, and they had had sex both nights and again before breakfast today, as Edmund had woken up with what, to his fiancée's great amusement, he called a 'morning glory'.

So everything was going very well on the engagement front. It was the social side of things that was giving Brianna Jade what Mrs Hurley picturesquely called the collywobbles, and all Edmund had meant to do was to try to reassure her that he certainly didn't expect her to organize huge house parties as an essential part of her duty as a Countess.

'*Excuse me?*' however, had been the biting response from someone who definitely *did* expect that from Brianna Jade. Tamra, who had been supervising the setting up of the bar in the morning room that led onto the terrace, stormed outside with a clicking of her high heels and a jingling of jewellery, placing her hands on the smooth curves of her hips and snapping that she hadn't spent all this money on doing up Stanclere Hall for the benefit of a few old farts from Rutland who wouldn't appreciate the taste levels she'd brought to the task if you buried them alive in a pile of *Architectural Digests* and *Style Interiors*.

'Tamra, I do appreciate everything you've done, and are doing,' Edmund had said, manfully standing up and confronting the gloriously angry virago before him. 'But you do need to realize that Brianna Jade and I may have a different way of doing things—'

'A *different way?*' Tamra had positively screeched. 'No no *no*! There is no damn different way! I didn't cross the Atlantic and work my way into high society and then throw millions at this place so you and BJ could cut yourselves off here! No *way*! This place is a *showpiece* now, or it will be when I get finished, and showpieces get *shown off*! I want to see BJ in *Tatler* every other month, throwing some party or some charity benefit here! *Definitely* hunt balls – Lady Margaret says people love those, and BJ wants to go hunting now—'

'I wouldn't mind that,' Brianna Jade had said quickly, eager to appease her mother; Tamra rarely went into full screaming mode, but when she did, she flattened everyone around her to the ground as if she were a tornado. 'I can't wait to get good enough at jumps to start drag hunting.'

It was like yelling into the wind: her mother didn't hear a word she said. The extraordinary thing was that Edmund wasn't just finding something Tamra was screaming about to agree with and apologizing profusely, as everyone else had always done in the past. Uniquely, he was standing there, his arms akimbo, his legs planted wide and solidly, shouting back at her. Brianna Jade had never seen anything like it in her life. Even Ken Maloney had ducked and begged for mercy on the few occasions Hurricane Tamra hit land.

'I refuse to let you simply dictate what happens in my house!' Edmund was barking, suddenly very much the Earl of Respers on his ancestral land. 'I and my wife will make our own decisions—'

'*Please*, this was *not* the deal!' Tamra interrupted. 'If I have to come down here every month and throw the parties myself, I will!' She tossed back her mane of glowing hair, narrowed her dark eyes and stared at Edmund with absolute challenge, not remotely intimidated by his status. While Edmund, arms still folded, jaw set, seemed to have decided that this was the moment he put his foot down once and for all.

'Actually that might not be such a bad idea, Edmund,' Brianna Jade tried once more. 'I mean, if Mom wants to do the organizing ... that's the bit I get worried about being able to do myself. I *like* parties, it's just putting them together I'm not so hot at.'

'I am very grateful to you, Tamra, but that does not confer a sense of automatic obligation!' Edmund said, going into pompous-aristo mode and completely ignoring his fiancée. 'If I need to put my foot down on this, I will!'

'Your foot? You can shove your big old foot in that hole in the roof over the east wing any time you want, to stop it leaking!' Tamra screamed back. 'Or you can recall that we made a deal – I want to see my daughter as high up in society as she deserves to be, and *you* need to get that damn roof fixed!'

'Your daughter is about to become my wife,' Edmund snapped back, 'and I *think* you'll find that when she and I are married—'

But Brianna Jade didn't stay to find out how Edmund planned to finish that sentence. Impressed as she was that he was the only person who'd ever been able to take on her mom, she disliked conflict so much that she always avoided it if it was remotely possible. She would almost rather Edmund had buckled under pressure from Tamra, like everyone else. This unexpected side of him actually made her uncomfortable. She had been easing her way across the terrace, unnoticed by either of them, and as she turned to slip down the stone steps the battle royale raged on above her, not requiring her presence at all.

Which was ironic, she reflected, because what they were fighting about was her; her wishes, her social status. However, neither of them was even bothering to ask her to contribute to the debate. Brianna Jade thought a compromise could easily be achieved, but, as she could tell, this wasn't about finding a compromise. It was, as they'd put it in the States, Tamra and Edmund throwing down.

She sighed. It was totally normal for Tamra to want to be in charge; she always did. Her daughter had imagined her married life with Edmund as being run, to some degree, by her mother, who would drop in regularly to tell the two of them how things should be done, and she'd thought that Edmund would be fine with that, because of the way he'd wholeheartedly approved of Tamra's makeover of Stanclere Hall. The revelation that Edmund was prepared to push back as hard as Tamra came at him was a very unwelcome shock for his fiancée. Many women would have been very pleased that their fiancés could stand up to their mothers. But Brianna Jade, who basically thought that all her mother's decisions were correct, didn't need a husband to fight her battles for her.

Because I don't have any battles. And I just hate fighting and quarrels and people yelling at each other. What if they go on like this for our whole lives? What a nightmare that would be!

And, of course, she was freaking out about the Barb situation more and more as well. Because Brianna Jade was increasingly worried that her strategy for dealing with Barb – keep her sweet till the wedding and, hopefully, the *Style Bride* cover – was beginning to wear as threadbare as Edmund's grandmother's towel. Money once a month wasn't enough: after being deluged with phone calls just two weeks after the initial Western Union transfer, Brianna Jade had had to make another payment on the clear understanding that Barb was never to ring the Hall phone again.

Barb now had Brianna Jade's mobile and her email, and she used both mercilessly to pressure her target into sending money every fortnight. Brianna Jade had managed to plead the difficulty of getting that big a sum without her mother knowing, to which Barb had responded instantly that she could give a shit about Tamra's being aware of what was going on: in fact, Brianna Jade *should* tell Tamra straight away, in order to ensure access to the principal bank account, and not just the pocket money that Tamra gave her daughter.

That tactic had backfired on Barb, however. Brianna Jade had become so hysterical that Barb had been forced to back off, at least temporarily. Tamra was not to know about this, Brianna Jade had screamed, and if Barb made any attempt to get in touch with her, Brianna Jade would have Barb killed – she wasn't joking. Ken Maloney hadn't become the Fracking King without breaking a *lot* of heads, and it wouldn't be at all difficult to find the people at Maloney Drill who wouldn't take at all well to someone trying to drag Ken's adopted daughter through the mud ...

Brianna Jade honestly didn't know where she'd got all this from: TV shows, maybe? Certainly she'd never heard a word about this kind of thing from Ken or her mom. But fracking didn't exactly have the best reputation – even Ken had admitted occasionally that some people who'd been, as it were, fracked, had had a tad of a rough deal, what with their water supply being all messed up and the gas fires breaking out. When Tamra had taken over, she had determined to move Maloney Drill in a much more environmentally friendly direction. It was out of self-interest, of course, as well as moral principle: Tamra was very well aware that if she wanted to relocate to the UK, with the anti-fracking movement so strong there, she'd have to reframe herself as a force for good, the figurehead of an energy company that no longer drilled near people's homes, dirtied their drinking water and set off gas explosions.

No question, however, that when Ken Maloney had been in charge, Maloney Drill, like almost all other energy companies, had practised tactics so dirty they amounted to black ops. This threat, which had popped out of Brianna Jade's mouth on hearing Barb trying to drag Tamra into her blackmail, did actually hold Barb for a while. Maybe it wasn't the threat itself so much as Brianna Jade's sheer fury. Barb might have decided that pushing her victim too far would mean that even if Barb wasn't killed, the golden goose would be: after all, Barb's revelation to the tabloids, her selling of the pictures of Brianna Jade in her pigskin jacket and Pork Queen sash, would be a big payday, but only a one-off. After that, nothing. Whereas if she kept milking Brianna Jade, and managed to keep her greed under control, she could maintain a steady income for the rest of her life ...

That was, at least, what Brianna Jade was hoping Barb had decided. But she was perpetually on edge nowadays, nervous about Barb changing her mind or deciding to contact Tamra through the offices of Maloney Drill, and the only time Brianna Jade could really relax, for some reason, was at the piggeries. Her footsteps had taken her automatically to her usual jogging route, or rather to the destination at the Hall in which she felt happiest and most secure. She crossed the bridge over the lake – the cracked stone had now been repaired, and Tamra had planned an elaborate set of photos on the bridge to be taken tomorrow for *Tatler* – vaguely noticing the rustles in the shrubbery as she passed, mutters and hisses as various protection officers communicated with each other to the effect that the Earl's fiancée was heading out for a walk and to stand down full alert. Princess Sophie was due to arrive in four hours and the officers were on patrol, staking out what they called 'areas of vulnerability'.

Princess Sophie due to arrive! The mere idea gave Brianna Jade heart palpitations. She had seen the princess before, at a party in London, and once in Loulou's, where Tamra had taken her before Brianna Jade went to the Cotswolds. Sophie looked intimidatingly thin, confident and haughty, though Lady Margaret had assured Brianna Jade that since Sophie's older brother, Prince Hugo, had married Princess Chloe and settled down to happy married life, Sophie had become considerably more friendly and approachable, a much needed change from her wild-child past. Brianna Jade hadn't quite understood how this alteration had been effected – something to do with Chloe's calming influence, though it didn't seem quite plausible that a new sister-in-law who had dated Sophie's brother for donkey's years should have had such an effect.

But Lady Margaret, who was always not only truthful but as blunt as a sledgehammer to the head, wouldn't sugarcoat anything for Brianna Jade; if she said that Sophie's manners and temperament had improved considerably since the days that she taunted her brother's then girlfriend for being a commoner, Brianna Jade could, as they said in the States, take that to the bank. It helped a little, but not a lot.

The thought of Princess Sophie, third in line to the British throne, arriving in the middle of an epic battle raging between Brianna Jade's fiancé and her mother, was enough to make the poor Countess-to-be, stuck in the middle with nobody listening to her, want to run away and hide out with another titled female. Brianna Jade was going to visit the Empress of Stanclere for the second time that day, scratch her back just where she liked it best, and pretend that she'd never have to go back to the Hall, dress up in sapphire Balenciaga and act as if she truly had anything to do with hosting this house party ...

'Brianna!' Abel, pushing an empty wheelbarrow which had until recently been full of slops, came round the corner of the pigshed and stopped dead at the sight of her. 'What're you doing here, then? You came by this morning already!'

'You really need to get some WD-40 on that wheel,' Brianna Jade said in a small voice.

Abel took in her expression, dropped the handles of the barrow and strode over to her, two big paces of his long legs enough to bring him to her side.

'You can't be here all dressed up smart like that, Brianna,' he said, shaking his head in emphasis. 'You'll get all mucky.'

Brianna Jade, who was on the verge of tears – something about seeing Abel's familiar, looming figure had made her want to cry – looked down at her outfit of pale blue silk-cashmere sweater, skinny jeans and pale gold suede Tremp loafers and huffed a laugh, instantly feeling a bit better. For her, this was everyday casual wear, stuff she pulled on after working out to hang around the Hall, but Abel was quite right about her look-ing smart, especially when she knew what the clothes had cost. The loafers alone, handmade for her and Tamra at the Tremp factory in Italy, were deceptively simple, their suede butter-soft, the label an in-the-know fashion secret: everyone knew about Tod's, but Tremp was for true fashion insiders.

'Your pretty little shoes!' Abel said, almost in wonder. 'They're like slippers! You can't walk through the muck to see the Empress in those. Here, come round to the cottage. Me and Gran'll give you some cider, that'll pick you up.'

He led her down a path she had noticed before but never taken. It ran down the other side of the piggeries, alongside the orchards where the pigs were let loose to forage for windfalls: the blossoms were long fallen, the heady scent of ripe apples and pears was faded, but the trees were still beautiful, the grass thick, and the sight of them calmed Brianna Jade further. By the time they reached the cottage, she was breathing regularly, no longer worried that she might burst into tears, and was able to exclaim in delight at how pretty it was. Wisteria climbed around its red-painted door and around the windows with their matching red shutters. It was like something from a fairy tale.

'Oh wow, you have a thatched roof!' she said, gazing up at it. 'That's so pretty! I feel like I'm in Hansel and Gretel or something.'

'No nasty witches here,' Abel said cheerfully, 'and the thatch is a right bugger, I can tell you. Looks lovely, but it costs Mr Edmund a fortune to keep up. We've got a thatcher in the village who's at it nonstop going round our cottages tightening all the roofs up – they need it once a year, and it's not a small job. Got to be cleaned all by hand, as well, you can't use rakes. The tourists love a thatched roof but that's 'cause they don't have to look after it. Backbreaking, it is.'

He grinned at her as he pushed the door open and stood back, gesturing for her to enter the cottage as he knocked the mud off his boots on the scraper outside. Brianna Jade, built on queenly lines, had to duck as she went in, and she couldn't help turning, once inside the tiny entrance hall, to watch Abel bending his entire head down to make his way into his home.

'I grew up here,' he said, knowing exactly what she was looking at, his grin deepening. 'Used to it by now, I am. But I had a big growth spurt when I was fourteen, and for a whole year I had a bruise right over my forehead like a line, where I kept walking into the lintels—'

Their bodies almost filled the hall, as if they were playing Sardines. Brianna Jade felt suddenly awkward, crammed in here with him; she smelt the light odour of pig on his clothes, a faint scent of his own fresh sweat, and found herself blushing and looking around for some space; her chest was nearly pressed into the big brass fasteners of his overalls.

'Kitchen's there,' Abel said efficiently, nodding sideways, and she crab-scuttled into the room with relief. It wasn't big

either, but she could sink into a wooden chair, one of two
pulled up at the table, which was painted the same colour as
the shutters and front door.

'I like red,' he said just as efficiently, reading her mind.
'Gran says I should have more yellow in here, to brighten up
the place on winter mornings, but the red always puts a smile
on my face. And I do a whitewash of the walls every spring, so
it's bright enough for me.'

Brianna Jade looked around the kitchen, whose walls were
certainly gleaming white. But then, everything gleamed, from
the modern white laminate fitted cabinets to the chrome top
of the compact stove and the glass of the cupboard against the
back wall where the good china was displayed. In the centre
of the table was even a bunch of yellow carnations, prettily
arranged in a cut-glass vase.

'It's really nice, Abel,' she said respectfully.

'Oh, you're seeing it at its best,' he told her. 'It's Gran's day
to pop round and tidy up for me, that's why it's so spick and
span. Where is she? Gran!' he yelled, his bellow so loud that
the china rattled in the cupboards. 'Where've you got to, then?
We have company!'

By this time, Brianna Jade was fully expecting a silver-
haired little lady in a gingham dress and apron, wearing round
wire glasses, to emerge; it was quite a disappointment when
the only point in common between her imaginings and Abel's
grandmother turned out to be that she was small. There was
a pattering of light, fast steps on the stairs, and a diminutive
figure bustled into the kitchen, dressed not unlike Brianna
Jade herself in a fitted sweater and skinny jeans, her hair cut
short and artfully blonde-streaked to balance the white, her
small features neatly made-up, and a duster in one hand which
she put down on seeing Brianna Jade standing up politely at
her entrance.

'My, you're a beauty, aren't you?' she said approvingly, looking the guest up and down without a hint of embarrassment
or deference. 'I heard you were like something off the telly,
but I thought everyone was egging the pudding. And I don't
read those gossip magazines, I've got better things to do with
my time. Abel, you never said the young lady was like a beauty
queen!'

Abel ducked his head forward again, this time shaking his
hair over his face as much as he could to conceal his blushes.

'Gran, *please* . . .' he muttered, shuffling his feet.

'Mr Edmund's done well, hasn't he,' his grandmother continued, quite unabashed. 'Money *and* good looks! We'll have
some downright gorgeous heirs up at the Hall soon, won't we?'

Now it was Brianna Jade who was blushing, and Abel lum-
bered over to the fridge, pulled out a big quart bottle and
busied himself filling glasses, his back turned to the room.

'It's lovely to meet you, Mrs Wellbeloved,' Brianna Jade said
politely, her hand held out. She knew that Abel's father was
dead, and his mother living in Wales with her new husband;
she and Abel had covered many subjects in their near daily
chats by the piggeries. And she remembered him saying that
his grandmother lived in a modern flat in Stanclere village,
preferring not to be miles away from most amenities down a
dirt track in the middle of the countryside.

'You too, miss,' Mrs Wellbeloved said, shaking Brianna
Jade's hand with a wiry grip. 'It's a pleasure to meet you. Abel
said you're right fond of the pigs, and all I can say is, rather you
than me. I couldn't wait to get away from them, nasty hairy
smelly things. Not that I mind a nice side of bacon, though!'

She winked at Brianna Jade. 'Sit back down, miss, do,' she
added, pulling up the other chair herself. 'Abel can stand –
won't do him any harm, lazy lump that he is!'

Brianna Jade started to protest at how hard Abel worked,

but instantly saw that his grandmother was joking by the loving look she shot her grandson, and obeyed docilely instead, duly sitting back down.

'But what're you doing here, then?' Mrs Wellbeloved asked, her bright eyes intent. 'There's the biggest to-do I ever remember happening up at the Hall. It's a party for you, isn't it? And here you are drinking cider instead with young Abel and me – shouldn't you be up there with the gentry?'

'It's a right old to-do, Gran, that's a fact,' Abel said with unexpected smoothness, setting down brimming pint glasses of cloudy golden cider in front of the two women. 'And Bri – *miss* – just needed a moment away from it all, what with her mum and Mrs Hurley running around like madwomen on a rampage. She's got Princess Sophie coming in later, believe it or not! You can imagine what it's like up there, can't you?'

Brianna Jade met Abel's eyes with almost wondering thanks at his understanding of her situation; he knew, of course, how nervous the party was making her, as they'd talked about it increasingly as the event came closer, but this summary of what she was going through made her feel as if a weight had been lifted off her shoulders.

He smiled back at her with great sweetness and said, 'A trouble shared's a trouble halved,' and nodded at the glass, picking up his own. 'Here, let's toast to happiness all round, a new Countess up at the Hall, and one of the best batches of cider I've ever made. Mostly Sweet Coppin and Court Royal apples, it is. Little bit of Stoke Red in too, to give it a bit of bite.'

'Nice and sweet, is it then, Abel?' his grandmother said gleefully, picking up her glass. 'You know I like it sweet.'

It was sweet as sugar and utterly delicious. Never had Brianna Jade drunk cider like this back home in the States, where they sold it in gallon jars at farmers' markets and the State Fairs. It was so good she drank practically the whole glass down in one go, relishing the rich taste, and when she set it down again on the table and looked up, licking her lips and beaming, she was taken aback by the appalled expressions on both Abel and Mrs Wellbeloved's faces.

'My life, miss,' Mrs Wellbeloved said, goggling at her. 'You can certainly hold your drink. I never saw the like from a young lady like you!'

'My *what*?' Brianna Jade realized that her smile was ridiculously wide and her head was spinning. Almost as if – no, *exactly* as if – she stared at the glass, suddenly realizing what had just happened.

'Wait,' she said. 'There's *alcohol* in cider over here?'

Both Abel and his grandmother collapsed with laughter. Abel had to put both his massive hands on the table to brace himself, his shoulders were shaking so hard, his messy thatch of hair falling forward over his face: his deep bass rumble and Mrs Wellbeloved's high giggle filled the small room, the table rocking as Abel's shoulders heaved. Brianna Jade looked in amazement at the foamy residue left in the glass: gingerly, she put out a finger, wiped up some foam and licked at it, which sent both Wellbeloveds into fresh spasms. Mrs Wellbeloved had, eventually, to reach for a clean tea towel to wipe her eyes, dabbing cautiously to avoid smudging her navy blue mascara.

'Oh, miss, *thank* you,' she said in heartfelt tones, still chuckling. 'I haven't laughed so hard since Abel fell over in the mucky pigpen some years back and the pigs tried to eat the overalls right off him! He kept trying to get up and slipping over 'em and falling back down – oh dear, that'll set me off again if I don't watch it. Better than the telly, it was.'

Abel raised his head, his cheeks pink, his eyes bright; he shook back his hair, a very characteristic gesture of his, probably because his hands were often so dirty that he didn't want to use them to push it off his face. His hazel eyes, Brianna Jade thought tipsily, were twinkling, which was a funny word, but fitted perfectly.

Not in the least perturbed by his grandmother's teasing, he said to Brianna Jade: 'You mean cider isn't boozy in America?'

'No, it isn't. It really isn't,' Brianna Jade said, slurring her words a little. 'You can get it in *Starbucks*!'

The cider, however, made the last word come out as 'Shtarbucksh', and set both the Wellbeloveds off again. Abel's eyes were tearing up too by the time he eventually calmed down, his enormous chest still heaving with laughter.

'Ten per cent, that cider is, my l— *miss*,' he said, knuckling his eyes hard. 'And you just drinking it down like it was nothing!'

'Oh dear, and she'll need to get back soon,' his grandmother added, looking at the clock. 'What with royalty arriving! I must say, miss, you and your mum've done wonders for the Hall and Mr Edmund. I don't mind saying we were all getting worried he'd have to sell it off to a hotel chain or something. We heard Mr Edmund had someone come from the National Trust to look it over, and they wouldn't touch it with a barge-pole. They've got too much on their plate as it is, and they said we didn't have enough history.'

A long, dismissive sniff showed exactly what Mrs Well-beloved thought of this slur on Stanclere Hall.

'But now it's like a palace, they say, and you've got Princess Sophie coming to stay!' she continued, her eyes gleaming. 'Ooh, if we had Prince Hugo and Princess Chloe visiting the Hall, I think I'd die happy that night. Do you think ...?'

She looked hopefully across the table at Brianna Jade, who opened her mouth to say that she had no idea, that Lady Margaret had been the motor to bring Princess Sophie to Stanclere Hall, but burped instead.

'Oh *dear*!' Mrs Wellbeloved exclaimed, as Abel stifled a laugh. 'She's in no state to get back, is she? You can see the young lady isn't used to drinking much, can't you?'

'I'm *not*,' Brianna Jade agreed seriously. 'That's Mom. Mom can hold her liquor, but I can't. I feel all wobbly.'

Mrs Wellbeloved tutted. 'She needs to lie down and then have some nice strong coffee,' she said to her grandson. 'I'd say she should do it here, but they'll be worrying about her back at the Hall, I shouldn't wonder. And it's not really proper, is it, the Earl's fiancée sleeping it off under your roof, Abel.'

'Isn't proper having her get drunk on cider here either, Gran, come to that,' Abel observed, grinning. 'Don't worry, I'll get her back safe and sound. Come on, miss.'

He put one huge hand under Brianna Jade's elbow and guided her gently to her feet; she stumbled, her head still dizzy from the strong cider, and was very grateful for Abel's close presence as he walked her from the kitchen, manoeuvred her through the little hall and outside. The fresh, chilly air helped, and she took in deep breaths, but then that made her feel dizzier, which made her stumble against Abel again and giggle, and she felt him shake his head above her.

'She'll never walk it, not if we're in a hurry,' he said thoughtfully. 'Gran, take her arm while I go and get the wheelbarrow.'

'*Abel Wellbeloved!*' his grandmother positively screeched. 'You can't take the Earl's fiancée back to the Hall in a wheelbarrow like a drunk sleeping off a night at the pub!'

'Thought you might say that,' he said, bending down and sweeping Brianna Jade into his arms as easily as if she were a child. 'Nothing for it then. I can't take her on the motorbike, can I? For a start she can't hold on properly, and then I'd have to loop all around the roads when it's ten minutes back to the Hall on foot. I'll carry her back and say she turned her ankle walking in her little slipper shoes if anyone asks.'

'Oh *dear*,' Mrs Wellbeloved wailed. 'Well, it's better than a wheelbarrow, and that's all that can be said for it. It was a real treat to meet you, miss, and congratulations on your engagement ...'

Brianna Jade's eyes were closed; after the momentary surprise of being swept off her feet, she had almost instantly relaxed into Abel's arms. She was very tired, she realized. It was blissful to shut her eyes and let someone else look after her. And she much preferred this to a wheelbarrow. There was something so reassuring about Abel, such a sense that he could cope in a crisis, that she didn't make the slightest protest about him carrying her back or how heavy she must be. The only thing she did mumble, her eyelashes fluttering up as his strong frame jounced her along, was: 'Abel, you called me "miss", and we said ...'

'Couldn't rightly call you by your name in front of my gran,' he said simply. 'She'd've raised the roof.'

That was more than reasonable. Brianna Jade nodded, closed her eyes and actually dropped off to sleep for a little while. Her nose was smooshed into the cotton of his undershirt, which smelt of soap powder, pig and himself, maybe not quite in that order, and was a little scratchy: *he needs to use fabric conditioner*, she thought as she dozed off. *But I guess men never think to buy it.* Abel maintained a steady pace, his rubber-soled work boots quiet even on the stone of the bridge, and it was as reassuring as being driven home in the back seat of a car after a party when you were small, falling asleep knowing your mom would get you home safe – though actually Abel's arms were more comfortable than the bouncing suspension of Tamra's ancient Hyundai, and his regular breathing considerably more peaceful than the rickety turnover of its engine.

I must remember to tell him that, he'll think it's funny, she thought drowsily, suspended in slumber, hearing him murmur over her head that the young Countess-to-be had slipped out walking and might have turned her ankle, so he was carrying her back just to be on the safe side, the background buzz of the Bluetooth earpiece an indication that Abel was addressing one of the protection officers.

The backgrounds of all the Stanclere employees who lived on the grounds had of course been cleared well before Princess Sophie's arrival, so the officer already knew Abel's identity. He could be heard muttering the information into his neck mike to his colleagues as Abel cleared the shrubbery and took a looping path around the edge of the lawns, pretty much hidden from the Hall by the massive oak trees; he was making a circuitous route so that he could deposit Brianna Jade at a rarely used side door and, hopefully, conceal her tipsy state from its inhabitants. And dusk had fallen now; they were quite unobserved as he reached the door, shifted her weight to free one hand, and checked that the door was unlocked.

'Here we are,' he said, tilting her down to the ground and holding her by her waist to steady her. 'Back home safe. You'd best take a nap, if there's time, and then get Mrs Hurley to make you a good strong pot of coffee.'

'Thanks, Abel.' Brianna Jade flashed him a gorgeous smile, and though he was used to these by now, the wattage had never been at such close range; instantly, he dropped his hands and took a step back as if she had burnt him. 'I can't believe you got me drunk!' she went on. 'That's so bad of you!'

She reached out to slap his arm playfully, missed and wobbled dangerously: Abel had to catch her again to steady her. She giggled tipsily, rocking back on her heels; the giggle turned into a yawn, her perfect teeth sparkling white, the ribbed roof of her pink mouth showing as she tilted back her head, arching her spine, the points of her breasts pressing against the blue sweater, almost touching his dungarees.

'I feel all woozy,' she said, sounding surprised. 'Ooh, Abel, you're so *naughty* to get me drunk!'

Abel writhed; still holding her with one hand, he reached out to push the side door open.

'You should get some coffee,' he said urgently. 'And have a cold shower.'

'And you carried me all the way back,' she said, still slurring her words. 'Oh hey, was I real heavy?' Her eyes opened wide with the classic exaggerated panic of someone under the influence. 'All the way from your cottage! Your arms must be so sore!'

'Don't you worry about that,' Abel said quickly. 'I'm used to carrying pigs around. Oh, I didn't mean—'

Brianna Jade giggled so loudly at this that he actually stepped forward and put a hand over her mouth to keep her quiet.

'Ssh! Everyone will hear!' he hissed. 'Look, go inside and get yourself into a cold shower, fast as you can.'

Nodding, eyes owlishly wide, Brianna Jade turned and went inside, steadying herself with a hand on the corridor wall. Abel closed the door behind her, but didn't walk away: instead he stood, staring at the closed door with its glass panes at eye level, watching her go down the corridor. Only when she had vanished from sight did he turn and retrace his steps back to his cottage, quite unaware that Milly, whose room was on the floor above, had been having a cigarette out of the window, curled up in the embrasure seat, and had heard the entire exchange.

Chapter Fourteen

There was no way Brianna Jade was ready to greet Princess
Sophie and her small entourage of friends when she arrived.
But mercifully for Brianna Jade, Tamra had already decided
that lining up everyone to meet the princess would look over-
needy and self-conscious. Instead, she and Lady Margaret were
sitting by the fire in the Great Hall, drinking cocktails and listening to the pianist play a witty medley of the latest R&B hits
arranged into easy-listening lounge music versions when Sophie,
her friends Lady Araminta Farquhar-Featherstonehaugh –
known as Minty – and Dominic de Rohan, Edmund's best
man, swept in, followed by Sophie's two protection officers.
The new arrivals promptly stopped dead and oohed and aahed
at the amazing transformation Tamra had effected at
Stanclere. The candles flickered in their silver branches, their
golden light reflected in the huge mirror over the fireplace,
and in others carefully positioned around the walls, even managing to pick out interesting details in the enormous and
rather boring tapestry of a hunt that hung opposite the fireplace. Behind Tamra and Lady Margaret, as they rose to their
feet, the fire itself crackled in welcome, and the pianist, on

strict instructions, only rose for a second in protocol before re-seating himself and continuing to play the lounge arrangement of Rihanna's 'Umbrella'.

'You should *totally* come and redecorate Buck House!' Sophie said to Tamra, kissing her on either cheek. 'My God, it looks simply fabulous! What does old Ed think of it?'

'*Old Ed?* Good Lord, Sophie, he's only thirty-four,' Lady Margaret said indulgently to her adorably pretty goddaughter.

'He always seems so much older to me!' Sophie, in her mid-twenties, said irrepressibly. '*Awfully* mature. Oh, hi, Ed!'

'Hi, Soph,' Edmund said, grinning at her as he came lightly down the stairs. 'I left my cane down here – do let me know if you happen to see it, or my false teeth. I'm getting so senile, I took them out and can't remember for the life of me where I put them.'

A maid appeared carrying a silver tray of frosted whisky sours and lemon drops: Sophie, Minty and Dominic took off their coats, handed them to a waiting footman – a real one, not a pro-tection officer in disguise – and fell on the drinks with gusto.

'God, this is bliss!' Sophie said, toasting Tamra. 'I can see you're going to spoil us rotten. We obviously need *way* more Americans coming over here and smartening us up! Honestly, if I weren't so keen on Chloe I'd be telling Hugo to divorce her pronto and snap up Brianna Jade instead.'

This was clearly so kindly meant that even Lady Margaret, who knew perfectly well how vile Sophie had been to her sister-in-law before the wedding, smiled at Sophie as Edmund greeted Dominic, an old schoolfriend of his, with a hearty man-hug and a slap on the back.

'Congrats,' Dom muttered to his host, his eyes never leav-ing Tamra's glossy golden figure. 'My God, I can't wait to start charming your ma-in-law into bed. I'm ready for some hot cougar action!'

'Honestly, Dom! Show some respect!' Edmund hissed back. 'I'm taking Dom off for a quick game of billiards before dinner,' he said more loudly for public hearing. 'We've got time, haven't we? I know Brianna's running a little late.'

He cast an apologetic look at Tamra: they had both been horrified when they realized that Brianna Jade had fled the scene of their fight, had apologized to each other and promised formally to reach some sort of compromise between Tamra's lust for society glory and Edmund's for a quieter life. Edmund had pointed out that he was going along without a murmur with Tamra's lavish engagement and wedding party plans, including the fact that Jodie Raeburn from *Style* was arriving tomorrow to organize both a photo and a video shoot of the engagement celebrations for *Style*'s extremely successful website, which meant that Edmund would have to spend most of the day dolled up in designer tweed posing on the bridge with his fiancée or recreating the proposal in the gazebo. Tamra in return had given him credit for not only submitting to all that, but doing it uncomplainingly.

So now Tamra's glance back at him was just as apologetic. Edmund, of course, didn't know that his fiancée had accidentally got drunk on cider with her pig-farmer friend and his grandmother; that was a secret that certainly shouldn't be shared with Edmund. But Tamra blamed herself even more than Edmund for upsetting her daughter so much that she'd run to the piggeries for comfort.

'Brianna Jade'll be down in a little while for cocktails,' she said faux-casually, 'but yes, there should be plenty of time for a quick game of billiards—'

'You really are the most fantastically gorgeous creature I've ever seen in my *life*!' interrupted Dominic, taking her hand and kissing it theatrically, quite eclipsing Edmund behind him. The two men were the same height, with very similar builds, but Dominic was as dashing and flamboyant as Edmund was quiet and buttoned-up in his sober dark suit. Dominic had a showiness possessed by some posh men, a dashing dandy style that the unfamiliar might confuse, from a distance, with being gay. But the sheer intensity of the look Dominic was directing at Tamra made his sexual preferences more than clear. Tossing back his curly black hair in a way he knew made him look like a sexy pirate, he narrowed his sparkling dark eyes and then winked at her to boot.

'Steady, tiger,' Tamra said dryly, detaching her hand. 'Keep your powder dry.'

'Rrrr!' Dominic growled like a tiger, shaped both his hands into claws and dragged them through the air in Tamra's direction. 'I'm in love!'

Edmund, rolling his eyes, hooked his fingers through the collar of Dominic's shirt and dragged his friend away, mouthing, 'Sorry!' to Tamra, who smiled back at him: *Lord, that smile said, men have been hitting on me since I was fourteen, don't you worry about him. And honestly, he's pretty cute.*

'Dom's always had a thing for older women,' Lady Araminta said in a nasty pinched voice which came from a ribcage equally constricted by the tightness of her bodycon dress: Minty certainly had an enviably thin figure, if you were going for the heroin chic look, but perpetual starvation did not have a good effect on what was already a fairly unpleasant personality.

Lady Margaret slanted her eyes sideways to watch Tamra's reaction to this, her weatherbeaten face cracking into a smile as Tamra answered: 'Oh, bad luck for you! I bet that really pisses you off. Never mind – if you like 'em young, dumb and full of come there should be plenty to go round this weekend.'

She flashed her best dazzling smile at Minty for the briefest of seconds and then turned it off again. This was always a terrifyingly intimidating tactic, like a Gestapo interrogation light

wielded by a beauty queen, and even Lady Araminta, used to
the snubbing stares of the highest echelons of the British royal
family, wilted beneath it. Tamra turned to Sophie, clearly signalling that Minty had been dealt with, and saw that the
princess was giggling.

'That put you in your place, didn't it, Minters?' Sophie said
cheerfully. 'And I *love* "young, dumb and full of come"! That's
perfect for Dom.'

'He's actually the same age as Edmund,' Lady Margaret
observed. 'But Edmund's had all the responsibility of Stanclere
on his shoulders for yonks, of course. Had to grow up fast.
Makes a difference.'

'Shall I show you to your rooms?' Tamra asked Sophie and
Minty: Edmund's disappearance with Dom had demonstrated
his willingness to assign hostess duties to Tamra, so not even
Minty could accuse Tamra of overstepping her authority in
Stanclere Hall.

'That would be *lovely*,' Sophie said, linking her arm through
Tamra's and looking around for somewhere to put her empty
glass: a maid appeared instantly with a tray to place it on. 'I
hear you've got five-star hotel bathrooms to go with the rest
of the do-over.'

'Sadly no jacuzzis,' Tamra said, in a light, self-mocking tone.
'Which, as an American, makes me feel *totally* uncivilized, but
the plumbing just wasn't up to it. I *am* hoping to get a hot tub
on the terrace as soon as I can convince Edmund ...'

'Ha ha!' Sophie giggled appreciatively. '*So* funny! I'll have
a go at him too. Every stately home should *definitely* have a
hot tub.'

Lady Margaret, sinking back down onto her comfortable
velvet sofa by the fireplace, reaching for a cigarette, watched
her friend and protégée with great appreciation as Tamra
escorted Sophie up the stairs. Tamra's manner was exactly

right, remaining herself, poking fun at her American identity and her vast wealth while also unabashedly enjoying all the good things that her wealth brought. She entertained her friends while giving no ammunition to her enemies: it was the perfect tactic. Just now, she was adding: 'Oh yeah, and these stairs are hell in heels. I need to figure out where to put an elevator. Or two,' as Sophie cooed in agreement.

'Minty! Sophie! Darlings, there you are!' called a clear, bell-like voice from the gallery that ran along the half-height of the Great Hall, the extension of the staircase wings: it was Milly, an ethereally beautiful fairy figure in white lace almost the same shade as her skin. Tarte Bellini gel blush and rose-pink lipstick, together with a lot of dark brown mascara, gave her features definition. Even Tamra, narrowly assessing her with a quick, stiletto-like glance, had to admit that Milly's clothes and make-up were extremely successful. Milly had been clever enough to copy almost exactly the look that had worked so well on her shoot with Tarquin. It was a textbook example of knowing what suited you best, rather than trying to compete with someone else's style.

'Hi Milly,' Sophie said as Milly flitted up to them. 'God, you look pretty. Are you going to be in the photos tomorrow?'

'Of course!' Milly said brightly.

'I'm *so* looking forward to it,' Sophie continued, quite unaware of the rivalry between Milly and Brianna Jade. 'Daddy gets grumpy when I'm in the mags too much, but I love having my photo taken, and he *so* approves of old Ed that I totally get a free pass with this one. You *are* lucky to be able to do real fashion shoots,' she added glumly. 'I'd really love to be properly styled in all those wacky outfits.'

She stroked back her long straight blonde hair wistfully. Sophie would not have made a true high-fashion model – she was not quite tall enough, and her features were too pretty –

but she could certainly have worked in perfume or jewellery spreads, or done the kind of *Tatler* photo shoots that were based on a certain celebrity status.

'I'm *totally* banned from modelling,' she complained. 'Minters does some and I'm always madly jealous of her. Come up and talk to us while we get dressed, Milly?'

'There's champagne waiting in your room,' Tamra said to Sophie. 'And just let me know if you need more cocktails sent up while you change.'

'Oh God, the bliss!' Sophie sighed again as Tamra led her and Minty along the gallery in the opposite direction from which Milly had come, towards the newly refurbished wing of the house.

Milly fell back, looping her arm through Lady Araminta's. They had made friends some years ago on the party circuit, recognizing a fellow capacity for bitchiness and back stabbing that meant they were much better off partnering up rather than becoming rivals, and also quite aware of the fact that the similarity in their names made them better known in tandem than apart: it was a form of branding. Milly provided access to actors' gossip, Minty the inside track on the aristocratic circuit, so that between them they were much more powerful than they would have been separately.

It was an alliance rather than a friendship, but since neither of them had the capacity for the latter, the former suited both girls perfectly. And, in a perfect example of how they operated, Milly was brimming with information that she wanted Minty to diffuse throughout the house party.

'You're never going to *believe* what I overheard earlier!' she hissed delightedly. '*Le scandale!* Just *wait* till we're alone!'

Chapter Fifteen

But though Milly filled Minty in on what she had overheard a short time before, the gossip did not spread until the next day. Minty had wanted to start dispersing it instantly, but Milly was much too strategic for that. The atmosphere that evening was too quiet, and Milly had no intention of wasting her powder. Tamra had made it clear that she expected everyone to have a fairly sober Friday night so that they would be fresh and energetic for the photo shoot: Saturday evening, to compensate, would be a bacchanalia.

It hadn't been a hard rule to impose, as even the most well-connected aristocrats were eager to follow Sophie's lead and appear in *Style*, the most prestigious high fashion magazine in the world. And one look at Brianna Jade, glowing and gorgeous after her cold shower and pot of coffee, had made the English girls realize that they needed to be in bed by midnight at the latest, Clarins Beauty Flash Balm or Guerlain's Midnight Secret worked into their faces and only a few drinks working their way through their systems, so they wouldn't look puffy-eyed and hungover next to Brianna Jade's healthy blonde radiance. None of the Brits worked out regularly, preferring the Three C diet – coffee, cigarettes and coke – and though they were all wafer-slim, the difference in their skin tone and Brianna Jade's was noticeable.

'I need to go to the gym more,' Sophie sighed as they were being made up, staring at Brianna Jade's flawless golden complexion in the clear white autumn morning light. 'By which I mean at *all*.'

'Oh, it's not just working out. I go to the dermatologist every month too,' Brianna Jade assured her, incurably honest. 'And I get tons of facials. With extractions.'

'Ow, that sounds horrible,' Sophie said.

'It *is*. You have to go straight home afterwards and lie low, 'cause you have little red marks all over your face. But it cleans out all your pores. Especially on the nose.'

Sophie, in the next make-up chair to Brianna Jade, squinted in more closely at her hostess's nose.

'It looks very smooth,' she agreed.

'God, she's practically *poreless*,' sighed Gary Jordan, one of the top make-up artists in the country, who was working mascara into the inner corners of Brianna Jade's eyelashes, coating every single lash with great care and attention. 'It's like making up a china plate. *Love* her. Don't ever believe us when we say we don't love working on the pretty people best, because we *do*.'

The morning room had been set up as a make-up room for the shoot because of its high French windows that faced east onto the best light: hence its name. It was also big enough to accommodate the racks of clothes that the magazine stylists had brought. Autumn colours were the order of the day, since the shoot was not for the magazine – which would usually have to be planned months in advance – but for the website, so that the images could be uploaded in just a few days, post-Photoshopping.

The racks held warm rusts and lichens and deep umbers, glowing richly against the range of russet and chocolate tweeds: Jodie Raeburn was obsessed with tweeds for the current A/W season, and practically living in the Prada tweed A-line skirt which was pretty much the only piece from the range that she could wear. Since she had conquered the eating disorder that had taken her below a hundred pounds and to a life-threatening size zero, she had settled back to a UK ten to twelve, and though she was much happier and healthier at this size, she still stood by the racks fingering the size six tweed trouser suits wistfully.

'You can't wear those, you silly bitch,' Gary called over to her: he was famous for his absolute refusal to be deferential to anyone, and the fashion pack loved him for it. 'You're not a stick insect.'

'You don't know how much I'd give just to be able to put this on for a day,' Jodie said gloomily, lifting the trousers of one suit, softly checked mushroom and beige threaded with a hint of green. 'It's just so *now*.'

She looked over at the line of women in the make-up chairs: they were already mostly finished. The *Style* team had arrived pretty much at dawn, and they were all crack operators, used to working fast and perfectly. Jodie herself had flown in from Milan late last night, otherwise she would have stayed at the Hall.

'I do wish we could have gone more Seventies with the hair,' she said, assessing the nearly finished results. 'But I know that would have knocked it over into too-styled, and with Your Royal Highness in the mix—'

'Call me Sophie, *please*,' Her Royal Highness said firmly. 'I'd have loved a big bouff too, but Daddy would kill me if I looked like I was modelling.'

Gary sniffed. 'I'd've needed to bring a hairpiece,' he said, picking up a strand of Sophie's fine blonde hair. 'Even after I've teased it to buggery, you've got no body here at all.'

Even Jodie's eyes widened at this lèse-majesté, but Sophie had built up a very good rapport with Gary over the last hour and a half of hair and make-up, and she giggled at this.

'I *know*, it's such a bore,' she agreed. 'Me and Minty both! Look at Brianna Jade with all her fantastic American hair ... Milly, yours is pretty, I love your ringlets, but she's just got so much of it!'

Milly and Minty exchanged narrow glances of fury at Sophie singing Brianna Jade's praises, something that didn't escape the sharp-eyed Gary.

'Right, you're done,' he said, pulling away the black shoulder cape that had been fastened around Brianna Jade's neck to avoid any loose powder spilling on her dress. 'Fabulous, if I do say so myself!'

Brianna Jade was wearing tweed, a carefully selected, tailored Roland Mouret dress that skimmed her statuesque curves. The trouser suits were for Sophie and Minty, skinny enough to carry them off, while Milly had been styled in a loose lace blouse and tweed mini-shorts, worn over dark green tights and Isabel Marant ankle boots. Their make-up was discreet, their hair as Seventies as the stylists had been allowed to go, done in the faux-natural, blown-out look which suited everyone. Though they were all blondes, their styles were very different: Brianna Jade, buxom and glamorous, was beauty-pageant gorgeous next to Sophie and Minty's pretty, foxy-featured little faces and Milly's saucer-eyed flower fairy look.

'I'm really happy with this,' Jodie said calmly, which made every single *Style* employee and freelancer shiver with happiness; that phrase was her highest accolade. 'OK, the guys are all done. Let's get out on that bridge.'

The men were gathered on the terrace, Tarquin and

Edmund chatting pleasantly about the past shooting season, while Dominic and Lance, the drummer from Ormond and Co, lounged against the balustrade, smoking, their eyes fixed on the French doors through which the women would emerge. The videographer, who had already shot 'candid' moments of everyone during their hair and make-up – all the subjects perfectly aware of when the camera was on, naturally – was waiting on the terrace to capture the moment, stationed on the top step down so that she could also pan to the men and see their reaction, which was duly impressed. The four young women, perfectly well aware of how good they looked, walked out at a self-consciously slow pace, their blown-out hair bouncing on their shoulders, their smiles wide, turning to glance at each other because they knew it would make their blonde hair bounce even more effectively.

'Whoa, it's an all-blonde Charlie's Angels goes to the country,' drawled Dominic, coming off the balustrade and flourishing an elaborate bow. 'Miladies, allow me to compliment you on your get-ups.'

But then, behind them, Tamra could be seen, exchanging a word or two with Jodie, both of them hanging back to avoid being in the shot. Tamra was not in this video, which was all about the engaged couple and what *Style* would describe as their 'connected country set'. Still, being Tamra, she was dressed and made up as wonderfully as if she were styled for the shoot, in a tweed jacket over jeans tucked into Tremp russet patent high boots, glossy as conkers, her rose-gold hair bouncing from a hot rollers set. Technically, the jeans were too tight for British country style, the jacket too fitted and nipped-in at the waist, but, as Tamra had already realized, she was much better off owning her glamorous American self rather than trying too hard to fit into a world whose rules weren't hers.

Dominic's gaze went to her like a heat-seeking missile and

he whistled slowly. Luckily, the angle of the camera made it seem as if his tribute was for the four younger women.

'I swear to God,' he drawled to Lance as the camera turned away from him, 'I'm bagging that cougar tonight. I bet she fucks like a runaway train.'

'She bloody terrifies me,' Lance admitted frankly.

'I tell you, Lance,' Dominic said, 'you'd go in there a boy and come out a man. Fucking that woman'll be like going to war. Death or glory. I simply can't wait.'

He caught Tamra's eye as she glanced out onto the terrace to see if she and Jodie could come out, and flashed a deep suggestive wink at her; he was rewarded with a full flirtatious smile that rocked him back on his heels.

'I'm in like Flynn,' he said complacently. 'I'd better bloody eat my greens today – I'll need all my strength for tonight, I can tell you.'

Jodie and her two stylists were bustling out now, shepherding the group down the steps in the direction of the bridge. Dominic lingered, hoping for a word with Tamra, but Minty linked her arm through his and dragged him off firmly, whispering in his ear. Milly had decided that the perfect tactical moment to drop the juicy nugget of gossip about Brianna Jade being carried home drunk by the pig farmer was just before the shoot, in order to destabilize her as much as possible, and there was no one better than Dominic for spreading gossip. This information was juicy enough to temporarily drive all lubricious fantasies about Tamra from Dominic's mind: his dark eyes widened, his jaw dropped and he beckoned Lance over to share the dirt.

This was exactly how the upper classes worked; they all had the love of gossip as part of their DNA. They moved in small, near-incestuous social circles, where fidelity was by no means a prerequisite for marriage, very much still in the tradition of the Edwardian country-house parties where a good hostess would always place the husband in a room as far from the wife as possible, so that it would be easy for them to conduct their affairs. The wives were ideally expected to ensure that at least the first two children were her husband's, but after that a blind eye was turned, and the parentage of many aristocratic offspring was an open secret, shared as much as possible.

'I say, the *pig farmer?*' Lance blurted out. 'You *must* be joking, Minters!'

'No, Milly actually *saw* them,' Minty insisted. 'She was drunk and giggling and he had to carry her back!'

'I *say*,' Lance breathed almost in respect for this incredibly rich piece of information.

'She didn't *look* drunk at dinner,' Dominic said dubiously.

'Oh look, if you don't believe me, I'll prove it.'

Minty flitted lightly up to Brianna Jade, who was a couple of steps ahead of them, chattering happily to Sophie.

'Brianna Jade, isn't this the way to the pig farm?' she asked in the classic high, carrying posh voice. 'I hear you absolutely love visiting it – Edmund was telling me you adore it there.'

Brianna Jade froze for a moment in mid-stride as Minty shot a triumphant glance back at Lance and Dominic.

'Uh, yeah,' Brianna Jade said carefully, continuing to walk along. 'It's been really nice to visit them. I go for a run most days and stop there to say hi to the pigs and do my stretches.'

'You *are* virtuous!' Sophie sighed.

'Most *days?*' Milly chimed in with perfect timing. 'Gosh, I thought I saw you coming back from there yesterday evening! Didn't you pop to see them later on? I could have *sworn* you did ...'

Only Brianna Jade's long experience with pageant bitchery enabled her to keep her legs underneath her and moving, to hold her head up and plaster some sort of smile onto her face.

'I do – I did,' she managed, but was temporarily saved by Edmund, who, having no idea what was going on, dropped back to take his fiancée's hand.

'She absolutely adores those pigs,' he said happily. 'I'm so pleased – she's taken to the farming life like a duck to water. She's always telling me how the Empress of Stanclere's doing.'

'The *pigs?*' Milly muttered with perfect, actress-skilled pitch, tailored to reach Brianna Jade's ears but not Edmund's. 'Oh, it's the *pigs* she adores?'

'Who looks after them?' Minty asked, emboldened by the fact that Brianna Jade had gone as white as a sheet. 'Is there some sort of rustic pig man or something? A horny-handed son of toil?'

'Ssst!' Milly hissed, a signal that Minty was over-egging the cake.

'Well, of course,' Edmund said, quite oblivious to any undercurrents, let alone the fact that his bride-to-be's clasp on his hand had loosened and that she was staring ahead of her as blankly as a newly made zombie. 'Abel Wellbeloved. The family's looked after our pigs for generations. He's a really good chap, solid as a rock.'

'*Wellbeloved?*' Milly purred, unable to resist this perfect opportunity. 'How *very* apt!'

'I'm not quite sure what …' Edmund began, his brow furrowing in confusion, but they were at the base of the bridge now, and the stylists were already calling them up, arranging them in a carefully chosen formation as Jodie and the photographic team set up on the lake's edge, calling out directions. Brianna Jade and Edmund were placed in the middle, of course, Edmund beaming at her and Brianna Jade sketching a ghastly bright smile that had Jodie and the photographer, even before a single shot was taken, exchanging worried glances. On

Edmund's other side was, of course, Sophie, out of respect for her status, Minty beside her, her smile as complacent as Brianna Jade's was panicked.

Looking from Edmund to Brianna Jade, Dominic wondered for a moment whether Edmund should be informed of what Milly had apparently seen. But he dismissed the thought almost immediately. Edmund and Brianna Jade's marriage was a mutually beneficial arrangement, and Lord knew what details they had worked out between themselves to keep the wheels running smoothly. Edmund certainly wouldn't thank Dominic, or anyone else, for putting a spoke in one of those wheels. Besides, Dominic didn't want anything getting in the way of his seducing Tamra that evening. What if Edmund got angry enough with his friend for spreading gossip that he insisted Dominic leave the Hall? Dominic was certainly not going to risk his chance of sizzling cougar sex. Turning to Minty, he smiled with her for the cameras. Discretion was definitely the better part of valour, he thought.

Meanwhile, now that she had pulled the rug out from under her rival, Milly was making sure that she and Tarquin presented the image of the perfect couple, his arm around her waist, her hand on his shoulder – the stylists had dressed all the men in Jermyn Street tweeds, and it was bliss for Milly to embrace her fiancé in a suit that didn't smell of ancient dog. She smiled up at him so sweetly that, enchanted, he bent to kiss her, their blonde curls mingling, an image so lovely that Jodie instantly clicked her fingers at the photographer, jerking her head, signalling him to take some shots. The videographer was already zooming in.

Eva, who had tailed the group down from the house, had to avert her eyes from the sight of Milly and Tarquin embracing so fondly. She had been asked to be in the shoot; her Jane-Birkin-meets-Françoise-Sagan look was very current, and Eva was slim enough to meet *Style*'s criteria. Although Jodie, with her own weight issues, was trying to literally broaden out the idea that a model needed to be reed-thin to work, it was a struggle getting designers to make samples larger than a size four. But Eva didn't like the limelight, and she had been firm in her refusal to participate. This way, also, she could walk away if Milly and Tarquin canoodling for the cameras became too much for her.

Tarquin lifted his head, his angelic blue eyes starry with love, and the photographer muttered: 'Jesus, that guy is *unreal.*'

'I know. He reminds me of a Raphael painting of a saint,' Jodie said. She might be a Luton girl with no university education, but she had educated herself very thoroughly since, especially in art history: it was crucial for a stylist to have a wide range of images on which to draw. 'Oh, that's given me a great idea: what about a shoot with the two of them as *Pre*-Raphaelites? We could recreate some of the most famous paintings. They've got just the right looks for that, and it feels really current. There's a big Pre-Raphaelite exhibition coming up at the V&A next summer.'

'I *love* it,' the photographer breathed. '*Definitely.*'

Eva turned and walked away, unable to stay to watch this. As arranged with *Style* before the shoot, Milly was wearing Milly and Me jewellery, and the leaf earrings in forest-green quartzite chimed perfectly with her outfit. There was nothing else Eva needed to do here professionally, and personally it was becoming harder and harder for her to see Milly with Tarquin. Milly had let slip some of the details of her rather unorthodox audition at the Charlotte Street Hotel, and Eva knew that Tarquin was absolutely unaware of the lengths to which Milly would go to further her acting career. Sometimes she was horribly tempted to spill the beans, but her loyalty was to Milly, and it wasn't her business to say anything.

And besides, it wouldn't get her what she wanted. Telling Tarquin Milly would cheat on him with a barn animal if it got her a part in a Hollywood film wouldn't make him fall into Eva's arms, wouldn't do anything but make him never want to look at Eva again. Miserably, she wandered off, wishing that she had never come to Stanclere Hall this weekend and wondering if she could somehow plead a family emergency and escape from what was just one source of pain after another.

No one noticed her go; they wouldn't have in any case, but they were all much too distracted by the pressing problem of the bride-to-be's frozen stare to pay attention to anything else.

'What's up with the bloody fiancée all of a sudden?' the photographer asked, wincing. 'Death warmed up doesn't *begin* to cover it!'

Jodie took in the scene on the bridge. From a distance, it was visually stunning. The pale grey stone was an architectural curve over the soft ripples of the darker grey water, and behind the lake, the rich autumn colours of the foliage rose up the slope beyond; it was already a beautiful image even without the eight young and handsome people clustered at the apex of the bridge, the girls' hair lifted by the autumn breeze, the young men dashing in their tweed suits, velvet waistcoats and contrasting slub silk ties. Sophie, Minty and Milly were all entrancing, the cream of young British aristocracy, blonde, slender, fine-featured, beautiful; Tarquin, with his wide blue eyes and tossing blond curls, could only be described as beautiful too, and Dominic, dark and dashing, his waistcoat deep red to set off his colouring, was a perfect foil. Edmund, in comparison, was merely good-looking, but his features were regular and his figure lean and muscled, and Lance's reddish beard, much as Jodie hated it, gave the whole picture a modern twist.

'What's *up* with her?' Jodie said, finally coming to the centrepiece, the point of this whole photo story: the blushing bride-to-be, ex-pageant queen, Miss America come to England to conquer an Earl. It was impossible for Brianna Jade to look anything less than stunning, but right now she looked like her own death mask. She might have been carved from stone, her eyes as blank as if they were painted on.

'Tamra?' Jodie looked round for Brianna Jade's mother. 'What's up with Brianna Jade?'

'Jesus, I don't know!' Tamra grimaced. 'She was fine a little while ago. Did anyone say anything to her?'

'Milly was talking about pigs, I think,' one of the stylists volunteered. 'Something about Brianna Jade liking to go and see them?'

Tamra's full lips tightened together in a way that boded very ill for Milly.

'That little *bitch*,' she muttered to herself. 'I should have *known* she was planning something.'

'Why don't we try a few shots and then we can mix 'em up a bit,' the photographer suggested. 'And if she doesn't unfreeze, someone could go and have a word with her?'

Tamra nodded grimly, seeing the glory that was this photo- and videoshoot slipping from her grasp. The whole point had been to put her daughter front and centre, to showcase Brianna Jade's dazzling beauty and make the point to Jodie Raeburn that surely Brianna Jade could be the only possible *Style* Bride of the Year. Look at her incredible social connections! Princess Sophie, third in line to the British throne, was visiting for the weekend and taking part in the shoot! Tamra had been sure that would clinch the deal. Look at Sophie right now, leaning on the parapet of the bridge, chatting to Brianna Jade, just as if they'd been friends for years!

It was Tamra's moment of triumph. She was at the peak of

her achievement, symbolized by her daughter's placement at the crest of the bridge, higher even than the royal princess. But, staring in horror at the ghastly fake smile on her daughter's face, she could feel this whole triumph flipping inexorably into disaster ...

However, Tamra was always brutally honest with herself. After she had pulled her daughter aside during the next set-up and barely managed to elicit a word from the seemingly mentally paralysed Brianna Jade, Tamra had to acknowledge to herself that this crisis was unsaveable. She had tried everything she could think of: compliments, encouragement, exhortations to ignore Milly's nasty jealous words, to pull herself together and suck it up.

But nothing got through to Brianna Jade, nothing at all. It was way worse than any pageant disaster, any sabotage some rival contestant had tried to pull. Whatever Milly had said – and Brianna Jade wouldn't or couldn't tell her mother why the words had had the effect they did – had hit its mark with absolute accuracy, the dart landing right in the bull's eye. In the end, Jodie and the photographer had conferred frantically and posed poor Brianna Jade in profile, where the strained fake grimace was much less obvious: thank goodness, at least, Brianna Jade didn't have a bad angle to her face, and both her profiles were equally good.

Still, with the bride-to-be as frozen and stone-faced as the statues in the gazebo, the process became much more work, and the last thing an editor wanted was extra work. Tamra was in pieces when they finally wrapped, though no one would have known that by her beaming smile, the way she congratulated the *Style* team and announced that there was chilled champagne along with a delicious light lunch waiting for everyone back at the Hall.

'What *happened*?' she hissed to her daughter as they all

trooped back. But Brianna Jade could only shake her head, her features still set tightly.

'Is it about the pig thing? We grew up in pig country – everyone knows that! We haven't made a secret of it!' Tamra whispered, at her wits' end.

But this just turned a knife in the wound, reminded Brianna Jade not just that she had been seen, drunk on cider, being carried back to Stanclere Hall by Abel in what could clearly have appeared to be a very compromising situation, but that she was also being blackmailed by Barb Norkus, and all she could manage by way of response was a terrible gulping gasp. She felt as if she were being squeezed in a vice. What if both stories came out? Not just the tacky photos of her as the Pork Queen, but a scandal about her and the Stanclere Hall pig farmer? How would she and Tamra ever survive the humiliation?

Her mother, realizing that her daughter was on the verge of tears, very sensibly backed off and focused her energies into charming the living daylights out of Jodie Raeburn as best she could, though she had a horrible sinking feeling that only half of Jodie's attention was on her; the other half was on the delightful vision of Milly up ahead. Adorable in her tweed shorts and dancing ringlets, hanging on the arm of her equally adorable fiancé, prattling away to him charmingly, Milly was doing everything she could to present herself as the obvious choice for *Style* Bride of the Year, a model who not only wouldn't freeze under pressure but whose fiancé was, miraculously, just as eye-wateringly photogenic as she was herself.

'That Pre-Raphaelite shoot's going to be *very* exciting, Jodie,' one of the stylists said deferentially to her editor.

'Yes, isn't it? Start researching that right now,' Jodie said, shifting her attention to the young man. 'Pull a ton of photos and have them on my desk by Monday afternoon. I want a whole lookbook to choose from. This'll be a lot of work to set up so the clothes look right – we need to get started on this straight away.'

She grinned. 'Victoria's going to scream her head off at me when I tell her I'm doing a shoot where Milly and Tarquin are lying down, draped over things! That's what all the people in those paintings are like – languid and stoned-looking. You know how Victoria is – everything has to be bodies in motion.'

The young man shivered. '*Oh* yes,' he murmured. 'I worked on the trampoline shoot she did over here for the Olympics issue. That's the only time I've felt sorry for models in my entire life.'

'Well, don't make a habit of it!' Jodie said, almost as crisply as her mentor, Victoria, would have done.

'Oh *no*, Jodie, of *course* not.'

Tamra's steps slowed down, the heels of her shiny polished leather boots tapping a slower pace on the path as the exquisitely painfully realization dawned on her, that not only had this shoot been a complete failure in sealing the deal with Jodie to make Brianna Jade *Style* Bride of the Year, but that it had possibly even handed that accolade to her daughter's rival. Already, Milly had been such a hit with Jodie that she was planning a shoot with Milly and Tarquin at the centre! That should have been Brianna Jade and Edmund! Jodie should have come away from this pivotal day impressed beyond measure with how beautiful and photogenic Brianna Jade was, how well connected; she should have been inspired to put her on a *Style* cover, not just as the Bride of the Year but *Style* magazine proper.

It wasn't even that the sheer effort to organize this day, this weekend, had all been for nothing, with Brianna Jade standing there looking even more frozen than the damn statues in the gazebo. It was Tamra's realization that her hard work had actually given a huge advantage to Milly. *That* was what burnt, deep down in her gut, as if she'd drunk a big slug of drain cleaner. *That* was what was making her swear revenge on that scheming little bitch with her golden curls, her big blue eyes, her butter-wouldn't-melt-in-the-mouth expression.

Tamra didn't know exactly what Milly had said to Brianna Jade to trigger her daughter's meltdown, but she was bent and determined on finding out. And whatever it had been, Milly would pay for it. *That* Tamra swore on her life. Milly had no idea who she was messing with, but she was about to find out. Big time.

Chapter Sixteen

'So you know how awful Daddy is?' Sophie asked the gathered house party after dinner. 'Really, he has the worst temper. He's famous for it. And he's not getting better with age. He threw a shoe at his private equerry the other day, can you imagine? So the chap's got all these little things he does to take revenge – secretly, of course, so that Daddy never realizes, but it sort of gets him back. Want to hear? They're awfully cunning!'

A chorus of 'yeses' immediately followed, of course; Sophie's audience was naturally very keen to hear a juicy piece of gossip about Prince Oliver, heir to the British throne, her notoriously short-tempered father. Even despite her profound disappointment at her daughter's meltdown at the photo shoot, Tamra couldn't help but be delighted at the success of her redecorating of Stanclere Hall: the cluster of guests was gathered in the Great Hall, curled up on the velvet sofas around the fireplace, sipping after-dinner drinks. The pianist was now playing versions of Barry White and Lionel Richie that had people hearing snatches of the chorus and swaying in their seats, humming 'Do It To Me One More Time' and 'Can't Get Enough Of Your Love'.

The lighting was soft and shadowy, a few huge silver-shaded lamps placed with care around the gigantic room, creating welcoming pools of light and equally enticing shadowy areas. Candles flickered in artfully tarnished mirrored sconces and candelabras, and the fire positively roared behind the high wrought-iron grate which bore the crest of the Respers family. Chocolates and petits-fours were piled on silver plates on the various tables. Waiters slipped up to the tables every now and then, refreshing drinks, taking new orders, perfectly trained not to interrupt the conversational flow: as Sophie reached the punchline of her anecdote, they hovered back at the far end of the hall.

'So, Daddy's a terrible, terrible spoilt fusspot, but of course he's much too lazy to lift a finger for himself; he makes his equerry do absolutely everything,' Sophie continued. She was fairly tipsy by now, her blonde hair partially falling down from her updo, her cheeks pink with both drink and proximity to the fire: she looked very pretty. Lady Margaret, sitting in an armchair in a wall embrasure a little removed from the group by the fire, smiled almost maternally to see her god-daughter not only so happy, but also able to party with her friends without reverting to the wild-child days full of scandal, bitchery and self-destructive behaviour.

'He won't put his own toothpaste on his toothbrush – you know that, right? He has to have the paste already squeezed onto the brush, ready and waiting for him, morning and evening,' Sophie told her eager listeners. 'And he's very particular about the kind – he has to have Colgate Total Plus or something. One of the whitening ones with the special stripe. So sometimes, if he's been really arsey that day, the equerry mixes in some Crest that he keeps specially – he puts it under the Colgate, so it tastes different but looks the same. He says Daddy goes mental, because he can't see the difference but he hates the taste, and the equerry gets all concerned and says does Daddy think it's a health thing – you know, tasting things differently – and Daddy gets all wound up because he's a huge hypochondriac. The equerry says he can't do it that often but it's absolutely hilarious when he does.'

'That's fiendish,' Dominic said, even drunker and more flushed than Sophie.

Tipsiness suited him just as it did her: his eyes glittered, his lips were moist and parted, his dark curls tumbling over his forehead, one leg casually hooked across the other knee. He was sprawling like a Georgette Heyer rake. If he'd been wearing a cravat, it would have been loosened; as it was, his shirt collar was open, his black bow tie dangling in debonair fashion. His arms were spread wide along the back of the velvet sofa, not just to demonstrate alpha-male credentials and to dominate his territory, but so that he could secretly reach far enough to stroke one thumb in slow, lazy circles at the back of Tamra's neck. She was next to him on the sofa, part of the main group, resolved to seem as bright and relaxed and happy as if her daughter hadn't been emotionally absent for the entire evening.

Because Brianna Jade had been like a gorgeous, glossy mannequin during drinks and dinner, almost completely silent. A casual observer would have thought that Edmund was planning to marry a very expensive blow-up doll. She had excused herself straight after dinner, saying that she had a headache, and gone to her room: Tamra had tried to ask her some questions after the shoot, but Brianna Jade had started vibrating like a tuning fork and very sensibly, Tamra had backed off fast, fearing that her daughter might actually break down if she pushed things any further. All Tamra wanted for the rest of the weekend was to achieve some damage control, and then she would sit down with her beloved daughter when all the guests were gone, find out what was worrying her so badly, and move heaven and earth to make it right for her.

Well, perhaps that isn't everything I want, Tamra thought, steeling her body not to react visibly to the pleasure of Dominic's thumb tracing those circles on her bare skin. It was utterly divine, heat and damp rising between her legs in delicious bubbles like a pot coming to the boil, and she shifted a little, catching his smug smile as he registered her reaction to his caress. *Thank God for Dominic. This is just what I need tonight, some cheap slutty boy to fuck so I can take the edge off, calm my nerves. Nothing remotely serious, no one who's going to fall for me and complicate my life. If there's anyone who knows the rules of a one-night stand, it's Dominic.*

To avenge herself for the smug smile, Tamra hitched the already short skirt of her blue velvet, off-the-shoulder 3.1 Philip Lim dress an inch up her thigh, ostensibly so that she could re-cross her legs, but actually to give Dominic, on her left, a swift flash of the elaborately patterned navy lace top of her hold-up stocking. One perfect leg scissored over the other, she adjusted her skirt demurely and settled back against the cushion behind her. Dominic's thumb was as frozen on her back as his eyes were glued to her upper thigh, and a quick sideways glance confirmed that his jaw was dropped. He looked as if he were about to drool.

All I can manage tonight is to get laid. I can't control what upsets my daughter, Tamra thought grimly. *I can't fix the past and make the photo shoot miraculously come out okay. Jodie Raeburn and her team have gone, dammit, and I was so bummed she couldn't stay over tonight, but honestly, with BJ gone emotionally AWOL, it's ended up being for the best.*

Shit, I could strangle that poisonous little Milly with my bare hands! But I mustn't think about that now, or I really will kill the bitch. I need to take all this angry energy and turn it into sex and fuck Dominic so hard tonight he won't be able to walk straight for three days ...

Some of this must have been conveyed in that swift look at Dominic, because his Adam's apple bobbed as he swallowed hard, and his arm retracted along the back of the sofa, his legs shifting as he sat up straighter, resettling himself so that the prominent bulge in his trousers was at least partially disguised from view. Luckily, everyone was listening to Sophie's story much too attentively to notice the short interplay between him and Tamra.

'But the best story's about Daddy's socks,' Sophie was saying. 'Did you know they're not just handmade, they're actually fitted individually? No, seriously, it's true!' she insisted to Edmund, who was sitting next to her and had murmured doubt at this information.

'They're made for the right and left royal trotter, honestly!' she giggled. 'So when Daddy's been a total petulant irritating bastard, this chap lays the socks out the wrong way round in the dressing room. You know, it's not super obvious, and Daddy wouldn't dream of doing anything so common as looking closely at his own socks, of course. But then he goes on to have a simply horrid day, feeling something's wrong but he can't work out quite what, and getting all fretful till he takes his socks off again ...'

Lady Margaret put down her whisky glass and shoved her cigarette into the corner of her mouth to free both her hands so that she could applaud this story loudly.

'Bloody perfect!' she said enthusiastically. 'I love this story! Top man!'

'Well, no one's going to beat that anecdote,' Edmund said, grinning and rising to his feet. 'Have we all digested the very excellent meal that Mrs Hurley regaled us with? I'm sorry to say that Tamra hasn't yet put in a heated pool or hot tub for us all to splash around in—' He winked at his future mother-in-law as play-groans of disappointment rose from the group of guests.

'Oh, that hot tub's coming!' Tamra said, laughing up at him. 'I just need to figure out the right place to put one in the grounds of a stately home.'

'God, you, me and a hot tub,' Dominic muttered in her ear, leaning towards her. 'The things we could get up to . . .'

'I'll test you out on a mattress first,' Tamra whispered back. 'See how you run in basic conditions before you get ambitious.'

'Christ,' Dominic murmured devoutly, whipping the hem of his dinner jacket over his crotch.

'But I think we could all do with stretching our legs a bit?' Edmund was saying. 'We've got billiards and table tennis, but my contribution to the entertainment's a rather fun idea I've been planning. does anyone feel like a game of croquet?'

'*Outdoors?*' Milly, who was very tiddly by now, squeaked in surprise.

'We've got torches set up all around the lawn, so we can see what we're doing, and to warm us up a bit,' Edmund revealed. 'And I ordered a set of glow-in-the-dark balls off the internet! Who's up for it?'

Almost everyone was. Dominic made a valiant attempt to convince Tamra to sneak upstairs with him and make a start on the mattress test-run, but she was fizzing with energy and loved the idea of outdoor croquet with glow-in-the-dark balls. She slapped him away playfully as he grabbed at her in the corridor outside her suite; they had all raced upstairs to change into warmer clothes and flat shoes for the women.

'I'll come and find you later,' he promised. 'Here, right? I'll come to your room?'

'Of course.' Tamra tossed her hair back. 'Do I look like a woman who has to sneak down corridors to get laid?'

'You look like fucking sex on legs,' he said, snatching her hand and pressing it eloquently to his crotch for a second, moulding her palm around the outline of his cock. 'Feel how hard you get me? I can't wait till I get you naked—'

But just then Edmund and some other house guests rounded the corner of the wing, and Tamra, saying: 'Hold that thought, tiger,' slipped through her door and shut it firmly in his face. For a second or two, she considered giving herself a quick orgasm or two, taking down the pressure that was pounding between her legs; she was swollen herself, the blood racing to her crotch, and the feeling of Dominic's cock had had almost exactly the effect he had intended. Almost: it hadn't been quite as big as she had been hoping for.

But hey, there are angles that'll work for that. And I'm always up for a good ass-fucking, she thought with a wicked smile. Best thing to do with an average-to-small dick. God, I'm horny!

Tamra had been so busy putting together the shoot and the house party, pulling Stanclere Hall into shape (or parts of it – the main guest wing and some of the public rooms; there were definitely doors that still needed to remain firmly closed to guests) that she hadn't had time to let loose, to ring Diane's agency and book herself in a boy or three. *Jeez, Dominic had better have been eating raw meat and working out to keep up with me tonight!* she thought. *I'm loaded for bear.*

Dominic was late to the croquet game, and when he did arrive his smile was even more devilish than usual. Even by the flickering light of the many torches, it was obvious that he had been up to something. Edmund asked suspiciously what the hell he'd been doing, but Dominic just smirked and wouldn't say a word. Edmund frowned, but Tamra just assumed that Dominic had, frankly, been knocking out a quick one before joining the game, and winked at him flirtatiously. She was hugely impressed with Edmund, who had not only put a great deal of effort into organizing this croquet game, but had done it all secretly, knowing that she had more than enough on her plate without adding this idea of his into the mix. She told him so as they awaited their turns, sipping hot mulled wine and rum toddies from antique cut-glass punch cups, their gloved fingers carefully clasping the miniature curved handles, another lovely surprise that Edmund had arranged with Mrs Hurley.

'It was supposed to be a treat for Brianna Jade,' he said rather wistfully as he blew on his toddy. 'She loves croquet, and she was talking the other day about the hot buttered rum drinks that you have over in America. I thought she'd really like all this. I did pop into her room, but she's lying down and says she has a terrible headache. It must have started before the shoot, I think, because she didn't seem quite her usual cheerful self when it was all going on ...'

'God, your British understatement,' Tamra said bitterly, slugging down her rum, her eyebrows raised. 'Not quite her usual self? She's in pieces! I don't know what went wrong today, but I'm going to get to the bottom of it, I promise you that—'

'Tamra! You're up!' Lance called, and Tamra handed her cup to Edmund and went off to take the stroke for her team.

Dominic, however, having turned up late, had found all the teams full and no chance to play; he compensated by drinking steadily for the entire duration of the game, and by the time they all strolled over the lawns back to the Hall, he was visibly reeling. A murmured word from Edmund: 'Old chap, you're totally bladdered and you stink of rum, I'd stick my head under the cold tap if I were you' – and Dominic staggered upstairs, hauling himself up by the balustrade, heading for his room to follow Edmund's advice.

He was just towelling off when the door of his bedroom burst open and his host stormed in.

'Dom, what the *fuck*!' Edmund shouted. 'I had a feeling you'd been up to no good when you turned up at the croquet court, so I went up to my room, and sure enough, you've been up to your old tricks! You put a bloody raw fish in my bed, you bastard!'

Dominic, whose head was spinning from the amount of rum he'd added to the whole bucketful of cocktails, champagne, wine, and brandy he'd already drunk before the lethal punch bowl had been produced, reeled back from this onslaught, clapping his hands to his temples.

'Really loud,' he moaned. 'Ow, Ed, no need to shout.'

'I'm not bloody sleeping in there!' Edmund yelled. 'I've got a poor maid coming to take the damn fish away, but I'm not sleeping on that mattress! Honestly, Dom, it's the total limit! How did you even get a fish – did you take one from the kitchen?'

His eyes fell on the cooler pushed against the bedroom wall.

'God, you planned this out enough to *bring* one?' he said incredulously. 'Dom, that's so bloody juvenile! We're in our thirties now, you know? I'm getting married, settling down ...'

An even more serious thought struck Edmund then.

'I tell you what, no way am I letting you anywhere near organizing my stag night,' he said with awful emphasis. 'You'll take me on safari in Africa, get me drunk, take my clothes off, tie me to a tree and shove raw chillies up my bum like Toby did to Plumpy Thurston.'

Dominic hung his head: this was indeed exactly what he had been envisaging for Edmund's stag night.

'Look, get your toothbrush and your pjs and whatever else you need,' Edmund ordered firmly, 'and fuck off into my room. You put that fish in there, and you can sleep with the smell – it bloody stinks.'

No problem, Dominic thought drunkenly. *I'll be ravaging that gorgeous cougar all night long in her palatial boudoir. I'll be fine – I won't need to spend the night in Edmund's stinky-fish room either.*

He couldn't tell Edmund that, of course; his friend had already made it clear that he took a very dim view of Dominic flirting with Edmund's mother-in-law-to-be. So Dominic gathered his toothbrush and picked up his pyjama case, which had been laid out for him by the maid on his four-poster bed, and made his way down the corridor to the master bedroom of Stanclere Hall. Even after the sluicing down with cold water, he wasn't feeling very well: on arrival, he shut the door behind him, took a couple of deep breaths and then staggered over to the imposing bed to put down his pyjama case.

Unfortunately, bending over to put the case on the bed was his undoing. It was the fish reek that did it. Edmund hadn't been exaggerating about the smell: it was as if, for extra stink effect, the fishmonger had gutted other fishes and shoved the entrails into the mouth of the one Dominic had bought. Lifting his head again brought on a violent case of the retches. Everything he had eaten and drunk that evening came up, suddenly and furiously, and it was lucky for Dominic that there was a wastebasket next to the bed, because there was no way he could have made it to the new en-suite bathroom. The contents of his stomach took quite a while to void, and the wastebasket was brimming with gelatinous gunge by the time he felt, gingerly, that the last clutching spasms of his upper colon were finally beginning to recede.

It was by no means the first time Dominic had upchucked, and it was very unlikely to be the last. He was fairly phlegmatic about the situation: these things happened when you partied hard. Better out than in. All he needed now was a little rest before he went back downstairs and completed his seduction of Tamra, that glorious American sex goddess. There was a large and comfortable leather armchair in Edmund's room, and Dominic subsided into it, closing his eyes.

Bit of shut-eye, and I'll be as good as new, were his last thoughts before he passed out, exhausted by his recent endeavours. *Wake up in twenty minutes, wash my face, brush my teeth, shove on some more aftershave, shag till dawn. Perfect.*

His chin dropped to his chest and he started to snore heavily. It was a deep, rumbling snore, a precursor to equally deep sleep: Dominic passed out completely until dawn was breaking and the smell of his own vomit woke him to a raging, dehydrated hangover.

Chapter Seventeen

No one else had hit the punch bowl as hard as Dominic; Minty and Sophie were not completely steady, but the cold air had balanced out the alcohol. Edmund proposed a game of Twister in the library, and Tamra shot him a very approving glance. This was how to run a house party, moving guests from one delightful activity to another, ideally ensuring that no one got too raging drunk along the way.

'You're doing a great job,' she said to him as they walked towards the library, leading the way. 'I really didn't expect you to be such a good host.'

Edmund grinned, his smile very boyish. 'You must think I'm completely devoid of all the social graces, Tamra,' he said teasingly.

'I love the way you guys talk!' she said, very amused. 'Like you swallowed a dictionary! You've got to admit, Edmund, all of that stuff you were spouting about not wanting to have parties in the Hall—'

'Not wanting to have them non-stop, when I have a farm to run,' he corrected her. 'But I must admit, I wasn't expecting to enjoy this weekend half as much as I am. Obviously posing for photos isn't really my thing ...'

'Hey, that's the price of the ticket,' Tamra said, flashing him a smile that teased him back.

'But yes, I do know that's the price of the ticket,' he agreed equably. 'And seeing the old place come to life like this is genuinely,' he considered for a moment, 'inspiring. Truly, I mean that.'

'Wow, Edmund, seriously?' Tamra put her hand on his arm, dropping the joking, her dark eyes fixed on his; in her four-inch heels they were almost the same height. 'That's the biggest compliment you've ever paid me.'

He patted her hand; the house guests flooded past them, pulling out the Twister mat from the box on the console table, arguing about whether they should all play at once or in a series of matches.

'I owe you an apology, Tamra, for being a bit of a grumpy bastard yesterday,' he said disarmingly. 'I realize, to be honest, that my parents weren't exactly gifted at entertaining. It always seemed like a terrible headache for them when we needed to host parties – and, to be even more honest, the state of the place was an embarrassment too. It felt like Mummy was always scrabbling around to manage something remotely decent, and failing, you know? Just sort of constant humili-ation, if I am being completely frank. This is worlds away from all of that.'

'Oh, Edmund!' She squeezed his hand hard, full of sympathy; she knew what it was like to be embarrassed by poverty. 'No wonder you didn't want to have parties!'

The Twister group had drawn lots, and Minty and Tarquin were the first up; already the spectators, perched on the Chesterfield armchairs or standing smoking by the fireplace, were collapsing in fits of giggles as Lady Margaret, who had taken command of spinning the pointer to avoid any pressure to play herself, announced: 'Right hand green!' and both Minty and Tarquin fell over each other competing for the same convenient dot of colour.

'You're gifted at being a hostess,' Edmund said simply. 'You make it look easy. Whereas Mummy made it seem like she was waging the Battle of Stalingrad every single time. I mean, if things are fun, it makes all the difference in the world.'

They both glanced over at the Twister mat, Minty and Tarquin spidered out across it, Minty's narrow hips piking up over Tarquin as she tried desperately to reach back with her foot to a yellow dot: even Lady Margaret had tears of laughter in her eyes as she spun the pointer again.

'I'd say things are definitely fun,' Tamra agreed. 'And now the Hall's running so well, I can pass the reins over to Brianna Jade. Once the building works are finished, of course. I just know she's going to love throwing parties just as much as I do ...'

She started strong, but the expression of doubt on Edmund's face made her tail off.

'Well, she will. In time. As she builds her confidence,' Tamra said more feebly.

'Tamra, she's more than fine as she is,' Edmund said gently. 'I'm not expecting her to be like you, and nor should you, if you see what I mean. She's finding her own place here.'

'Yes, at the damn pigsties,' Tamra murmured crossly. 'I swear, it's her favourite place in Stanclere.'

Edmund laughed. 'I love it down there too, you know,' he said reassuringly. 'You have to let her be herself, Tamra.'

'Oh, shut up!' Tamra slapped his arm. 'How dare you make more sense than me, when I'm kinda the mother and you're the son? That's completely the wrong way round!'

'Tamra, stop saying that!' Edmund said, irritated. You're

only a few years older than me. It makes me feel fantastically awkward, to tell you the truth.'

'I'm sorry. I only do it because it annoys the crap out of you,' Tamra said, her smile dazzling. 'You know I do. And now I need a drink, dammit!'

'And I need to go to bed,' Edmund said, smiling at her. 'I keep farmer's hours. Thank you again for turning the old place into something so warm and welcoming.'

'Fuck it, now I need a drink or I'll cry,' Tamra said, slapping him again. 'Go get your beauty sleep, farm boy!'

She went over to the drinks tray a footman had brought in and poured herself a stiff two fingers of neat vodka, dropping ice into it with tongs, and wondering where the hell Dominic had got to. He'd looked pretty drunk when he was staggering upstairs: she hoped and prayed he was sobering up.

I'll give him fifteen more minutes so it doesn't look too obvious, she decided, *and then I'll head up to find him. Maybe he's waiting for me in my room? I swear, if he's too drunk to get his shit together, I'll whale the hell out of him. He'd better not have got me all wound up with nowhere to go.*

She drank half the vodka in one go.

Think positive, Tamra. It'll be okay. You'll get your jollies tonight.

Chapter Eighteen

Meanwhile, outside on the library terrace, Eva was beginning to feel that she would never get her jollies again. The first round of Twister was over. Minty had triumphed, and was now taking on Sophie: Tarquin had rejoined Milly, who was sitting on his lap, curled up like a cat and looking as smug as if she had not only licked up her own portion of cream but everyone else's too. Eva was fully aware of the extent of Milly's triumph today, had heard about Milly seeing Brianna Jade and the pig guy last night and seen how effectively Milly had played that card, just at the right time to panic her rival before the shoot.

Eva seriously doubted that Brianna Jade was cheating on Edmund, let alone with the pig farmer; she just didn't seem that kind of person. She actually didn't think that even Milly believed it. But that hadn't stopped Milly using the information to her advantage, rather than keeping her mouth shut, or having a quiet word with Brianna Jade to let her know that she'd been seen coming back tipsy from a drink with a friend.

Tarquin would hate what Milly did today, Eva thought now. He would loathe the thought that his fiancée was capable of pulling such a dirty trick. But who was going to tell him?

Again, not Eva. She sat on the terrace balcony, dangling her long legs over the edge, her hair falling over her face, chain-smoking as she contemplated jumping down onto the grass and running away; no one would miss her, she thought miserably.

In that, at least, she was wrong.

'Hey, there you are! I was looking for you!'

It was Lance, emerging onto the terrace. Walking up beside her, he leaned on the wide stone balustrade, turning his head to look at her.

'You look like a French film star,' he said. 'Or a model. One of those cool ones who goes out with rock stars.'

I wish.

Eva swallowed hard. 'Thanks,' she muttered.

'You're not playing Twister?' Lance asked. 'Not your kind of thing?'

'Not really.'

'Yeah, you're too cool for that,' Lance said, and Eva bristled for a second, thinking he was making fun of her, and then realized he wasn't, which was worse.

'I'm really not,' she mumbled. 'I'm just ... quieter.'

'I think you're amazing,' Lance said. 'And you're just as pretty as Milly. Honestly, to me you're much prettier. I think you should model for your jewellery, not just her. You know, a lot of your pieces work better on you than they do on her. You're so much hipper. I've been wanting to say this for ages.'

'Oh. Um, thank you!'

Eva was taken completely aback by this unexpected praise. She swivelled a little to look at Lance, feeling that she owed him that after the compliment; she shoved back her hair from her face, not realising that Lance would take this as a cue to straighten up, lean forward and kiss her.

His beard rubbed against her skin, his lips soft in their

surround of bristly hair. It wasn't the first time Eva had kissed
a man with a beard, of course; facial hair on men had been
fashionable for years, and there were plenty of beards in her
Hoxton/Brick Lane social circle. She didn't pull back instantly,
and Lance, encouraged, managed to get his arms around her,
twisting himself to press against her torso without pulling
her off the balustrade; it was awkward, but the awkwardness
would only have lasted a few seconds if Eva had fully co-
operated, swivelling more to face him.

As it was, he was kissing her, and she was merely letting him.
Letting him hold her, letting the pressure of his lips open hers,
letting his tongue slide inside, trying to convince herself that this
was what she wanted. The human contact, the physical sensation of being held so close to another warm body, of being
desired after all her lonely months of desiring someone who
didn't want her, was, for a very little while, hugely compelling.
She went slack in his arms, trying to give herself to the embrace,
to relax into it and hopefully feel something building inside her
that would prompt a response to Lance's obvious eagerness.

He was so keen that he interpreted her limpness as full
acquiescence; his tongue started thrusting in and out of her
mouth, his beard rubbing against her entire lower jaw, his
arms tightening around her narrow torso. Eva bore it as long
as she could, until she was completely sure that she couldn't
fancy Lance, couldn't endure this a second longer; then she
shifted, managing to lift her arms enough to push him back.

'Too much? God, I'm sorry. Too fast?' Lance babbled. 'Did
my beard scratch you? I'll shave it right now if you want me
to ... Just say the word, Eva, and I'll shave it off, it won't take
me much time at all ...'

Oh shit. It was dawning on Eva that he really liked her,
wasn't just trying for a hookup at a house party; that he'd
clearly had a crush on her for a while.

'You're so beautiful, and you look so sad most of the time nowadays. I want to make you happy, I've wanted that for so long!' Lance continued. 'Kissing you was a dream come true for me.' He grabbed her hand. 'I think you're the most beautiful, most spiritual girl I've ever met.'

Great. Now I feel even worse than I did before, like I led him on by letting him kiss me.

'I just don't feel the same, Lance, I'm sorry,' she blurted out. Eva was incapable of anything but frankness; if it couldn't be said directly, she wouldn't say it at all. 'I was trying to feel something, but I couldn't.'

'It's the beard, isn't it?' Lance asked, grasping at the only straw he could find.

'It isn't the beard, Lance. I'm sorry.' She sighed. 'You're a really nice guy. I wish I could feel the same as you. It would make things so easy. But I just can't.'

She swung her legs down from the balcony and dropped to the terrace.

'I should go to bed,' she said gloomily.

'Oh no, now I've chased you away. I'm so sorry, Eva.' Lance sounded on the verge of beating his head against the stone wall of Stanclere Hall.

'It's okay,' she said, her voice dull. 'I was tired anyway. Goodnight.'

Poor Lance was left behind on the terrace, nursing his wounds, staring out into the night and mentally writing lyrics even more miserable and poignant than most of Ormond and Co's current output. The song, titled 'Balustrade of Tears', would eventually become a ballad on their upcoming album, not strong enough to be a single, but generally considered not only very moving but considerably easier to understand than Tarquin or Elden's lyrics.

Eva's re-entrance was completely unnoticed by the raucous

crowd in the library, now in a foursome Twister competition that Lady Margaret was refereeing with brusque snapped orders, like a staff officer trying to keep control of an increasingly rowdy mess party. She slipped through the room and back to the Great Hall, surprised to see Tamra about to ascend the staircase; she had assumed that Tamra was back in the library in the Twister group.

'Going to bed?' Tamra said, seeing Eva approach, and reading her disconsolate expression with the skill of a woman who had spent years observing pageant competitors in every possible emotional state.

Eva nodded.

'I'm not really a Twister person,' she said, managing to summon up a feeble excuse, as if there were a current diktat at Stanclere Hall that the guests' only activity choices were Twister or bed.

Tamra was kind enough to nod politely and accept Eva's words at face value.

'I'm turning in myself,' she said as they went up the staircase together. 'It's been a long day.'

This made no sense to Eva: Tamra was so vibrant and so fizzing with a glowing golden energy that it seemed impossible that she might be ready to go to bed. But Eva nodded equally politely, and at the top of the stairs they bade each other goodnight, Tamra turning left towards the central part of the Hall, Eva right towards the unmodernized guest wing.

Nice girl, Tamra thought as she picked up the pace, walking swiftly towards her room, where she assumed Dominic was waiting: *shame she's so close to that bitch Milly. She'd be a great friend for Brianna Jade otherwise. And I like how she dresses. She knows what works for her, and I always respect that in a woman ...*

And then all thoughts of Eva fled as she opened the door of her room, and saw, even by the dim light of the flickering fire and the bedside lamps which the maid had switched on when she came by to turn down Tamra's bed that evening, that the pristinely smooth coverlet and crisp white sheet were not sullied with the presence of a lounging Dominic de Rohan, preferably wearing nothing but a come-hither smile and grasping his stiff cock in one hand.

'Fuck!' she said between gritted teeth. 'Fuck, fuck, fuck!'

Tamra was a woman of swift decisions and great determination: she wasn't going to give up on her plans to get laid tonight until she had exhausted the possibilities. Instantly, she stripped off all her clothes and pulled on her Loro Piana cashmere dressing gown, sliding her feet into matching slippers, grabbing a handful of condoms from her vanity case and slipping them discreetly into her pocket.

All she had to do was check that the corridor was empty, all bedroom doors shut, before she slipped into Dominic's room, and that was exactly what she did, gliding down the carpet that ran down the centre of the polished hallway as silently as a ghost. This whole wing of Stanclere had been redone with en suites to every room: no one needed, thank God, to leave their room to use the bathroom any more. So she was quite unobserved as she shot a quick glance around, turned the handle and nipped inside.

The room was almost completely dark, just a few glowing embers in the fire by which she could make out the shapes of the furniture, the drawn curtains of the four-poster bed. For a moment, she thought that Dominic wasn't here at all, and then she heard slow, steady breathing from behind the heavy brocade curtains and realized that the bastard had, instead of sneaking into her room, come back to his and gone to sleep.

How dare he? Well, if he thinks he can turn me on and leave me hanging, he's got a second thought coming! I'm going to ride him like a bronco for this!

The cashmere dressing gown fell from Tamra's perfect silky shoulders and puddled on the carpet. She kicked off the slippers and, naked and angry, condoms in hand, stalked to the four-poster bed, pulled open the curtains and climbed up onto the mattress beside the man she thought was Dominic.

Edmund, who had been fast asleep, stirred into semiconsciousness at the brief glimmer of light as the curtains parted. They fell closed behind Tamra, and the next thing he knew, the covers were being pulled off his recumbent body, and a warm hand was reaching decisively into the slit of his pyjama bottoms and taking hold of his cock in a way that meant business.

'Christ!' he mumbled sleepily, feeling himself respond instantly. 'Oh, God ...'

She was tickling his balls now with the fingers of her other hand, working them expertly, making him moan even as he managed to say:

'I thought you went to bed.'

'Ssh!' She was very conscious of her daughter sleeping in the next door bedroom, didn't want Brianna Jade to hear a thing. 'Keep your voice down!'

Straddling him, she bent down to silence him with a kiss which she deliberately turned into a sharp, punishing bite that had his cock springing up, rock-hard now.

'I don't care what you thought, you fucker,' she whispered against his lips, her voice so like her daughter's that, at this low pitch, it was indistinguishable from Brianna Jade's. 'Stop thinking and get ready. I'm going to start fucking your brains out in about thirty seconds, so you better brace yourself and hang on for dear life.'

Brianna Jade had never, ever, talked dirty to Edmund during sex. Actually, no one had. No one had bitten his lips or pulled on his cock as if she owned it, or told him that she was going to fuck his brains out, and he realized immediately, as his balls throbbed and tightened, that this was exactly what had been lacking from his entire adult life. She was ripping open a condom wrapper, rolling it onto his cock, and he felt like he might burst already: he reached up for her, closing his hands around her breasts for a wonderful moment, the skin so soft, the nipples so tight and hard at the centre, before she actually slapped his hands away.

'No touching me,' she hissed. 'Not yet. You haven't earned it. Fuck me good this time, and then maybe you can.'

And the next thing he knew she was lowering herself onto him, so hot and wet that he groaned in utter pleasure, his arms thrown wide, his hands splayed and gripping the sheets and the mattress to hold on, just as she'd told him to do, as she started to ride him so hard and fast that it hurt, and that hurt felt better than any sensation he'd ever experienced in his life. She was grinding her arse down onto his balls, taking him in right to the root with every stroke, her strong, lean muscled legs making the movements seem effortless, and Edmund's fingers sank so deep into the mattress to get some purchase that he pulled a button loose with the force of his clutch.

'Oh God,' Tamra panted above him, 'fucking God, this is so good ...'

His cock was considerably bigger than it had felt through his trousers, which was weird – maybe it had been the angle? – but definitely a positive thing. She'd driven down on it so hard as it entered her that she already felt bruised, but that was wonderful, just what she needed, extreme sensation: she wouldn't care if she woke up tomorrow morning covered in bruises just as long as she left marks on him too. And there was something about him that made her want to do that, to bite him, to spank him and have him spank her back, some wild energy that had sparked between them the moment she touched his cock. She felt him trying to rear his hips, to fuck her like she was fucking him, and she reached down and slapped the side of his bum as hard as she could

'I told you not to fucking move!' she hissed. 'You dirty bastard, don't you dare!'

It was a total power game: she drew that hand between her legs, starting to make herself come, knowing that he could tell what she was doing. His groans grew louder, his cock swelled inside her, and she was so excited that she came almost straight away, her pussy throbbing around him, came again and again just to torture him, knowing that he was doing his best to hold out, until finally she collapsed onto his chest, sank her teeth into his lower lip and whispered: 'Come on, you bastard, shoot inside me ... come on, you dirty bastard, do it, shoot your load ...'

She gasped as she felt his cock swell even more, as his hips did jerk now, pumping come so hot that she could feel it through the condom, his hands grabbing onto her hips and pulling her even further onto him: she screamed silently at how deep the tip of his cock drove for a split-second before he arched his back, grunted and went limp beneath her.

His chest hair was already sweaty under her breasts. She loved it, the dampness, the coarse hair against her sensitive skin. She bent to lick the salty sweat from the pool in his collarbone.

'Well?' she whispered. 'Did I fuck your brains out?'

'Uh-huh.'

He shifted her off him so that he could take off the condom. Brianna Jade sometimes got him to use them for a few days if she'd accidentally skipped her Pill, or even taken it late – she was paranoid about getting pregnant before the wedding – so he assumed this was what had happened today.

'So, um, is this what we're doing tonight?' he whispered; for some reason she wanted to keep it down, and the sex had been so amazing that he'd go along with pretty much whatever she said. 'Fucking each other's brains out?'

Just saying the words sent a rush of such excitement through Edmund that he thought he might get hard all over again, his cock still wet with come from the last fuck. *The last fuck.* He'd never dared use this language to a woman, had always felt that it was disrespectful. But here was Brianna Jade, somehow transformed by the stress of the day, and maybe the utter darkness around them, into a total sex vixen, insulting him, biting him – God, his cock twitched just *thinking* about her biting him – and it had liberated something inside him he didn't even realize had existed.

'Have you been drinking?' he said, finding the gap in the curtains, tying the condom up by the faint firelight and managing, to his great satisfaction, to chuck it squarely into the bedside wastebasket. He was still trying to work out the reason for the metamorphosis of his sexually modest fiancée into a full-blown porn fantasy woman.

She laughed deep in her throat.

'No more than you,' she said, which Edmund naturally took to mean 'not much at all'.

'So what happened to get you all—' he began, but at that point his arm was grabbed, he was pulled fully back into the darkness of the curtained bed, and Tamra's mouth closed on his.

'Stop talking,' she said, kissing him deeply. 'Finger me.'

Edmund's cock surged again; her commands were delicious, her new-found confidence incredibly exciting. But he realized that he wanted not just to follow along with her wishes, but to exert his own will too. This was the moment he needed to do it, or she would take over completely. He needed to flex his own muscles too, to give his own commands. Without even thinking about what he was going to do, he slid his thumb into her mouth.

'Suck it,' he said, wondering if she would get furious at his daring to order her around as she'd been ordering him: when her warm wet lips folded over her teeth and she started to pull on his thumb, sucking it just as he'd told her, right up to the base of the second knuckle, he groaned loudly in surprise and pleasure, his balls tingling, growing fuller. His other hand slid down her body, squeezing each breast as he went, first tentatively, but then, as she arched wordlessly beneath him, he squeezed harder, his thumb flicking the nipples, his head lowering to close his teeth around each one in turn, hearing her moan around his thumb as he did so: she liked it as rough as he was learning that he did, and, realizing that, he narrowed three fingers together, parted her wet lower lips and drove the fingers inside her with barely any preliminaries.

She surged right up around his hand, fast and furious, pumping her hips against him. He rubbed his thumb against her, trying to feel what she wanted, what she needed, and apparently it was a series of steady quick strokes, making her pump her hips right off the bed, reaching desperately for the orgasm that was just about to come, and did, and then the next one, and the next one, waves and waves, Edmund determined not to stop although his hand was cramping, determined not to give up first, to wear her out before she wore him out, not to give in: he found a rhythm of licking and biting her nipples that finally made her head arch right back, his thumb slipping out of her mouth as she hissed out a ragged series of 'Fuck you!'s at the brocade tester overhead, her pussy contracting ever more tightly around his hand. The rush of moisture around his fingers, the scent of her sweat and come was so intoxicating that he was hard as a rock again by the time she finally subsided, trembling with the aftershock, onto the mattress.

He wasn't sure if she was ready for him yet: probably not.

He pulled himself back up to lie beside her, his own breath coming fast, but hers much louder, as he listened in utter happiness to the physical state to which he had reduced her. Never had she responded like this to him before, nor him to her: tonight was some sort of alchemical reaction, a magic that had somehow sparked in the pitch-black of this bed.

Maybe that was it, the fact that they were in neither of their bedrooms, that this bed was neutral ground: maybe that was why she felt so free to let go? He assumed, of course, that she'd gone to his room first, found Dominic passed out and snoring on the fish-stained bed, and realized what must have happened; maybe the fact that she'd come to find him in the night, something she'd never done before, had set this connection between them fizzing like an electric cable?

He wanted to ask her, but his cock was demanding some sort of attention more urgently than his brain, and he heard himself say: 'Can I – are you ready to, um ...?'

'Oh hey,' she murmured drowsily, 'don't pussy out on me now, boy! Say what you want!'

She rolled over, reached down and closed her hand around his stiff cock. He felt like wailing with pleasure, but somehow managed to keep it to a more manly groan. Her voice was smug as she said softly, 'Well, *you're* good to go again, aren't you?'

'I'm gagging for it,' Edmund said, leaning forward, finding her mouth, plunging his tongue into it deeply, exactly what he wanted to do with his cock. Her hands came up and twined in his sweat-curled hair, pulling it closer, kissing him back, their tongues battling for supremacy, their teeth biting each other's lips. He buried his hands in her long hair, pulling it, hearing her moan, pulling it harder, twisting it into a rope, really dragging it now, feeling her pressing even tighter against him. Obviously she liked this, wanted it badly, and he was hugely grateful because he absolutely loved it, was horrified by how much he did love it, how pulling her hair made him even harder, even keener to fuck her as hard as she'd fucked him.

'Fuck me up the ass and pull my hair!' she said, managing to wrest her mouth from his. 'Do it, fuck me up the ass, now, *do it*!'

Edmund had never done this before in his life, and her words made his balls tighten in soaring anticipation.

'Go slow at first,' she said, turning over and pushing up her bottom. 'That's a big cock you've got there. Take your time and then fuck me with everything you've got.'

He didn't need to be told twice: he was already behind her, reaching between her legs for her own moisture, working it into the cleft of her arse, again and again, making it a series of caresses, hearing her wail and push against his hand, her face, he assumed, buried in a pillow, because her pleas of 'Fuck me, fuck me, do it, please fuck me now' were muffled. He took his time until he thought he had enough lubrication not to hurt her too much, and, to be honest, enjoying torturing her, making her beg for it until she was screaming in frustration into the pillow; and then, finally, when he couldn't bear it any more himself, dipping the tip of his cock for a second into her pussy for extra wetness and then dragging it up to where she wanted it, easing it in.

'Oh Jesus fuck!' he said as her body closed around him, the sensation of entering the tight ring of muscle incredibly intense. He could feel how snug the fit was, understood what she'd meant, did his absolute best to go as slowly as he could, feeling as if his head was going to explode with the sheer excitement of doing something this taboo, of fucking his fiancée in the arse. He leant forward, felt for her mane of hair, grabbed it and pulled back – Jesus, burying his cock in his fiancée's tight arse while tugging on her hair, starting to fuck her like she'd told him to with everything he had ...

She was screaming her head off into the pillow now, a

stream of filthy encouraging curses, calling him a dirty bastard, a fucking dirty animal, her arse pumping back against his balls, clearly loving what he was doing to her. Emboldened, he twined her hair around one of his wrists, pulled harder, forcing her to arch up off the pillow, and with his other hand he landed a hard slap on her arse cheek.

It sent her even more wild. She bucked beneath him frantically, and it sounded as if she'd stuffed one hand into her mouth to keep from shrieking. 'Yes, yes, fuck yes, oh fuck yes, do it, fucking do it!' He heard her crying into her knuckles, and he lifted his palm and spanked her again, a whole series of spanks, her firm flesh quivering every time, his cock pounding inside her, finding a rhythm where he drove deep, pulled out almost to the tip, landed a slap and then thrust inside her again. It was ecstasy, it was the most intense thing he'd ever done, it was actually going to burst the top of his head right off if he didn't tell himself he could come almost immediately, his balls were so tight it was agony ...

He managed, somehow, to reach around, to grab her mound in his palm and find her clit with his finger and bring her off: she went absolutely limp as she came, as if all the bones in her body had dissolved, and once he knew she was done he let go and came like a runaway train hitting the buffers at full blast. It was as if his cock actually blew up, exploded inside her for good, like a bomb detonating. He knew exactly how she'd felt, coming, because he went limp too, collapsing on top of her with his entire weight, something he would never normally do because it was so ungentlemanly to crush a woman like that, as if she were the mattress ...

But then, nothing I've done with her has been remotely gentlemanly. And the more I acted like an animal, the more she liked it – and God, the more she acted like an animal, the more I bloody loved it ...

They were both running with sweat, her back wet with it, his chest plastered to her shoulder blades. His heart was pumping out of his chest, and beneath him he could hear her panting, feel her own body heaving as she also struggled to catch her breath. His head was resting on her upper back, and he licked her sweat, tasting it, her salt mingled with his, and he felt her tremble beneath him just at this touch of his tongue.

He had never been so reluctant to slide his cock out of a woman in his life. He held on as long as he could, till he couldn't help it, and even then she moaned softly as his shrinking cock eventually slipped out of her. They turned on their sides as one, and he pressed himself against her back, spooning her, trying to get as much of himself as he could against her smooth skin, her wonderful round arse, wrapping an arm over her and closing his hand over her equally wonderfully round and heavy breast. He was going to kiss the back of her neck, but then he thought better of it, opening his mouth instead and sinking his teeth just fractionally into the damp skin, rewarded by the sensation of her whole body trembling in response.

'I need to sleep, tiger,' she mumbled, already halfway there by the sound of her voice. 'Give me a couple of hours and then I'll suck you off.'

Edmund groaned. 'Not fair, when we need to sleep ...'

'Who said I was fair?' she mumbled.

He put his lips to her ear and whispered:

'I bet you'll like it if I bite your pussy when I go down on you, won't you?' and this time it was she who moaned, unable to help herself writhing against him.

'Fuck yes,' she sighed. 'You bastard.'

And she did.

Chapter Nineteen

Tamra glided down the main stairs of Stanclere Hall at eleven that morning, heading for the lavish, American-style brunch which she and Mrs Hurley had planned – muffins, waffles, bacon, pancakes, Bloody Marys, exactly what everyone would dig into gratefully after a hard night's partying. She had a smile on her face that nearly stretched from ear to ear. It was almost painful. But then, what part of her body didn't ache deliciously?

The soles of my feet, she thought naughtily. *That's pretty much the only bit of me that doesn't hurt.*

Her smile became so saucily full of reminiscence of last night's activities that a maid, changing the candles in the huge silver branch on the piano, looked up at Tamra descending the stairs and was hypnotized, unable to take her eyes off Tamra's face: it was as radiant as the sun, as bright as the rays of morning light that were glittering across the Great Hall, thrown down at angles from the high arched windows. Tamra didn't even notice the maid's rapt gaze as she headed around the base of the stairs, towards the dining room, happily anticipating her first Bloody Mary of the day, made, according to her orders, in New Orleans style, with plenty of horseradish and pickled green beans.

With Edmund's agreement, she had promoted Mrs Hurley to housekeeper and allowed her to hire cooks to replace her in the kitchen. Mrs Hurley had taken to her new role like a duck to water, having effectively been cook/housekeeper of the Hall for years, and was very enthusiastically embracing all the new elements Tamra wanted to introduce to Stanclere, pickled green beans and all. By now, in fact, Mrs Hurley's emotions for Tamra could best be described as heroine-worship. Tamra's money was preserving the Hall and keeping it out of the hands of hotel developers who would probably want to drain the lake to build a golf course, and Tamra's taste was dragging the Hall into the twenty-first century, making it into a showplace that was the wonder of the County.

Mrs Hurley was in the dining room, supervising the breakfast buffet and taking orders for omelettes, as Tamra tripped in, sleek in her tight jeans, beige sweater and hair arranged in a glossy curled ponytail, barely any make-up on her face. Even brushing her hair, pulling it back and wrapping a lock around the elastic to cover it, had been a little sore: her scalp was tender from the enthusiasm with which Dominic had dragged back her hair last night. He had, as promised, sunk his teeth between her legs, which no one had ever done before, and her cheeks flushed pink as she remembered it: he had driven her almost literally out of her mind. It had been unquestionably the best sex she'd ever had in her life.

I mean, I could tell he'd be kind of a dirty fuck, but who knew we'd have chemistry like that? Shit, that was off the charts. That kind of chemistry happens once in a lifetime, if you're lucky.

And to think I was assuming that'd be a one-night stand! She wanted to whisk him off somewhere for at least a couple of weeks – maybe the Maldives, she'd never been, and everyone said they were stunning. They'd fuck each other's brains out non-stop for a while, then see if there was anything more than just the sexual connection between them, if it would burn out with time or whether there was something else beyond it ...

Tamra poured herself a Bloody Mary and loaded a plate with bacon and cheese muffins. That was food she would never normally touch, of course, but last night she must have burnt so many calories she was frankly going to allow herself to eat whatever she damn well wanted. She flashed Mrs Hurley a dazzling smile of appreciation and floated over to the dining table. Only Lady Margaret was down yet, and Tamra took a seat next to her, a footman pulling out the chair for her as she settled in and ordered coffee.

'You look like the cat that got the cream,' Lady Margaret observed, as Tamra sipped her morning cocktail.

'Honey, I got the cream about five times in every conceivable place!' Tamra said naughtily, but at a pitch low enough for none of the staff to hear. Her friend spluttered out cappuccino foam. 'Dominic turns out to be the biggest stud ever. Honestly, I may never need to pay for it again!'

God, I wish I were still up there in his room, she thought wistfully. It had been so tough to get up at dawn and slip out without waking him. She'd struggled with the temptation to pull back the bedcurtains, to see him in a sliver of the morning light that was filtering in through a crack in the curtains at the high-framed window: but the light might have woken him, and he'd have pulled her back for another bout – mmn, morning sex, slow and sticky and languid – and then Stanclere Hall would be stirring, which meant someone might have seen her sneaking down the corridor, like a teenager coming back from doing her boyfriend under her parents' roof. Which would be way too humiliating.

I wonder how he felt when he woke up and realized I wasn't there? I hope he missed me.

She grinned at how pathetic she sounded, like a sixteen-year-old with a mad crush. God, she hadn't felt like this since she didn't remember when!

'Darling, you need to get a grip on yourself,' Lady Margaret said, her eyebrows raised. 'You look positively giddy.'

'I *am* giddy,' Tamra said, thanking the waiter bringing her coffee with so beautiful a smile that he almost tripped as he put it in front of her. 'Which is fabulous. You know I don't want anything serious – this guy's perfect. I'll fuck his brains out for a few weeks or months, see if it burns out or not. Have a lovely time and no expectations. What could be better?'

'Well, if you put it like that ...'

Her friend raised her own Bloody Mary and clinked it with Tamra's.

'These are delicious, by the way,' Lady Margaret said approvingly.

'Good and spicy,' Tamra said with great satisfaction, extracting a pickled green bean from her glass and biting into it with a snap of her perfect white teeth.

Then she paused, the second half of the bean still between her fingers. Dominic had entered the dining room, and he didn't look remotely as she had expected. After the night they'd had, the sheer volume of orgasms, the amount of blood rushing to their faces, the sheer delight they'd given each other, he should have looked as glowing as she did: tired, maybe, but also smug, his eyes meeting hers with conspiracy about their shared secret.

But Dominic, instead, just seemed – hungover. His eyes were bloodshot, the bags underneath them were large enough to store bowling balls, and his gait was shambling: not in an

I-fucked-a-hot-cougar-all-last-night way, more I-passed-out-in-an-armchair-and-my-back-is-fucking-killing-me. Tamra stared at him in disbelief. His curly hair was plastered to his forehead, damp and unattractively sweaty.

'My God, what did you do to that poor boy?' Lady Margaret huffed out a laugh. 'He looks like a shell of his former self! Honestly, Tamra, he looks like you sucked his brains out through his cock!'

Tamra couldn't help a giggle at this, even as she stared, bemused, at Dominic. His hair was so curly: surely she'd remember that texture between her fingers? His lips were full, pouty – they hadn't felt that wide and luscious when she kissed them, bit them, when they fastened between her legs last night and made her scream with pleasure. And the cock he'd pressed her hand against in the corridor, she recalled, had felt considerably smaller than the one that had driven itself, on her orders, up her ass last night as she wailed and bit down on the pillow—

She was on her feet without even realizing it, the heavy dining chair rocking back as she jumped up reflexively, picking up her cup of coffee in one hand, the Bloody Mary in the other, walking swiftly over to Dominic and saying to him: 'Come outside on the terrace for a moment, okay?'

Close up, he was even more pitiful-looking; the whites of his eyes were pink as an albino rat's, his skin was greyish with fatigue and he didn't smell as fresh as he could have done. Tamra's brow was furrowed in confusion as she led him to the terrace doors, nodded at him abruptly to open them, walked outside, leaning against the balcony in the sunshine, the cool air was a sharp relief to her overheated face. Dominic winced at the sunlight, turning himself with his back to the east, hunching his shoulders against it. Tamra handed him the coffee, saying sharply: 'Drink that up and tell me what the hell happened last night.'

Too sharply: Dominic coughed on his mouthful of coffee, dribbling it down his shirt front.

'Look, I'm sorry,' he said, when he finally managed to swallow some. 'What d'you want from me? I drank too much and passed out. I've got the most hellish hangover, if you must know. I woke up in a room reeking of the smell of my own puke.'

Tamra blinked frantically, trying to process this information. The glass in her hand was shaking; she looked down at it as if she had no idea what she was even holding.

'What room?' she heard herself say. 'What room did you wake up in?'

'Why is this even a question? Why does it *matter*? Fuck, my head hurts like buggery,' Dominic whined.

Tamra took the coffee cup from him and handed him the Bloody Mary instead.

'Try that,' she snapped.

'Oh, hair of the dog.' Dominic cheered up a little as he took a long pull on the cocktail. 'Nice one.'

'*What room did you pass out in?*' Tamra hissed at him. Through the French doors, she saw her daughter come in for breakfast, sitting down next to Lady Margaret.

'I don't know why you're making such a fuss about this,' Dominic said fretfully. 'It's not like I put a rotting fish in *your* bed, is it? Look, I'll leave something extra for the maids if that's the problem here. Did one of them come and complain to you? Bloody sneaking if she did. It's Ed's house, when all's said and done, and if I put a fish in my host's bed as a joke, that's between him and me.'

'A *fish*?' Tamra repeated blankly.

'Bit of a traditional thing here when someone gets engaged,' Dominic said. 'Going to have a fish in your bed for the rest of your life – see how that works? Jolly funny, really. Bastard couldn't take it like a man, though, complained about the stink and made me swap rooms with him—'

His face convulsed suddenly and he thrust the glass back at Tamra as if it were burning him.

'Feel a bit sick – that fish smell was really strong when I woke up,' he muttered, and turned to dash down the stone steps to the lawn, where he could be heard gagging.

Tamra actually envied him: she wanted to throw up too. Wordlessly, she lifted the glass to her lips and drained it, then she walked like a zombie back to the terrace doors, a footman coming forward to open them for her, since both her hands were full. She handed the glass and coffee cup to him and sank into a seat at the table opposite Brianna Jade and Lady Margaret, her face as frozen as Brianna Jade's had been yesterday.

'Mom?' Brianna Jade said, worried. 'Are you okay?'

Say something, you have to say something – everyone's staring at you.

'Uh, I'm pretty grossed out by Dominic,' Tamra managed to say. 'He just told me he put a rotten fish in Edmund's bed last night as part of some disgusting British tradition for when men get engaged.'

'Oh yuk!' Brianna Jade exclaimed, her lovely eyes widening with shock. 'That's *totally* gross – why would anyone do that?'

Lady Margaret was frowning deeply as she looked at Tamra, but she was too intelligent to say a word until she had worked out exactly what was happening.

'Good morning!' came a very cheerful, ringing masculine voice from the doorway, and in strode the Earl of Respers, his face lit up like a hundred-watt bulb, his grey eyes glowing as they lighted on the face of his fiancée. 'Hello, darling!'

A few swift paces brought him to Brianna Jade's side, and

he bent to plant a passionate kiss on her mouth: she let out a little yelp, a hand rising to her lips, and Edmund looked briefly embarrassed as he pulled up the chair on her other side and sat down.

'Sorry,' he said. He lifted her hand and brought it to his lips as Mrs Hurley sighed fondly by the buffet table. Brianna Jade looked at him in great confusion as he kissed it, staring deeply into her eyes, then he jumped up, saying: 'God, I think I'm hungrier than I've ever been in my life! I'm absolutely starving!' He winked at his fiancée. 'I can't think why I've worked up such an appetite!'

For a moment, Tamra and Lady Margaret's eyes met across the table in outright, horrified understanding. Tamra bit her lip so deeply she tasted blood.

'Oh, good morning!' trilled Milly, flitting into the dining room on a cloud of Anaïs Anaïs; she had decided that the perfume was so out it was in again, and that it would give her an extra, trendsetting edge to be the one to bring it back into fashion. 'How's everyone doing? Brianna Jade, sweetie, are you feeling better? Such a shame you weren't feeling well last night!' She leant in towards her victim. 'Maybe you should have taken a nice stroll outside and got some fresh air? That seems to, um, pick you up, doesn't it?'

This was a catastrophic misjudgement on Milly's part. Emboldened by her success at the photo- and videoshoots the day before, she had quite lost sight of the fact that her target was sitting with her mother and Lady Margaret. Tamra's head rose slowly to look at Milly, her eyes two dark dead black holes in a pale face, the high blonde ponytail bouncing, the very image of a psychotic Barbie.

'Oh *goodness*,' Lady Margaret breathed, setting down her coffee cup as Tamra rose slowly to her feet, pushing back her chair.

Milly blanched as white as her floaty shirt-dress. Tamra's expression was as terrifying as if she'd actually been the cougar Dominic called her: all her protective, tiger-mother instincts for her daughter surged to the fore, propelled by the rush of absolute, burning horror at the realization of what she had done the night before with her daughter's fiancé. Her own sense of the terrible betrayal she had committed made her shiver from head to toe as it sank in. She leaned forward, her palms on the table for support.

To Milly, it looked as if Tamra's fury was caused entirely by her own words, and she flinched back in fear as Tamra hissed at her across the width of the table.

'*Get. Out.*'

'I – I—' Milly stammered. 'I didn't mean—'

'*Oh yes you did,*' Tamra breathed. 'I know exactly what you meant! Get out of this house – now, before I throw you out! How *dare* you come in here as a guest and deliberately try to upset my daughter? You've already done enough damage – get out without saying another word, or I'll tear your face off!'

Milly was used to actresses throwing tantrums, make-up artists being bitchy, directors yelling in frustration or trying to seduce her. But she was a sheltered girl brought up in an upper-middle-class household, and never, ever, had she been confronted by a working-class woman used to scrapping down and dirty. Milly couldn't move: she stood there, paralysed, as Edmund turned from the buffet table with the baffled expression of a man who's suddenly found himself in the middle of a catfight.

'Wait, what's all this about?' he said.

'Let Tamra deal with this, Ed,' Lady Margaret said quickly to him, seeing how Tamra's eyes darkened even more at the sound of Edmund's voice. 'Stay out of it.'

Taking Milly's inability to budge as a sign not of fear but of defiance, Tamra stormed around the head of the table, and Milly actually squealed in panic and darted behind Edmund, thinking that Tamra was coming for her. Instead, Tamra swept magnificently out of the room and could be heard tearing up the staircase. It sounded as if she were taking the treads two at a time. Irresistibly, drawn as if by a powerful magnet, every guest and most of the staff present in the dining room filtered outside into the Great Hall. No one dared to follow Tamra upstairs, but a degree of crashing and banging could be heard from the unrenovated guest wing, and in just a couple of minutes, Tamra emerged on the long balcony that led to the staircase, clasping an armful of clothes, two terrified-looking maids following her, laden with more clothes and Milly's luggage.

'Here!' Tamra screamed, opening her arms and dropping Milly's clothes theatrically down the two-storeys-high well of the staircase. 'Take all your boho hippy-dippy crap and get the hell out of here!'

Underwear, tights, blouses, jeans tumbled down onto the polished wood floor. Tamra reached for the second bundle the maid was carrying and grabbed a pair of shoes in one hand, at which everyone shrieked and ducked back against the wall.

'Mom, no!' Brianna Jade yelled.

Tamra was breathing so hard that everyone could hear her panting: apart from her daughter, the rest of the spectators were keeping as silent as they could to avoid drawing down her wrath on their own heads. Courageously, Brianna Jade stepped out into the hallway, directly into Tamra's line of fire, crossing her fingers that Tamra wouldn't see a blonde head and start chucking shoes at it before she realized her target was her own daughter.

'Mom, stop!' she called. 'You've made your point, okay? She'll go! Don't throw any shoes! Or Jesus – Mom, put down the curling tongs! Put them *down*!'

'I think you should probably nip out the back to the garages,' Lady Margaret said to Milly in an undertone. 'No point staying here now, is there? We'll find Tarquin and send him out to you. I'll get a maid to, er, re-pack your cases.'

'Clearly, this is a terribly awkward situation, but even with my duty as a host to guests under my roof, I have to second Tamra's decision,' Edmund said gravely, walking out to stand next to Brianna Jade, his deeper voice and his quiet authority drawing every eye. Even Tamra, who had snatched Milly's curling tongs from the pile the maid was carrying, and was poised with one arm back, rather like the statue of the discus thrower in the gazebo, still panting as loudly as an athlete in the middle of a race, stared down at him, his serious grey eyes meeting hers for a moment before he turned to encircle her daughter with one arm, regarding Brianna Jade with great devotion.

'My fiancée comes first,' Edmund continued, as Lady Margaret hustled Milly away before Tamra could send the tongs or the shoes hurtling down towards her target's blonde head. 'I can't permit anyone, even an invited guest, to treat Brianna Jade with anything less than the respect she deserves. I did notice how upset you were yesterday,' he added to Brianna Jade more quietly, 'but I didn't realize it was Milly causing it. I do apologize for not asking you about it yesterday, but I'm so glad you came to find me last night.' He squeezed her tightly.

'I don't understand—' Brianna Jade started to say, looking up at him in puzzlement.

'What's going on?' Sophie's voice came from up above them, and they both craned back to look at her. 'I heard screaming – is everything all right?'

'Tamra's chucking Milly out for winding up Brianna Jade,' Dominic said, strolling out from the dining room. He had a full glass of Bloody Mary in one hand, a cheese muffin in the other, and looked a little better: after his last retching fit had proved abortive, with practically nothing left to come up, he was proceeding to re-line his stomach.

'Oh, fair enough,' Sophie said, leaning on the balcony and heaving a long yawn. She was wearing a towelling robe, and her feet were in fluffy mules. 'Milly *was* being pretty vile yesterday. Did she finally go too far?'

'Clearly,' Dominic said, shrugging his shoulders.

Behind Sophie, down the corridor, the footman who had brought the breakfast she had requested to have served in her suite slipped out, tucking his shirt into his trousers and buttoning his waistcoat, heading down towards the service stairs with a very self-satisfied smile on his face: Sophie had always had a taste for working-class men in uniform.

'Oh, breakfast was *delicious*, by the way,' Sophie added with an equally satisfied smile, checking out of the corner of her eye that the footman had made his escape discreetly. 'Thank you so much, Tamra. I must say, your hospitality is first-rate in *every* respect ...'

'Dom, would you go and roust out Tarquin?' Edmund asked. 'Tell him I'm sorry and all that, but one simply can't have this kind of thing going on.'

'Absolutely,' Dominic said, starting to climb the stairs, leaving a muffin crumb trail scattered behind him as he went. He winked at Tamra as he passed her. 'Look, sorry about last night,' he muttered, reaching out to give her a discreet pat on the bottom. 'I'll make it up to you tonight, eh? Believe me, when I'm not completely blotto, I know how to give a girl a good time. Got a lot of tricks up my sleeve. This time tomorrow you'll be telling everyone that was the best shag you ever had – trust me on that.'

Tamra made such an awful choking sound that everyone down in the Hall looked up, concerned that she was having a fit. The shoes and curling tongs fell from her hands. One high heel nearly tumbled through the open balustrade and down onto the maid who was now, under Mrs Hurley's instructions, on her knees swiftly gathering up Milly's scattered clothes; the maid screeched in fear, but Dominic, showing great aplomb, punted the shoe aside just in time, knocking it back onto the hallway carpet.

'Nicely done, if I do say so myself,' he observed complacently.

Tamra turned and ran. Down the balcony and into the corridor that led to the main wing of Stanclere Hall, heading with a sprinter's speed for her rooms, slamming the door behind her and, her whole body shaking, grabbing the tasselled cord on the wall of her living room and tugging on it so hard that if it had been one of the old bell-pulls it would have come straight out of the ceiling in a cloud of dust and plaster. But this had been one of her innovations when this wing had been remodelled, to keep the idea of old-fashioned bell-pulls, so familiar to everyone from *Downton Abbey*, and she had organized the rewiring of the ancient system so that it was now electrically operated: a tug on the cord rang pagers clipped to the waist of three maids who, between them, were responsible for the main wing on a shift system, two on duty at any time during the day.

The maid who was closest flicked a switch indicating to the others that she was answering the summons, and in under a minute she was knocking on the door, terrified of Tamra's current state of mind but even more frightened of arriving late. She found the Earl of Respers' future mother-in-law sitting on the wide upholstered seat of the curving bow window, staring out to the park beyond, and was very grateful that Tamra did not turn her head to look at her: the reflection of Tamra's face in the glass was paralysing enough. The absolute stillness, the black holes that were her eyes, the dead-white face, as if all the golden tan had faded at the speed of light ...

'Pack up all my things,' Tamra said to the window in a voice as dead and emotion-free as her facial expression. 'And have my car brought around. I'm going back to London immediately.'

'Yes, madam,' the maid said, hurrying into the bathroom, beginning to sort Tamra's toiletries and perfumes into her matched set of red lizard Aspinall of London vanity cases while paging Tamra's driver to bring the Bentley to the side entrance where the suitcases could be loaded into it.

The window recess had been turned into a cosy bower to Tamra's specific design, pale grey velvet seat cushions piped in matching silk, with throw pillows in shades of darker grey velvet and slub silk scattered artfully around, sea-green velvet curtains framing the stone alcove. And yet Tamra, curled up, hugging her knees, was utterly oblivious to both the comfort surrounding her and the beauty of the newly tended park beyond, the soft colours of the oak trees in autumn and the deep green of the lawns. She stared at the mullioned window panes, her entire body aching: she felt as if she was just a shell, as if someone had hollowed her out, harvested every organ, leaving her effectively a zombie who could walk and talk but whose eyes were blank and sightless.

All I can do is pretend that it never happened. Leave Stanclere at once, and do my best not to come back until the day of the wedding, not to see him –

She shuddered from head to toe.

Not to see him until he marries my daughter.

Chapter Twenty

'So *this* is where the red carpet will go?' Milly asked. 'That's terribly important, you know – everyone will be wearing heels. And besides, it'll look much better in the photographs ...'

'Of course!' both Ludo and Marco Baldini, the very dapper local agent who was Ludo's fixer in Chianti, assured the bride-to-be.

'The carpet will run up the little hill to the oratory,' Ludo added, winding his arm through Milly's. 'And we'll have another one crossing it, as it were, when you make your entrance from the side of the church and walk around it all the way to the gazebo. But darling, we don't want to cover *all* the grass in carpet, you know? My suggestion for my more rustic spring and summer weddings is that the ladies wear heels but bring a lovely pair of elegant flat sandals as well.'

He winked confidentially at Milly's pretty face, which was framed delightfully between her white mohair beret and the matching fur collar of her rose-pink wool coat.

'You know, when one's had a little too much champagne, and one is dancing, it can get a little slippy on the dance floor.

Flats are *always* a good idea, actually – I like to check that the bridal party has them just as a backup.'

'This is *so* beautiful!' Eva sighed to Tarquin, following behind Milly as they walked up the little slope to the oratory of the Madonna della Neve d'Agosto. The exquisite little church nestled in the heart of the Chianti hills, fifteen minutes down a narrow, winding dirt road whose rises and falls Marco Baldini's Range Rover had navigated expertly on the last leg of their trip from Pisa airport. On their right, the hillside fell sharply away to a spectacular view of the Chianti valley below, the tight marching lines of the vineyards, the vines now stark and black, pruned back after the September harvest, and the fluffy grey-green olive trees, their fields busy with workers on ladders hand-picking the fruit.

'Sadly, all that is left of the castle that once was here is this church,' Marco Baldini was explaining to an uninterested Milly. 'The Castello of Montagliari was the noble seat of the aristocratic Gherardini family – their name will be most famous to you from the portrait of the *Mona Lisa* by Leonardo da Vinci, because it is believed that the original of that lady was Lisa Gherardini, of this family. But when that was painted, her family castle was no longer here, because the Florentine Republic became so jealous of the power of the Gherardinis that they razed the castello to the ground, leaving only the church and a well.'

'A well?' Milly repeated blankly.

'For water, darling,' Tarquin said, coming up behind her and dropping a kiss on the top of her head, or rather on the beret. 'Rather important, water, you know? Can't really manage without it.'

'So did the Mona Lisa live here?' Milly asked, having tuned out almost all of the historical information. 'That would be *fantastic* for publicity!'

'No, darling,' Tarquin told her patiently. 'Marco just said that the castle wasn't here any more, and she could scarcely live in the church, could she?'

'She lived in Florence,' Marco explained. 'She was married very young to a rich silk merchant and had many children. Her husband was called Francesco del Giocondo, which is why the portrait is also known as *La Gioconda ...*'

But he tailed off, seeing that Milly had lost interest again. She was walking up to the medieval oratory, a pale yellow building that dated back to the thirteenth century, with a wide and gracious portico running round three sides, the space generous enough to comfortably accommodate dining tables and chairs; the high loggia had arches, providing a series of frames through which diners would look out and see the jaw-droppingly beautiful Tuscan landscape beyond as dusk fell and the sun set.

'Isn't this *exactly* the small scale, rustic setting that you wanted, dear?' Ludo said, keeping pace with her. '*Very* intimate and charming – *totally* original, they've only just opened it as a wedding venue, so you'll be the first celebs to use it – and the food will be absolutely spectacular. Not just delicious, but *utterly* photogenic. Gabriella, who owns the place and runs it with her son Leonardo, is the most extraordinary chef.'

'Will it be as special as Keira Knightley's?' Milly asked anxiously. 'You know it needs to be like hers, but better.'

'Of *course*, dear,' Ludo sighed. 'I haven't forgotten that we're looking at *Style Bride* taking photographs and covering this wedding! It will all be one hundred per cent *Style*-worthy. I know this unbelievably talented designer called Antonio di Meglio in Milan who makes chandeliers from semi-precious stones – we're going to commission several from him to hang in the portico, especially for the wedding, *and*,' he said with great satisfaction, 'listen to *this*! I'm going to get him to use the same pearls and turquoises that are going to be sewn on your dress! White and pale blue are your colours, of course – but just *think*, the chandeliers actually echoing the bride's dress and jewellery! How fabulous will *that* be? And I see lemons, too,' he added thoughtfully. 'In those antique birdcages you're so obsessed with. I'm going to put them on the table and fill them with Sicilian lemons.'

So they look less bloody twee, he thought to himself but naturally didn't say.

'Oh, that sounds lovely!' Milly clapped her hands girlishly. They were clad in suede gloves, pale pink to match the coat: it was a pleasantly temperate day in Tuscany, lit by a pale yellow November sun, but there was enough of a breeze to justify the hat and gloves, and Milly had been determined to wear the full outfit she had planned, as Eva was tasked with taking plenty of cameraphone photos for Milly to put on social media. Tarquin, hearing the muffled clap, looked up from where he was standing with Marco and Eva, hearing more about the history of the church, and smiled happily on seeing how delighted his pastel-clad fiancée was with the destination that Ludo had selected.

'And the wild flowers in the vintage teapots?' Milly asked eagerly. 'Have you worked out where to source those from? I've set my heart on bluebells and lilies of the valley. You know, white and pale blue – our colours – and they'll look great with the lemons and the china and the birdcages.'

Ludo had a minor coughing fit; when he recovered, he said smoothly:

'Sorry, dear. It must be the wind. Are you sure you're set on the vintage china side of things? I just wonder if that *and* the antique birdcages might veer just the *slightest* into cutesy territory ...'

'Oh *no*,' Milly assured him very positively. 'They'll all look wonderful together! I've got a huge moodboard in Eva's office with lots of pictures of the teapots and cups and saucers and birdcages and wild flowers, and I just *sigh* with happiness every time I see it, because it's so perfect and *totally* on brand.'

'What does Eva say about it?' Ludo asked, casting a side eye to Milly's best friend, who, in her skinny jeans, slouchy leather jacket, shaggy fringe and ankle boots, was considerably more fashion-forward than the rather over-girlishly dressed Milly.

Milly paused briefly.

'She gets the whole branding thing,' she said firmly, 'and that's positively crucial. I mean, sometimes our aesthetics don't completely blend, but that's fine, and she really knows what she's doing for the jewellery line. Everyone always says how on trend she is. But it's my wedding, and I'm selling me and Tark together, *our* brand, *our* image, and I know what I'm doing. You should *see* what my followers on Instagram like! It's all the pretty, girlie, boho-chic stuff! That overdone bitch Tamra Maloney might call me hippy-dippy, but it's *in* right now, and my fans love my style!'

She was breathing a little faster now: the memory of having been thrown so unceremoniously out of Stanclere Hall still rankled, even though, technically, it had been because she had won a huge victory. She had destabilized Brianna Jade enough that very few of the photographs from the *Style* online shoot had been usable, or at least the ones with Brianna Jade front and centre: Ludo's connections at *Style* had reported back that considerable work had had to be done to tweak the photo shoot enough for it to be posted on the website. There could be no question of killing it, of course, not with the styling work that had gone into it, let alone the presence of Princess Sophie: but working around Brianna Jade's frozen features and rictus smile had definitely presented a challenge that only a team as professionally skilled as *Style* could have managed to pull off.

Ironically, the video from the shoot had come out much better. There was a natural liveliness to images in motion that the editor had succeeded in cutting together so deftly that even Victoria Glossop had nodded approvingly when she watched it. Milly, Sophie and Minty looked absolutely charming as they laughed, hugged each other, jumped into Dominic, Tarquin and Lance's arms, and posed playfully on the statues in the gazebo. They were so charming, in fact, that they carried the more staid Edmund and the near-paralysed Brianna Jade along with them. But Victoria and Jodie could clearly see how much Milly and Tarquin stood out, and how Brianna Jade and Edmund faded into the background.

Perfectly aware of how well she had come out of the *Style* shoot, and how poorly her rival had done, Milly was floating on Cloud Nine, very confident of snagging the prized, first ever *Style Bride* cover and all the attendant publicity. Still, even though it had been her own fault that Tamra had thrown her out of Stanclere Hall, even though Milly should have left well alone after upsetting Brianna Jade at the shoot and not continued to goad her the morning after, it still rankled with Milly that she had been chucked out, let alone with her underwear scattered all over the hall carpet in front of a royal princess. Milly knew perfectly well that Minty and Sophie had told the story all over London with great amusement, and even though Milly herself would have recounted all the gory details in similar circumstances, she still reserved the right to be angry about Tamra's dramatic expulsion of her.

Ludo cleared his throat, seeing that any further attempt of his to persuade Milly to lose either the vintage china or the birdcages would fall on deaf ears. He switched to another bone of contention instead.

'Dear, the lilies of the valley and bluebells that you keep mentioning?' he said. 'I *have* managed to find a florist near here who's going to grow them on special order. The price he quoted is frankly astronomical. I wouldn't be doing my job if I didn't let you know that.'

'Oh, Tark makes absolutely *tons*,' Milly said lightly, resting one hand on Ludo's arm. 'And there's plenty of family money too.'

'Of course there is!' Ludo said, cheering up as he mentally added his customary mark-up of 20 per cent to the florist's bill. *When life gives you lemons,* he told himself, *call them organic Meyer citrus specialities imported at great cost from California and charge the client accordingly.* 'Isn't it just wonderful?'

'We have the ceremony here, in the gazebo,' Marco Baldini was saying to Tarquin and Eva, indicating the pretty white iron structure set on the grass to one side of the oratory. 'It will be hung with white curtains of course, muslin, to blow a little, very romantic. I will show you photographs over lunch – my wife Alice and I were married here last August, it was the first wedding they have here, and that gave us and the owners the idea to make it a special place for the ceremonies. It will be very exclusive – just a few couples every year, so that we can take time to make it very carefully, with all the details just how the clients choose. And the dance floor will be on the other side, overlooking the valley, with the wonderful view and a band to play music. You will have prosecco before the ceremony, then a buffet of antipasti after, with more prosecco, of course, and then dinner in the portico of the church.'

'What does the name of the church mean?' Eva asked, wrinkling her brow. 'Madonna of the Snow in August?'

'Correct!' Marco smiled at her. 'That is exactly right. There is a legend that God makes it snow here in August, many centuries ago. Which is of course a miracle, because it never can snow in August! And this –' he gestured towards the stunning sweep of view beyond the church, the glorious escarpment, thick with trees, and the white ribbon of dirt road winding around the slopes – 'this is exactly the same view that we have seen here in Chianti for many, many centuries, a panorama which Leonardo da Vinci painted in 1473, a landscape drawing in ink. The picture is now in the Uffizi Gallery in Florence. We have a copy of it here to show you, of course. You will see it does not change at all.'

'Wow, a Leonardo of this very place,' Eva breathed. 'Can we go and see it while we're here?'

'That would be wonderful,' Tarquin said eagerly. 'We could go tomorrow, before the flight.'

'Oh, I'd love that!' Eva exclaimed.

Ludo, walking back with Milly to rejoin the little group, was smiling smugly at the expression of enchantment on both Tarquin and Eva's faces. He had deliberately not given his clients much information about where he was taking them, because he knew that the extraordinary history of the church – painted by Leonardo da Vinci, no less! – would be most effective as they stood in front of it, taking in the breathtaking beauty of the place and its setting.

This was a principal reason why Ludo was one of the most highly paid wedding planners in Britain, with an impressive list of celebrity clients. Not only did he know his job backwards and forwards, he also had a finely developed, theatrical sense of how to present those clients with the solutions he had found for their requests. This location, this perfect little church nestled in the heart of the Chianti hills, was exactly what Milly and Tarquin had wanted, fairy tale without being in any way a cliché. The oratory would give them all the privacy they wanted, tucked away in a fold of the Montagliari hillside so perfectly that it could barely even be seen from the gravel and dirt road that approached it.

'It's perfect,' Tarquin observed seriously, turning around in a circle to take in the full beauty of the vista. 'Simple, magical, isolated. Like a gem in a perfect setting.'

Marco Baldini nodded gravely. 'That is very beautiful,' he said. 'You are a poet, Mr Ormond. We know this from your excellent music.'

'The main thing is that Milly must have everything she wants,' Tarquin said with great earnestness, his eyes wide, as his fiancée settled herself to nestle in front of him, smiling with great satisfaction at his words. 'Money really is no object.'

'Of course, dear,' Ludo said, patting Tarquin's hand. 'What Milly wants is the only thing in *any* of our minds. And Eva's here so that she can be Milly's voice, as it were, when you're off touring and Milly's filming in Portland.'

'Great!' Tarquin's smile was angelic as he glanced over at Eva, tall enough in her ankle boots that her eyes were on a level with his. 'I trust Eva implicitly, and so does Milly.'

Milly's smile deepened at Ludo's reference to the fact that she had snagged the coveted part in *And When We Fall*: filming started in January.

'Why don't Marco and I talk logistics for a little while,' Ludo said smoothly, 'and let you three wander round the church? And then we can show you the rooms here behind the church, where you'll be staying for the weekend of the wedding. Gabriella has decorated them truly beautifully. There's a villa just down the road where more guests can stay, and hotels in the nearby village for the overflow. But of course, there won't be *that* many. The portico seats about seventy, which is what you said you wanted?'

Tarquin nodded.

'We don't want this to be a big spectacle,' he said even

more seriously. 'It's for Milly and me, our spiritual bond being sealed for ever, and for our close family and friends, you know? It's not at all about the world outside. This is why this spot is so perfect for us. It's a jewel, like I said, but hidden away. Like a diamond inside a locket, kept only for the few people who know where it is, but even more special because of its secrecy and intimacy.'

'Truly poetical,' Marco Baldini said with appreciation. 'I salute you, Mr Ormond.'

Ludo was overcome with another coughing fit.

'Excuse me,' he said, pulling out a silk handkerchief. 'Some late-autumn allergies ... this weather is a little damp. I'll just wander off with Marco here and work out where we can set up the *Style Bride* photographers and the videoshoot for this very secret wedding that isn't going to be a big spectacle at all in any way.'

But the last words, of course, were buried in his handkerchief as he turned away, and were not for any ears but his own; as devoutly as an atheist could, Ludo wished that Liam had been with him to appreciate the full irony of the moment. Although Liam loved to reprimand Ludo for his cynicism and exert the due punishment required for Ludo's lack of reverence for the holy institution of marriage, even Liam would have shared Ludo's amusement at Tarquin so solemnly speechifying about the intimacy of the wedding ceremony which his fiancée was scheming to splash all over the cover of one of the best-selling fashion magazines in the world.

'I loved what you just said,' Eva murmured to Tarquin as the three of them strolled over the grass to look up at the carved wood birdhouse hung above the gazebo. 'It really captured the magic of this place.'

'It's terribly special, isn't it?' Tarquin said, his eyes sparkling. 'This is absolutely *it*. I knew it really even before we arrived, as we were driving here bumping over that road, you know? Marco kept apologizing for the dirt road, but to me that makes it even more lovely.'

'Yes, the journey's hard but that makes the destination even more worthwhile,' Eva agreed eagerly. 'That's exactly how I felt too.'

'I love the chandelier idea,' Milly said, turning to look at the oratory, quite uninterested in Tarquin and Eva's elevated discussion. 'Can't you just *see* them? Handmade with semi-precious stones and pearls. *Style Bride* will love that detail!'

'Pearls and turquoises,' Tarquin said dreamily, pulling Milly back in front of him, wrapping his arms around her; he was easily distracted. 'Like the blue seahorses, jewels of the sea ... turquoises, it's almost a rhyme with horse ... hmm, that can go into the wedding song I'm going to write for us, Milly, because turquoise is your favourite stone ...'

With Tarquin unable to see her face, Milly grimaced at Eva, rolling her big blue eyes; the engagement ring meant that Milly had to go along with the turquoise theme, and it did fit with the whole rustic-chic, bluebells-in-vintage-china wedding décor.

Turquoise is her favourite stone? My God, you don't know Milly at all, Eva thought, staring at Tarquin's blissed-out, unearthly beauty with a cold, unusual clarity that took her by surprise. *You have absolutely no idea who you're marrying. You fell in love with a pretty face – a pretty façade*, she corrected herself. *The girl you think Milly is doesn't even exist. You've made up a whole fantasy about her, and you're so in love with your own creation you don't listen to the things she says, or look at the things she does which completely contradict the fantasy.*

Staring at Tarquin, this revelation rushing through her, Eva realized something else.

It's not even just that Milly's such a pretty face – Tarquin's in love with her partly because she looks so like him. He's fallen for his own image in the mirror.

Tarquin was still burbling away, his gaze up and to the right, accessing the creative part of his brain as new lyrics bubbled to his lips: he was beatifically unaware of how assessing Eva's gaze had become.

Oh God, I'm right, I'm absolutely right, Eva thought in misery, *and it doesn't change anything. I can see that he's not really in love with Milly at all, not her as a person, that he's been shallow enough to fall for her because of her looks and the image he's projected on her – and I still love him. It hasn't changed anything at all.*

I'm still head over heels in love with him.

Chapter Twenty-One

Lunch consisted of *pici al aglione*, oversized spaghetti with tomato and garlic, and *cinghiale*, wild boar stew, washed down with local red Sangiovese wine at a delicious local restaurant called Le Panzanelle to which Marco took them. Afterwards, the four Londoners were whisked down the winding Chiantigiana road to Florence and the luxurious surroundings of the Grand Hotel Villa Cora, a nineteenth-century mansion in its own grounds, set in the hills that surrounded the city. From its terrace, the view of Florence was laid out before them in its breathtaking beauty, the terracotta and white cupola of the Duomo, just beyond the Arno River, glittering in the late autumn sun.

At Ludo's suggestion, they checked into their junior suites and then assembled on the terrace to sip *prosecco* in the warmth of space heaters and the weak afternoon sun, reviewing detailed ideas for the wedding arrangements: now that his clients had approved the church, Ludo had sketches and menus to show them, spread out on the square white leather pouffe in front of them. But although Milly was paying close attention to Ludo's sketches of how he planned to arrange the birdcages on the tables, lemons spilling out artistically, the designs for place cards that would cunningly echo the 'snow in August' miracle, the wrought-iron canapé holders that Gabriella, the chef, was having made to her own design to best display her signature puff-pastry truffle wraps, Tarquin and Eva were not.

It was the history of the oratory and the Gherardini family, and of course the Leonardo da Vinci connection, which had entranced them both. Marco Baldini had thoughtfully provided them with some sheets of information about the church, and Tarquin and Eva, sitting in white leather chairs pulled up together, pored over them, exclaiming happily at details of the carved wooden chancel and the various frescos and paintings inside the church.

'*Such* a shame that we can't get married inside the church,' Tarquin sighed. 'I so love Baroque architecture, and the altar is so striking! But I do understand, of course, though I'd almost convert for a chance to have the ceremony in the oratory!'

'It's not like there are Leonardos inside the church,' Eva said consolingly. 'It's the landscape outside that he sketched. Look, you can see the church here ...'

She pointed to the reproduction of the sketch which had been attached to the information sheets. In sepia ink, the landscape was very dramatically rendered, with the gorges and trickling rivulets of water that characterized Tuscan hill country picked out in detail, little castles dotted at the tops of the peaks.

'I can't wait to see the real thing,' Tarquin said, his eyes radiant. 'To *think* that we're getting married in a da Vinci landscape!'

'It's the most amazing thing,' Eva said quietly. 'I know Ludo kept saying the place he'd found would blow you away, but I had no idea it would be like *this*.'

'I don't like to oversell a location before I show it to my clients,' Ludo said smugly, raising his head from his iPad, where he had been showing Milly photographs of smoked salmon and chive *cornetti*, made to look like ice-cream cones, which Gabriella had sculpted for Marco and Alice's wedding and was proposing to offer as part of the antipasto buffet for Tarquin and Milly's ceremony. 'I prefer to present the place first, so clients don't have preconceived ideas. Of course that means I have to make sure I've got it completely right, but,' he smirked, 'I haven't found *that* to be a problem.'

'You really have surpassed our expectations,' Tarquin said, pushing back his blond curls and smiling at Ludo. 'And it's so interesting to read about the history of the family and Montagliari. Milly, you must look at this. After the castle was razed by the Florentine Republic, the family split into two branches, and one of them ...'

But Milly had had quite enough of her fiancé not only directing most of his attention to another woman but talking about things in which she had no interest at all. Standing up, swirling her coat around her dramatically, she clasped her fur collar to her throat with her gloved hands, flashed a brilliant smile at Tarquin, and cooed in her best girlish, seductive tones: 'Darling, I'm getting a little chilly out here, and I'd *love* a lie-down on our gorgeous big bed before dinnertime. Why don't you come down with me and keep me company ...'

Tarquin was on his feet at once, apologizing profusely for not having noticed that Milly was cold and needed a rest.

'Well, I wouldn't quite say a *rest*,' she purred in satisfaction at having snagged Tarquin away from a discussion that he had found so absorbing. 'I think we should fill that *huge* marble bath with bubbles and see where we go from there ...'

Ten minutes later, it was very obvious where Milly had been headed, and fairly unlikely that a bath had been involved at all; there simply wouldn't have been enough time for them to run it and get in. Not only that, the bathrooms of the suites didn't have windows, and there was no question that, from the volume of the noise she was making, she was either very close to a window or had actually opened one in order to ensure that the sounds circulated as thoroughly as possible.

'Oh God, yes!' she was screaming happily, her high voice rising quite clearly up to the terrace, where Ludo, Eva and quite a few other hotel guests were ensconced. 'Oh Tark, yes, like that, oh God! Yes, yes, *yes*!'

'In retrospect, perhaps booking them into the fourth-floor suite wasn't the best idea,' Ludo commented to Eva, refilling their glasses from the bottle reposing in the ice bucket by their table. 'It's just below us, and I rather suspect Milly of being perfectly aware of that, don't you?'

Some guests were grinning now as Milly's screams rose in volume: Tarquin could just about be heard muttering, 'Darling, *darling, God,*' at a comparatively low pitch, but it was Milly, an actress to the core, who was aware of her audience and working it to the maximum. Her wails of delight were building expertly to a climax. An older couple, the woman in furs and frowning deeply, summoned a waiter over and were clearly telling him in strong terms that the management needed to have a word with the offending pair of lovebirds: the waiter bustled away swiftly as the couple rose and with great dignity removed themselves from the scene.

'So good, so good – yeah, like that, oh my God, ohmyGod, I love you, Tark, I love you so *much* – yes, *yes* ...'

'Quite the little performer, isn't she?' Ludo said dryly as he sipped at his prosecco. 'No need to say "Sing out, Louise!" to that one! And a talented writer too – that monologue is *definitely* scripted. Who yells out "I love you" in the throes of passion?'

Then he looked more closely at Eva's white, miserable face, and sighed.

'Oh dear,' he said. 'I rather suspected how things were. She wasn't terribly keen on you and young Mr Ormond's art appreciation society, was she? She *does* rather need to be the centre of attention at all times.'

'*I love you* – oh God, yes, that's so good – baby, *yes*, I love you so much, ohmyGod ohmyGod ohmyGod!'

Ludo's comparison was on the money; Milly was positively singing out the words by now.

'*Cosa dice?*' asked an Italian woman two tables down.

'*Bimbo, ti amo cosi tanto,*' her female friend, swathed in Fendi leather, translated, giggling. '*Poi, o Dio mio! O Dio mio! O Dio mio, eccetera eccetera.*'

'On second thoughts, maybe she's *not* such a talented writer,' Ludo observed. 'Rather repetitive. Drink up, dear, it'll help. And sit up straight and stop hiding behind that very fashionable fringe, you're beginning to look like Cousin It.'

Eva spluttered out some of the mouthful of prosecco she had just obediently taken, but she did sit up rather than slumping, and she shook the heavy fringe out of her eyes.

'I just …' she started, but couldn't find the words to continue; Ludo held up his hand to indicate that she didn't need to. Milly had now progressed to wailing:

'Baby, baby, *baby, baby!*' on an operatic, soprano crescendo, which the second woman at the next table was imitating with a series of '*Bimbo, bimbo, bimbo!*'s which was making her friend, and the people at the table next to them, howl with laughter.

'It'll be over in three … two … one …' Ludo held up three fingers and started pulling them down. 'And … *now*,' he predicted, a split-second before a silver cascade of screams poured down the side of the villa, much like the streams of mountain water in the da Vinci sketch. A few groans from Tarquin were faintly audible below Milly's triumphant coloratura cadenza, but there was no question who was the star of the show.

'And to think *he's* the singer,' Ludo commented, as the Italians at the two tables beside them broke into ironic applause, their gloved hands pattering together.

'*Molto dramatico!*' the first woman commented approvingly.

'It won't last,' Ludo said, reaching forward to touch Eva's arm lightly. 'It never does with the Millys of this world. They move from step to step, man to man. Right now she sees the wedding as being a great publicity opportunity. Tarquin's very famous and very rich. But dear, what is being married to a musician going to do for her acting career?'

He shrugged and drank more prosecco.

'Very little, frankly. And do you think he'll be understanding of her having all those little necessary flings with directors and producers and co-stars that oil the wheels of climbing the Hollywood ladder? Oh dear, *listen* to my mixed metaphors!'

Eva was staring at him, some colour now back in her cheeks; but it was at least partially caused by embarrassment at her secret desires being so very clear to Ludo.

'Am I really that obvious?' she muttered, ducking her head again to hide behind her fringe.

'Tut tut, Cousin It!' Ludo said. 'Really, dear, I'm *never* this nice and it won't last long, so stop slouching and listen to me. I give them two years max, as our American friends say. They'll never see each other, for a start; she'll always choose her career over her marriage, as frankly she should at her age. He'll be touring all the time, it's how the bands make their money now. And she won't get pregnant – I don't see *that* young lady taking any time out at all for years to come, not until her star's fading and she thinks that having a baby or two will get her back on the covers of *OK!* and *Hello!*. She'll meet someone else who can give her more publicity and a career boost and she'll be off as fast as you can say *please respect our privacy and give myself and Tarquin some space during this difficult time.*'

Eva drank more prosecco, staring at Ludo as if entranced; the waiter, having gone away to hide during Milly's performance, had now re-emerged and was circling the terrace to see if any of the guests needed his services. He paused for a moment at their table, decided that the raptly absorbed young woman and the sleek gentleman who was busy seducing her should be left alone for now, and moved smoothly on.

'So what should you do, I hear you ask,' Ludo continued smoothly. 'A very apropos question. Obviously now, nothing at all. You stay quiet, you facilitate the wedding, because absolutely nothing on God's green earth is going to come between Milly and her *Style Bride* cover, and, if you really feel you can't get over him, you wait it out until it all goes blooey and he needs a shoulder to cry on. Though even then, you do rather risk being his rebound. Frankly, I'd suggest moving on if you can. You've got a couple of years to do it. You're young, and you're very attractive in that hipster Hoxton way that's currently all the rage. I'm sure there's a whole array of boys with artistic piercings and artfully wayward facial hair lining up to buy you microbrewery beer and kale chips in Hackney eco-pubs that make their own tofu in the back room.'

Eva had to giggle, not only at Ludo's having nailed the current trendy climate, but at his own shudder of distaste as he described it.

'Really, dear, that's the better option,' Ludo said kindly. 'Go forth and date widely. They have a lovely expression in Italy – *chiodo scaccia chiodo*, which means, more or less, "one nail drives another one down". And as far as I'm concerned, the more nails the merrier, eh?'

He looked at her, his gaze sharp.

'I know that my words are going right through one ear and out the other without being absorbed,' he said. 'But one sows the seeds, you know? It's all one can do. Now I advise you to go back to your suite, put on one of the very luxurious robes with which this fabulous hotel provides us, pop to the spa and see if they have any last-minute cancellations for treatments. It's all going on Mr Ormond's bill, and his fiancée assures me his credit card can take it, so I suggest you hit the hammam and the plunge pool with everything you have.'

'Thank you,' Eva finally managed to say, putting down her glass.

'Mmn-hmn. You're very welcome,' Ludo said. 'Look, dear, if you find you simply can't get over him and need to play the waiting game – I do see that he's quite a catch: he's terribly pretty to look at, means well, has tons of money, and is probably the only musician one actually thinks won't avail himself of all the available groupies.'

He reached out for the bottle: the waiter was there before him, however, his white-gloved hand pulling the green prosecco bottle from the ice bucket and finding it empty.

'*Ancora, signore?*' the waiter asked.

'*Si, un' altra bottiglia, per favore,*' Ludo said. 'Don't worry, dear,' he added to Eva. 'I'm perfectly capable of finishing the whole thing on my own. Where was I?'

'Um ... the waiting game?' Eva mumbled, pulling her jacket around her more tightly, and not really because she was cold: the subject under discussion was so close to her heart that even the mention of her possibly being coupled with Tarquin made her shiver from head to toe.

'Oh yes.' Ludo looked grave. 'Eva, you know my situation, don't you? You've met Liam.'

Eva nodded, finishing her prosecco: she wasn't a big drinker, and her head was spinning now from the wine at lunch and the afternoon aperitifs.

'He's never going to come out officially, and he's never going to leave the Church,' Ludo said sadly. 'So what's a boy to do? I love him more than anything in the world, and he loves me more than any other person. But being a priest is equally important to him as being with me, and I can't change that. Here I sit, planning everyone's perfect weddings with their antique teapots and lilies of the valley, God help me, when what I want more than anything is to plan my own. But I can't, and I probably never will. Not as long as I'm with Liam. I know the new Pope's making nice noises about being gay-friendly, but the gulf between "you're not all going to hell" and "feel free to get married and settle down" is still *gaping* wide.'

He sighed.

'Not to whinge on, of course,' he said as the waiter returned with a bottle dewed with cool drops from the chill of the terrace's wine fridge. 'But just to make the point that sometimes one finds oneself in situations that one simply has to accept. If you really think you can't stand to be with anyone else but Tarquin, the waiting game is all you have left. And you're going to have to hold your chin up and smile so successfully that sarcastic queens like me don't spot that, as Aretha Franklin sings so wonderfully, you're laughing on the outside, crying on the inside. Because most of us, I'm sorry to say, will mock you horribly for it.'

Eva nodded, her eyes wide and concentrated.

'I'm so sorry about—' she started, but Ludo was already waving her away with a sweep of his hand.

'Please! We don't dwell,' he said firmly. 'And we *certainly* don't apologize for things that aren't our fault. Now pop down to that spa like a good girl, have a steam and a nice cry and get it all out so you can look bright and fresh for dinner and like you don't have a care in the world, while I ring my beloved and tell him that Thunderbirds are Go for Chianti next spring.'

He suited the action to the word, picking up his iPhone and flickering his fingers over the touch screen as Eva obediently stood up and proceeded to follow his instructions exactly as he had laid them out. Ludo was quite right. Crying her heart out in a hammam turned out to be the single most therapeutic thing she had ever done in her life.

Chapter Twenty-Two

Stanclere Hall, February

'Miss Brianna?'

Mrs Hurley put her head round the corner of the library door, her voice sounding unaccustomedly tentative. But then, everyone had been on tenterhooks around Brianna Jade for the last couple of months, even Edmund; ever since the engagement party, the staff and master of Stanclere Hall had been walking on eggshells trying to keep her happy, and failing. Naturally, they all assumed that the key issue was the abject failure of the *Style* photo shoot, and they also took for granted that Tamra's storming out immediately after evicting Milly meant that Tamra was furious not just with Milly, but with her own daughter.

Because Tamra had not been back to the Hall since then. All the energy she had pumped into the first phase of the renovations, all the detailed plans and loving care that she had brought to the magnificent redecoration of the central wing and the public rooms, had now dissipated in a puff of smoke. Instead, she was travelling widely, photographed in the gossip columns tossing back her hair and smiling for the cameras, a different handsome tanned young man by her side in every new photograph: from the Sandy Lane Hotel in Barbados to Cabo San Lucas in Mexico to the Amanpuri resort in Phuket, she had spent the last couple of months hitting a whole range of the most exclusive winter-sun holiday destinations, partying hard, sometimes with Lady Margaret, sometimes with the latest gigolo of choice.

The building works at Stanclere continued, of course, according to her instructions, now supervised by a project manager hired by Tamra. Ironically, although Tamra had previously driven the workers crazy with her relentless drive for perfection, now that she was absent, everyone missed her. With Tamra in charge, they had all known that they were doing their absolute best, because there was no alternative: if they didn't execute a task perfectly, they would have to tear it out and do it all over again. This had swiftly raised standards all over the site, especially because Tamra, a very successful businesswoman, had been as swift with praise as she was with criticism, and had wielded her power to give bonuses with the skill that came with experience of managing people. The works had flown along before: now they chugged at a slower pace, done perfectly competently, but without Tamra's taste and flair.

If anyone had expected Brianna Jade to step up to the plate and take over now that her mother had gone AWOL, they learnt their lesson fast. After a few attempts by the project manager and Mrs Hurley to consult with her, they had both backed off, it being very obvious that the questions were bouncing off Brianna Jade. All she could offer was a weak smile and a muttered: 'Just do what Mom would do, I guess,' in answer to every question. The poor girl was under the impression that her mother was so angry with her failure to connect with the *Style* photo shoot that she had packed up and taken off for London, washing her hands of her daughter. Tamra had even refused to come back for Christmas and New Year, which had been a huge blow to Brianna Jade: they had never been apart for the holidays before, and Tamra had been planning a lavish fortnight of celebrations and parties at the Hall before the disastrous weekend of the shoot put paid to all that.

Instead, Tamra and Lady Margaret had celebrated Christmas in London at Lady Margaret's house in Eaton Square and then flown to Barbados to see in the New Year: Tamra had told her daughter airily in a phone call that she felt that, in order to bond with Edmund, Brianna Jade really should spend the holidays with her fiancé without her old mother getting in the way. Brianna Jade had sobbed and protested and told Tamra that she was ridiculous even to *think* that, let alone say it, but Tamra had been utterly unyielding, even when her daughter asked in tears if she could come to London to see her mother for Christmas: all Tamra would repeat in reply, like a robot parrot, was that Brianna Jade and Edmund needed to bond without her in the way.

No matter how much Brianna Jade begged and pleaded and pointed out that Edmund was very fond of her mother, respected her drive and energy, was happy for Tamra to treat Stanclere Hall like her own country home, Tamra would not be swayed. The only moment Tamra had strayed at all from the robot parrot script was when Brianna Jade, desperate now, had suggested that Edmund himself call his future mother-in-law to reassure her that she was always welcome at what was now his and Brianna Jade's home.

That, for some reason, had made Tamra utterly hysterical. Brianna Jade couldn't imagine why, and she didn't get an answer, no matter how much she asked. She barely even knew

if her mother had heard the question. Tamra screamed inco-
herently that Brianna Jade had no idea what she was talking
about and that she and her daughter needed a break, before
pretty much hanging up on her.

It was the first fight they had ever had – not that it was even
really a fight, as Brianna Jade hadn't been able to get a word
in edgeways. She'd stared at the phone in her hand as the line
went dead, unable to believe what had just happened. *Needed
a break?* What did that even mean? How could a mother and
daughter who loved each other as much as the two of them
did possibly need a break? What could Brianna Jade have done
so badly wrong that her mother didn't want to see her any
more? Had freaking out at the photo shoot really been such
a terrible crime that Tamra couldn't forgive her? Oh God,
would Tamra *ever* forgive her?

Ever since then, Brianna Jade had effectively been in mourn-
ing. Her relationship with her mother was the only close one
she had ever known, and it had been the greatest source of
love, companionship and trust she could imagine. Tamra might
have dragged her daughter round every pageant conceivable,
taken her on the road when Brianna Jade, a homebody, would
much rather have stayed in Kewanee, but there had never been
any doubt in Brianna Jade's mind that her mother was doing
everything for her daughter's benefit.

*All Mom ever wanted was to see me happy and settled with
no money worries,* Brianna Jade thought miserably. *But how
can I be happy without her? Of course we can't live together for
ever, just the two of us. I know that! I was totally fine sharing a
house with her and Ken, and I'd be just as fine if Mom came
and went from Stanclere Hall, kept her rooms here, kind of lived
here half the time, came for all the holidays. And Edmund would
be too!*

I just wish she hadn't reacted like that when I said he could call her and tell her he wanted her to come for Christmas. It's like she's mad at both of us now.

As far as bonding with her fiancé went, Brianna Jade could not deny that Edmund was being as lovely, sympathetic and understanding about her grief at her mother's disappearance from her life as she could possibly have wanted. Seeing Brianna Jade's misery, Edmund had bent over backwards to treat her with kid gloves, spending much more time with her than he had before, and although Brianna Jade was very grateful for his care and attention, she couldn't help feeling a little odd about it. She loved the company, was highly relieved that Edmund was devoting his time to her, and yet it was as if he wanted something from her, was *waiting* for something from her, that she couldn't figure out and so didn't know how to provide. There was an air of anticipation, of excited expectation, that hovered around him for the first month or so after the photo shoot, and he was being so sweet and thoughtful to her that she really tried, even through her sadness, to give him whatever it was that he wanted in return.

However, Brianna Jade might not have the business smarts and organizational skills of her mother, but she was clever and intuitive, and she couldn't help sensing that whatever Edmund was waiting for, he wasn't getting it. He was as kind and considerate as ever, but the anticipation seemed to fade, replaced by a sort of ... *resignation*, was how she would have put it.

She'd made some attempts to ask him if there was anything missing from their relationship, and he had assured her that there wasn't; that night, when they were having sex, however, there had been a very odd moment when she had suddenly screeched because, apparently, his watch strap got caught in her hair, pulling it nearly out by the roots. It had been really painful; he had apologized profusely and explained what had happened, because it was night-time and so dark she couldn't see a thing. It had been the next day before she had had the even odder thought that Edmund never actually *wore* his watch to bed . . .

Which had made Brianna Jade wonder nervously if Edmund was secretly into some sort of kinky sex stuff that she definitely would not welcome at all. A previous boyfriend had wanted to spank her with a hairbrush once, and she'd told him exactly where to shove it; she wasn't judgemental at all, was more than happy for everyone to get on with doing whatever they wanted with whomever they wanted, but no one was going to spank her or pull her hair or do anything freaky with her, thank you very much. The boyfriend had derisively called her vanilla, to which she'd snapped back that it was her favourite ice-cream flavour and not to let the door hit him on his way out.

However, since that scream of shock at what was hopefully an accidental hair-pull, Edmund hadn't tried anything like that again – if in fact he had even tried it in the first place – and things had settled back into the normal, regular, vanilla sex routine, which Brianna Jade found perfectly satisfactory. She found herself wanting sex more than ever these days, probably as a compensation for Tamra's absence; the physical contact was hugely comforting, the cuddling afterwards maybe even more so. She was leaning on Edmund so much for comfort at the moment, and could only be grateful that he was responding.

Because, since being informed that Milly had spotted her being carried back to the Hall by Abel after getting tipsy on cider, Brianna Jade had decided that her visits to the pigpens would have to become much less frequent. In a series of sly asides during the *Style* shoot, Milly had implied some truly nasty things about Brianna Jade's friendship with Abel, things that had made Brianna Jade feel dirty and sordid. Not only would she never dream of cheating on her fiancé, but to imply that her happy, guilt-free friendship with Abel was sordid and creepy in some way, that Abel had some sort of designs on her, that he had got her drunk deliberately so he could make a pass at her ... that was just *horrible*, and it had completely tainted Brianna Jade's ability to hang out with Abel as she had done before.

She knew, of course, that none of it was true. She and Abel had simply made friends because of their mutual love of animals in general and pigs in particular, and not only had Abel not got her drunk on purpose, his *grandmother* had been there the whole time! Nothing could have been more innocent, and yet Milly's nasty little quips about Abel's size, dungarees and ability to sweep Brianna Jade off her feet had somehow poisoned the well, made it very difficult for her to feel as easy and natural and unaffected with him as she had been before.

So she had cut right back on her visits to the pigpens and to the Empress of Stanclere, and honestly, she almost thought sometimes that she missed them as much as she missed seeing her mom. Which was ridiculous, of course, but she couldn't help feeling it. In fact, when Mrs Hurley popped her head round the door, Brianna Jade had been struggling with the urge to take the old route for her daily run, swing by the pigpens and see what Abel, the Empress and the rest of the pigs were up to; there would definitely be fewer now since the pre-Christmas pig slaughter. The impulse to visit the remaining ones was so strong that she greeted Mrs Hurley's intrusion with huge gratitude for the distraction, her smile almost as bright and welcoming as it had been before she had effectively lost both Tamra and Abel from her life.

'What is it, Mrs Hurley?' she asked, sounding encouraging enough for the housekeeper to smile back in relief and come fully into the library.

'I didn't want to disturb you, miss,' Mrs Hurley said, 'but

there's a visitor asking for you. Says she's your cousin from America.'

She cleared her throat, the well-trained servant's way of indicating disbelief without actually saying a word.

This was not, in itself, impossible. Brianna Jade had a lot of cousins in America: both Tamra and the late lamented Brian Schladdenhouffer had had numerous siblings who had gone on to produce numerous spawn. And yet Brianna Jade very much doubted that one of her many Schladdenhouffer or Krantz cousins, or whatever surname of predominantly Scandinavian or German extraction taken on marriage by the female Schladdenhouffers or Krantzes, had decided to fly across the Atlantic and make their way to Rutland County for the purpose of visiting their very estranged relative without even so much as a phone call first.

No, this female 'cousin' could be only one person. And suddenly, Brianna Jade found herself wishing devoutly that her only problems were the absence from her life of her mother and her best friend at Stanclere Hall.

'She's called Barb, right?' Brianna Jade said, a sense of doom enveloping her as thickly as if a dark blanket had been dropped over her head.

Mrs Hurley nodded.

'That's right, miss. I think she rang you here, months ago, didn't she? So she *is* your cousin?'

She managed to pitch the second sentence so perfectly between a statement and a question that Brianna Jade could have chosen not to answer it if she hadn't wished to; it wasn't Mrs Hurley's place to query her employer, but at the same time, as the housekeeper of Stanclere Hall, it was her business to know how to treat every guest who came below its hallowed roof. Considering the appearance and demeanour of this new visitor, her relationship to the Earl's fiancée would certainly make a difference to which bedroom might be assigned to her, or whether she merited a maid's unpacking her suitcase.

'Not really. Sorta,' Brianna Jade muttered in confusion. Barb had a hold over her: Brianna Jade couldn't directly contradict something Barb had said. 'It's, uh, a big family on both sides. She's kind of ... anyway ...'

'Brianna Jade! Honey, you in here?'

Behind Mrs Hurley's apron-clad figure, Barb Norkus burst into the library, grinning from ear to ear.

'Wow, look at all these books! Have you read 'em all? Sheesh, this place is so *old*! Hey, you've come a long way from that tumbledown shack of the Lutzes', right?'

Barb's voice was as sharp and nasally inflected as ever, but she was much thinner and paler than Brianna Jade remembered; her face was greyish, in fact, and although Barb had made an effort to outline her eyes in black pencil and gloss her lips, the use of concealer to hide the dark circles beneath her eyes and the rough reddish skin around her nostrils would have been considerably more useful in improving her appearance. You couldn't grow up where Brianna Jade had without being familiar with the signs of meth use, and she had no doubt, looking at the skinny figure before her, the jeans and sweater Barb was wearing hanging off her bones, that a lot of the money Brianna Jade had been sending Barb had gone up her nose or into a pipe.

'Would you like a cup of tea?' Brianna Jade said automatically: she was so accustomed by now to asking this question of British guests that it popped out of her mouth, and she could have bitten her tongue off when Barb burst into raucous laughter.

'Get *you*, lady of the house!' she said maliciously. 'I guess you've been watching *Downton Abbey* to learn all this British shit!'

Barb's hair was freshly bleached, with barely any roots showing; she had pulled it back into a long ponytail and her nails were newly done. She had made some effort to spruce up before dropping in on Brianna Jade. The jeans and sweater looked new as well, and the big bag slung over her shoulder, which she now dumped onto the library table, was a Coach ripoff from Macy's; it was obvious that Barb had come up in the world financially. But you would never have looked at her thin frame and imagined for a moment that she had once been Corn Queen of Watseka. You needed curves to be a beauty queen, and curves were not what a diet of cigarettes, meth and diet sodas got you.

'A plate of sandwiches, please, Mrs Hurley,' Brianna Jade said, standing up and managing to summon some sort of outward composure as her brain raced frantically. 'And, um ...'

Tea had been refused, but if she suggested water, Barb would laugh in her face.

'A pot of coffee,' she decided. 'This is my, uh, distant cousin, Barb Norkus.'

'Coffee'd be good, and I gotta say, I'd kill for a beer!' Barb grinned, displaying a mouthful of teeth that bore painful witness to her meth habit. 'What you got?'

Brianna Jade ignored this question, and so did Mrs Hurley: while rich Americans entertaining at home liked to show off their abundance of supplies, Brianna Jade had learnt that when visiting British aristocrats you simply accepted wine, or beer, or a cocktail when offered, without doing anything so vulgar as treating their home like a restaurant and asking for specific information on what you were about to receive. Mrs Hurley reluctantly withdrew, closing the door behind her.

'Do you have any luggage, Barb?' Brianna Jade asked as politely as she could manage.

'Nah, travelling light.' Barb grinned even wider. 'I figured I could pick up whatever I needed here. Or borrow stuff from you.'

'You won't fit into most of my clothes now, Barb. You're so slim,' Brianna Jade said, hoping that Barb would take this as a compliment; she didn't want to lend Barb anything, as she clearly wouldn't get it back.

Barb preened, running one hand through her bleached fringe: it was so crispy and fried with the harsh treatments that it looked as if it might snap off under her fingers. She sank into a deep leather armchair opposite Brianna Jade's, one of a set arranged around a low inlaid circular table.

'Wow, this is real cosy,' she said admiringly, her arms splayed out along the wide, buttoned arms of the chair. 'If it had a footrest, it'd be better than a La-Z-Boy.'

'What are you *doing* here, Barb?' Brianna Jade blurted out, as Barb reached for her bag and fished out a pack of Marlboro Reds and a plastic lighter. 'This wasn't the deal at *all*! You were supposed to stay in the States – I mean, we never even talked about you leaving, I totally assumed you wouldn't come over here – it never ever entered my mind! I can't believe you'd just turn up here without even being *invited*.'

'Hey, if I waited for you to be nice and ask me to visit, I'd have gone old and grey first, amirite?' Barb said, lighting up without even looking around to see if there was an ashtray near her. 'So I figured I'd turn up and give you a real nice surprise. Bet you're glad to see me! Finally you can let your hair down after having to suck up to all these British snots. Boy, that has to be the biggest pain in the ass!'

Brianna Jade stared at her, dumbfounded by Barb's shameless attitude. She had clearly decided to walk into Stanclere Hall as if she belonged here, brazening it out with barefaced cheek, and it was working: Brianna Jade was letting her make herself comfortable, had ordered her refreshment, was even now standing up to retrieve an ashtray from the console table by the wall so that Barb wouldn't get ash all over the carpet ...

'So you've got somewhere I can bunk down here, right?' Barb said, not even bothering to acknowledge Brianna Jade's putting down the ashtray in front of her. 'I mean, it's the country and all, not much going on, but this place is totally cool. I can see myself crashing here for a nice long time. Hey, I bet you've got, like, a whole *wing* I could stay in!'

'You can't stay here, Barb,' Brianna Jade managed to say, shaking her head in vigorous denial. 'You just can't. Sending you money was supposed to mean you'd stay away and wouldn't bother me, not turn up here! This is, like, the *opposite* of the deal!'

'Well, I guess the deal just got changed then, didn't it?' Barb blew out a cloud of smoke. 'Tough titty.'

Brianna Jade bit her lip, hard.

'Let me guess,' she said. 'You had to get out of town 'cause you owed money to someone. You thought you had some bottomless money pit with me, and you just spent like there was no tomorrow, and you got caught out and had to leave in a hurry. I bet it's your dealer you owe, now I think about it.'

She watched Barb's eyes as she spoke, and could see that she was getting it right so far.

'Whatever,' Barb drawled, looking down at her cigarette. 'I *am* all cleaned out, to tell the truth. The trains here cost, like, *tons*. They were all like, if you book in advance you save loads of money, but I was like, well, what the fuck, you know? I'm here now! So with that and the cab from the station, I'm totally broke.'

A tap on the door signalled the arrival of the food and drink. Brianna Jade called 'Come!', prompting a derisive snigger from Barb, and a footman entered carrying a big silver tray, which he placed on the inlaid table between the two women. Brianna Jade noticed that Mrs Hurley had provided two water glasses and two coffee cups in case the Earl's fiancée wanted some refreshment too, but only one frosted glass for the bottle of Belgian beer; as always, Mrs Hurley had judged things perfectly.

'I'll pour, thank you,' Brianna Jade said to the footman, who duly withdrew, not a flicker on his well-trained face as he got a good look at the unexpected arrival who claimed to be Brianna Jade's cousin.

'All these servants need to take *major* chill pills,' Barb said, reaching for the beer and swigging it straight from the bottle. 'They've got sticks up their asses so far they're practically coming out of their mouths.'

'Barb, shut up!' Brianna Jade snapped. 'You're disgusting.'

'Whatever,' Barb said again, shrugging. 'Your accent's showing, by the way. I can hear all that posey Brit crap slipping away the more you talk to me.'

Brianna Jade set her jaw, determined not to be distracted: the only thing that mattered was getting Barb out of here as quickly as possible.

'You can't just walk in here and dump yourself down and be rude like that and expect to stay!' she said.

'Really?' Barb put the empty bottle down on the tray with a slam of glass against metal. 'You're kidding, right? 'Cause I was under the impression that I can do whatever the hell I want, just as long as I don't spill about you being Pork Queen and show those photos of you standing in the back of that pickup in your blue satin dress and pigskin jacket, dropping the Oreos for the pigs to race, you know?'

She snuffled with laughter as she stubbed out her cigarette.

'Wanna see? I've got them right here in my bag. Oh, and I made copies – don't think you can just throw them into the fire or something. Seriously, take a look.'

She pulled out a cheap plastic Walgreens photo folder from her bag and tossed it over at Brianna Jade.

'Hey, who do I have to blow around here to get another beer?' she added. 'All this travelling's made me *real* thirsty!'

Chapter Twenty-Three

Brianna Jade simply didn't know what to do. She was at her wits' end. She wanted to handle the situation herself, and if it had been just her and Edmund at risk of being laughed at in the media, she would have told Barb to shove her photos up her ass, get out of Stanclere Hall and never come back. Edmund, as she had known he would, utterly backed her up in this when she finally escaped from Barb, leaving her 'cousin' ensconced in the library working her way through a six-pack of beer and her Duty Free stash of Marlboro Reds. She found Edmund on the farm, picking her way towards him in her new Le Chameau wellies over the ruts his equally new John Deere tractor was ploughing in even lines across a wide, muddy field.

It was unprecedented for her to interrupt Edmund while he was hard at work. So, as soon as he spotted her, he switched off the machine, pulled off the earmuffs he was wearing for hearing protection, and jumped down to meet her as she came stumping towards him. The expression on her face told him at once that it was serious: he strode towards her, enfolding her in his arms, and hugged her so tightly that the buttons on the flap pockets of his waxed Barbour jacket dug into her.

Brianna Jade burst into tears, the cold air making them tingle on her cheeks as she sobbed against his shoulder. Eventually she wiped them away with the handkerchief Edmund gravely handed her and managed to tell him the entire story in a stuttering flow of words, interrupted by frequent pauses to blow her nose and blot the tears away. It all came out, every single detail about the Pork Queen title, the details of what was in the photographs that Barb possessed.

'I'm not at all ashamed of it!' she said passionately, looking directly into his clear grey eyes. 'I was *proud* to win that title – it's pretty much the only one I ever *did* win.'

She couldn't help a snuffle of amusement at those words.

'You know, it's my past, and I worked real – *really* hard to win that pageant,' she continued. 'I wouldn't care at all if the photos were all over the papers.'

'Nor would I,' Edmund assured her with a vigorous shake of the head. 'No one who cares about you would give a damn, darling. You might get some good-natured teasing around here when we go out to dinner, but if you take it in the spirit that it's meant, it'll fade pretty quickly. I mean, we've all got embarrassing photographs of ourselves when we're young, haven't we? And if this so-called *friend* of yours takes money for selling photos of you – well, that's the worst form imaginable. People will positively rally round you in support, I promise.'

She'd known that Edmund would take this position, but the relief was still huge. Her body relaxed in his arms, and she hugged him back fiercely.

'Thank you,' she said. 'I was *sure* that's what you'd say.'

'But you weren't,' he said, frowning in concern. 'Or you'd never have given this awful woman a penny.'

'It's Mom!' Brianna Jade explained, her voice rising into a wail. 'She's loving her big social life, you know? And those people might not be as cool with this as you and people in Rutland are! I heard Minty and Sophie used to call Princess Chloe "Dog Rose" when she was Prince Hugo's girlfriend, before they got married, because her surname's Rose, and they were calling her a social climber, you know? Think what Minty and her group could do with all the Pork Queen stuff!'

'"Friends" like that aren't worth having,' Edmund said with great contempt.

'But this matters to Mom – she loves all the society side of things, and she'd hate to know people were sniggering at her and me,' Brianna Jade said fervently, trying to make Edmund understand.

'You know, the whole Eurotrash world is full of social climbers,' he said gently. 'I can't imagine this making much difference to them. And your mother's best friend is Lady Margaret, whose pedigree is absolutely impeccable. All Lady M would do on seeing photographs of you with a Pork Queen sash on is laugh her head off and then forget all about it.'

Brianna Jade's pretty forehead was corrugated with worry now.

'I want to protect Mom,' she explained. 'Don't you see? She's protected me all my life, looked after me, kept me safe, worked her ass off to make money for us, married Ken so we'd never have to worry about that again. Now *I* want to take care of *her.*'

'So you're going to pay blackmail to this awful woman for the rest of your life?'

Centuries of aristocratic breeding showed in the Earl of Respers' voice and demeanour as he looked down his long nose at the mere thought of allowing oneself to be blackmailed. Like the Duke of Wellington when the famous courtesan Harriette Wilson threatened to name and shame him in her memoirs, Edmund's response would instinctively be the same: 'publish and be damned'. It was near impossible for him to imagine a situation where he would pay someone even once to keep silent about a secret of his, let alone for years and years.

'I don't *know*,' Brianna Jade wailed feebly. 'I need time to think about it.'

'And in the meantime, Brianna, what happens?' Edmund asked inexorably. 'She can't stay at the Hall with us. There's simply no way in the world that I'm extending my hospitality to some piece of moral refuse! She can't sleep under my roof – it's utterly impossible.'

'Not even one night?' Brianna Jade said in horror.

'No! Absolutely not! Brianna, you don't know what you're asking. You give this woman an inch and she'll take a mile. You have to put your foot down now, and letting her stay when she's turned up on our doorstep like this is completely the wrong thing to do,' Edmund said with extreme seriousness. 'I understand that you're trying to protect Tamra, but this is not the way to do it. Do please listen to me.'

Brianna Jade felt that she was being pulled in so many directions at once that she could barely breathe. She knew that Edmund was quite right: Barb shouldn't be allowed to stay at the Hall, should never even have been let inside. Once Mrs Hurley had told her who her visitor was, Brianna Jade should have got up immediately, marched to the front door and told Barb to get out and stay out.

That's what Mom would have done, no question, she reflected sadly. *But I'm not Mom. I wish I was as tough as she is – she's so good at knowing the right thing to do, and she's always brave enough to do it, too. I just blunder along, never taking the initiative, and now that means I'm totally stuck.*

'Shall I come back to the Hall now and we'll throw her out together?' Edmund asked. 'Screw your courage to the sticking point, darling!'

Brianna Jade didn't recognize the Shakespeare reference, but she knew she wasn't ready for the kind of terrible screeching throwdown with Barb which the announcement that she was no longer welcome at Stanclere Hall would inevitably provoke. She stared mutely at Edmund, silently begging for some reprieve, an agreement that Barb could stay for a night or two and postpone not only the awful confrontation, but the equally inevitable splash of the Pork Queen revelation all over whichever paper or magazine Barb chose as the buyer of her story.

But Edmund didn't budge. Of course, he was right: how could she imagine eating meals with Barb, for instance? How could they be under the same roof and not exchange a word? But then, if they did speak, what could they say to each other?

What kind of Countess of Respers will I make if I can't handle a crisis properly? she thought in panic. *Look at me, I'm going to pieces! How am I ever going to handle running the house and the estate and dealing with stuff that comes up when Edmund isn't around?*

'I'm not ready yet,' she managed. 'I think I need to go for a walk.'

Edmund nodded slowly, more in acknowledgement of his fiancée's upset state than in agreement that her decision not to confront her blackmailer was the right one.

'Come back and find me when you're ready,' he said quietly. 'I won't go back to the Hall until we're together. We should deal with this as a couple, Brianna, don't you think? I'll be by your side when you tell her she needs to leave. She needs to see that I'm backing you up, that I don't care a jot about whatever threats she might make.'

Edmund was the perfect fiancé, which was wonderful: the trouble was that she wasn't good enough for him. She wasn't up to the pressure of being the Countess of Respers. She had been skating along, letting her mother arrange everything; she didn't have one useful thing to do in the Hall, and she knew it. The only place she had ever felt truly at home was where her footsteps took her as she turned away from Edmund and plodded across the rutted field, over the stile and onto the dirt road that looped around the estate, down a path that led off it, knowing exactly where she was going by instinct, even though she had never taken that precise route before.

She was headed to the piggeries.

And watching the slim figure of his fiancée move across the newly ploughed field, not towards Stanclere Hall but away from it, avoiding Barb Norkus and the confrontation that awaited her, Edmund slipped his phone out of his pocket and dialled Tamra's number.

It had been months since Brianna Jade had visited the pigpens, and yearning and anticipation rose in her as she approached them. She could hear the familiar grunting noises, start to smell the warm, ripe scent of the pigs, which, to Brianna Jade, was wonderfully familiar. Memories of home, happiness, security instantly flooded back: running barefoot in the dusty earth of the Lutzes' farm, helping to feed the pigs and the chickens, long sunny Illinois summers with the scent of fresh hay and blue skies above. Even though today was a chilly February day with a flat grey lid to the world, the cloud cover so low that it seemed as if you could almost reach up and touch it, the scents and sounds of the pigs still lifted her spirits, and as she rounded the turn in the path, her heart raced even faster at the sight of Abel's huge figure leaning on the rail of the sty, forearms propped on it, his shoulders hunched as he stared disconsolately down at the Empress of Stanclere.

It didn't occur to her to turn back while she still could, while Abel hadn't noticed her approach. Her need for comfort was too extreme, the company of both the pigs and Abel exactly the solace she needed. She wasn't just escaping from the crisis at the Hall, from Barb's unwelcome presence; she was heading towards the dead centre of the place where she felt most relaxed, most wanted and needed in the world. Putting that into words would have scared her to pieces, so she instinctively shied away from it, telling herself that she'd just stay for a few minutes, catch up with Abel and the Empress and then go back to the Hall and face the music ...

The thought of having to confront Barb, even with Edmund backing her up, made her walk even faster, almost breaking into a run, as much as she could manage in her wellington boots. Hearing the squelch of her rubber soles in the mud, Abel looked up, his expression changing from hangdog to joyous in a flash as he caught sight of her; his eyes lit up, he stood up straight, automatically reaching a hand up to push his thatch of hair out of his face. He was dressed in his denim dungarees, a big cable-knit sweater underneath them to ward off the February chill, the legs tucked into a pair of rubber boots so gigantic that they would have made almost every other man apart from a professional wrestler look as if he was wearing waders.

'Brianna!' he exclaimed unguardedly. 'Oh, it's nice to see you! Me and the pigs've really missed you.'

'I've missed you all too!'

In her eagerness to reach his side, she skidded in the mud, nearly slipped and fell, flailed her arms in the air for balance, and only just managed to catch a rail of the pen in time to steady herself. They should have been laughing about it; the near-pratfall was potentially hugely comic, the yelps Brianna Jade made as she slid and thrashed around, the dive for the rail, the splashes of mud her boots kicked up, the way she grabbed and held on grimly as her legs threatened to slip from under her, should have had them both collapsing in fits as soon as she was stable.

But neither of them laughed, not at all. Brianna Jade, gripping onto the rail, getting herself straight, gazed up at Abel with an utterly serious expression in her brown eyes that mirrored exactly the way he was gazing at her; he hadn't reached out to help, even though, huge as he was, he could easily have extended a long arm to steady her. The Empress, a bulky pale mass beneath the rail, looked optimistically at the new arrival, recognizing Brianna Jade and hoping for an extra treat, or at least a nice scratch on the back. But after a few moments her head dropped again and, disappointed but resigned, she returned to working her way through the brimming contents of her trough.

'Were you angry with me?' Abel asked simply.

'What do you mean?' Brianna Jade looked puzzled. 'Why would I be angry with you?'

'You stopped coming round,' he said. 'To visit us. Me and the pigs. I thought you were angry with me – because of the cider. I didn't mean to get you tipsy. Me and Gran were so sorry that happened. We didn't think anything of it, but then you never came back. I thought maybe I should come up to the Hall to see you, but Gran said to leave well alone.'

'Someone saw us,' Brianna Jade blurted out. 'When you carried me back. She was really snarky about it, and I thought I maybe shouldn't come for a while. And then it went on for longer than I meant, and I felt so weird about it ... I just feel so confused about everything, and I didn't know how to handle it – but that's my problem.'

She started to cry again.

'That's *it*,' she said hopelessly. 'I don't know how to handle things. I'm not up to this. I can't deal with stuff like Mom can, and I don't think I'll ever be able to ...'

Her shoulders slumped in depression and she leaned on the rail, her forehead resting on her hands, tears dripping down her fingers. Her sobs grew louder and louder, her back heaving, as she cried out her sense of failure; she couldn't cope with Barb, had fled from Stanclere Hall rather than confront her, and she had come here in a pathetic search for comfort from the pigs and the pigman she had abandoned months ago.

When Edmund had hugged her a short while ago, it had felt good, reassuring, a safe place to let out her tears. However, when Abel awkwardly placed a huge hand on her head, stroking her hair as if she were an animal whose pain he was trying to ease, Brianna Jade, to her surprise, did not feel reassured at all. Instead, it was as if he had touched a pressure point, like the Shiatsu massages she had had with her mother sometimes; when the massage therapist accessed, even lightly, a point of great sensitivity, it could make you nearly buck off the table with the shock, like pressing deeply on a bruise.

But it was pain and pleasure so deeply mixed together that you could never separate the two. The therapist would keep pushing on the spot, and release would start to flood through Brianna Jade's body, rebalancing her meridians like a hot rush that made her head spin dizzily. Afterwards, the therapist would know what to do to put Brianna Jade back together again, working down a series of other, rebalancing pressure points. Now, though, she didn't even feel as if she could have stood up without the rail of the pigpen, which she was gripping tightly for support. Her legs were so weak she could hardly feel them beneath her; it was as if they'd dissolved the second Abel touched her. His hand was cupping her scalp now, so warm it was like a miniature electric blanket, deliciously hot, and all she could think of was turning to him, curling up in his arms like a cat, absorbing more and more heat from his big body on this miserably cold day, heat that seemed to be scorching away all the sadness she was feeling . . .

What exactly was she crying about? She couldn't remember. She turned to look at him, and he reached out with his other hand and started, with his wide, spatulate finger, to stroke down the trails the tears had left on her skin. They dried almost on contact with his touch; looking down at her with great tenderness, he placed both thumbs on either side of her perfect straight nose, just below her eyes, and drew parallel, caressing lines around the curves of her cheeks, blending in the last traces of her tears, making them vanish into the smooth surface of the pale golden skin that had been made perfect that morning by her daily application of BB cream.

'Don't cry, Brianna,' he said softly. 'You shouldn't ever cry.'

That did it. She arched up towards him, her arms coming up, pulling down his head towards her; for a split-second he resisted, but Brianna Jade was absolutely determined, had been from the moment his hand had cupped her head, and a heartbeat later, her lips met his. He was so tall that even the statuesque Brianna Jade had to stretch up to keep kissing him, go on tiptoes in her wellington boots, but it was utterly worth it. His arms wrapped around her like two woven cables, lifting her a little more, his hands stroking her back, long steady caresses from her shoulders to her waist that made her melt against him; it was the most reassuring, entrancing thing a man had ever done to her.

Eagerly she pulled his head down even more, kissing him deeper and deeper; his tongue shyly touched her lips, and she responded to it instantly. It was as big as the rest of him, which was maybe why he was shy; slowly, carefully, it met hers, sliding further into her mouth, making her gasp around it, almost unable to breathe but feeling so completely filled by it already that she trembled, pressed herself against him, opened her lips still further.

How long they kissed she had no idea. Wrapped in his arms, Abel's big body sheltering her from the elements, she didn't even realize that it had started to rain, slowly, the occasional large, splattering drop that presaged a long steady shower to come. As the rain began to drip down inside the ribbed neck of his sweater, Abel raised his head and looked down at Brianna Jade very seriously.

'You should go back,' he said. 'Rain's coming.'

She shook her head vehemently, grabbing the straps of his dungarees. She couldn't find the words: all she could do was indicate as clearly as possible that she wasn't going to let go of him and make her way back to the Hall on her own. Not now, at least. Abel closed his huge hands for a moment over hers, feeling how strong her grip was on his dungaree braces; his immense strength could easily have made her loosen her hold, but instead he let out a deep sigh, bent, and swung her off her feet as easily as he had done before, turning to carry her down the cart track, his stride steady, Brianna Jade's head nestling blissfully into the rollneck of his scratchy woollen sweater, her lips resting on the strip of white skin exposed above it.

She closed her eyes, feeling raindrops start to patter on her head, determined not to think about what was happening. If she started to think, she would have to stop, and the one thing she didn't want to do, more than anything else in the world, was to stop, so that meant that she couldn't think, which was more than fine with Brianna Jade, because thinking really didn't seem to work for her anyway ...

A barn door creaked open, shouldered by Abel as he carried Brianna Jade inside, out of the rain, and turned to kick it shut again. A few long steps and he had reached a big bale of hay, sitting down on it with her on his lap; instantly, she started kissing him again, reaching for the buckles on his dungaree straps and sliding them down to unclip them from the brass buttons, pushing the straps back over his shoulders, grabbing his sweater and pulling it and the T-shirt underneath it up in great folds so that she could feel his bare skin. It was hot as a furnace and lightly hairy; she tangled her fingers in the hair as she stroked his back, trying to give him the same pleasure that he had given her.

They wrestled together in the hay, not to take each other's clothes off – even with Abel's body heat, it was too chilly in the barn for that – but to get their hands where they wanted to go. From then on not a word was exchanged, just pants and sighs and moans as Abel unzipped Brianna Jade's padded gilet, pulled up her sweater, closed his hands over her breasts, the warmth of his palms even through her silk bra hitting her instantly with the same force as when he had touched her hair; she gasped, leaned back into the hay, lying down, pulling him on top of her, wanting to feel that heat and heaviness all over her, on top of her, inside her. Her hands went to the denim dungarees, pulling them down impatiently: so much fabric, so hard to drag it down far enough, especially when he was caressing her breasts with the same steady, hypnotic rhythm, his thumbs tracing small circles on her nipples, his fingers larger, wider ones, as if he instinctively knew how to do Tantric massage.

She had the dungarees down to his hips now, and, lying on and over her, his body almost completely blocking out the light, he raised his bottom to help her push them down; unlike her, Abel didn't seem to be in a hurry. She was the desperate one, the one craving to have him inside her, to have his hands sink lower and lower. They were sliding slowly down her ribcage, and she moaned as his thumbs reached the waistband of her jeans, the circles widening, the heat rising.

Abel wasn't teasing her, she realized; this was just his way, slow and steady, in no rush to get where he was going. By the time he unbuttoned and unzipped her jeans and eased them down her hips, her silk knickers coming with them, she was so frantic for him that her head was thrashing from side to side on the hay, a steady stream of whimpers coming from her parted lips; her hands were gripping his wide, bare, muscular waist, but they slid up to his shoulders as he went lower, hardly able to make any dent in the solid flesh over even more solid muscle, now beginning to be slippery with sweat.

He put one entire hand over her crotch, and she screamed out loud at the sensation as he began to trace the same circles, his four splayed fingers overwhelmingly hot, his thumb, as it gradually, slowly, inexorably, began to slide inside her, finding her dripping wet already. She dragged furiously on his shoulders, pulling him down on top of her, finding his mouth with hers, kissing and kissing him, her hands now in his hair; she couldn't find words, but she could tell him with her actions that she wanted him inside her, and as his tongue once more filled her mouth, he groaned deeply, his hips lifting, his thumb circling against her so exactly in the right place that she started to come, her eyes squeezed tight shut, concentrating in utter bliss on the sensations that were rippling through her. Abel's slow build of stroking and circling meant that when the orgasms came, they truly were almost Tantric; she lost herself in them, arching and arching against his hand, taking everything he was giving.

Abel was infinitely patient. It was only when she reached down, trying to pull him onto her, into her, that he slid his hand from her, licked his fingers one by one with great satisfaction, and then positioned himself to kneel over her, taking his cock and butting it between her legs. She widened them to make room for him, but her eyes flew open again as she felt him moving inside her, almost a millimetre at a time, making sure that she was fully wet and willing and ready.

It was unbelievably intense. Abel was built fully to scale, never necessarily a given; he was probably, she realized, so used to going slowly and steadily not just because of his strength but his size, needing to pace himself to avoid overwhelming his partner. A gentle giant, who was being careful to lower his hips in gradual stages, getting her used to the sheer size of him, the weight of his pelvis on her, his heavy, hairy thighs; it *was* overwhelming, and she loved it, wrapped her arms around his back, as much as she could, encouraging him to do it, to do what he wanted, to begin to move back and forth, to start really, fully, truly—

Abel was reaching his hands under her buttocks now, tilting them a little, finding the right angle, still careful, still in control of himself; Brianna Jade, spreadeagled beneath him, clinging to his shoulders, thought dizzily that he would always be in control of himself, and that that was okay, because he was clearly getting exactly what he wanted, and God knew she was more than happy with what he was doing. He started to rock them both together in the same rhythm, rubbing against her on every up-beat, barely pulling in or out but staying firmly lodged inside her, anchoring her legs with his, gradually, relentlessly, working them both to climax, refusing to speed up no matter how much she pounded on his shoulders and tried to rock her own hips faster. His sheer weight, bearing down on her, held her at his own pace, and when she finally trusted that pace, let go and stopped trying to rush him, she felt the orgasm building so fast that in a few more seconds it was fully on her, rippling between her legs and out to her stomach and thighs like a tide that was sweeping inevitably to shore.

Whether Abel had been waiting for her to come again or

whether her body's juddering beneath him tipped him over the edge, she didn't know. She heard him groan, felt his body heave up and out of her, and she wailed in disappointment, even as she came, because he was no longer inside her. He managed to hold out just in time to come into the bale, kneeling awkwardly just beside her as his cock spurted into the hay: then he reached for his T-shirt, tugging it free from his sweater, wrapping it around his still-huge cock to wipe it clean before he collapsed on his side by Brianna Jade. Stretching his big frame fully out onto the bale, he spooned her as she wriggled into his embrace, pulling her sweater down for extra protection against the chill. One muscled arm wrapped around her, weighty as a heavy rope winding around her waist, pulling her even closer so he could rest his forehead against her mass of hair. Their breathing slowed, became more even, and in the comparative silence they could hear the rain pattering down on the barn roof.

'We'll wait out the weather, eh?' he said into the back of her head.

She nodded, settling even deeper into the hay bale, which held the warmth their bodies had just generated. Firmly, she told herself to relish these moments, this body heat, this nest they'd made for themselves, because this was as much as she and Abel would ever have: one afternoon in a rainstorm. She was going to marry Edmund. Her mother hadn't worked so hard all these years to contrive a fairy-tale marriage for her beloved daughter only to have Brianna Jade let her down with the kind of epic, nine-days-wonder scandal to which the revelation of what she had just done would inevitably lead.

Abel knew it too, she could tell. This could never happen again, which meant she could no longer visit the piggeries. She would be up at the Hall, Abel would be down here, and they would both get on with their lives and be absolutely fine.

Edmund would make her a wonderful, kind, sympathetic husband, while Abel would doubtless find a lovely girl with whom he could share his fairytale cottage.

But the most important thing was that Brianna Jade would, finally, have achieved what her mother wanted, realized her mother's dreams for her. Tamra had spent so many years, made so many sacrifices, to make Brianna Jade happy. Finally, Brianna Jade had been presented with a sacrifice she could make to return everything her beloved mother had done for her, and there was no way she was going to back down from the challenge.

The only way she could handle this was to tell herself, very simply, that there was no alternative but to continue along the path laid out for her. No choice, no decision for her to make, because God knew, she was incapable of making them. She was going to marry Edmund and become the Countess of Respers, and that was all there was to it.

Chapter Twenty-Four

By late afternoon, the rain had stopped and the cloud cover had opened enough to let a watery winter sun come filtering through. Enough, too, for Barb Norkus, having spent a very pleasant several hours in the library, snoozing off her jet lag on the big leather Chesterfield sofas, ordering more sandwiches and cake from the footman and washing them down with beer, to wake up, notice the weak sunshine outside, and decide that this would be the perfect opportunity for her to take some photos of herself outside to add to her Facebook and Twitter feeds. She had already Facebooked and Tweeted pictures of the beer and sandwiches arranged on the silver tray, plus a couple of selfies of her lounging on the sofa, cigarette in one hand, beer in the other. Her friends back home had posted appreciative comments already.

But the majesty of Stanclere Hall did not convey itself just with a couple of interior shots of the library, and now that Barb had had a nap and refreshed herself with another beer or two, she was ready to dazzle her social media acquaintances with the high life into which she had so successfully infiltrated herself. She wasn't remotely concerned that Brianna Jade had left her to her own devices for several hours; she assumed, quite correctly, that her reluctant hostess had been thrown into so much emotional disarray by Barb's sudden appearance on her doorstep that Brianna Jade had retreated somewhere to have a cry and a lie-down. Though, of course, Barb could not possibly have imagined the precise circumstances of either ...

Picking up her phone, she strolled out into the Great Hall, and after a quick survey of the area, she set the timer, put the phone on the piano, dashed up the staircase and stopped half-way up, sticking out her tongue to one side, flashing the V-sign with her right hand while her left held a half-empty bottle of beer. Pleased with how that photo had come out, she decided to go outside while there was still light and recreate the pose with the whole of Stanclere Hall behind her.

Drafting a photo caption in her head that managed to get in both *Downton Abbey* and the pop star Miley Cyrus, whose tongue-out pose Barb had shamelessly imitated in her selfie, Barb dragged open one of the huge front doors and, with her usual self-protective instincts, made sure that she would be able to open it again, propping it just fractionally ajar, before tripping out and down the big stone flight of steps. She crossed the gravel drive, heading for the huge stone fountain at the centre of the green grass circle around which the drive made a loop before continuing on to the stables and garages. The fountain, which had also come over from Greece cen-turies ago in dubious circumstances, depicted Hercules wrestling the river god Achelous for the love of Princess Deianeira of Calydon. It wasn't currently switched on; Tamra had had the pump replaced, and the stone thoroughly cleaned to remove all the algae, but there was still the risk of sub-zero temperatures causing the water to freeze and pipes to crack, so the fountain was always drained over the winter. Over the last few months, however, rainfall had filled up the wide stone bowl, since the base was plugged up to avoid water filtering into the pipes.

The statue could not have been more eye-catching. Achelous was depicted by the sculptor in the form of a snake, and the very muscular Hercules – who for some reason had decided that it would be a brilliant idea to wrestle a snake god while completely naked – was doing his best to strangle his opponent. Princess Deianeira cowered away in an exaggerated pose of fear as Hercules, legs straddling the circular plinth like a Colossus, leant forward triumphantly, seeming quite unbothered by the fact that the curls of the big snake's body were wrapped around one of his ankles in an attempt to trip him up.

The strapping Abel Wellbeloved could have posed as the sculptor's model for Hercules, with one significant difference; as with all classical statues of naked men, the genitalia were depicted in near-minuscule proportions to avoid the male clients who had commissioned them falling into serious depressions at the sight of a resting penis larger than theirs. Cunningly, however, the sculptor had symbolically circumvented this restriction by using the huge rearing snake to represent Hercules' tiny member. The gigantic, wrist-thick body of the serpent came up right between Hercules' legs, and Hercules was gripping it in a way that could not have been more phallic. Barb had a lot of fun with that: she boosted herself up onto the fountain lip, grabbed onto the wide body of the snake with one hand, and reached back with the other enough to get a picture, which she happily captioned: *Me and some naked dude jerking off a snake! Hotttt!*

She tried a few other shots and eventually climbed down again, positioning her phone on the far edge of the fountain so that it would capture an image of herself on the steps of Stanclere Hall with the statue in the foreground. Happy with the angle she had achieved, she set the timer again and positively scampered around the fountain, over the lawn, onto the gravel drive and up the steps, with a second to spare before she struck again the tongue out and V-sign pose. The beer was finished by now, so she flashed the V with both hands, arms thrown wide, one bony hip jutting out, her head at a side angle to show off the blonde ponytail of which she was very proud.

The flash went. Barb was heading down the steps again to check the shot when a deep, humming noise in the sky above made her tilt her head back to look for the helicopter that had to be the source of the approaching sound. It came into view almost immediately, a dark spot on the horizon that swiftly resolved itself into the familiar dragonfly shape and in a few seconds more was almost over Stanclere Hall. As it reached the grounds of the Hall, it slowed, hovered, the markings on its undercarriage now clearly visible, and began to sink down, the whirling rotor blades cutting through the air as loudly as a buzz saw.

Barb clapped her hands to her ears and watched, fascinated. She had never seen a helicopter land before, and it was way more deafening and dramatic than it seemed on TV. The extended landing skids below the body of the cabin reached out like delicate arms, finding their way down to the lawn onto which the helicopter was lowering itself. The skids trembled briefly under the impact, settled into the grass, and landed, the pilot so experienced that it looked as easy as parking a car.

Barb imagined this would herald the arrival of the Earl of Respers at the very least. Maybe even Princess Sophie! Barb, of course, had been Googling Brianna Jade on a daily basis, had seen the *Style* shoot go up online: those images had been what had prompted her to buy the air ticket and come to the UK. Well, that and, as Brianna Jade had guessed, needing to leave town because of what she owed her dealer. Jealousy had risen in Barb again at the sight of Brianna Jade hanging out with Princess Sophie and Tarquin Ormond. Brianna Jade didn't just have it all – money, an Earl to marry – she had more than Barb had even imagined possible.

Hanging out with Princess Sophie and a famous pop star! Brianna Jade wasn't just rich and classy now, she was part of a stellar celebrity inner circle! It had been more than Barb could bear. This visit to Stanclere Hall hadn't just been a move to prompt Brianna Jade to raise Barb's stipend: it had been an act of revenge, rubbing Brianna Jade's nose in where she had come from, a deliberate attempt at humiliation which, so far, had succeeded wonderfully.

The cabin door of the helicopter opened and someone jumped down lithely: a woman swathed in a camel fur-trimmed coat, slim jean-clad legs flashing, snakeskin high-heeled boots zipped over the jeans. Her blonde hair was pulled back into a ponytail so lush and well-groomed that Barb's hand instinctively rose, sheepishly, to her own thinner, stragglier version. The woman's glorious hair bounced like a shampoo advertisement as she strode towards the Hall, high-stepping like a runway model to counteract the sogginess of the rain-soaked grass: she stopped when she saw Barb's phone propped up on the edge of the fountain, picking it up in one suede-gloved hand.

'Hey, that's mine!'

Barb started down the steps, walking towards the fountain. Because the statue was so sprawling and elaborate, she was halfway round it before she realized the identity of the woman, who was standing waiting for her, hands on hips, the phone firmly grasped. Barb reared back as if she had been bitten – very much, in fact, as if the gigantic snake Hercules was so heroically throttling had suddenly uncoiled itself and hissed in her face.

'Well, hello, Barb,' Tamra said, her voice colder than the wind whipping from the rotor blades.

Barb froze, still in the rearing-back position. She had known, of course, that a clash with Tamra was inevitable, but she had envisaged it very differently. In her imagination, she had pictured it somewhere like the Stanclere Hall library, with herself lounging across one of the sofas like a Bond villain, pulling her photographs out of the Walgreens plastic folder, fanning them over the coffee table with gusto as Brianna Jade cried and turned to Tamra, and Tamra, holding and comforting her daughter, writhed and raged, but impotently, knowing that she had no choice but to accede to Barb's demands in order to keep her daughter happy.

But Brianna Jade was nowhere to be seen, and Tamra's mouth was set in a firm line, her dark eyes as narrowed and beady and menacing as the snake that, in Barb's mind, she was strongly resembling right now.

'Uh, Brianna Jade said—' Barb started, her voice not as strong or assured as she would have liked.

'My daughter isn't here, and you won't be dealing with her any more,' Tamra said, even more icily.

Behind her, the rotor blades of the helicopter slowed down and stopped, the pilot turning off the engine.

'What about the Earl? He around?' Barb tried, pulling her thin jacket around her instinctively. It wasn't that cold in England in the winter, nothing compared to the minus thirty degree Fahrenheit conditions common in Illinois around this time of year. And yet there was something about the look Tamra was giving her that made Barb shiver.

'I'm the only person you'll be dealing with, Barb,' Tamra said. 'And it's going to be a damn short conversation.'

She raised Barb's phone to look at the screen.

'I see you've been taking even more photographs,' she

commented, starting to scroll through them. 'Any of them for blackmail purposes?'

Summoned by the noise of the helicopter, a footman appeared in the doorway of Stanclere Hall, naturally assuming that Tamra had arrived, unexpectedly, for a visit; seeing her and Barb standing by the fountain in the cold, he stood watching to see how developments would play out.

'I don't need any more photos,' Barb said angrily. 'I've got plenty right here!'

She pulled the Walgreens folder out of the back pocket of her jeans; she hadn't wanted to leave it in the library when she went out.

'You wanna look at them, Tamra? You've come a ways since then – you might have forgotten some of the details of the whole Kewanee Hog Days shindig,' she added, smirking. 'I bet you wouldn't like all your smart friends over here getting a look at what you were wearing – let alone your hairstyle.'

Tamra took the folder out of Barb's hand and, still keeping her eyes fixed intimidatingly on Barb's face, threw it into the fountain with a back flip of her wrist.

'I have copies!' Barb blurted out furiously. 'I have copies online, I scanned them in – I'm not a fucking *idiot.*'

'*Oh yes you are,*' Tamra hissed through her teeth, her eyes darkening to black as Barb watched her in growing fear. 'You're the *biggest fucking idiot in the world,* because you took me on, you stupid little bitch! I don't give a *shit* what's in those photos! None of them shows my daughter doing anything she needs to be ashamed of, and that's all I need to know! Unlike you on this phone – I'm willing to bet that if I have a look through here, I'll find a lot of photos of you flashing your boobs, doing drugs, all sorts of crap.'

She continued drawing her finger over the screen, such a sneering expression on her face that Barb's blood began to boil.

'Hah, I knew we'd get there!' Tamra exclaimed, emitting such a contemptuous, scornful laugh as she looked down her nose at the image she'd found that Barb could no longer contain herself. Furiously, she lunged for Tamra, hand outstretched to snatch her phone. A mere second later it dawned on her that she had reacted exactly as Tamra wanted: Tamra neatly side-stepped Barb's run at her, sending Barb off balance, slipping on the wet grass, and flailing helplessly. The next thing she knew, she was being spun around and pushed, face-forward, towards the fountain.

Barb thrashed around wildly, reaching for some purchase on the stone fountain edge. She grabbed onto it, but she was no match for Tamra, who had one hand in the small of Barb's spine and the other twisted powerfully in the girl's hair.

'Take a breath!' Tamra said viciously.

Barb opened her mouth to say: 'What? Let the fuck go of me!' but the second half of those words turned into bubbles as Tamra bent Barb in two over the fountain and dunked her head thoroughly into the ice-cold water.

It was the worst shock Barb had ever had in her life. She came up sputtering, her face and head tingling as if the skin had been pierced by a million tiny needles. Water trickled out of her mouth and snorted from her nostrils.

'Fuck you, bitch!' she coughed out, and promptly went under again. Tamra ducked her deeper this time, and water flooded into her nose. Tamra didn't hold her under for long, but this time when Barb came up the ache of the cold water up her nasal cavities was so intense that all she could do was pinch the bridge of her nose and wail.

'Fuck *you*!' Tamra retorted, standing back, as Barb was jumping up and down now, trying to get the water out of her ears, releasing some of the unbearable pressure, her wet hair splattering drops in all directions. Tamra waited until Barb's

breathing was less frenzied, though she was still gripping her
nose and grimacing in pain.

'I'm packing you off, and if I ever see you again, I'll have
you arrested for blackmail,' Tamra said evenly. 'And convicted.
Believe me, I'll do it. The courts take blackmail extremely seriously. I talked to a lawyer this afternoon. It carries a maximum
penalty of fourteen years in this country.'

This was enough to freeze Barb's blood all over again.

'But the publicity—' she started feebly, only to have Tamra
cut through her as sharply as a Japanese Ginsu knife.

'We don't give a shit about that,' she said calmly. 'Big fucking deal. Who cares?'

'The Earl wouldn't want people to know—' Barb gestured
widely to the pomp and circumstance of Stanclere Hall behind
her. Turning to indicate it, she saw that what must be half of the
entire staff had gathered in the doorway and on the steps to
watch, summoned urgently by the footman: more faces were
pressed to the windows that faced out onto the drive.

'And everyone who works for him ...' she went on, feeling
self-conscious now.

'Please! I pay the salaries of everyone who works for him and
my daughter,' Tamra snapped. 'They're *extremely* loyal to us. He
doesn't give a damn about Brianna Jade's being Pork Queen,
and nor does anyone else who knows us! Now I'm sending you
back to London and putting you on the first plane back home.
My secretary's waiting in the helicopter. She'll pay for your
ticket back to the States herself and make sure you check in and
go through Departures. After that, you're on your own.'

'I don't want to,' Barb started sulkily, blowing her nose on
her fingers.

Tamra burst out laughing.

'Why the fuck would I care what you want?' she said,
almost pleasantly. 'Get on the plane or be prosecuted for

blackmail. Your choice. Believe me, I'd *love* to see you go to prison after what you've put my daughter through. Seriously, don't tempt me!'

Barb's shoulders slumped in defeat.

'I need my bag,' she muttered.

Tamra smiled in triumph, her eyes glittering now like dark stars.

'Get in the helicopter. Someone will bring it to you,' she ordered. 'Oh, and you'll probably want this too.'

She opened the hand she had been holding closed in a loose fist by her side: out of it fell the fake ponytail that Barb had been wearing, which had come off when Tamra had gripped her hair to duck her in the fountain. Barb's face puckered, a wail coming from her lips as she shot her hand around instinctively to check the back of her head: sure enough, all that remained was the short stub of hair which she had pulled back and wound an elastic round so that she could attach the hairpiece to it. She hesitated for a moment, her pride battling with her wish to retrieve it, and the latter won out: dropping to her knees on the grass in front of Tamra, she scooped up the miserable lank strands of acrylic hair and shoved them in the pocket of her jacket.

As she did so, she heard an unmistakable click. She looked up to see that Tamra had taken a photo of her down on the grass.

'Here,' Tamra said, handing the phone to her with a grim little smile. 'A last souvenir of your trip. If I ever lay eyes on you again, Barb Norkus, I'm calling the police.'

Sullenly, Barb snatched the phone out of Tamra's hand.

'You're such a bitch, Tamra Krantz,' she muttered.

Tamra's smile was positively beatific now.

'Tell me something I *don't* know,' she said, turning on her heel and sweeping off magnificently towards the main doors of Stanclere Hall.

As she approached, the staff fell back inside, bustled along by Mrs Hurley. Strictly speaking, none of them should have been watching in the first place, but the Earl himself, back from the home farm, had joined them, and that gave tacit approval to the group of spectators; he even exchanged smiles of sheer enjoyment with them as they shot back to their assigned duties. The priceless scene of the interloper getting dunked in the fountain and packed off would be related with glee for years to come at Stanclere Hall.

The Earl was the only person remaining as Tamra came up the steps. Leaning against the balustrade, he was clapping his hands slowly in tribute to her.

'Marvellous,' he said appreciatively. 'Absolutely marvellous. Think if you'd gone into the armed forces, Tamra – you'd be a general by now.'

Tamra could barely make direct eye contact with him, but she had to laugh at this comment.

'More like a mercenary,' she said, flashing him the swiftest smile imaginable. 'I'd get court-martialled by the Army for my brutal methods. Where's BJ? The helicopter's coming back for me after it's taken Barb to Heathrow, and I've got to see someone in London by close of business tonight. So I don't have that much time, and I want to talk to you both about all this.'

Edmund followed her back into the Hall, a footman waiting to close the door behind them. Tamra gave him quick instructions about taking Barb's bag out to the helicopter, and Edmund affectionately took her arm, meaning to wrap it through his; both he and the footman were horrified when she screamed and pulled it away as if he'd burnt her.

'My God, Tamra, I'm so sorry—' he started.

'No! I'm fine! It's nothing! Sorry.' She caught her breath, managing another smile, but unable to look at him at all this time. 'Just – nervous after that scene with Barb, I suppose.'

She glanced at the footman.

'Look, get someone else to take the bag to the helicopter and bring me a dry Martini,' she said. 'Gin, no olives, a twist. Make a whole pitcher.'

'Tamra, you're never nervous,' Edmund said, puzzled. 'What on earth—'

'I just need a drink,' she said wildly, taking off her coat and practically throwing it at the waiting footman, 'that's all. I just need a drink!'

'*Mom!*' Brianna Jade, entering the Great Hall from the side staircase, and looking very dishevelled, spotted her mother and came tearing towards her, throwing herself into Tamra's arms. 'Oh Mom, I'm so glad to see you! I've missed you so much! Things are so terrible! Barb's here, and she—'

'Not any more,' Tamra said, hugging her daughter. 'I've seen to that.'

'Tamra was fantastic,' Edmund said enthusiastically. 'I wish you'd seen her. She grabbed that woman by the hair and dunked her head in the fountain twice; it was like something from a soap opera! We all piled out to watch – it was positively superb.'

Brianna Jade pulled back a little from her mother, looking at her with wide eyes.

'Mom, really? But won't she go to the papers, sell the photographs ...'

'I don't give a damn if she does,' Tamra said impatiently. 'That's what I wanted to tell you. Edmund said you were worried about protecting me, and that's completely ridiculous.'

'I told you so, darling,' Edmund said, putting an arm around Brianna Jade's shoulders, only to have her, too, jump as if she'd been stung.

'My God,' he said, backing away. 'I'm definitely like Kryptonite to the Maloney women this afternoon.'

The footman arrived with a silver tray bearing a pitcher of Martinis and three frosted glasses.

'We'll have it here, in front of the fire,' Tamra instructed: she had such natural authority that it never occurred to her that it was for Edmund or Brianna Jade to give orders in their own home. Edmund, who was not easily offended, grinned and obediently followed her and the footman to the coffee table in front of the fire, surrounded on three sides by velvet armchairs and sofas.

'The Fracking Queen commands, and we obey,' he muttered cheerfully under his breath.

'Here's what I'm thinking,' Tamra said, not looking at either of them as she drank half her Martini in one gulp. 'This is going to come out eventually, the whole Pork Queen thing. I say we might as well turn it to our advantage. I've been mulling things over for a while, trying to think of a way the estate can get more self-sufficient. I can keep pumping money into it, but I hate the idea that I'm just pissing it away down the drain, you know?'

Edmund started to say something, but Tamra held up one perfectly manicured hand.

'Please! I made the deal and I'll stick to it – no need to defend yourself,' she said. 'But it'd be *great* if Stanclere could start generating some income, and this whole mess with Barb gave me the germ of a really good concept.'

Now she did look from Edmund to Brianna Jade, her eyes flashing in triumph as they always did when she made a great business point.

'Organic sausages!' she said. 'We'll start with them, anyway. We can even use Brianna Jade's Pork Queen past as publicity – neutralize any negativity at one stroke. If the Duke and Duchess of Devonshire can run a thriving business out of Chatsworth – farm shops, holiday rentals – I don't see why you can't do the same here. I know there are some empty cottages on the estate that would make great holiday lets, and I can do those up – but building the whole Stanclere brand will be what gets people making bookings. Sausages and bacon are the first things I thought of, obviously, but I did some research on Chatsworth and Dayleford Organics on my iPad in the helicopter, and I have tons of ideas for products. Jams, biscuits, cakes, liqueurs – Mrs Hurley would *love* to supervise the kitchens – not here, of course, we'd need a proper, purpose-built kitchen on the estate – then we'd get the products into Fortnum's and Selfridges and start a mail-order business. There's a company called Dukeshill that has a great website – cuts of meat plus bacon and pies; we should look at that in detail and analyse their business model.'

'Abel would definitely enjoy expanding the piggeries,' Edmund agreed appreciatively as Tamra finally ran out of breath. 'We're just producing pork for the needs of the house at the moment, which really isn't using his considerable skills to the best advantage.'

'And Brianna Jade loves the pigs. She's always visiting them, aren't you, honey?' her mother said. 'See, this is a way no one can tease you about that any more – you can hang out there as much as you want. Oh, look, you have some straw on you. Were you helping out in the barn?'

She reached over to pick the straw off her daughter's sweater. Brianna Jade's face went as red as the embers glowing at the heart of the fire.

'I think this is wonderful,' Edmund said, leaning forward to touch his fiancée's hand. 'Don't you, Brianna? I know I'd feel much prouder of Stanclere if it were starting to at least try to pay for itself, rather than living on your money, wouldn't you?'

Brianna Jade managed a nod.

'You know I've been reading all the nineteenth-century

novels about American heiresses coming to Britain and marrying into the aristocracy,' Tamra said with increasing enthusiasm – she had finished her first Martini by now and was pouring herself another. '*The Buccaneers, The Duke's Children, The Shuttle* – there are tons! I've given Brianna Jade copies of all of them. I don't know if you've had time to get to any of the books yet, honey?'

Brianna Jade shook her head. *Time?* she thought. *More like inclination! Come on, Mom, I'm not you, I've never been a reader.*

'Oh, I love Trollope,' Edmund said appreciatively. 'We have his entire works here in the library – do borrow any that you'd like.'

'Cool!' Tamra said, driving on however with the point she was making like a juggernaut. 'But you know what's missing from those novels? Apart from Bettina in *The Shuttle*, what *isn't* in them is the business brains those girls inherited from their tycoon dads who made the big bucks in the first place. You know? Those guys were first-generation millionaires, robber barons, they made truckfuls of money. No way would their daughters not have inherited their brain power. Those girls would have come over the Atlantic, married their Duke or Earl, rolled up their sleeves and got to work making their estates productive!'

Her eyes gleamed with excitement at her literary observation, her hair shone in the firelight; she looked positively resplendent. Edmund gazed at her in admiration.

'I must say, Tamra, I never thought of that,' he said. 'And I've read the Trollope and the Wharton books. Very good point! This idea of yours is brilliant. I feel an idiot for not thinking of it myself.'

He turned eagerly to Brianna Jade.

'Darling, how do you feel about taking over the whole sausage and bacon side of things, as it were?' he asked. 'You could liaise between Mrs Hurley and Abel, work on increasing production and flavours for different sausages. We'll do research, look at the companies Tamra mentioned and see how they run things. You'll be able to spend your whole time at the piggeries if you'd like.'

With a choking sob, Brianna Jade jumped to her feet, clumsily manoeuvred between the sofa and the coffee table, then ran across the Great Hall and up the stairs, disappearing from sight.

'What on *earth*?' Edmund said, staring after her, a frown creasing his forehead. 'Do you think I should go after her? Did I say something wrong?'

He looked back at Tamra, who promptly ducked her head and took another long pull at her cocktail.

'To be frank, Brianna Jade's been on edge since you upped sticks and left us alone here,' he said. 'She's missed you horribly, Tamra. I must say, I have too. You bring a wonderful energy to the Hall – we've *all* missed you. Mrs Hurley in particular.'

'I just felt I should leave you two kids alone for a while,' Tamra said into her glass, staring down at the lemon twist and swirling it around as if it had suddenly become the most interesting thing she had ever seen. 'Or we'll start playing out a rerun of some nineteen-seventies sitcom called *And Mom Makes Three*.'

She cleared her throat, setting down the glass.

'But say hi to Mrs Hurley for me. I'd get her to oversee the whole production side of things here if I were you. She deals amazingly with new challenges, and when the renovations are finished, just housekeeping the Hall isn't going to be a big enough deal for her.'

She was on her feet now, visibly uncomfortable at having a tête-à-tête with Edmund.

'The helicopter should be back soon,' she said, not meeting

his eyes. 'I might just go wait for it. I have an appointment in London this evening – well, not an appointment, but someone I have to see. I'm *determined* to get Brianna Jade the *Style Bride* cover.'

Edmund rose as well, too much of a gentleman to stay seated while a lady was standing.

'But if the helicopter's going to Heathrow and back, it'll still be quite a while till it returns, won't it?' he asked, his forehead furrowed in confusion. 'You haven't even finished your drink!'

'Uh – look, Edmund, I think you should go and check on your fiancée,' Tamra said. 'You know, bond with her? Like I keep saying you should do?' She heard the slightly hysterical note in her voice, and caught herself. 'And I'll go say hi to Mrs Hurley, how's that?'

'Well, of course that's fine,' Edmund said, still confused but too polite to question his mother-in-law-to-be about her sudden mood swings. 'It was such a pleasure to see you, Tamra. I do hope you'll come back and spend more time with us in future.'

He leaned forward tentatively, to see if he would be allowed to give Tamra his customary kiss on the cheek, but by now he was aware that Tamra was evincing symptoms of sensitivity so extreme that she was as likely to slap him across the face as let him kiss her, and he signalled his intentions so clearly that he gave her plenty of time to execute a defensive manoeuvre. Which was exactly what she did, making a great play of grabbing her bag and holding it in front of her to ward him off.

'It's been a pleasure,' he said courteously. 'Literally a flying visit! Thank you so much for dropping in – oh look, I did it again – and sorting out our problem for us. I really don't think Brianna Jade would have managed it on her own. She was so keen to protect you, you know. Honestly, I don't mean to be self-deprecating, but you really are her first priority. She's so grateful to you for all the sacrifices you've made for her.'

The choking sob Tamra gave on hearing these words was identical to the one Brianna Jade had emitted just a short time earlier, and so was the speed at which she shot across the Hall in the direction of the servants' wing and Mrs Hurley's office. Edmund stared after her, struggling nobly with what he knew was a sexist impulse to assume that both women, so physically alike, were also synchronized in their monthly cycles and were simultaneously suffering with uncharacteristically nasty bouts of premenstrual tension.

But frankly, he thought, *it's the most flattering explanation as far as I'm concerned. Otherwise I really do have to assume that I not only forgot to wash this morning, but for the last three days, and I pong like a laundry bin full of schoolboys' socks and jock-straps after a rugby match.*

As the thought occurred to him, he actually raised his arm and sniffed under the armpit. The relief of securing empirical evidence that he had, in fact, not only washed but applied his Nivea For Men Sensitive 48 Hours deodorant stick that morn-ing, as always – they could call it '48 Hours' all they wanted, but Edmund, a fundamentally cautious soul, wasn't prepared to live that dangerously – was blotted out as soon as he real-ized that he had just committed the most appalling breach of etiquette. Blushing from head to toe at having just sniffed his own armpit in the middle of his own Great Hall for anyone to see, the Earl of Respers went upstairs to find out if his fiancée was in any mood to receive him, or if she were, perhaps, going through some particularly awful women's problem and the sight of him would only exacerbate it for some unknown reason.

Chapter Twenty-Five

Jodie Raeburn was working late, as she did for the three days every month when the latest issue of *Style* was due at the printers. Plus the two days a month when *Mini Style* was ditto, plus the days when she had to oversee special issues ... She worked late more often than not, frankly. But there was no need to rush home, as her fiancé was still in New York: hopefully he would be moving to London later this year. Currently he edited the fashion pages of *Style Men*, and the plan was for him to transfer to the parallel role in London when the job came free and his visa was issued.

Though she missed him, Jodie was fine with the temporary separation: these were the crucial career-building years for her, in which she needed to devote much more of her time to her job than to her private life. Luckily her fiancé, having met her at work, fully understood how driven she was.

Jodie had never made any secret of her ambition to one day take over from Victoria Glossop as editor of *US Style*, and she was well on her way to achieving it. The plan was to follow Victoria's career path, which meant working like a dog in her twenties, then get married and try for children in her early thirties. After which time, hopefully, Victoria would have loosened her hold on the reins in New York enough to consider Jodie fully qualified to take over from her there as editor ...

Though Victoria had to pull the move of going to Harper's *for a while, raise her value until Dupleix caved in and asked her back,* Jodie reflected. *I might have to do that too. It wouldn't at all hurt me to work outside Dupleix for a while – and God knows, Victoria responds to nothing so well as a show of power.*

'Jodie? I'm so sorry to disturb you while you're going over proofs.'

Jodie looked up to see her assistant, Catalina, standing half in her office, half out, her figure so slim that this meant that her body was barely visible. Jodie really did try to employ *Style* staffers who were not sample size, but, annoyingly, Catalina had been by far the best qualified candidate on paper, and equally impressive at her interview; Jodie had had no choice but to hire her. She *did* make sure that there were plates of elegant little sandwiches and tasteful nibbles lying around the *Style* offices to counteract any idea that *Style* demanded that its personnel all maintain a UK size four, but so far Catalina hadn't put on a pound, rather to Jodie's annoyance.

'What is it?' she said abruptly, her concentration entirely on the images and text in front of her.

'It's someone called Tamra Maloney,' Catalina said. 'She says she doesn't have an appointment, but she wants to see you anyway, and she's brought—'

'Cocktails!' Tamra announced, swirling into Jodie's office not by pushing Catalina aside, but by fully opening the door and using the considerable space that Catalina's skinny frame left vacant. Behind her came a young man wearing the black trousers, white shirt and black waistcoat of the professional waiter: he was carrying an ice bucket containing a bottle of champagne in one hand, and a tray in the other which bore two martini glasses and a silver shaker.

'They're Pimm's Cup Martinis,' Tamra continued, gesturing to the young man to put down the tray on the white laminated table between the two burgundy Fritz Hansen 'Egg' chairs. 'With a champagne float.'

'How did you get into the building?' Jodie asked, her brows drawing together. 'Security's very strict. I'm sure no one here gave you entry clearance.'

Catalina shook her head in confirmation as Tamra said airily, 'Oh, you wouldn't expect me to tell you if I'd slipped some poor underpaid security guy a fifty and told him I was a friend of yours come to buy you a drink while you were working late, would you? Because then you'd have to sack the guy, and that would be totally unfair when he thought he was helping to give you a lovely surprise.'

Jodie assessed Tamra Maloney's Prada camel coat, her Ferragamo boots and Reed Krakoff bag, her experienced fashion editor's eye identifying every single label and season instantly. She had met Tamra, of course, at Stanclere Hall the day of the shoot, but Jodie's focus, in such a tight schedule, had been entirely on the logistics of making the day work, and the girls who would be modelling for her, as well as the particular challenge of working with royalty. And Tamra had not been trying to stand out from the crowd: for her, that day had been all about Brianna Jade.

But Jodie had certainly noticed Tamra then: it was impossible not to. Her particular kind of burnished golden perfect-featured beauty might not be model-fashionable from Jodie's perspective as a magazine editor, but it was unmistakable.

Christ, she really does wear clothes well, Jodie admitted. *So much poise. If we were back in the 1980s, she could have been one of the classic supermodels. She's got that whole Christie Brinkley/Cheryl Tiegs American blonde confidence.*

Something else was tugging at Jodie's memory as she looked at Tamra standing there in the middle of her office on the bright Marimekko rug, coat pushed back so that she could put her hands on her jean-clad hips, and the image in Jodie's head wasn't of the Amazonian, Versace-clad beauties who had walked the runways in the 1980s. Eventually she located it, and it came as quite a shock: although Tamra and she looked nothing alike, and Tamra exuded much more confidence than Jodie had done then, Jodie was remembering herself, standing in this very office, in front of Victoria Glossop, the then-editor of *Style*, years ago, interviewing for the position of Victoria's assistant.

Then, as now, Victoria had liked to rule by fear, although her new relationship had certainly softened many of her rougher edges. And she had conducted the interview with Jodie by adding and subtracting points, out loud, when she approved or disapproved of something Jodie was saying or wearing.

Ten points, Jodie thought now. *Tamra just admitted to bribing the guard downstairs and stopped me from sacking him in a couple of sentences. That was very well done. I get people trying to force their way in to see me all the time, and no one's ever pulled it off like this woman has.*

'I should get security to chuck you out,' she said, testing Tamra just as Victoria had tested her years ago.

'Oh, poor Michael,' Tamra said, smiling beautifully at both Jodie and the young waiter. 'He had this huge balancing act carrying everything over here from Claridge's, and all the way up in the elevator – you're not going to make him take it all back again, are you? At least let him pour the drinks!'

Ten more points. The Pimm's Martinis did sound delicious.

'Catalina, it's fine,' Jodie said, releasing her poor assistant from limbo: Catalina had been following the dialogue between her boss and the interloper like a trapped mouse at a catfight. She positively scrambled to get out of the office and close the door behind her. Michael, after a nod from Tamra, filled the glasses from the cocktail shaker, leaving a good centimetre on top for the Pol Roger, which he opened with the tiniest, most elegant of pops and then trickled carefully on top of the pale cinnamon Pimm's-tinged martini.

'You can go, Michael. Thank you,' Tamra said.

She had already taken care of the tip: the waiter smiled and followed Catalina out of the office, leaving Jodie and Tamra together.

'I'm not going to put your daughter on the cover of *Style Bride* just because you did a home invasion on my office and brought me a drink,' Jodie said, keeping her face straight and serious.

'Well, of course not!' Tamra said, apparently shocked that Jodie would even think such a thing. 'May I sit down?'

'Go ahead.' Jodie gestured to the Egg chairs.

Tamra took her coat off, draped it over a side table and sank so elegantly into one of the chairs that Jodie, less naturally graceful, couldn't help but envy her.

'Did you ever do any modelling?' she found herself asking.

'No,' Tamra said simply. 'It was all about my daughter. I was a single mom, and I wouldn't leave her behind to go try my luck with a modelling agency in a big city. I'd've loved to do pageants, though, believe it or not. They're real fun if you've got the right temperament, and you can use your title as a great platform to take you where you want to go. I bet the editor of *Style* thinks pageants are totally old-fashioned – hell, you've probably got way worse words for 'em than that – but I'd really have enjoyed 'em.'

She winked conspiratorially at Jodie, picking up a glass and holding it out to her in invitation.

'And I could *totally* deal with all the girls scheming behind my back and being bitchy to my face,' she added. 'I bet you get a lot of that in your job.'

'Sometimes you're your own worst enemy,' Jodie heard herself saying, much to her surprise, as she stood up, came round her desk and sat down in the other Egg chair, swivelling it to face Tamra and taking the glass the latter was proffering. 'At least, that's been how it's worked for me.'

Tamra nodded with sympathy as she picked up her own glass and chinked it with Jodie's.

Ten more points! Sod it, twenty! Jodie thought as she sipped some of the cocktail. *She just got me to tell her something personal, let down my guard – wow, she's really good.*

'This is great,' she admitted, setting down the glass.

'Yay!' Tamra flashed her stunning teeth. 'I'm so glad you like it! Now, I can see you're working, so I won't take up more than a few minutes of your time.'

'You've got as long as it takes me to drink this,' Jodie said, returning the smile for the first time. 'And I really like it, so I may drink it pretty fast.'

Tamra's smile was appreciative now.

'So let me get right to it,' she said. 'What you saw of Brianna Jade at the shoot wasn't really who she is. Brianna Jade's done a shitload of pageants. She can get up on stage and smile for the cameras and pose her ass off at the flick of a switch. I'm not going to tell you what went wrong with her that day, because it would sound like I'm making excuses for my daughter. But she can bring it – she's incredibly photogenic – and there's no way she's not going to do it on her wedding day.'

Jodie sipped some more of her cocktail, not saying a word:

it was a technique she'd learnt from Victoria, the silence that intimidated her interlocutor but also instructed them to keep talking. She was unsurprised to see that Tamra was not ruffled in the slightest by this treatment. Instead, she continued, crossing her legs and sitting back, the picture of relaxation and elegance:

'Maybe Milly and Tarquin's wedding would be right if you were picking a cover for *Mini Style Bride*. In fact, it totally would. I can see that: she's got that flower-power boho vibe that the tweens and teens are really keen on right now. But she doesn't look grown-up enough to be on the cover of *Style Bride*, does she? I know you're pursuing a policy of avoiding really young models, which as a forty-year-old woman, by the way, is *fantastic*, and thank you for that! But little Milly, with her Shirley Temple curls and her Little Lord Fauntleroy fiancé – oh God, I can't *even*! I mean, that's *before* you start picturing what my sources tell me's going to be some wild-flower-and-vintage-china hippy-dippy puke-fest in Tuscany ...'

Jodie, drinking some more of her cocktail, had to use all of the self-control she had learnt working as Victoria Glossop's assistant not to spray her Pimm's and champagne martini out through her nose at this.

'I mean, how can that even *compare* with a wedding in the Stanclere Hall chapel, attended by Princess Sophie?' Tamra concluded triumphantly, reaching into her handbag and pulling out her iPad from its Italian leather croc-embossed sleeve, drum dyed in a pale gold. Jodie's eyes went straight to the sleeve: she hadn't seen quite that pebble-effect leather before, and it was highly covetable.

'Here's the sketch for Brianna Jade's dress,' Tamra said, clicking on the screen and laying the iPad in front of Jodie on the white table. 'Designed for her by Sartoria Massimo in Milan. We have the first fitting next week. Lace georgette and silk gazar, in perfect clear white. Brianna Jade's colouring can take that, unlike most. It's really going to pop in photos.'

Jodie gazed down at the exquisite sketch on the screen. The bodice and cap sleeves were in heavy lace georgette, the base of the bodice scooped into an elegant curve that would follow the line of the breasts: below that, silk gazar flowed down, snug to the line of the perfect figure outlined in the drawing, which, for once, was not a flattering elongation, but an exact reproduction of the shape of the bride. Below the hips was a wide band of lace georgette, under which more silk gazar, with a lace underlay, flowed out into a flounce which was gentle in the front but spread out into a train at the back; it would actually be a double train, the silk layered over the lace, a striking effect which was only earned by the simplicity of the dress and the fact that both materials were used so effectively.

'The silk will be sewn invisibly to the lace of the train, so one flows out over the other,' Tamra said, watching Jodie's face with great satisfaction. 'And it'll be weighted, of course. This is couture, all handsewn by Massimo's seamstresses in his Milan workshop. Exquisite, isn't it? Of course, only someone with Brianna Jade's figure could carry this off. The lace inserts would cut up a shorter girl.'

She didn't need to say that Milly could never wear this dress, would be drowned in it. Jodie reached out and scrolled across, seeing another sketch; it was Tamra's mother-of-the-bride dress, also designed for her by Massimo: a stunning silk satin wrap dress, sleeveless, with a huge handmade silk flower on one shoulder, the wrap opening over an embroidered lace underskirt. It subtly echoed Brianna Jade's dress, while clearly acknowledging the two women's different roles at the ceremony, as well as their respective ages. But in the wedding photographs there would clearly be a beautiful coherence of the entire aesthetic.

'In deep rose-pink,' Tamra said. 'I don't do pastels.'

Perfect, Jodie thought. *Wedding-suitable but fantastic with her colouring. Wow, everything I'm looking at is just … perfect.*

'Bridesmaids?' she asked, not looking up.

'Two flower girls. Edmund's nieces,' Tamra said efficiently. 'Throwing white and deep pink roses. Keep going. Oh.' She placed a USB stick on the table. 'Copies of the sketches for you. Just in case you want to take a look at them later.'

Jodie's eyebrows couldn't help but rise as she gazed at the next sketch: Massimo had pulled off the very demanding challenge of designing a scaled-down version of Brianna Jade's dress that managed to be suitable for an eight- and a ten-year-old and avoided even the faintest hint of cutesiness. No sashes, no frills, but a pretty little cluster of deep pink silk flowers at their waists which echoed Tamra's huge shoulder appliqué. It was a triumph.

'I'm not familiar with his work,' she admitted, handing the iPad back to Tamra. 'But I will be now.'

'His stuff doesn't date,' Tamra said. 'And you always look a million dollars in it. But it's all word of mouth recommendations. He doesn't advertise. He doesn't need to.'

Jodie nodded, understanding Tamra's point: a fashion editor was driven very much by brand considerations when making choices for editorials. You had to use your advertisers, first and foremost, and those were the designers who drove fashion trends, because they functioned by constantly driving change, telling women shoppers that they needed to continually update their wardrobe in order to look modern. Yet the bulk of their income came from diffusion sunglasses and handbag lines that were much less fashion-forward than their catwalk collections. Massimo's style was the opposite: he and many smaller designers flourished by making beautiful couture outfits for clients who wanted primarily to wear clothes which flattered them and expressed contemporary style without being dominated by it.

'I'm on the last sips of my drink,' she observed, picking up her glass.

'So you are!'

Tamra rose to her feet, coming up onto the high spiked heels of her boots with such effortless grace that Jodie had to agree that Tamra would have been a raving success in the pageant world. Picking up her coat, she shrugged it on, wrapping the fabric belt around to hang smoothly down over the knot like a runway model showing off an outfit, a gesture of such panache that Jodie almost wanted to applaud.

'Someone from Claridge's will come by for the tray tomorrow,' Tamra said. 'Thanks so much for agreeing to see me – I can only imagine how busy you are!'

She extended a hand to Jodie, who was also on her feet now, and the two women shook hands, exchanging a glance of mutual acknowledgement for the very astute businesswomen they both were.

'It's been a real pleasure,' Tamra said, turning and whisking herself from the office before Jodie could even agree with her. 'I'll leave the door as it was when I came in, shall I?'

Thirty points! Jodie thought, staring at Tamra's blonde ponytail, lightly curled at the ends, bouncing over the fur collar of her coat as Tamra said goodbye to Catalina and was buzzed out through the main double glass doors to the lobby with its bank of lifts. *My God, she went before I was ready for her to go – she left me wanting a little more. No one's ever pulled that off before!*

Jodie leaned over and refilled her Martini glass from the shaker; there was enough for another, and honestly, it was too good to resist. Carrying it and the USB stick back to her desk, setting it down beside the proofs, she realized that she was shaking her head slowly in appreciation of Tamra's mistress-ful technique.

No wonder she's the Fracking Queen! she thought. *That woman could sell Crocs to Louboutin.*

And instead of returning to her proofs, she found herself clicking on her computer, pulling up the gorgeous, smiling, and, as Tamra had observed, hugely photogenic images of Brianna Jade which Veronica, Tamra's publicist, had sent Jodie months ago on first pitching for the *Style Bride* cover, and she sat staring at them very thoughtfully indeed.

Chapter Twenty-Six

Tuscany, late May

'Eva! Shit fuck fuckety fuck! Help!'

Eva was sitting in the elaborately carved wooden swing in the grounds of the Madonna della Neve church, watching the workmen installing the shiny wooden dance floor and bandstand: they were being very careful not to step back too far and fall over the edge of the stone retaining wall that kept the church lawn from tumbling down onto the dirt road below. She looked round to see Milly running towards her from the side of the oratory. Milly, who was carrying an iPad, was clad in a high-necked, slightly see-through blouse and shorts cut so high on her slim legs that a workman looked round and muttered '*Madonna!*' so devoutly that one might have thought he was contemplating the Virgin Mary in the frescos painted in the portico, rather than the young woman rapidly approaching.

Flinging herself onto the seat of the swing with her usual dramatic flair, Milly kicked off her Bisue ballerina flats and curled up girlishly in the other corner of the seat, dropping the iPad to bury her face in her hands and letting out such a wail that the other workmen, who had failed to notice her arrival, were now alerted to her presence on the swing: the moan cut through the loud clicking noises they were making as they locked together the panels of the parquet floor. They all tilted their heads to the same angle, focusing on the crotch of her tight shorts. Eva didn't even bother alerting Milly to this. Years of being best friends with her had made her fully aware of Milly's extreme need for attention.

If anything, it's worse now she's wrapped that film, Eva thought gloomily. The month-long shoot of *And When We Fall*, which sounded as if Milly had spent most of it stark naked with her face buried between another actor's legs, had, if anything, intensified Milly's exhibitionism. Presumably, the fierce competition to stand out among Maitland Parks's carefully selected troupe of hot, up-and-coming young actors had meant that Milly had learnt to further exaggerate all her little flirtatious tricks.

Certainly, Eva was finding her almost completely unbearable nowadays. Eva had made a decision: they would get through this wedding, making it so wonderful and magical that *Style* would crown Milly its Bride of the Year. And then Eva would not only use the consequent publicity to build sales for Milly and Me, but start a line of her own that didn't have Milly's name on it. She just couldn't take being tied so closely to her any more.

Milly peeked through her fingers to check if everyone was looking, saw they were, and, with another wail of despair, let her hands drop to her lap, thus calling even more attention to the tight crotch of her denim shorts and the fact that the hems rode up almost to her pubic bone when she sat down. If she had not been so slim, the sight would have been positively obscene; the fact that she had barely any bum cheeks to flash was the only saving grace. She looked at Eva expectantly, her big round eyes wide, but Eva was so exhausted by Milly's antics that she didn't have the energy to ask what was wrong.

Eventually, rather petulantly, Milly whined: 'Oh Eva, it's so awful! Tark's just dropped a *bombshell* on me! He's saying we're going to write our own *vows*. You have to help me! I'm so rubbish at the kind of thing! It's all right for Tark, he writes his own lyrics, even though no one can understand what they mean, but I'm an *actress*. Other people write words for *me*!'

No way, Eva thought instantly. *I'm absolutely, positively, not helping her. She's going to have to do this all on her own.*

Her thick, straight dark brows formed a single line under her heavy fringe as she said: 'But Milly, you were always going to write your own vows. That was planned as part of the ceremony: the mayor does the official bit, Father Liam comes in to do the blessing, you say your own vows and then the mayor pronounces you husband and wife. Ludo said that ages ago.'

'I've been *sooo* busy,' Milly moaned, pressing her hands prettily against her cheeks. 'Just, like, *rushed* off my feet with all the filming—'

At the start of the year, Eva noted to herself.

'—and then learning my lines for Nina *sooo* unexpectedly—'

Which you don't even start rehearsals for until the end of June.

'—*such* a hurry, though lucky me about Melody getting pregnant!'

Milly brightened up, temporarily forgetting about the woes of having to write her own vows to the man she was promising to love and cherish till death did them part. Melody Dale, the young British actress, had discovered she was expecting a baby, due in November, which put the kibosh on her plan to play Nina in *The Seagull* on the London stage for a two-month run starting in August. Despite the fact that Nina's role revolved around her getting pregnant by a famous actor, the entire pregnancy subplot took place in a time lapse between acts, and, as the ingénue, Nina could not possibly be visibly pregnant onstage.

Melody was so happy about the pregnancy that she had barely batted an eye at having to surrender a prized role in one of Chekhov's most famous dramas, and her loss had been Milly's gain. She couldn't help glowing with excitement every time she mentioned it.

'Lucky Melody,' Eva said wistfully. 'She's got it all – great career, lovely husband, and now a baby on the way.'

'What?' Milly stared at her blankly. '*I'm* the lucky one – I get to play Nina. She has some *great* monologues. Anyway, the vows! Look, Eva, what would you say if you were me?'

The transition was so fast that Eva, taken by surprise, blurted out a stream of consciousness before she could remember that she'd sworn two minutes ago not to help Milly with her vows in any way. Of course, the words were so close to her heart that it would have been hard not to say them; on the eve of watching the man she loved get married to a woman she was sure wasn't worthy of him, Eva had been unable to stop imagining herself in the place of the bride, and what spilled out was exactly what she would have said if she were marrying Tarquin.

'The Leonardo da Vinci connection,' she said instantly. 'I'd talk about this place being the ancient family seat of Mona Lisa's family, the Gherardinis, and how her portrait's become one of the most famous in the world, and how Leonardo painted her and the church – well, sketched the church – and a miracle happened here, snow in August, and how you and Tarquin having found each other is a miracle, because it's so hard to find love, lasting love, and when you do, it must feel like your own special, personal miracle ...'

Milly had grabbed the iPad and was making fast notes, but Eva didn't realize. She was staring ahead of her, at the landscape, the stream tumbling down the side of the hill, still full from the winter and spring rains, the same stream depicted by Leonardo da Vinci in the exquisite, sepia ink drawing in the Uffizi, Florence's main art museum. A curator had shown it to her and Tarquin last year, when they had visited on the special tour arranged by Marco Baldini. Milly, naturally, had been much too busy to join them.

But Eva and Tarquin had exchanged a long look full of awe and anticipation as the curator slid open one of the narrow drawers in the print cabinet, eased her fingers under the acid-free paper that enclosed the drawing, and very gently extracted the landscape, bringing it to a lightbox table so that the visitors could examine it in detail.

Eva and Tarquin both had photographs on their tablets, taken of the church and its setting so that they could compare the view then and now, and they were both amazed at how unchanged it was: Marco telling them it was still the same, and the visual proof, were two very different things. Time and again, switching back and forth between the inked landscape drawing and the photographs – which Tarquin had suggested viewing in black and white to make the parallels clearer – their eyes had met, sparkling with the same excitement. Their words babbled over each other's, expressing their wonder at the sense that the day before, at the Madonna della Neve d'Agosto, they had been standing in a place that was almost out of time, the past and the present overlapping each other, the only missing element the castles that had been razed to the ground.

And then Tarquin's expression had gone dreamy as he fell silent, with that special, faraway look that meant his lyric-writing impulse had been triggered. One never knew what would set him off, and Eva had watched him in awe, imagining the creative process swirling behind those big blue eyes, so proud and elated to be sharing the moment with him ...

But now she was called back to the present by the rocking of the swing: Milly was kicking her heels against the base of it in sheer happiness.

'This is *great*!' she exclaimed, having transcribed Eva's words onto the iPad. 'Thanks *so* much, Eves. Top stuff! I'll work all that in and then just google something sort of poetic about love and marriage to add to it. You're a star!'

She leant over, planted a smacking kiss on Eva's cheek and dashed off again. Eva bit her lip, unable to believe what had just happened. Yet again, she'd given Milly what she wanted despite resolving not to do it.

Am I ever going to be able to stand up to her? she wondered miserably. It was a pattern that had been set since they were kids – Milly got what she wanted from Eva whenever she wanted it.

'May I join you?'

Father Liam's voice startled Eva: he had approached over the grass, and was standing next to the swing, politely waiting for her to approve his sitting down next to her. She nodded automatically, and he hitched up his perfectly pressed black trousers and took a seat. Father Liam was as immaculate as ever, his reddish-brown hair brushed straight back from his high forehead, his black clerical shirt ironed as crisply as his trousers, the white tab at his neck bright and spotless.

'Eva, let me ask you a question you'll think is very random: are you familiar with the play *Cyrano de Bergerac*?' the priest asked. 'There was a film version with Gérard Depardieu, and another one, some time ago, a comedy version with Steve Martin. You're probably too young to have heard of him.'

Eva frowned, trying to think. She hadn't heard of Steve Martin, but the name Cyrano definitely rang bells.

'I'm not sure,' she admitted.

Father Liam nodded.

'Well, this is the plot,' he said. 'A young man called Christian, very handsome but not very clever, falls in love with a young woman called Roxane. She, being a tremendous blue-stocking, will only give her heart to a man who can court her with clever words and poetry: merely being good-looking isn't enough for her. But Christian, being a bear of little brain, is quite incapable of satisfying her demanding requirements, so he turns to his friend, the poet and wit Cyrano de Bergerac, to help him out. Cyrano gives Christian exactly the right poetic script to say to cause Roxane to fall into his arms. Cyrano can't resist the opportunity to see how his words affect her because, you see, he's madly in love with her himself.'

There was a long pause.

'Why can't Cyrano court Roxane himself?' Eva asked after a while in a very small voice.

Father Liam grimaced. 'He doesn't think he's attractive enough for her. He has an enormous nose. Almost a deformity.'

Gently, he reached out and pushed Eva's hair back from where it had been partly obscuring her face.

'Not an issue with you,' he observed. 'No deformities here.'

Eva went bright pink.

'Milly's just bubbled up to Ludo and me and informed us that you've been a world of help to her in writing her vows, so I'm not to worry she won't be ready for the ceremony tomor-row after all,' Father Liam continued. 'I was very sorry to hear this, as you can imagine. To be frank, I wouldn't at all mind if Milly were *not* ready for her wedding; they're clearly a very mismatched couple. I'm being very frank with you, Eva, and you must be wondering why. But *I'm* wondering why you'd help her with something so intimate as writing her vows?'

'I'm so used to it!' Eva said, fixing her eyes on the priest's, wanting to make him understand. 'I was just thinking, *I won't help her with her vows*, I *won't*, and then I got distracted and she asked me and it just all popped out! I don't want to help her any more, I didn't mean to, I have to work out how to stop ...'

Father Liam reached out and took her hand, holding it between his own.

'That sounds like an excellent idea,' he said. 'I'm so very glad that I haven't just raised this subject out of nowhere, as it were.'

The workmen had finished assembling the stage; wondrously, the pieces of wood they had carried up to the lawn were now one smooth shining parquet square, raised on an invisible frame to keep it level, two shallow steps leading up to it. They jumped down from the edge, too manly to use the steps, and filed past the swing, each of them bowing their heads in respect for Father Liam's calling as they went.

'Ludo already talked to me about this when we first came to Italy,' Eva admitted. 'Not the Cyrano, putting-words-in-her-mouth part, though. I didn't think of that until you pointed it out. He could see what my feelings were about ... about Tarquin. He was really nice and sympathetic.'

'You clearly struck some kind of nerve with him,' Father Liam commented wryly. 'No one *ever* says that about Ludo!'

Eva managed a little laugh.

'No, he really *was* nice,' she confirmed. 'He said that the marriage was going to go ahead because Milly was so set on it, and I shouldn't get my hopes up that it wouldn't, but that it wasn't going to last long and so I should sort of wait it out and hope to ... hope that when it broke up, I could ...'

'Hope to catch Tarquin on the rebound?' Father Liam clicked his tongue crossly. 'What very typically cynical advice of Ludo's! I'll have to haul him over the coals for that. Please, for your own good, and for the good of the ill-assorted pair whose union I will be blessing tomorrow, leave them to sink or swim on their own. Marriage brings with it many

challenges, and if they can't communicate with each other
properly, it won't last. Eva, don't give Milly any more poetic
words she can parrot back to Tarquin like Christian to Roxane.
Stop playing Cyrano.'

Eva hung her head.

'Take care of yourself,' he said kindly. 'Direct all your energies into putting yourself first and foremost.' He stood up,
smoothing down his shirt. 'This is an emotional subject, and
it'll take a while to absorb, I'm sure. Do please feel free to come
and talk with me further if you want or need to, won't you?'

Eva looked up at him, the sun in her eyes, and nodded.

'Thank you,' she said quietly. 'I'm going to sit here and let
it all sink in.'

'Good, good,' Father Liam said, smiling. 'Very good.'

But his smile faded as he walked across the lawn and up the
steps to the portico, where Ludo was conferring busily with
Gabriella and Leonardo on last-minute catering decisions.
Further down the long table, the handmade chandeliers,
decorated with pearls and turquoises, were being very carefully unpacked, foam packing peanuts tumbling out as the
magnificent, sculptural creations were lifted out of their boxes
by their creator, Antonio di Meglio, a tall Italian silver fox so
handsome that, busy as Ludo was, he couldn't help occasionally glancing over appreciatively.

This was not the cause of Father Liam's frown, however; it
was quite taken for granted between him and Ludo that male
beauty was there to be admired. As he snapped out: 'Ludo?
May I have a word?' his abstracted boyfriend didn't think for
a moment that there was any jealousy behind the priest's curt
tone.

'Can it wait?' Ludo replied. 'I'm just going over the
antipasto buffet arrangements—'

'*Now*, please,' Father Liam said, pleasantly, but with enough of an edge that Ludo instantly obeyed. The priest had already turned and was heading down the path to the road, and Ludo scampered to follow.

'Why are we going for a walk all of a sudden?' he asked, catching up with Father Liam. 'Not that I don't love a country stroll, but I really have quite a few things to do today.'

'I want to make sure that we can't be overheard when I tell you exactly why I'm cross with you,' Father Liam said under his breath, striding fast along the uneven surface of the road, which passed a large house set back behind a high wrought-iron fence, and then promptly dwindled into a narrow, tree-lined path that led into what almost immediately became a forest. Strict conservation laws meant that any new building in the Tuscan countryside was utterly prohibited, and the oak trees which surrounded Father Liam and Ludo after a mere couple of minutes would not only have been there when Leonardo da Vinci was sketching the landscape, but many centuries before.

'Ooh!' Ludo perked up at once. 'You're cross with me? Am I going to have to do penance?' He looked around him. 'This path's a bit too public, especially with you in your dog collar, but we could nip up that slope behind one of those lovely big trees ...'

'*Ludo!*'

Father Liam rounded on him, stopping dead in his tracks.

'For God's sake, get a grip!' he said angrily. 'What do you think – that I suddenly became overcome with desire after having a talk with that nice little Eva and brought you out to the woods in broad daylight, while we're planning a wedding, to get my cock sucked?'

'Well, I *did* rather hope—' Ludo started optimistically.

The priest put his hands imperiously on his hips.

'Ludo, be *quiet and listen to* me!' he commanded. 'Eva's just told me that you instructed her to sit around and wait for

Tarquin and Milly's marriage to fail and then try to sneak in and catch him on the rebound.'

Ludo shrugged.

'What's wrong with that?' he said. 'It's very good advice. Tarquin's the kind of man who needs to be in love with *someone* – he's a love junkie, frankly – and Eva's a much better match for him than Milly is. I know she's rather wet, but so's he, you know?'

'Ludo, do you not understand how cynical you're being?' Father Liam said angrily. 'And it's not just your own cynical attitude to marriage, but that you're visiting it on that sweet little girl and corrupting her too – encouraging her to think of marriage as something comparatively meaningless, like a casual relationship that one picks up and puts down on a whim. Tarquin and Milly are going to make vows to each other, serious vows! I find it very distressing that you – '

'*I* find it distressing!' Ludo exploded quite unexpectedly. 'Liam, *I'm* distressed at being lectured about the morality of marriage when it's something you and I will never, ever, be able to do! You just called me cynical – well, why *wouldn't* I be cynical, when a Pope's allowed to retire and live cosily in the Vatican with his devoted,' he raised his fingers and made apostrophes in the air, '"private secretary", but I can't, even officially, live with you? All these gay scandals positively *swirling* around Vatican City – cardinals living in apartment blocks above gay clubs, Pope Francis even talking openly about a gay lobby in the Vatican – but no hope for us! Of *course* I'm bloody cynical about marriage, when that Church of yours is covering up for gays in power but making us live in an awful limbo for our entire lives. Talk about corruption, it's not *me* being corrupt here!'

Father Liam opened his mouth to try to refute some of what Ludo was saying, but his boyfriend, triggered into a very uncharacteristic display of emotion, was unstoppable.

'I know you'll never leave the Church,' Ludo was saying passionately, 'I know that and I've made my peace with it, as much as I can! We talked and talked about this when we first got together and I made the bargain that you were worth it, that *we* were worth it as a couple, for the sacrifices I'd have to make – because they're mostly on my side, Liam, you must admit! I'd love to be out as a couple, to have us written up in the magazines, to show off my handsome husband – yes, I'm shallow that way, but that's no surprise to you, I'm sure. I see my friends getting married now, properly, not just the civil partnerships but proper marriage, and I may joke and say it's all fabulous, darling, we've got our full rights now *and* I'm making a mint off all the new ceremonies I'm organizing, lucky me, but I don't *feel* lucky when I see all these gay couples happily getting on with it and I know I never will – because there's nothing I'd love more than to plan our wedding and walk down the aisle together, hand in hand!'

Ludo was in tears by now, and the last sentence was blurred; Father Liam stepped towards him, his own eyes welling up, and drew his boyfriend into his arms. Ludo was shorter than the priest, and his head snuggled into the priest's neck, held fully in Father Liam's embrace as, over Ludo's head, Father Liam said against his hair: 'I'm sorry, my love. I'm so sorry. I was insensitive and thoughtless. I'd give the world to be able to marry you too.'

'I don't know what came over me,' Ludo managed through his tears. 'I don't know ...'

Father Liam heaved out a long sigh, one hand coming up to stroke Ludo's hair, tangling his fingers in Ludo's curls, as Ludo's tears kept falling, dripping down his face and wetting Liam's shirt till the starched white clerical collar was limp and sodden with his lover's tears.

Chapter Twenty-Seven

Stanclere Hall, later that day

'Honey!'

Without waiting for a summons, Tamra swept into Brianna Jade's bedroom, her eyes bright with the excitement of her daughter's impending nuptials. Today had been a whirl of activity. All the house guests had arrived, including a team of photographers and videographers preparing to record the wedding for *Style Bride*; after Tamra's visit to Jodie Raeburn, it had been agreed that Brianna Jade would still be in the running for the coveted Bride of the Year cover, and Tamra's fingers were very tightly crossed that her daughter would pull it off. After all, Brianna Jade had been very calm and self-controlled for the last few months, ever since Tamra had rung her in excitement after her incursion into Jodie's office and said that she thought Brianna Jade was in with a chance of making the cover.

What Tamra didn't know was that, the day after Tamra had first thrown out Barb Norkus and then pitched the idea of the Stanclere estates becoming a self-sufficient farming brand, with particular emphasis on pork products, Brianna Jade had made an appointment with a GP two villages over and secured herself a regular prescription of Valium. It had been a lot easier than she'd thought; she had literally just started with 'I'm feeling really stressed at the moment because ...' and the busy, harassed-looking doctor had needed to hear no more before typing a prescription into his computer and printing it out for her. Brianna Jade had discovered that a Valium first thing in the morning, another with a glass of wine at lunch and a couple more glasses during dinner, kept her on an even keel, allowing her to keep smiling and happy and floating above the path that she was on, the one that led inexorably to marriage to Edmund and residence for the rest of her life at Stanclere Hall, with the knowledge of Abel's presence in his cottage just down the lane ...

In order to avoid having to get involved in the plans to market Stanclere Sausages, as Tamra and Edmund had decided to call them, Brianna Jade had thrown herself into wedding organization with an attention to detail that had not only thoroughly impressed her mother, but reassured Tamra that her daughter was truly committed to her upcoming wedding. Brianna Jade couldn't demonstrate excitement – the Valium was preventing that – but she could certainly spend a great deal of time painstakingly working through every little issue that came up with the wedding planner, pretty much taking the entire responsibility off Tamra's shoulders for the last few months.

Because, desperate to avoid being forced into contact with Abel, Brianna Jade had maintained that she had no business skills, but could take over the wedding and honeymoon planning and free up her mother to help Edmund start up Stanclere Sausages. Tamra seemed oddly reluctant to visit the Hall, let alone stay overnight, but she was very happy to immerse herself in research about what would be needed for all the various aspects of establishing and promoting an online food retailer.

She had land maps of the estate, and had identified a barn that could be converted to a catering-sized kitchen, another two that could be knocked together to make the farm shop, and four disused cottages to be renovated and converted into holiday lets. Edmund was even more in awe of her drive and energy now he saw it directed, not just to rescuing Stanclere Hall, but to making its estates economically productive.

'Hey, Mom,' Brianna Jade called back.

She was in the bathroom, massaging Amorepacific Moisture Bound Vitalizing Masque into her face and neck, her body already slathered in Sisleÿa Anti-Aging Concentrate Firming Body Care. It was a long way from the cheap Jergens body lotion which Tamra had trained her daughter to work into her skin every night when she started doing pageants and the Dove cold cream she'd used on their faces, but Brianna Jade honestly wondered if there was much of a difference, apart from the fact that the pricey stuff smelt much nicer.

'I won't stay,' Tamra said, walking into the bathroom and nodding with approval as she saw her daughter dutifully taking good care of her skin. 'I just wanted to kiss you good-night for the last time as a single woman.'

She hugged her daughter tightly as Brianna Jade turned from the mirror to embrace her mother.

'Tomorrow you'll be Edmund's, and not mine any more,' Tamra said into her daughter's hair, stroking the shiny blonde waves as Brianna Jade ducked her head into her mother's neck. 'I know that sounds crazy, but it's how I feel. I'm so happy for you, but I'm losing you in a way ...'

She swallowed.

'But you're going to be a Countess! I still can't believe it! My little girl a Countess! Oh, baby, we've come so far together, we really have.'

Brianna Jade nodded vehemently into her mother's bosom.

'I'll be crying my heart out with happiness when I see you walk back down the aisle with Edmund as the Countess of Respers. I'll be so proud of you!' Tamra said. 'Oh shit, I'm about to lose it just thinking about it. Thank God the chapel's in the house so's I can run back to my room to touch up my make-up. I'm going to be such a mess!'

Brianna Jade lifted her head, smiling at her mother's ingenuous admission that she was concerned about her own looks at her daughter's wedding.

'What?' Tamra said, faking indignation. 'I find you a great husband who just so happens to be an Earl, I do up your stately home so you guys have the most gorgeous place to live, I spend months researching the pros and cons of commercial kitchen sausage stuffers – seriously, there are tons of them! – and all I get is being laughed at because I don't want to look like a sobbing clown at your wedding?'

'Oh Mom, you'll be the most beautiful woman there,' Brianna Jade said, hugging Tamra even tighter. 'I love you so much!'

'I love you too, baby,' Tamra said. 'Always and forever. It's all been for you, you know that? Everything I've done and worked for, it's been to make you happy. And you are, aren't you? He's a really good man.' Her voice softened. 'Really, *such* a great guy. I couldn't wish for a better husband for you.'

'He *is* a great guy,' Brianna Jade agreed so strongly that Tamra didn't realize that her daughter hadn't answered the question she'd asked: Brianna Jade hadn't confirmed that she was happy.

'I brought you an Ambien,' Tamra said, finally, reluctantly, detaching herself from her daughter. 'Here.'

She filled the cut-glass tumbler by the side of the marble sink and handed it to Brianna Jade, pulling a vial of pills from the pocket of her dressing gown and tipping one out.

'You need your beauty sleep,' she said fondly. 'I want you all bright-eyed and bushy-tailed tomorrow, and I bet you've got a million and one things running through your mind right now.'

Brianna Jade swallowed the Ambien, hugely grateful for her mother's thoughtfulness. Her brain *was* racing madly, though not with the kind of natural, pre-wedding nerves that her mother was assuming. Tamra kissed her on the forehead and slipped from the room; Brianna Jade, more sure than ever that marrying Edmund was the only way to give her mother the happiness she wanted, finished her bathroom ritual and poured herself a small glass of brandy from the carafe on the console table.

This was the worst time of all, just before going to sleep, whether she was with Edmund or not, because lying there in the dark she couldn't help thinking about Abel. The brandy helped tip her over the edge into unconsciousness before her thoughts could take hold; she climbed into bed and resolutely, as if it were medicine, drank down the whole glassful. She didn't actually like brandy, but it was better than sherry, and those seemed to be the two socially allowable options that a Countess was permitted to have in her bedroom.

She was just about to turn out the bedside light, her head swimming from the fortified spirit, when she heard a tap on her door.

'Brianna? Can I come in for a moment?'

It was Edmund's voice, and he sounded nervous. *He wants to call it off!* Brianna Jade thought, her heart pounding, jumping to a far-fetched conclusion she wouldn't have reached if she hadn't been woozy with the Ambien and brandy on top of the wine at dinner. *He wants to call it off, and it won't be my fault, so it won't be me breaking Mom's heart . . .*

'Yes? Come in!' she called, a sudden hope rising in her, irrational though it might be. And Edmund's hangdog appearance raised her hopes still more; he looked deeply awkward.

Lady Margaret had declared it a ridiculously bourgeois idea for either bride or groom to have to go to a hotel, or a friend's house, when they had their own separate suites at Stanclere Hall and were going to be married beneath their own roof; the wedding planner would coordinate bride and groom's movements the next morning to avoid them seeing each other before they met in the chapel. So Edmund was in his dressing gown and slippers, about to turn in for the night.

'I won't be long – I know we both need to get a good night's sleep. I just wanted to get something rather important off my chest,' he said, closing the door behind him. 'Something that's been on my mind. Can I?'

He crossed to the four-poster bed, and Brianna Jade nodded sleepily, indicating he could sit down.

'This is a bit – well, embarrassing, but I'm going to plough right in,' Edmund said, reaching out to take her hand. 'I haven't been able to stop thinking about that amazing night we had last year. It was so ...' He cleared his throat. 'Well, out of the ordinary for us. And it switched something on in me. I simply can't stop thinking about it, how incredible it was. I've sort of tried since then to ... well, to recreate some of the things we did ...'

He couldn't meet her eyes.

'But you haven't seemed, um, *receptive*, is probably how I'd put it. And I backed off, because I didn't want to push. But honestly, having had that amazing time with you once, I genuinely don't feel that I could be satisfied spending the rest of my life without it. I've been mulling it over, and I, um, did think that it might have been the different surroundings – you know, not being in my room or yours – and the fact that it was a party, and we'd both had quite a bit to drink. I know I'd certainly had more than the usual, all the punch and so on, and you were definitely a bit tipsy, in the best way possible. I could taste it when we kissed – the punch, I mean. I assumed you'd popped down and had some – very nice, wasn't it?'

He cleared his throat again.

'So I just wanted to reassure you, in case you were embarrassed, not to be. At *all*. It was phenomenal. Really, as if you were quite a different person. Um, I was thinking that I could possibly have Mrs Hurley make the punch again? What do you think – was that, um, the trigger?'

Brianna Jade was barely taking in what he was saying: waves of drugged sleep were hitting her hard, and her head jerked forward, pulled by gravity. She caught herself and raised it again, but Edmund took the gesture as a 'yes', and was instantly emboldened.

'Great! That's wonderful!' he said excitedly. 'Or on honeymoon – they must have drinks like that in Mauritius – rum-based drinks. God, this is absolutely fantastic! I've been so frustrated not knowing what was, um, the key, and this is really – God, I can't *wait* till tomorrow night!'

Brianna Jade nodded again, another sleeping-pill-fuelled bob of the head. Edmund picked up her hand and kissed it.

'This is so wonderful,' he said, standing up. 'You're going to make me the happiest man in the world tomorrow. I just can't wait!'

Beaming from ear to ear, he left the room as if he were walking on air, a complete contrast to his demeanour on entering. Brianna Jade was already sliding down the pillows, her eyes closing, so knocked out that she passed out then and there, the bedside light still turned on, and only the haziest sense of what her fiancé had just said, and what she'd agreed to, running through her mind.

Chapter Twenty-Eight

Tuscany, the next day

Although the ceremony was not taking place in the church of the Madonna della Neve d'Agosto, Tarquin and Milly's guests, walking up the little rise and seeing for the first time the way the grounds had been decorated, gasped and murmured admiration to each other as softly and respectfully as if their feet had been on hallowed ground. Or, perhaps, as if they had been in a museum: Ludo, Gabriella and Leonardo had done such an exquisite job that the oohs and aahs that followed every new discovery were as respectful as if the invitees were at a design exhibition.

Ludo had particularly excelled at integrating Milly's list of demands into his own aesthetic. The Sicilian lemons that filled the birdcages were what stood out, not the over-curlicued cages themselves, and the abundance of lilies of the valley and bluebells that filled the antique teapots disguised the cutesiness of the receptacles. To further undercut any potential for over-prettiness, Ludo had decided not to use tablecloths after all, and the bare rustic oak tables that ran round three sides of the portico were shining with lavender-scented polish, the chairs upholstered in pale blue linen that matched the napkins and the Chinoiserie pattern on the china plates. An array of Riedel glasses glittered at each place setting, light sparkling off them from the rock crystals trembling delicately from the chandeliers above, scattered artfully among the pearls and turquoises for maximum effect.

Red carpet had been laid up to the portico and along the lawn, just as Milly had wanted, a wide strip leading from the apartment entrance, tucked behind the church, past the dance floor to the gazebo. Hung with muslin curtains trimmed with pale blue ribbon, its wrought-iron struts had been freshly painted white, gleaming in the spring sunshine, and little iron chairs with blue cushions were lined up on either side on wide red carpets for the guests to sit on while watching the ceremony. On its far side, tables were laid out in the shape of an L, ready for the antipasto buffet to be brought out after the vows had been said; currently they were stacked with prosecco bottles gleaming in huge ice buckets and a mass of gleaming glass Riedel prosecco flutes.

The *Style Bride* team which Jodie had assigned to this wedding had been here for hours already, capturing all the details: journalistic coverage of weddings, more than anything else, required an almost OCD level of attention to even the tiniest minutiae of the decor. Brides-to-be all over the world would be avidly consuming every single piece of information that they could about this celebrity wedding, deciding which frill or furbelow they could afford to copy directly, which they could scale down or which they could find as a knock-off cheaper version. The arrangements of the flowers, looking so simply done but actually hugely studied, the way a few lemons spilled so seemingly carelessly from the open doors of the birdcages onto the glossy wood of the tables, the stunning, handmade chandeliers – images of all of these would be torn out of the magazine, printed off the internet, taken to a wedding planner or propped up in front of a bride as she grimly wrestled wild flowers into an old teapot bought from a boot sale, determined to recreate some of the more evocative design elements of Milly and Tarquin's wedding.

The photographer and video crew were positioned in the portico initially, capturing the arrival of the guests, the delight on their faces as they took in the exquisitely transformed grounds; but once everyone had arrived, the cameras began to circulate, capturing spontaneous-looking moments which the guests, very well aware of the constant press attention, knew perfectly well how to stage. They clustered around the gazebo, posed charmingly, chatting on the swing, threw back their heads and laughed, prosecco flutes in their hands, acting the parts of perfect, beautifully dressed wedding guests they had been cast by Milly to play.

Only Eva hung back, avoiding the lenses. She wasn't under any obligation to go outside yet. As chief bridesmaid, it was bad enough that she had to precede Milly down the red carpet, walking towards Tarquin as if she were his bride, seeing him smile at her for a brief moment before his eyes shifted focus, went dreamy and soft as they gazed at the ethereal vision that was Milly, approaching him as lightly as a feather blowing behind Eva's taller and lankier frame.

Eva had seen Tarquin that morning when he had been breaking dry spaghetti into as many pieces as possible, a tradition that was supposed to ensure a long marriage: each broken piece symbolized another year together. He had been looking ridiculously handsome in his white shirt and periwinkle-blue waistcoat, the wide lavender silk floppy tie that was due to be arranged into a loose bow hanging dashingly around his neck, his golden curls a halo framing his angelic face; she thought he was the most beautiful thing she had ever seen. But Milly, she had to admit, was almost as lovely in her off-white lace dress, whose broderie anglaise layers were intended to lift lightly in the breeze. Jewelled butterfly pins in semi-precious bluebird and cornflower quartzite, rock crystals and mother-of-pearl, designed by Eva for Milly and Me, were set into Milly's hair, piled up in a mass of curls on the crown of her head, and a cluster of pretty little butterfly brooches were scattered over the bodice of the dress as if the bright winged creatures had settled for a moment on the bride.

Eva had talked Milly into the butterfly concept and persuaded her that the semi-precious stones from their own brand would work much better than the diamonds Milly secretly wanted. And Eva had been absolutely right. Milly twirled in front of the full-length mirror, hair and make-up done, testing out that she had enough hairspray, that the hairpins were securely fastened, but also glorying in her fairy-tale prettiness. Copies would be made of Milly's dress by bridal designers; her hairstyle would be much imitated, and hopefully the butterfly pins and brooches would fly out of the display cases of the retailers who stocked Milly and Me, thousands of brides all over the world trying to imitate Milly's look, that of a nymph who was going to marry Prince Charming.

He is *Prince Charming,* Eva thought half an hour later as, to the accompaniment of Elden on theorbo and Tristram on bass, playing an arrangement of 'Blue Seahorses', she stepped out onto the red carpet and led the other two bridesmaids down the path towards the man with whom she herself was in love. At least she knew that her pale blue dress suited her perfectly; she had picked it out, of course, and the Twenties-style dropwaist flattered her narrow hips, made her long waist less noticeable. Tangles of lavender beads, caught together with the same butterflies that Milly was wearing, were draped around her neck; Eva had the height to carry them off, and in her dark hair, pulled back into a side bun, a couple more butterflies were affixed.

Appreciative gasps greeted Eva's appearance as all the guests, now marshalled into the seats on either side of the gazebo, turned to watch the bridal procession arrive. The bouquet of delicate wild flowers she carried was tied with a narrow silk ribbon wrapped with a circle of rock crystal and bluebell quartzite beads, strands of which dangled down decoratively, another touch that future brides would be sure to copy.

I've put the effort into this ceremony that I should have used for my own wedding, Eva thought sadly. Glancing over to the back of the gazebo, where Father Liam stood next to the mayor of Greve-in-Chianti, she met the priest's eyes for a moment and knew that he was very aware of what she was thinking. *I'll do what he told me. That was such good advice. From now on, I have to put myself first.*

Eva had been trying not to look at Tarquin but, of course, it was unavoidable. As one of the two witnesses, she had to sit down almost directly opposite him, in a chair parallel to Lance's, who was Tarquin's best man. Lance cast Eva a swift glance in which admiration was mingled with the gloomy disappointment that she had politely turned down his advances again the night before. The other two bridesmaids fanned out to each side, their pretty pale blue dresses and blue and white bouquets forming a little frame in which the advancing Milly posed beautifully, glancing down modestly for the cameras, then smiling shyly yet eagerly at her groom.

Tarquin's face glowed in the gentle warmth of the late-May sun as he took in his bride, his eyes as blue as the sky behind him, the loose bow of his tie lifting just fractionally in the soft breeze. He held out his hands to Milly, who, passing her bouquet to one of the little bridesmaids, gave a pretty burbling laugh and, holding out her own hands, ran the last steps to his side, moving easily in the blue suede, ribbon-trimmed ballerina flats that made her look like a charming little doll.

Ludo, watching from the portico, where he was waiting to cue Elden and Tristram for the post-ceremony music, covered his mouth with his hand to avoid a tiny, involuntary, retching sound. *God, she's really pushing it*, he thought. *That run was terribly* Princess Diaries.

But the audience – or the guests – sighed, charmed by Milly's seemingly impulsive little rush. The mayor came forward to conduct the legally binding part of the ceremony, smiling paternally at the bride and groom, gesturing to them to sit as he read out the required Italian legal statutes; programmes rustled as the guests all opened theirs and followed along with the printed English translation inside. His voice was sonorous and he smiled from bride to groom, clearly thoroughly enjoying conducting this celebrity wedding.

Eva was mercifully unable to see Tarquin's expression most of the time, but occasionally he would glance at Milly and the joy on his face, even in that fleeting profile glimpse, was almost too much for Eva to bear. She ducked her head and stared down at her bouquet, dreading having to get up and read the poem that Milly had selected as her chief bridesmaid's contribution.

She was so lost in misery that she only realized that the legal side of the proceedings had been concluded and the blessing was beginning because Milly had pushed back her chair and was standing up. Father Liam had replaced the mayor at the wrought-iron lectern, and he was looking very seriously at Milly, gesturing for her to turn to Tarquin and recite her vows.

Milly tossed back her head, relishing that the spotlight, as it were, was entirely directed on her. Flashing a brilliant smile at Father Liam, she fixed her round blue eyes earnestly on Tarquin, raised the sheet of paper on which her vows had been printed, and began.

'Let me not to the marriage of true minds admit impediments,' she quoted from Shakespeare, her trained actress's voice appropriately soft, but carrying like a clear silver bell. She tilted her head to the side, smiling at Tarquin. 'And that's us, darling. True minds. We must be the two luckiest people in the world to have found each other. It feels like a miracle to me, and I know it does to you too! And here we are in these amazing surroundings, where a miracle happened all those centuries ago, the miracle of the snow in August, and we're living in our own miracle. Having found each other.'

She paused for effect.

'Finding lasting love truly is a miracle,' she went on. 'A thing of beauty is a joy for ever, as Keats said ...'

I see she's been hitting the miracle of Google hard, Ludo thought, rolling his eyes.

'... and with the amazing connection of Leonardo da Vinci to these surroundings, it feels like we're just encircled by beauty and love!' Milly read. 'The *Mona Lisa* was painted for Lisa Gherardini's husband, out of love, and that love has made it the most famous painting in the world. And her family came from right here, would have worshipped in this beautiful church, which was sketched by Leonardo. Every time I look at that drawing, so precious and unique, which shows this stunning landscape all around us at this very moment, I feel the wonder at the miracle that happened here and our love, which is *just* as precious and unique—'

'But you haven't really looked at it,' Tarquin said very quietly, so quietly that only Eva and Lance, the closest to the bride and groom by virtue of the seating arrangements, could hear him. They exchanged brief, startled glances as a blissfully unaware Milly carried on:

' – and which, like great art, enfolds two people who've found each other, two real true minds and hearts as miraculously joined as I am with you, Tarquin darling—'

Abruptly, the groom took a step back.

'Milly, I'm feeling really uncomfortable!' he blurted out, interrupting his bride in mid-flow. 'Something's not right.'

Muffled gasps from some spectators greeted his words, but Tarquin was oblivious to anything but Milly's shocked face.

'Did you write your vows yourself?' he continued, his voice trembling. 'Because that's what we said – what we agreed on. I wrote a song for you called "Turquoises in the Snow" that I was going to sing.'

Eva realized now why there was a guitar case propped beside Lance's chair, when Lance himself was a drummer; clearly, Lance was going to pass the instrument to Tarquin so he could accompany himself while singing. A rush of envy raced through her, jealousy that Tarquin had written a song specially for Milly and their wedding day.

Dots of red had appeared on Milly's cheeks, pinging out like little distress beacons.

'Yes, I wrote them!' she said quickly. 'Of course I did, darling. Look, there isn't much more.'

'No, I meant—' Tarquin pressed the back of one hand against his forehead. 'You wrote the words, I suppose, but the *thoughts*, the *ideas* – are those yours? Or did you have help?'

By now, the spectators were frozen in their seats. The natural shifting and fiddling with programmes and re-crossing of legs that always happened at any kind of ceremony had completely ceased. The muslin curtains had been looped back around the top struts of the gazebo to give everyone a clear view of the wedding, so the drama that was playing out was as visible as if on stage.

Mobile phones had been banned from the wedding, because *Style Bride* insisted on an exclusive for the ceremony, but the magazine's cameras were still clicking away, the video running. Eva was craning to try to see Tarquin's face, but at the angle at which her chair was placed she could only see his profile. She did, however, have a perfect view of Milly. The bride's spaghetti-strap dress left her collarbone bare, and it was very obvious that a red rash of embarrassment was breaking out on her pale chest.

'Yes, of course I thought of them myself!' Milly said, after a pause. 'Look, Tark darling, just let me finish and we'll talk about this later.'

She was very aware of the reaction from the guests, the stares that were swiftly becoming horrified as the situation dragged on, as Tarquin didn't just kiss her and let her continue; she darted her eyes from side to side, taking in the scale of the problem.

'But the thing is – you *didn't* see the drawing,' Tarquin said bluntly. 'The Leonardo of the church. You've never been to see it.'

'I saw it in the papers they gave us about the church!' Milly's voice rose frantically. 'And online! I've looked at it lots, just like I said in the vows! Darling, *please* just—'

'We've been back twice since we chose this place to get married in,' Tarquin carried on, 'and both times I really, really wanted to go to the Uffizi to show you the drawing – but you always had something better to do. And yesterday I said that Marco said there was a guide who could take us on a private viewing, and you said you were too busy with wedding stuff, and then you went shoe shopping in Florence instead.'

Milly swallowed hard. Leaning towards him, she put a hand on his arm.

'I didn't know it meant so much to you, darling,' she said softly, controlling herself with a huge force of will. 'We'll go as soon as we're back from honeymoon, I promise.'

Tarquin shook his head vehemently.

'But you talked about it like you'd seen it,' he said simply. 'I know in my heart that you didn't write those vows all by yourself.' He tapped his chest with one hand. 'Those *aren't* your thoughts, your ideas. And when I asked you just now, you said they were.'

Tears brimmed in his eyes.

'You lied to me at our wedding, Milly,' he said. 'At our *wedding*! If you'd admitted that you had help writing your vows, I could forgive that. I truly could. But *lying* about it . . .'

As Tarquin mentioned Milly having help with her vows, Milly's glance slipped involuntarily to Eva for a second, and Tarquin, seeing this, turned to look at Eva too. Eva's eyes met his, full of panic: would Tarquin blame her for what Father Liam called playing Cyrano? But as the tears started to fall down his cheeks, Eva saw no blame, nothing but misery and grief in his expression.

'How can I ever trust you again if you've lied to me at our wedding?' he asked Milly with terrible simplicity.

'Tark – Tark, *please*.' Milly, now in utter panic, grabbed onto his arm. 'Tark, *wait*! We can work this out – you know how sensitive you are! When you calm down and think it over, you'll realize this is a storm in a teacup. Please, *please* let's just finish the wedding!'

Tarquin looked down at her tiny fingers grasping the pale grey sleeve of his jacket. You could have literally heard a pin drop on the stone floor of the gazebo as he very gently raised his own hand and detached her grasp, letting her nerveless, limp fingers fall by her side. He drew the back of his sleeve roughly over his eyes and the fabric came away wet with tears.

'It's over, Milly,' he said in a low voice. 'You can keep the ring.'

This prompted not only very audible exclamations from the people seated at the front but, even worse, urgent requests from people in the back rows to repeat what Tarquin had said. As guests swivelled round to pass on the shocking news, hissing, 'He says it's off! He says she can keep the ring!' Tarquin turned away from his dumbfounded bride and walked slowly from the gazebo. He paused for a moment, standing just outside it, drawing in a deep breath, and seeming to Eva, who was gazing up at him in a kind of paralysed wonder, to be considering something very deep and serious.

Finally, he exhaled, slowly, steadily, and looked down at Eva. He was very pale, but his cornflower-blue eyes were no longer brimming with tears.

'I need to go for a walk,' he said softly. 'Will you come with me?'

She couldn't say a word. For a second, she couldn't even move. But then Tarquin, very gravely, held out his hand, and she found herself rising to her feet, putting her fingers into his, and walking, by his side, away from his aborted wedding, down the slope that led to the road and to the woodland path beyond.

'It's a *different* kind of miracle!' Ludo muttered to himself, shaking his head in amazement.

The red blotches on Milly's slim chest had now spread up her neck in a flush of absolute mortification. She stared wildly after her departing groom.

'I don't understand!' she wailed. 'What just *happened*?'

She turned to a horrified Father Liam, who was coming forward to comfort her.

'Did we get married?' she asked, clutching frantically onto the faintest of hopes. 'Is it legal? Did we actually get married?'

Father Liam shook his head sombrely. And Milly's shrieks of frustration and fury on hearing this news were so high and piercing that the white doves enclosed peacefully in the dovecote, waiting to be released at the end of the ceremony, became so agitated, flapping their wings and shuffling around, that a stream of bird poo started running down the side of the pretty wooden birdhouse.

Chapter Twenty-Nine

Milly and Tarquin's wedding ceremony had taken place mid-morning, to allow for lunch afterwards and then dancing until dusk on the outdoor dance floor, before the guests adjourned to the villa behind the church when the May evening became too chilly for comfort after sunset. However, Brianna Jade and Edmund's wedding, scheduled for the same day so that Tamra could be sure that Princess Sophie would attend this one and not Milly and Tarquin's, did not have to consider the same weather constraints as an outdoor marriage in Tuscany. Tamra and the planner had chosen an early afternoon timeslot, which allowed guests to arrive up till lunchtime on the day itself and gave plenty of time for the second *Style Bride* team to potter happily around through Stanclere Hall with their cameras and videocameras.

A journalist with a Dictaphone followed the photographer, dictating a near-constant stream of notes into the machine, trailed by an assistant to the wedding planner who was trying to answer her questions as fast as she could ask them. The Great Hall alone was enough to keep *Style Bride* occupied for days: it had been transformed into an entrance arbour, many of the sofas removed to make room for two rows of huge flowering white magnolia trees in china pots, towering above the guests, perfuming the air. Clusters of white Claire Austin roses, selected for their strong scent of meadowsweet, heliotrope and vanilla, were arranged in low silver vases on the polished tables and on the gleaming black piano. In the fireplace was a dark pink Gertude Jekyll rose bush, entirely filling the space where the grate had been: Tamra had specified that the dark rose colour of her dress and of the flowers the little bridesmaids would throw should come through in hints throughout the decorations, a subtle contrast to the main theme of white flowers and glossy green leaves.

'Jekyll spelt like Jekyll and Hyde?' the journalist was asking the assistant when a text came in for her.

'Yes, I've got it all on a spreadsheet for you – I've emailed you the Excel document. And the roses in the chapel are Claire Austin too,' the assistant was answering, only to be cut off as the journalist gasped, having just checked her phone.

It was from her counterpart at Milly and Tarquin's wedding, who was dying to share the incredibly juicy news with as many people as she could: as a *Style* employee, she was almost the only person at the wedding to have a mobile phone to hand, the other guests having been relieved of theirs.

'Oh my *God*!' the journalist exclaimed, staring down at the screen. 'Best gossip of the year!'

'What?'

The wedding planner's assistant eagerly leaned over and the journalist tilted the phone over to her. She gasped.

'Bloody *hell*,' she said, shaking her head. 'Because she didn't write her own *vows*? That's rough.'

'It looks like he went off with the maid of honour!' the journalist said, scrolling down. 'This is crazy! And I can't Tweet it – shit, I'd get so many RTs, but Jodie would kill me.'

She looked up to see that the assistant had disappeared: the latter, very well aware of which side her bread was buttered, had shot off to deliver the news to Tamra. Busy supervising the final touches being put to the flower arrangements in the chapel, Tamra initially greeted this information with unabashed joy. The collapse of Milly and Tarquin's ceremony meant, of course, that there was no longer any competition for Brianna Jade to take the *Style Bride* cover. A few minutes later, however, when more details of the events in Tuscany were conveyed, Tamra was, like the journalist, shaking her head in disbelief.

'She didn't write her own vows, so he left her at the *altar*?' she repeated, looking at Lady Margaret. 'I don't get it.'

'He's always been *terribly* sensitive,' Lady Margaret said, pulling a grimace so exaggerated she looked like a gargoyle.

'But Margaret – I mean, come *on*. Lord, I know I threw Milly out of the Hall for being a total bitch, but no one deserves that! You think she cheated on him or something?'

'He went off with the maid of honour!' the assistant said breathlessly.

Lady Margaret shrugged. 'Nice girl. Can't blame him.'

'What a *disaster*,' Tamra sighed. 'Thank God Edmund's not going to pull a stunt like that.'

'No, he's solid through and through,' Lady Margaret said gruffly, looking at Tamra under lowered brows. 'Stick by his word no matter what, that's Edmund. Like all the Respers. Very responsible family. Knew that when I suggested him for Brianna Jade. Though I—' She stopped. 'Well, never mind that. You don't need to worry about Edmund.'

'Oh, I'm not,' Tamra said quickly. 'Not at all.' She smiled distractedly at the assistant. 'You did a great job coming to tell me,' she said. 'I'll make sure you get a bonus for this.'

'Thank you, Mrs Maloney,' the assistant beamed, dashing out of the chapel to resume her normal duties.

'Well, I guess I better go tell Brianna Jade that she's *Style* Bride of the Year!' Tamra said, her face flushed with excitement from the news, her dark eyes sparkling.

But Brianna Jade, when duly informed of the bizarre turn of events in Tuscany, was not as gleeful as her mother had expected.

'Honey, this is *it*!' Tamra crowed. 'Don't you get it – you're guaranteed the cover! It was down to the two of you, and no way can Milly be *Style* Bride of the Year now that this has happened. Even if Milly and Tarquin patch things up, they're selling happy weddings, not a walkout at the altar, you know?'

Brianna Jade, who was sitting on a stool in her lavish bathroom, her hair in curlers being put up by two stylists, her face already a perfect, eerily smooth mask of natural-looking make-up, couldn't nod with four hands winding rollers onto her scalp. She managed to say: 'Wow, Mom, I can't help feeling sorry for Milly. I mean, being left at the altar – that's as harsh as it gets.'

'I know, hon. But hey, it's still great news,' Tamra said exultantly. 'What can I say – you're nicer than me. That's not exactly a newsflash to anyone.'

'Tamra, sweetie, leave the girl alone,' Lady Margaret said, sweeping her friend away. 'Let everyone do their work. She should be thinking about her own wedding, not someone else who made a total cock-up of theirs.'

The hairstylists, plus the make-up artist who was waiting to do final touch-ups on Brianna Jade, burst into excited babbling about this incredibly juicy piece of gossip: the make-up artist was already checking Twitter on her phone and posting what she'd just heard. But Brianna Jade, facing the mirror as the hot curlers were removed and the bouncy curls brushed out and pinned into place, wasn't really absorbing the fact that her *Style Bride* title was assured. Her attention was entirely directed towards trying, as best she could, to reconstruct the conversation – or rather, the monologue – that Edmund had had with her last night.

She had only started to remember it halfway through the morning. She had debated taking her Valium, and decided not to: she surely ought not to be on anti-anxiety medication the day of her wedding. And she felt quite calm, because there was so much on her schedule today that she didn't have any spare time to wander around wishing that she were down at the piggeries ...

She dragged her thoughts away from that avenue, focusing instead on what Edmund could possibly have been talking about. She'd been racking her brains to try to remember a night where she and he had gone at it in a much kinkier way than usual, which seemed to be the gist of what he'd been saying.

But she couldn't. She really couldn't.

Edmund had said that she hadn't seemed like herself, which was gradually beginning to make her think that the woman he was talking about hadn't been her at all, bizarre though that sounded. But how, and when, could a misunderstanding on that scale have happened? Who could the other woman have *been?*

Because Brianna Jade had been so zonked as she fell asleep last night, Edmund's words were only coming back to her in fits and starts. There had been something about punching – no, that couldn't be right.

'*Punch,*' she said out loud. 'Not *punching. Punch.*'

'You what, love?' The hairstylist looked down at her. 'What was that?'

'Nothing,' she said, used enough by now to having her hair and make-up done to know not to shake her head.

He returned to his work, and Brianna Jade to her thought process: *punch,* she repeated to herself. Punch had been served that night of the house party at the weekend of the photo shoot, Saturday night, after Milly had derailed Brianna Jade so completely with those nasty little side digs about her and Abel, which had turned out to be right on the money ...

Anyway – she bit her lip hard, smearing the lip gloss – she had gone to bed early that night, hadn't participated in the croquet or the Twister or the late-night partying. She hadn't had any of the punch. And as she recalled, Edmund had said the woman he'd thought was her had seemed tipsy – that was right, he'd definitely said 'tipsy'. Another little piece falling into place. So a drunk woman had – what? Staggered into Edmund's room and got into bed with him for some random reason? Brianna Jade had been in her own bed, fast asleep, but how would some other woman know that Edmund's fiancée wasn't in bed with him already? And even if she did somehow know that Edmund was alone, why would she suddenly decide to have sex with him? It didn't make sense.

Could the mystery woman have mistaken Edmund's room for someone else's? That seemed a lot more likely, but it was the master suite, so it would be hard to make that sort of error ...

Wait. She took a breath. *The fish.* The horrible stinky fish that Dominic had put in Edmund's bed that night, some sort of icky British posh custom that, to do him justice, Edmund hadn't defended because of tradition or any bullshit like that. It had taken ages to air the room out, the mattress had been ruined, Edmund had slept in the guest room down the hall until the smell was—

The guest room down the hall. The room to which Dominic had been assigned, but which Edmund had insisted on swapping with him. *So Dominic was in Edmund's room, and Edmund was in Dominic's – which means the woman who had sex with Edmund thought she was having sex with Dominic!*

Brianna Jade let out a long breath of triumph. She wasn't

at all accustomed to having to work through a string of clues, come to the only logical conclusion, and she felt as satisfied as if she'd solved one of the British crime mysteries she liked to watch in the afternoons on TV. Miss Marple and Poirot, explaining to a selected group of people at the finale why the empty bottle of tanning lotion had been thrown out of the window of the hotel, or the reason the colonel's wife hadn't taken her handbag when she went to visit the vicarage. In fact, Brianna Jade was so busy being pleased with herself that it didn't occur to her that a crucial factor was missing from the puzzle she had just nearly completed: any jealousy on her part that Edmund had, by mistake and through no fault of his own, had sex with someone who wasn't her, and which had clearly been infinitely better than the sex he had with his fiancée ...

She reached for her phone, which was lying on the marble surround of the huge sink, and scrolled through the contacts list. She had a feeling that she had Dominic's number in it from a weekend Edmund had spent shooting with him up on the Isle of Harris, where mobile service was famously patchy for Edmund's network and he'd wanted her to have Dom's number as well just in case she needed to reach him. Yes, here it was. She dialled it, putting Dom on speaker, because she couldn't hold the phone to her ear due to the activity going on around her scalp.

'Hey!' Dom answered. 'What's up? Bride emergency?'

'No, not at all,' Brianna Jade said. 'I was just—'

'Oh, great!' he said jocosely. 'I wasn't looking forward to having to tell old Ed everything was off at the last minute.'

Brianna Jade frowned. 'Dom, just focus, will you? I wanted to ask you something.'

'Need a last-minute shag before married life begins?' He guffawed. 'No probs, babe, I'll be right up.'

'No, my hairstylist needs sucking off,' Brianna Jade said

curtly; she wasn't going to put up with that. 'Can you get up here and do that for him?'

It was the male stylist's turn to guffaw, and to do him credit, Dom did too.

'God, it's been a while since school!' he said cheerfully. 'Still, I'm sure it's like riding a bike, you never forget how. Right, what can I do you for?'

'You know that night you put a fish in Edmund's bed and he made you crash in his room?' she asked.

'Ugh, the pong! Don't remind me! I can't believe the bastard made me sleep in there. I hurled my bloody guts out.'

'Was there someone you were going to hook up with that evening?' Brianna Jade asked, ruthlessly ploughing forward.

There was a pause.

'Look, you've got me on speakerphone, right?' Dom said. 'You might want to take me off it, if you're asking what I rather think you're asking.'

Baffled, Brianna Jade gestured to the stylists to back away and clicked the speaker off, mentally running through the list of women guests at the party as she did so. Milly was so tiny there was no way Edmund could have mistaken her for Brianna Jade, not for a moment. What about Princess Sophie? She was almost Brianna Jade's height, though thinner –

That's it! Edmund had sex with Princess Sophie! Weirdly excited to have figured it all out, Brianna Jade wiggled the phone under a remaining curler and said: 'Okay, shoot. No one else can hear.'

'Sweet girl, it was your *mother* I was after!' Dom said. 'That's why you're asking, I imagine? Is this a very roundabout way of warning me off? Because if so, I think that's awfully unfair. She's an absolute stunner and doesn't look her age at all. I mean, she isn't that much older than me anyway, is she? Why shouldn't she have some fun?'

Brianna Jade's jaw dropped so far that her entire mouth sagged open.

'We had a hot rendezvous going, but I'm afraid I rather blew it by getting totally plastered,' Dominic continued, 'and she's been giving me the cold shoulder ever since. Any chance you could put in a word for me?' His voice brightened. 'Wait, is that why you're ringing me? Did she mention me at all? Were you trying to get the lay of the land?'

He chuckled. 'I say, that's very good! Lay of the land! Look, I damn well will be if she just gives me a chance – tell her that, will you?'

But he never got an answer to his question, because Brianna Jade had hung up.

'Okay to keep going? We're on a deadline, you know,' the stylist said, bustling back.

If Brianna Jade had been sightless before, now it was as if she had laser vision. She stared at her beautiful reflection as the hairstylists finished their work, sculpting the thick, silky rolls produced by the curlers into smooth waves that were as elegant and as emphatically non-pageant in style as Tamra had specified. She wanted to be absolutely sure that no one could point to Brianna Jade on her wedding day and see any connection between her and a Miss America contestant.

The bride rose, the hairstylists fluttering around her with extra mirrors, showing her every angle conceivable of the sleek, fashionable updo they had spent over an hour creating. Trailing a halo of Elnett hairspray, she moved through into her bedroom, where Massimo Panuccio himself of Sartoria Massimo was waiting with her bridal dress on a padded hanger. The smile of triumph on his handsome Italian face deepened as, carefully, he unzipped the dress and held it for Brianna Jade. She took off her dressing gown, and, in her smoothing slip, bra and stockings, stepped into the silk and lace creation. Massimo zipped her up, stood back, sighed with happiness: the make-up artist and the hairstylists all made noises of appreciation and wonder. Massimo's assistant was removing the custom-made white silk shoes from their box, and kneeling down in front of Brianna Jade, holding them out for her to slip her feet into, lifting the folds of the dress so that the delicate lace wouldn't catch on the kitten heels.

On her earlobes were fastened the antique diamond and pearl earrings that had been in the Respers family for generations; around her long neck, the matching necklace. The jewellery was not as large as Tamra would have liked, but its Respers family heritage made it an impeccable choice, and Massimo had designed the dress with photographs of Brianna Jade wearing the earrings and necklace to ensure that they would work perfectly together.

'Honey!'

Tamra swept in, so stunning in her dark rose dress that everyone who had been marvelling at Brianna Jade, the most beautiful bride that could possibly be imagined, turned to look at her mother and goggled in equal appreciation. The huge silk flower on Tamra's right shoulder would have overwhelmed a woman with less height and poise, but on Tamra it was magnificent, her blonde hair fabulously twisted into an asymmetric arrangement that balanced out the flower, her eyes huge and dark, her mouth boldly coloured a bright fuchsia that only she could have carried off.

'Oh my *God*,' she sighed in bliss on seeing her daughter. 'Oh my *God*. Massimo, honey, if I weren't all dressed up already I'd get down on the ground and kiss your feet. She's going to be on the cover, you know! This is the *Style* Bride of the Year you're looking at. My little girl! Oh Jesus, I am *not* going to cry, I'm *not*.'

She was holding a jewellery box which she handed to Brianna Jade.

'It's mine,' she said. 'So I'm lending it to you for today, get it?'

One dark eye closed in a wink, the ridiculously thick lashes fluttering down to her perfect cheek and up again.

'After today, I *might* just let you keep it, if you ask me nicely,' Tamra went on, smiling naughtily. 'See what I'm doing here?'

Brianna Jade opened the box and gasped: it was a sapphire and diamond hair clip whose simple, formal lines echoed the design of the Respers jewels she was wearing.

'But Daniel just did my hair,' she said, even as Daniel, smiling conspiratorially, came forward to take the box from her.

'Tamra and I've been planning this as a surprise for you,' he said. 'I did your updo so the clip would fit just under the chignon.'

Expertly, he fitted the sapphire and diamond clip exactly where it was meant to go and stood back with a smug expression on his face.

'Oh, that's perfect!' Tamra exclaimed, as the *Style* crew, who had entered with her, busied themselves in a whole series of candid shots of Brianna Jade being shown her hair clip, the final touch that was both borrowed and blue, in the bathroom mirror, Daniel holding up a hand mirror for her, Massimo standing back, admiring with great complacency the way his dress flowed around Brianna Jade's perfect figure. The little bridesmaids, looking adorable in their white dresses, were brought in by their proud parents; more photographs were taken of them, mostly goggling in dumbstruck awe at how beautiful the bride was.

A procession formed: Tamra at the head, then the little girls, then Brianna Jade. Slowly they made their way out of the room, down the corridor and to the head of the majestic staircase, whose banisters were wrapped in white ribbon and adorned with roses. The guests had all been shepherded into the chapel by this time, the groom and best man waiting there for the *Style Bride* team to ensure they had all the photos and video they needed of the bride's party first posing at the top of the stairs, then descending slowly, Brianna Jade's weighted train spreading out wonderfully. Massimo, seeing it in motion, sighed in bliss at how successfully the white silk layered over the lace, at the wonderful effect it made against the dark polished wood and deep plum of the carpet.

Brianna Jade felt as if she were in a boat on a river being inexorably swept along. Everyone in it with her was confident, sure of the way, and she was the only one aware that around the next bend was not the open sea, as they all thought, but a drop to a cascading waterfall that would upset the whole craft. She wanted to tell them to stop, that they needed to row the boat to the shore: but the river was too strong, and her years of pageant training, where you smiled and smiled and walked up and down steps and over stages and hit your mark and stopped and smiled some more, making sure that you were posed at exactly the right angle and that your dress was perfectly arranged, made it impossible for her to break through the sheer waves of expectation that surrounded her.

The florist handed her and Tamra their bouquets, and she smiled as she took hers, smiled as the river carried her along the hallway, down the side wing of Stanclere Hall to the chapel at its far end, pausing so the little bridesmaids could make sure they were holding Brianna Jade's train exactly right. Tamra waited in the doorway of the chapel until she got the whispered confirmation that the bride was ready and the signal was given to the organist to begin.

The music was an arrangement of Mendelssohn's 'Wedding March', very traditional, but that was what Tamra wanted for her daughter. The first chords were sounded, the familiar melody began, and Tamra set back her shoulders and started the slow walk down the aisle, her fuchsia lips curved into a proud smile.

The Stanclere Hall chapel was unusually large, having been built for the farm workers to attend Sunday services as well as the household staff, so there was room for about fifty guests plus selected staff members – like Mrs Hurley – who had been with the Respers for so long that they had as much right to be present at the Earl's wedding as family members. More, in fact, considering that the Respers family had many branches, not all of which had been invited. There would be a much larger party thrown after the ceremony, a dinner for three hundred with dancing afterwards, but it was tradition for the Earls to be married here, in this chapel with its marble pillars and carved marble altar over which was draped the linen altarcloth embroidered in gold thread by the ninth Countess. On it was set the two gilt candlesticks and statues of angels which had stood there since the eighteenth century.

Lozenges of blue and red and green and yellow fell across the altarcloth from the stained-glass windows set into the curved apse at the back of the chapel, sumptuous arrangements of roses clustered at their base. The vicar stood on the low marble step below the altar, smiling, a carved wooden lectern in front of her, and Edmund, in pristine morning dress, blinked hard at the sight of Tamra approaching, a glorious beauty in her dark rose dress, the exquisite silk flower at her shoulder no competition for Tamra's glowing face under her red-gold hair, her vivid dark eyes and perfect bone structure.

Murmurs of appreciation trailed her approach, which yielded to sighs of pure wonder as Brianna Jade stepped forward and the congregation realized that, no matter how many weddings they attended, they would never again see a bride this perfect. Tamra, nodding at Edmund as she gave her bouquet to Lady Margaret in the front pew and waited to take her daughter's, was so riven with conflicting feelings that she could only be grateful to the ritual of the wedding ceremony that laid down for her exactly what to do. On Edmund's face, as he took in Brianna Jade in all her white silk and lace glory, diamonds glinting in her ears and around her neck, was an almost rueful smile of pure appreciation. He shook his head briefly, as if he were amazed that this vision of beauty was actually about to marry him.

Brianna Jade reached the altar, swivelling to hand her bouquet to her mother, and her lips parted, about to say something: but straight away Edmund stepped forward, taking his bride's hand, turning her back to face the vicar. The organ music faded away, the vicar began to speak.

'Dearly beloved, we are gathered together here in the sight of God, and in the face of this company of witnesses to join together this man and this woman in Holy Matrimony; which is an honourable estate, instituted of God ...'

Edmund's hand was warm in Brianna Jade's, his face gentle as he looked down at her. The vicar's voice was mellow and quietly confident as she spoke about mystical unions between Christ and His Church, miracles in Cana and St Paul.

'... therefore, not entered into unadvisedly or lightly, but reverently, discreetly, soberly and in the fear of God. Into this Holy Estate these two persons present come now to be joined ...'

Reverently, discreetly, soberly: those words all sounded like instructions to Brianna Jade to be quiet, not to say anything, to let the river keep carrying her along. But there was a waterfall coming, she could see the spume rising from the rocks over which the cascades were starting to tumble, the splashing, the rough edges of the stone—

'If any man can show just cause why they may not lawfully

be joined together, let him speak now or forever hold his peace,' the vicar said, and paused to look over the congregation.

The *Style* photographer, in one corner of the chapel, and the videographer, in the other, where they had excellent views of both the congregation and the bride and groom, panned around to catch the smiles of mutual amusement exchanged between the guests. They had all been to numerous weddings, heard this admonition numerous times, and they enjoyed both the frisson that came with the words and then the silence that greeted them, prompting the vicar to continue with the wedding vows.

No one had ever actually heard an interruption. That only happened in Richard Curtis films, and the whole point of Richard Curtis films was that they were as unlike real life as they possibly could be, which was why they were so enjoyable. Sophie, sitting next to Minty, even allowed herself a rather unprincessly wink at her friend which said that, of all the marriages they'd attended, this one, arranged for mutual benefit, was the least likely of all to have anyone object to it.

So it was the most enormous shock when, even though she wasn't a man, and was actually panicked for a second that, because of her gender, it wouldn't count if she said anything, Brianna Jade opened her mouth and blurted out: 'Wait. This isn't right.'

Edmund's hand froze in hers.

'*Brianna?*' he said disbelievingly.

'Edmund.' She turned to look at him directly. 'This isn't right. It's not what you think. *I'm* not what you think.'

'You *are*,' he said, looking very confused. 'I don't understand.'

Every member of the congregation was leaning forward, their heads almost in the pews in front of them; just below Brianna Jade, Tamra was trying to get up, but Lady Margaret was pressing her back.

'Edmund ...'

Brianna Jade looked around her, at the fifty-plus faces all tilted in their direction, at the cameras trained on them from the back corners of the chapel, and dragged her fiancé around the altar to the curved apse where they were partially concealed behind a marble pillar. She was as tall as him in her heels; she didn't need to go up on her toes as she leant towards him and whispered in his ear, the colours from the stained-glass windows playing over both their faces.

'That night you were talking about yesterday? The one that you couldn't stop thinking about, that was the best thing that ever happened to you?'

She took a breath, knowing the news she was about to deliver would shock him profoundly.

'Edmund, it wasn't me with you that night!' she hissed. 'It was *Tamra*!'

Edmund gasped out loud at this revelation. He took an instinctive step back, his shoulder knocking into the window. Brianna Jade reached out to steady him. Even with the multicoloured light streaming in, she could see he had gone white as paper with the shock.

'It's no one's fault,' she whispered. 'I'm okay about it. It was an honest mistake. Tamra thought you were Dominic, and you thought she was me.'

The Earl of Respers was speechless, the congregation, unable to hear a word, agog. The vicar, deciding that an intervention might be needed at this point, started to walk around the altar towards the bride and groom, but Brianna Jade waved her impatiently away.

'Mom?' she said. 'Can you come over here?'

That request was all Tamra needed to jump to her feet, practically tearing around the pillar to get to her daughter.

'What's happening?' she begged. 'Honey, why on earth—'

'Mom! Listen to me!' Brianna Jade interrupted. 'I just told Edmund: that night you had sex with Dominic after the party – it wasn't Dominic, it was *him*!'

She took in her mother's stricken expression, reading the guilt rather than the expected surprise.

'Oh my God, you already know!' she exclaimed. 'But why didn't you *say* anything?'

'Honey, it was your *fiancé*!' Tamra said, pale with shock and guilt. 'I felt so terrible – worse than I can possibly tell you. I didn't want to do anything to mess up your future ...'

'Oh, so *that's* why you took off so suddenly!' Brianna Jade gasped. 'That's why you stayed away for so long! Oh, yay – I thought you were pissed with me. Wow, now I get it. I get *everything*!'

She turned back to Edmund, who was still propped against the window for support.

'Edmund, it's okay,' she said in utter happiness. 'It's more than okay. I don't want to be Countess of Respers, and honestly, no offence, I don't want to be married to you either – I really don't. Mom, it's the God's honest truth!'

Words were spilling out of Brianna Jade faster than they had ever done before, her tone now louder, passionate, reaching wedding guests in the front pews: everyone was unashamedly craning forward to listen, and the *Style* photographer and videographer had both sneaked up the sides of the chapel to get closer views of what was going on.

'I wouldn't be a good Countess at all,' she said, her smile huge. 'I mean, we all *know* that, right? It's totally not my skill set – if I even *have* a skill set.'

'Honey—'

Tamra started an attempt to reassure her daughter, but Brianna Jade was far beyond needing reassurance. She was taking out the earrings, unfastening the necklace, reaching back to undo the sapphire and diamond hair clip, and putting them all down on the altar.

'It's *you* who should be marrying Edmund, Tamra! Don't you *see?*' Brianna Jade looked from her ex-fiancé to her mother. 'It's you two who've got all the stuff in common. You read the same books – those ones about the heiresses and whatever – and you can talk for hours about Stanclere and making it run properly, and Edmund actually really liked the party you threw. Well, of course he did, considering what happened at it . . .'

Edmund and Tamra glanced at each other involuntarily, went the dark pink of Tamra's dress, and kept looking at each other.

'I mean, it's obvious! It was staring us all in the face,' Brianna Jade continued, delighted. 'Just look at the two of you! Okay, I'm getting out of here.'

'You're *what?*' Tamra dragged her eyes from Edmund's grey ones.

'I have somewhere to be,' Brianna Jade said with even greater delight. 'Someone to see. The right guy for me.' She grinned in sheer happiness. 'Seriously, no offence, Edmund. But you're the right guy for my mom, and *he's* the right one for me, and I need to go find him right now.'

Reaching out, she took her mother and Edmund's hands, put them together, picked up her train and swivelled around. Kicking off her heels, she started to run down the aisle. The wedding planner, the florist, and a few others who had been stationed at the back of the chapel jumped aside just in time as Brianna Jade flung open the doors and tore through them: the chapel was at the end of the east wing, and there was a door to the outside almost directly opposite. In a second she had reached it and pulled that one open too, and, in her stockinged feet, she dashed away over the lawn, the silk and lace wedding dress so well cut that it moved beautifully with her even as she tore along with the speed of a natural athlete.

Guests poured out of the chapel, riven with curiosity as to where Brianna Jade could conceivably be going.

'Well, she's not going to throw herself in the lake,' Dominic drawled. 'It's completely in the other direction.'

'Ohmygod, ohmygod, do you think she's going to the pig guy?' Minty said, actually jumping up and down in excitement, forgetting to care about her high heels sinking into the grass and getting ruined. 'That would be the absolute best gossip moment ever in *history*!'

'It really would,' Sophie agreed as Brianna Jade took a path that skirted the ha-ha. 'I must say, this is beyond epic.'

'Lucky Ed,' Dominic said enviously. 'He gets the hot cougar and probably even *more* money! God, I'm never going to get to shag her now, am I?'

Brianna Jade vanished from sight behind the shrubbery, and the *Style* journalists turned from capturing her flight to recording the reactions of the guests.

'I must say,' the wedding planner commented ironically to Massimo, the designer, 'your dress looked really beautiful in motion.'

Massimo threw his hands wide, hunching his shoulders: Brianna Jade had hitched up her train, but there was no question that his exquisite creation was going to get torn up as the runaway bride raced through the bushes. At least he could take some satisfaction in the knowledge of how wonderfully his tailoring was coping under pressure.

It truly was. Brianna Jade was tearing along at a positive sprint, and though sweat was dampening the silk and lace, and her stockings and feet were getting ripped up by the occasional twigs and stones on the path, she didn't even notice because adrenalin was pumping a constant stream of energy and excitement around her body. Later she would realize how cut and bruised her soles were, but right now she was like a ballet dancer who breaks bones in her foot during a performance and doesn't even notice until she comes offstage after the final curtain call.

The path looped into the cart track, and the cart track led to Abel's cottage. She passed it without even checking, as sure as she could be that Abel would be at the piggeries at this time of day. As she took the turn into the narrow lane that served the piggeries, her heart rate sped up so fast that she felt almost frantic with the need to see him, and overcome with fear that she might not, after all. What if he'd gone down to Stanclere village to drown his sorrows at the pub, or taken off on holiday? Worse – what if that afternoon in the barn hadn't meant as much to him as it had to her, and he didn't care at all that she was getting married today? What if, God forbid, he had a girlfriend who was hanging out with him?

And when she didn't spot his large figure beside the Empress of Stanclere's sty, she could have sobbed aloud in misery. She'd told everyone that she was going to find him! He *had* to be here, he *had* to make those crazy, romantic, elated words come true—

She could see the Empress now, her enormous shape in the middle of the sty, another enormous shape beside her. For a moment, she wondered if Abel had imported another pig to keep the Empress company, but why would he risk the Empress having any competition for the epic quantity of food she needed to consume in order to win the Fattest Pig silver medal at the County Fair? And then, as she neared the sty, the shape resolved itself into not a pig at all, but a very large man squatting in front of the Empress, scratching her between the ears, his head ducked down disconsolately.

'Abel!' she managed to yell, though she didn't have much breath left. 'Abel, it's me!'

His head rose and he stared at her in utter disbelief, this blonde vision racing towards him, her white dress hitched up to her knees, her muscled legs rising and falling even faster as she saw him jump to his feet, start striding towards the gate in the side of the sty. But Brianna Jade was there first, and she couldn't wait for the gate to get opened: she reached the rail, put one hand on it, and vaulted over it in a titanic jump that did, at last, succeed in tearing her dress. Abel stepped aside just far enough to miss her feet and legs, catching her body as it shot through the air towards him: she landed in his huge arms with an 'Oof!' of breath and an audible ripping sound as her train, flying out behind her, caught on a splinter of wood and shredded the lace trim.

'I didn't get married!' she said ecstatically. 'I nearly did but then I didn't!'

Pulling his head down, she kissed him fiercely. When she finally let him go, he was breathing as rapidly as she was, his eyes shining.

'Your lovely dress,' Abel said idiotically, beaming from ear to ear. 'You tore your lovely dress!'

'No problem – I'll get it cut down and wear it for our wedding!' she said, feeling absolutely drunk with love and happiness. 'You don't mind if I don't have a train, do you?'

He goggled at her, his mouth open. She couldn't help laughing: his expression, plus his mess of hair and the dungarees he was wearing over an old T-shirt, made him look exactly like the dozy yokel that she knew he was far from being.

'Hey!' She stuck her tongue out at him. 'I just proposed to you, Abel Wellbeloved! It's rude not to say anything back!'

'But Brianna—'

'You can put me down if you don't want to marry me,' she said.

His massive biceps swelled as he shifted her higher on his chest.

'Of course I want to marry you,' he said, as if it was the most obvious thing in the world. 'But you can't marry me! I'm just a pig farmer!'

'That's one of the main reasons I want to marry you,' she said blissfully. 'I'm *dying* to be a pig farmer too.'

He nodded seriously: this was, at last, something that made sense to him.

'So that's a yes?'

He nodded again, this time with great enthusiasm.

'But—' he began.

'I'll tell you everything later,' she said, reaching up to kiss him again. 'But right now I want you to carry me back into that barn we were in before and put me down on that hay bale we were on before, and fuck my brains out just like you did before. What?'

Because, even as he started to walk towards the barn, Abel was frowning deeply.

'We're going to be married, Brianna,' he said firmly. 'I love you. People who are getting married, in love, don't use that word. We make love.'

'Fine!' she said, delirious with happiness now, at the supreme achievement of having finally taken charge of her own life and made a happy ending come true not just for herself, but her beloved mother. 'Take me into the barn and make love my brains out!'

And he did.

Chapter Thirty

Back in the chapel of Stanclere Hall, Edmund, Tamra and the highly confused vicar were the only three people left inside. Everyone else had raced outside to watch a sight they would only see once in their lives: the near-mythical spectacle of a runaway bride. As soon as the exodus had taken place, Lady Margaret had stationed herself at the chapel doors to make sure that no one went back inside again, and though attempts were made, no one was capable of breaching her very capable defences.

Edmund, holding Tamra's hand, stared down at her.

'That night was…' he said eventually, in a very soft voice.

'I *know*,' Tamra said equally softly.

The vicar, deciding that something very important was calling her away, slipped as quietly as she could down the aisle and out of the chapel, where she joined Lady Margaret in barricading the doors.

'I haven't been able to get it out of my mind,' Edmund confessed.

They were both still bright pink, and Tamra's colour didn't

dissipate at all as she said: 'Me neither. It was …' She gulped. 'It was …'

'I *know*.' He paused. 'Brianna Jade was completely right about everything, I think. I mean, you've been the biggest boon that could ever have happened to Stanclere. Which is *not* the reason I'm about to say what I'm going to say.'

'Edmund, this is *crazy*,' she said, her voice rising nervously. 'You were just about to marry my daughter!'

'I know – can you believe it?' Edmund shook his head in disbelief. 'She's the loveliest girl in the world, but she's not *you*. Honestly, Tamra, now I think about it, I realize that without you around, things would never have got this far. I suppose I saw Brianna Jade as being a younger version of you. As if I was hoping she'd grow into you, become the woman that you are. That was what convinced me to marry her, you know. I've known that for quite a while, actually.'

If Tamra could have flushed any more with pride, she would have. Edmund secured her other hand in his.

'It was that night between us that kept me going, frankly,' he said. 'It was just … phenomenal. I kept thinking: *She does have that passion for me, it'll come out again, somehow, some way* … I was waiting and waiting, trusting that it would come back – but I'm such an idiot, I should have realized that the passionate woman I was craving, the one who wanted me as much as I wanted her, was right under my nose. As soon as Brianna Jade told me just now, all the pieces fell into place. To think I once thought I wanted a restful life!'

He smiled down at her with immense fondness.

'Tamra, don't tell me I've actually managed to strike you dumb,' he said teasingly.

'All these months,' she said slowly, 'I've been thinking I'd have to keep the secret for ever. The relief that I don't have to any more is just amazing! I've been feeling so guilty and miserable about wanting you, but if I'd said anything, Brianna Jade would have lost everything I had worked for ...'

Edmund's grip tightened, and he drew her closer, bending down to kiss her. It was just as mind-blowingly good as the last time; they had to pry themselves away from each other at last, Tamra's hands clasping the lapels of Edmund's morning suit, Edmund resting his forehead against hers, his breath coming fast.

'I'm having to think of really awful things,' he said to her. 'I mean truly terrible, disgusting, revolting things, like that fish Dom left in my bed – for which, by the way, I owe that bastard the most enormous debt – because any moment now someone's going to come in here and see that I've got an erection that's bursting through my trousers.'

'*Edmund*,' she said, trying to sound reproving.

'God, I wish you could do something about it right now,' he said, his grey eyes gleaming.

'*Edmund!*' She dragged her hands away from him and took a step back. 'Shit, I'd *love* to – no, don't you dare touch me again, don't you dare – we're in the damn *chapel*, for fuck's sake, you sick, twisted pervert!'

'For some reason,' the Earl of Respers said, 'I get even harder when you swear like a trooper. Why do you imagine that is?'

Tamra looked at him, her eyes shining dark and full of mischief.

'How the fuck would I know?' she said deliberately.

Edmund promptly grabbed her again. By the time the vicar, aware that twenty minutes had passed and feeling that, since the bride hadn't come back, she really ought to check on the groom and the bride's mother, pushed one of the chapel doors open again, making as much noise as she could to give them due warning, most of Tamra's hair had fallen down, the flower on her dress was bent askew, and a considerable amount of her fuchsia lipstick was smeared, clownlike, over Edmund's mouth.

'Ahem!' the vicar said, clearing her throat and trying to avert her gaze from the dishevelled state of the two lovebirds. 'Lady Margaret and I were thinking ...'

'We sent all the guests to start tucking in,' Lady Margaret said briskly, following the vicar in and showing not a whit of the latter's middle-class embarrassment at Edmund and Tamra's considerable state of disarray. 'Thought it was for the best. God knows where Brianna Jade's gone off to, but it doesn't look as if she's coming back any time soon.'

'I have a notion where she went and who she's with,' Edmund said, as Tamra, realizing how much of her lipstick had transferred to him, exclaimed in horror and reached for the handkerchief in his breast pocket to wipe it off. 'And you're not going to like it much if I'm right, Tamra.'

'As long as she's happy,' Tamra said, licking the handkerchief to get more of the lipstick off.

'Don't *do* that,' he muttered at the sight of her tongue. 'I'll hold you to those words,' he said, louder, tucking her arm through his and turning to face the nave of the chapel. 'Vicar, Lady Margaret, I think it's pretty clear that Tamra and I will be getting married as soon as we can get the banns read. All very unexpected and unorthodox, but it is what it is, and to others it'll be a nine-days wonder, I'm sure. It's not as if everyone at the Hall isn't dying to have Tamra as its official mistress already.'

Tamra smiled at him with such grateful sweetness that even Lady Margaret couldn't help muttering, 'Aww,' to herself.

'Edmund!' Tamra exclaimed suddenly. 'We can't – Edmund, I'm forty, and you're going to want heirs. I might not be able to get pregnant ...'

Edmund shrugged with great nonchalance.

'Tamra,' he said easily, 'like everyone else who's ever met you, I believe that you can do absolutely anything you set your mind to. And if it doesn't happen, who cares?'

'*I* do,' Tamra said firmly. 'I didn't bring the Hall back from rack and ruin just to see all my work inherited by some cousin of yours.'

'Fine.' He grinned down at her. 'So we'll adopt if necessary. Really, darling, relax, will you? I'm not marrying you because you're going to give me heirs, or because you've got pots of money. I'm marrying you because, as you know perfectly well, you give me—'

Tamra clapped one hand over his mouth.

'*Edmund!*' she said firmly. 'In front of the *vicar*! Will you fucking shut up!'

Epilogue

A few months later, the Harrods Bridal Boutique was packed to the gills with a glittering group of guests celebrating the delayed launch of the first-ever edition of *Style Bride*. The lavish space had been decorated by a crack team of Harrods' in-house designers and *Style* event planners, and the result was a world away from the frou-frou and frilliness that often characterizes bridal salons: instead, from the ceiling were suspended floaty, underlit clouds, semi-transparent and glittering gently, which gave the entire room a sense of drifting magically in space. Strategically arranged lighting glowed in silvery globes around the walls, and Jodie had made the decision to banish anything as obvious as cupcakes and flowers from the launch.

Instead, the theme was a symphony of white. The cocktails were elderflower White Ladies, made from Cointreau, gin, lemon juice and elderflower syrup, whipped egg whites making them foamy and opaque; the canapés were bite-sized cream-cheese blintzes and ricotta puffs, and, for those with a sweet tooth, silvered mini-meringues. Models circulated among the guests, wearing Hervé Léger, Alexander McQueen and Marchesa wedding dresses, each dress more exquisite than the last.

Jodie stepped up onto the central podium. It was the kind on which a bride-to-be would usually stand while trying on a series of dresses, curved panels of mirrors behind her that reflected her from every angle. She looked down at the super-fashionable, skinny-thin, wonderfully dressed crowd and couldn't help wishing for a moment that her bottom wasn't being reflected to all of them, even held in as it was by Spanx and a very flattering Nina Ricci sheath dress: then she took a deep breath, told herself firmly – as she had to do at least once a day in her job – that size twelve wasn't fat, and tapped the microphone to get everyone's attention.

The DJ muted the background music, the people in front of the podium hushed and looked up at the *Style* editor, and Jodie, knowing that at these events you could never expect the people at the back to stop talking, smiled for the cameras and said: 'Ladies, gentlemen, thank you so much for coming out this evening! *Style* is so excited to be hosting this event together with the wonderful people at Harrods and their beautiful Bridal Boutique.'

She paused briefly for applause.

'Honestly, this is so overdue, isn't it?' she went on. 'We should have launched *Style Bride* years ago! If there's ever an opportunity for the style-conscious woman to put together an event which really speaks about how she sees herself, her partner, and their particular aesthetic, it's a wedding and everything that surrounds it. And for this first issue we've loved being part of that process for the brides whose weddings we've covered. I don't think it's any secret to all of you here that some of those weddings were a lot more ...' she took a beat for effect, knowing there would be some anticipatory laughs – 'well, let's say it, *dramatic* than we anticipated! This is why we're launching later than originally planned, of course.'

Which is a shame, as we pretty much missed bridal season – but ironically, Milly and Tarquin's fiasco, plus Brianna Jade's runaway bride moment, actually got us even more publicity, she thought happily. And publicity translated into more advertisers, which raised *Style Bride*'s page rates. Everyone wanted to run an ad in the magazine that had the exclusive to both sets of photographs.

Because, naturally, Jodie had run photographs from both weddings. Milly and Tarquin's publicists had tried to prevent the magazine from using theirs, but the contract they had signed was locked down tight; *Style* had the best lawyers going, and there was no clause to say that if the wedding vows weren't completed, the photos couldn't be used. It had been done tastefully, of course, mainly shots of the church set-up, the chandeliers, the spectacular antipasti, Ludo's wonderful table settings, the swing, the gazebo. There had been a few photographs of the bride and groom, though none of the actual ceremony; and plenty, from the British wedding, of Brianna Jade's dramatic sprint across the lawns of Stanclere Hall. When living in New York, Jodie had loved the American saying 'if life gives you lemons, make lemonade', and she'd billed the first edition of *Style Bride* as 'High Drama, High Romance'.

'I'd like to thank my amazing team, as well,' Jodie added. 'For obvious reasons, we had a real scramble to pull this issue together, and we're hugely proud of it. In fact, we're so proud of it that our supreme leader, as I like to call her, would like to say a few words about it, live from New York!'

Oohs and aahs came from the audience, hardened London partygoers, journalists and socialites as they were: access to Victoria Glossop carried such cachet that they were perfectly aware of what an honour this was. Unprecedented, in fact.

But the sheer level of publicity and advertising money that this issue had pulled in was exceptional, and Victoria was always driven by the bottom line.

Jodie gestured to a side wall, and the oohs and aahs increased in volume as the guests realized that, while Jodie had been talking, a screen had been discreetly lowered. On it was the very familiar image of Victoria: it was a reveal worthy of a stage play, and Jodie smiled happily at how well it had worked.

Sensibly, Victoria had chosen not to be filmed in her white office, knowing that its background, plus the white clothes in which she almost always dressed, wouldn't work in this context. She was standing against a dark wall, and her white tailored trousersuit made her look like a 1940s film star. Her hair was in its classic blonde chignon, her lipstick freshly applied and redder than usual so it would pop out on screen, a huge necklace visible beneath the lapels of the suit jacket.

Murmurs of admiration rose as she said in her crisp transatlantic accent: 'Hello, everyone, and welcome to what I'm sure is a wonderful party! Harrods always throws a superb event, doesn't it?'

That's Victoria, Jodie thought. *Always on the ball, thanking the sponsors straight away. I learnt that from her.*

More applause for Harrods; cocktails were raised and the girls from the press office smiled happily.

'It's certainly been a winding road as we got this issue to press, as I know you're all aware,' Victoria continued. 'But at *Style* we love a challenge, and I truly think the first ever issue of *Style Bride* is better because of it. Not only do we have the most stunning cover, but we're telling a really compelling love story with it. Weddings aren't just about the day, the dress, the flowers, the table settings, wonderful fun though all of those are. They're about the couple in question and the fit they make together, their love story, which is why we're so happy with the choice we finally made for our cover. Talk about an original love story! I know you're all dying to see it – ' Victoria reached down to a side table beside her and picked up a copy of the long-awaited magazine – 'so here it is! The first, but *definitely* not the last, *Style Bride*!'

In another carefully choreographed piece of staging, other, smaller screens had been lowered around the room during her speech without the audience noticing. Victoria always compelled the gaze. The clouds overhead opened, and a delicate shower of silver glitter rained down on the guests as, in perfect synchronicity, every screen lit up at once.

It's like the reveal of the winner on the finals of America's Next Top Model, Jodie thought, looking at the picture of Tamra on the cover of *Style Bride*, her head thrown back in a laugh, her hair and skin glowing golden. She was wearing the same deep pink dress she had worn for Brianna Jade's wedding, though Massimo had made her a new version: Edmund had manhandled the first dress so much getting it off that it couldn't be worn again.

It was the perfect dress. Both Tamra and Edmund had agreed that it was the only possible choice. It was the dress that she had been wearing on the most fateful day of their lives, the day when, as Edmund put it, the miracle had happened. And Tamra certainly wasn't going to wear white. The fuchsia colour had been a gift to the *Style Bride* art designers, as it lent itself perfectly to the white and silver background that a bridal magazine demanded, and the silk flower was appropriately dramatic. Choosing Tamra for the cover had been hugely strategic: not only did she incarnate beauty for the precise demographic of women who bought the expensive goods advertised in the magazine, the story of her and Edmund's whirlwind romance was as shocking as a plot twist in a soap opera, and Jodie had insisted on an exclusive interview with the couple.

They had been more than fine with that request. *Style Bride* was guaranteed to give its cover star and her new husband a favourable article. Besides, as Veronica, Tamra's press adviser, had said, they needed to give their version of the crazy bride-switch to *some* interviewer. And, as Tamra had added happily, it would be the best publicity in the world for Stanclere Hall as a brand, its holiday lets and Stanclere Sausages ...

'Our cover star and her new husband, the Earl and Countess of Respers!' Jodie said, and Edmund and Tamra, to much applause and even more excited comments, appeared behind the podium and walked up onto the stage.

In her magenta ruffled-crepe Philosophy di Alberta Ferretti gown, her hair pulled to one side in a single twist, her make-up American-immaculate, Tamra looked like a goddess. Beside her, Edmund beamed with pride. He was wearing a Savile Row suit that he had had to have newly made; he had lost nearly half a stone since the day of his first, aborted marriage. Tamra, he said happily, was wearing him out in bed; he was a shadow of his former self. Tamra grumbled that she hadn't lost a pound, and he told her firmly that she was perfect as she was. Certainly, gazing at her right now, it was clear that he thought she outshone every woman in the room.

'She looks *amazing*,' Ludo said, raising his glass in tribute. 'Diva-tastic. My God, that woman knows how to wear clothes. Wouldn't you love to have a lifesize doll of her? Think of the outfits you could dress her up in!'

Father Liam, by his side, smiled at this. Since Ludo had broken down in tears in Tuscany, Father Liam had tried to be more understanding of Ludo's needs in the relationship, had agreed to accompany his boyfriend out more socially, and the launch of a bridal magazine, after all, was appropriate to his profession.

'They certainly make a very handsome couple,' he said. 'Look how happy they are! It's a pleasure to see.'

'When I think of Milly and Tarquin . . .' Ludo shuddered. 'I must say, even though it would have been a coup for me, seeing her doing her ingénue face on the cover would have rather turned my stomach.'

He was talking quietly enough not to be overheard by the crowd, and Father Liam nodded.

'We can only be glad that didn't come off,' he said. 'Oh, I forgot to tell you! I heard from Eva today. She emailed me.'

'Ooh, how are they?' Ludo said eagerly, always keen to hear gossip.

'Still on their walking tour,' Father Liam said. 'It sounds perfect for the two of them.'

Ludo grimaced. 'Lord, first a monastery and then the Highlands with a backpack! Rather them than me.'

The monastery had been Liam's idea: he had suggested that, after the collapse of his nuptials, Tarquin go on a retreat for some much-needed privacy, quiet and time to reflect on the disaster of his personal life. It was the perfect solution. Apart from the religious environment suiting Tarquin's meditative nature, the paparazzi were unable to get any shots of him behind the monastery's high walls.

Naturally, the scandal of the failed wedding had spread like wildfire, trending on Twitter for days, spreading instantly to the online gossip sites and the weekly magazines. A couple of guests, inevitably, had defied the *Style* ban and sneaked their mobiles into the ceremony, managing to catch some photographs towards the end of Tarquin's confrontation with Milly, which they then sold, along with their versions of events. Tarquin's walking away with Eva had been the icing on the cake, a twist that added intrigue, gave Tarquin an extra motive for leaving Milly at the altar, and swayed popular sentiment strongly towards her.

'He should have issued a statement,' Ludo sighed. 'Everyone thinks it was his fault. Milly's been playing the betrayed innocent very successfully ever since.'

Father Liam pursed his mouth.

'I hear the film she's in is absolutely pornographic,' he said disapprovingly. 'That must surely contradict her playing the innocent?'

'Oh, everyone's doing full nudity sex scenes now,' Ludo said lightly.

'It's Eva I was concerned about,' Father Liam said. 'But I must say, she's dealt with it better than I thought she would.'

'You gave her *very* good advice,' Ludo pointed out, knowing that these words always pleased his boyfriend tremendously and wanting to give something back in return for Father Liam's accompanying him out tonight. 'Telling her to give him some space while he went to that Cistercian monastery. I bet all the monks had *huge* crushes on him,' he added irrepressibly. 'Making him wait until he'd got at least some of the Milly fantasies out of his system.'

'It's always harder loving a real person than a fantasy,' Father Liam observed. 'I hope that isn't the case for Eva.'

'No, I don't think Tarquin was ever a fantasy for her,' Ludo said. 'She's really very like him, just more sensible. Women are always more sensible than straight men, after all.'

By the side of the podium, Brianna Jade, dressed simply in a Jonathan Saunders knee-length frock, her hair pulled back in a ponytail, hung on Abel's arm, looking up happily at her mother. Various celebrities, sponsors and advertisers were being brought up and introduced to Tamra, an endless stream of people and photo opportunities, and she smiled with equal delight at each one, making conversation while ensuring that she mentioned the Stanclere brand as much as possible, Edmund hovering behind her.

'Do you wish that it was you up there?' Abel asked.

Brianna Jade turned to her fiancé, who was wearing a custom-made suit from Edmund's tailor: nothing off the rack could have fitted him.

'No way,' she assured him.

She had moved into the cottage and was living in domestic bliss, relishing doing her own cleaning and cooking, running her own little house with no servants to make her feel useless and unnecessary. Abel, quite accustomed to living on his own, cooking his own dinners and washing his own clothes, was taken aback by how little his fiancée knew about the basics, having grown up in near-poverty, then gone on the road at fifteen, living out of motels and after that in the lap of luxury; she'd barely used a dishwasher or a washing machine, had only learnt to cook the most basic recipes.

Which, as it turned out, was very positive for their new relationship. Brianna Jade might be a millionairess, but she didn't even know how to wash her own sweaters or bake a pie, and Abel and his grandmother thoroughly enjoyed the process of teaching her. Abel, who had initially been very dubious about whether Brianna Jade could really be satisfied with a tiny cottage after the luxury of Stanclere Hall, was relaxing more and more each day as he saw how happy their life together was making her. Especially as it was blindingly obvious how much she loved pig farming. Tamra, who had tried to no avail to get her daughter to read novels, was amazed to see Brianna Jade in the Stanclere Hall library with her nose in *Whiffle: The Care of the Pig*, looking for extra tips to fatten up the Empress.

The highlights had grown out of her hair, her nails were

short and ragged from farm work, and that was just how she liked it. Tamra dragged her to a hairdresser and manicurist before parties, lectured her about wearing sunblock at all times, and Brianna Jade listened and smiled and went back to mucking out the sties.

'You know I couldn't be happier,' she told Abel now. 'I *chose* you! I ran out of my wedding to find you without even knowing if you'd be there, or have a girlfriend, or anything! Honestly, what more do you want?'

He grinned down at her, running a hand through his hair and ruffling it all up again; Tamra would despair when she saw him. Nothing could make Abel look fashionable, and he begged off all invitations to parties at the Hall, attending only family dinners, but Tamra insisted on him brushing his hair back when he did come out. Though he did it to please Brianna Jade's mother, he always forgot and messed it up into his customary thatch after a while.

'Hey, it's Mom's big day.' Brianna Jade reached up and pushed back as much hair as she could. 'Don't give her a heart attack.'

'Brianna Jade, could I ask you a few questions?' said an eager voice beside her. 'I write the gossip column for the *Herald*, and I'd love to have a little chat with you.'

'I'm sorry, I don't do interviews,' she said with her best pageant smile. 'Plus today's all about my mom.'

'You're happy for her, right? Doesn't it feel odd at all that she's marrying your ex-fiancé?' the young man asked.

Brianna Jade looked back at Tamra, up on the stage, the cynosure of all eyes, with Edmund by her side, his grey eyes full of admiration and delight in his bride.

'You know what?' she said to the diary writer. 'It could not feel more completely and totally right.'

Ludo, who had realized that Brianna Jade was present and

dragged Father Liam over to get a closer look at her, was eavesdropping shamelessly.

'She's really lovely,' he said sotto voce to his partner. 'And ooh, look at the size of her farmer! Lucky girl! Still, Tamra definitely has the pop and fizz. She'd make a fabulous drag queen.'

'Ludo,' Father Liam said, and his voice was suddenly so grave that Ludo turned away from contemplation of the Maloney women and focused on his partner's face.

'What's wrong?' he said nervously. 'Are you cross with me?'

'One day, this will be us,' Father Liam said with great conviction. 'I promise you. One day, you and I will be able to get married. I believe that from the bottom of my heart. We see changes all around us, even in the Vatican. It has to come. Even if we're both in our eighties and tottering up the aisle on walkers, we'll get married one day, I'm sure of it.'

'Oh, *darling*.' Welling up, Ludo took his partner's hand and squeezed it tightly.

'Everyone, thank you so much again for coming,' Jodie said into the microphone. 'There are copies of the issue in goody bags for everyone at the door.'

And I hope you're feeling strong, she thought. *We pulled in so many ads that thing's not only two centimetres wide, it weighs more than a coffee-table book.*

'I'll leave the last words to the Earl and Countess of Respers,' she finished, 'who've been generous enough to share their story with us – exclusively to *Style Bride*.'

On this excellent note, she handed the microphone to Tamra, but Edmund reached over for it instead.

'My wife usually does the talking, and that's more than fine with me,' he said to the crowd, grinning down at Brianna Jade, who smiled back. 'I'm discovering that one of the advantages of marriage is that one barely needs to say a word any more.

I'm sure some of the men here will know how restful that is!'

This sally drew a laugh, and he went on: 'Marriage is simply the best thing that's ever happened to me. I can't recommend it enough. The main thing is to apologize for absolutely everything, constantly. And I have an apology to make to my wife right now. Darling,' he said, looking directly at Tamra, his eyes so full of love that she couldn't meet them for fear of bursting into tears, 'when I met you, you were the Fracking Queen.'

He took her hand and kissed it.

'And now, you're just a lowly Countess. I'm going to spend my lifetime trying to make you forgive me.'

Tamra hadn't expected this speech, so spontaneous, so funny and loving, and it took her completely off guard. Edmund hated speaking in public, had done his duty at their wedding, but it had been as formal and traditional as was appropriate for the Earl of Respers in his family home, surrounded by half the County and all the Stanclere dependants. This was such a demonstration of how much he loved her that she was almost overwhelmed by it.

Pregnancy was already making her extra-sentimental; she had been just the same when she got knocked up with Brianna Jade, crying at the least little thing. She hadn't told him yet, had been saving it up for later tonight. She was only a few weeks late, but she knew her own body, and she was absolutely sure.

She bit her lip, hard, and, low enough so only he could hear, she hissed at him: 'Hey, Edmund? Guess what? I'm pregnant,' and watched with triumph the effect of her words. If he was going to knock her off-balance in public, she was damned well going to pull the same trick on him. They had found that they had the same give and take when talking as they did dominating each other in bed, each taking great pleasure when they scored a point. Tamra had certainly managed to do that now.

He gulped as the impact of her words sank in. Jodie, seeing that they were going to say no more into the microphone, retrieved it and went down the steps to get a much-needed cocktail which the efficient Catalina had ready for her.

Edmund and Tamra remained on the podium, staring at each other. Eventually, Edmund said, straight-faced: 'I do hope it's mine?'

Tamra burst out laughing.

'You win,' she said, as her husband pulled her towards him and kissed her, their reflections splitting in the mirrors behind them into hundreds of Edmunds and Tamras, wrapped in each other's arms, kissing as passionately as a pair of teenage newlyweds.

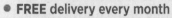